MAGEBORN

BOOKS BY JESSICA THORNE

MAGEBORN

JESSICA THORNE

bookouture

Published by Bookouture in 2020

An imprint of Storyfire Ltd.
Carmelite House
50 Victoria Embankment
London EC4Y 0DZ

www.bookouture.com

ISBN: 978-1-83888-098-9
eBook ISBN: 978-1-83888-097-2

To my always-hero

Prologue

Ripples and waves of light danced on the roof of the cave, the churning maelstrom of the glowing pool beneath reflected on the centuries-old rock worn smooth by the passage of time and water. The boy with the sword stopped in the entrance, mouth agape at this wonder. The king watched, his chin resting on his fist. He might have been a statue, sitting on his broken throne in front of the pool, bathed in the shifting light. The polished obsidian rock from which the throne was carved mirrored that light like a living thing, and he was a shadow, a void, an empty space upon the seat. Outside, the roses adorning the approach had all burned days ago, incinerated by the magical wildfires which had consumed the valley beyond the cave. Only the thorns remained, black and brittle. The boy had cut his way through them.

It came down to this. All his power, all his might, armies born of magic to command, godhood coursing through his veins – and a boy with a sword come to stop him.

He didn't look like a hero. He definitely didn't look like a would-be king.

The Maegen – that source of magic, light and dark, that place where anything was possible – stole the intruder's breath, making the king forget why he was here in hiding. He could kill the boy now, in this moment.

But the Hollow King didn't move. To do it was to forsake everything he was, everything he could be. To do it was to fall. He sat as still as stone.

'Kill him,' the Little Goddess whispered from behind his throne. Her voice was sweet and beguiling, but her words were terrible. He heard the echo of otherness in her, the Deep Dark, that which was infecting all the mageborn and driving them to acts too terrible to continue.

'Kill him, or let us have him,' the Deep Dark whispered from behind her.

The Hollow King wasn't fooled. He'd resisted them this long. He held up his hand and forced them back into the shadows. It was harder every time.

The strain must have shown on his face. The boy gazed at him with dark eyes, black like the polished obsidian on which the king sat. But not cold. There was compassion there. Warmth.

'You're him, aren't you?' he said. Not the voice of a warrior. The Hollow King had no knowledge of human lives, of human years or ages. But he recognised youth. And innocence.

'They told me you were a monster,' the boy said.

A broken laugh echoed around the chamber and the Maegen rippled, throwing up a rainbow of lights into the darkness. It took a moment for the Hollow King to recognise that laughter as his own.

'I've been called worse. What do you want, boy?'

A flicker of annoyance passed over his delicate features. 'I'm fifteen.'

Fifteen. Only fifteen years in this world and he thought he could defeat a god. Was that common for humans? That belief? That arrogance? Probably.

'Congratulations.'

He couldn't keep the sarcasm from his tone. The Little Goddess edged forward, slinking past him and showing all her teeth, white and gleaming like wet bone. The circlet crowning her head glittered like a starry midnight amid her thick curls.

The boy's face paled. His grip on the weapon tightened. A ridiculously long sword. He could barely lift it.

His sister, the Little Goddess, laughed. 'This? This is what we hide from?'

No. Not this. This was just the surgeon come to deal with the source of the infection. What they hid from was much worse. The Deep Dark had made it and it would consume them all. But she could not see that. Not when it consumed her as well.

It would take him too. It was only a matter of time.

'Run away, little boy,' the goddess sang to him. 'Run back to your mother's skirts.'

Something tightened in the boy's face. Something hard and bitter, determined. 'My family are dead. The mageborn killed them all.'

'The mageborn are beyond control now,' the Hollow King sighed.

'Not for you,' the boy said. 'I want… I'm here to offer you a way out.'

The Hollow King pushed himself up from the broken throne. The Maegen called him. The Deep Dark called him. It whispered words of comfort, sweet enticements. It was running wild through his mageborn people and soon it would take him too. It was inevitable. Why fight it any more?

There was no way out. This child of hope knew nothing. The Hollow King took off his crown. He cradled it in his hands, staring from it to the luminous waters of magic beneath.

All it would take was for him to finally give up. Break the crown. Fall. Be consumed and lost. Do what they wanted at last.

'Please,' the boy cried. In a fit of despair, he dropped the ridiculous sword and threw himself forwards. The crown cracked before he made it.

But his hands shot out, almost touching the Maegen, and he caught the pieces before they could vanish into it. He knelt beside the king, holding them back, holding *him* back.

'Please,' he said again. 'Please listen to me. I want to offer you a deal. A pact. Please.'

The Hollow King stared down into those endless dark eyes, so full of faith and hope. And for a moment he too believed. Maybe... maybe... there was a way.

'Don't!' his sister cried out. 'Please, my liege, don't do this.'

He was so tired. Tired of being a king, tired of the struggle, tired of trying to make it right. Besides, he knew better than to listen to her. She could make you think day was night if it served her purpose. And it never ended well.

'What's your name?' he asked the boy.

'Larelwynn. Lucien Larelwynn.'

His hands shook as he held the pieces of the broken crown. He was terrified. But he wasn't running away. Larelwynn believed in something.

If his belief had bid him to come here, face a monster, and save the crown – or what was left of it – perhaps the Hollow King could believe as well.

Belief was power. But more than that. Belief could save them all.

'And what is this pact?'

Chapter One

The body looked like nothing more than a tangled heap of flesh. That wasn't the worst of it. The first thing that hit Grace as she entered the coffin-narrow house was the smell, that lingering sweet-sickly stench which meant she already knew what she was going to find by the time she stepped into the murky room. Nothing good.

It was never anything good.

'Daniel, check out the back and meet up with Ellyn. Kai, with me.'

The big northerner fell into step with her, his eyes downcast. He was half her height again and twice her width, all broad shoulders and brawn. But he wasn't here for his physical strength. Kai's skill with magic was second to none. And that just made this harder for him. He looked tense, on edge, but he had been the whole way here. He knew what to expect, too.

So by the time they made their way through the door and saw it, saw what had been left behind for them to find, the urge to throw up was largely under control.

It still sickened her. She would have been worried if it didn't. Really worried.

Nothing moved inside the hovel they'd been led to. Not even the air. It was a morass of pain and misery, of destruction, that made her skin itch beneath the surface. It lingered there, in the air, in the shadows.

Kai's face had turned ash grey, drained of colour, miserable. The collar around his neck was a stark line of black leather, softened with age. It marked him for what he was. Mageborn.

'Talk to me,' she murmured, the way she'd talk to a spooked stallion. She tried not to fiddle with the line of sigils on her belt. She didn't want to activate them too soon. 'What can you sense?'

'Not much,' he admitted grudgingly. 'He took his time. Enjoyed himself. There's a stink all over this. Worse than the last.'

An understatement.

She assessed it. A poor home in the cheap end of the city, deep in Eastferry, poorest of the poor quarters. Lots of immigrants, lots of desperate people, lots of victims, everyone jumbled together. No one asked too many questions. No one dared. The killer knew this. Damn him.

'I know.'

Four bodies so far, over four weeks, always in parts of the city where the most wretched lived. His prey were all women and all mageborn. Nothing dark or dangerous about them, attending their days of homage without fail, using their powers for the sake of all. Every one of them left like this. In the dark, alone, twisted and broken. Not dead. Not yet.

That would have been a mercy.

As Grace looked down on the mangled shape of the victim, she moved. Just for a moment.

The whimper was unmistakable. Broken, barely human. Not any more.

'Shit,' Kai said. It wasn't shock or surprise. It was despair.

Grace felt her heart sink as she knelt down. They'd had to do this before, Kai once, her the other time. They hadn't realised with the first one until it was too late.

'It's okay,' she whispered and reached out to hold what had once been a hand. Her skin recoiled at the taint of the magic coursing through the woman's flesh. But with Kai there, blocking the worst of it, she knew she was safe. 'I'm going to make it stop now.'

A pulse of hope, a slight press on her fingers. Another smothered whimper. *Please.*

Her knife was quick and practised. The little blood on it was black and congealed. He'd even mangled the blood in her veins.

Kai muttered a prayer and nodded as Grace looked up. The pain on his face was evident, the pressure all around them making her teeth ache. As this was magic, illegal and uncontrolled, it took a lot to push it back.

Did he feel it the same way she did? Did the magic in him amplify it as he tried to block it out? Was it a constant battle?

And then she heard it, a movement upstairs. Her gaze shot up to the damp-mottled ceiling. The abandoned house wasn't a large building, little more than a shack when you got down to it. This room downstairs and maybe two smaller ones up the steps that were closer to a glorified ladder.

'Find the others,' she told Kai in a voice soft as a lover's sigh. 'Secure the exits.'

'But…'

Grace didn't wait to hear him protest. She knew what he would say, and he was right – she shouldn't be going alone, especially not in this case. But the moment he said it, it would be real and she didn't want to hear it. She didn't give him the chance.

They'd hunted this one for weeks and he'd always been a step ahead. Always. And now he was here. He *had* to be here. His magic still twisted away inside his victim. He'd want to wait until she died, to feel the last connection die with her.

If Grace hesitated, even just long enough to get the others, he'd give them the slip again.

Grace forced her muscles to uncoil, loosening limbs honed to fight for as long as she could remember. She deepened her breath and let her senses extend around her. She told herself it wasn't magic. Not really. Just a knack she had, and not one she felt particularly inclined to share with her superiors. The team knew, or at least guessed, that she could do it. But it wasn't magic. A remnant perhaps, a ghost of what she had once possibly been. It gave her an edge. That was all.

And she needed it. Every time.

Her free hand brushed against one of the sigils and she felt it hum into life. Other officers – mundane, quotidian officers without a drop of magic coursing through their veins – had to wait for a mageborn to be in range before they could fire up a sigil. Luckily for her, she had that one small advantage. It had kept her alive on more than one occasion.

The shadowy figure lurched towards her the moment her head came level with the top of the stairs and she bent back to evade him. She swung up, launching herself into the air. There was barely enough room but she twisted at the last moment and came down like a cat, facing him in the unfurnished attic room. The sigil unfurled from her hand and flew at him, perfectly aimed, heading right for his throat.

And impossibly, moving so fast she barely saw, he dodged it. The sigil reformed, changing from a streak of light back into metal, and thudded into a beam behind him.

He drew back his lips in a semblance of a smile. Or a snarl. 'Well now, secrets of your own, eh?'

Her quarry's voice was thin and guttural, barbed with laughter even as it chilled her blood. He wasn't tall, strong, or impressive, and he didn't look like a monster, just a mediocre man with a horror inside him. No one would ever have picked him out of a line-up; a round face, glossy with a sheen of sweat, and vicious eyes which gazed at her too intently.

She pulled a second sigil free. She just had to get it around his neck. She just had to keep him busy. A sigil acted almost like a Leech, although whereas that particular branch of the mageborn drained magic, a sigil would merely contain it, turning the body housing it into a prison. This was shaped like a triple spiral and its weight was perfect for throwing. At her touch it glowed, the power in her bringing it to life. 'Give it up, *Gore*.'

Call the monster what he was. Name him and know him. Let him know you recognise him. It was the best way. Craine had taught her that.

But he just laughed. 'Insults will get you nowhere, girlie.'

He lashed out at her, his hand glancing against her arm but recoiled as she brought the sigil up. He bent backwards like a dancer and almost grabbed her neck. If he touched her she was going to be in real trouble. A Gore could control the blood, and if he could control the blood he could control the body. He could stop her heart, collapse her lungs, twist and reshape her limbs and flesh the way he had the girl downstairs. And all the others. Or maybe not. He wouldn't be able to take the time to indulge himself, not with her squad here. She just had to hold on until they arrived.

But he could make it hurt. Oh yes, he knew how to make it hurt. 'Grace?'

Shit, it was Daniel. She could hear him on the steps. Panicked. His voice was wretched with it. Her oldest friend, oldest alive anyway, she should never have agreed to having him on her squad. But she couldn't say no to him.

'Your boyfriend?' the Gore teased, seeing her slight turn, her alarm. 'Want to watch me turn him inside out, girlie? I'll do it slow for you. Imagine what fun we'd have, eh?'

As Daniel's head came over the edge, the Gore dived, reaching for him like a toy at a fair, but Grace was quicker. She threw herself forward with a snarl, bringing the Gore down in a heap, grappling to keep his hands away from her, with her own hands on the oily fabric of his sleeves. She slammed into the hard wooden floor and rolled instantly, forcing him under her and pinning his legs. The sigil slipped from her fingers. She couldn't risk letting go of him to get the third.

'Get Kai!' she yelled at Daniel's startled face. 'Get Kai now!'

Daniel took one look at the situation and ducked back down, yelling for the rest of the squad.

The Gore snarled at her, twisting like a wild animal. He spat, cursed, but she held on like a stone.

Stay calm, don't lose it. Stay calm.

'In the name of the crown I arrest you and charge you with the crime of being an unregistered and unsworn mageborn. You will submit to examination and yield up your magic for the greater—'

'You really believe that crap?' he spat. 'The way they treat us?'

I believe it. I know what monsters like you can do. I've seen it. The evidence is downstairs. But the law does not bend, and cannot break. Truth and justice, that's what matters.

She slammed him down against the floorboards again, adjusting her grip as he struggled for freedom. 'And yield up your magic for the greater good. In the name of the king.'

He cackled at her, his mouth wide, his chest heaving. 'The greater good? The greater good of *what*?'

Why was he laughing? He shouldn't be laughing. Not now. Not when she had him.

His hand twisted, stretched in an impossible motion, and a finger brushed against the inside of her wrist. Like an ersatz lover's caress. Skin to skin, just a single touch.

Grace's whole body went rigid before her mind even caught up with what was happening. Wires of pain lanced down her limbs and twisted around her chest, crushing the air out of her lungs. She gasped, trying to breathe through the pain. Failing.

The Gore slid out from underneath her, slipping through her grip like the slime he was. 'Ah poor girlie, you tried. The Little Goddess knows you tried.' He kicked the sigil she had dropped out of reach – not that she could have moved to reach for it anyway. The third, on her belt, might have been a million miles away for all its usefulness now. 'How does it feel to be locked away inside yourself? Time to share. That's what all your little Academy tricks would have done to me, isn't it?'

That same wet laugh slithered over her and her skin crawled. She could feel her blood pounding in her veins, burning inside her in rage and defiance. He crouched down before her, studying her, drinking down her defeat, and he smiled, his teeth like yellow tombstones, his breath choking her as surely as his magic.

Reaching out, he pressed his hand against her cheek. Almost gentle, but drenched in threat, his dry skin dampened by her sudden tears.

'It's a shame to twist such a pretty face. We could have had some fun, you and I. Some real fun.'

Real fun. Sure. She'd show him real fun.

A jolt like lightning fired through her and her blood ignited, not with pain this time, but something else. It coursed along her veins, boiling, raging. The Gore froze, his eyes widening, his mouth falling open in shock.

Behind him, Kai clamped a huge hand around the Gore's neck and jerked him back from her. He held him for a moment and then she saw him grit his teeth and unleash his own magic.

It wasn't a sound but an absence of sound. It wasn't a force, but a vacuum, sucking everything out of the Gore, whether Kai wanted it or not.

What does it feel like being a Leech? she had asked Kai once, when they first met, when he'd been assigned to her, the collar still fresh around his neck, red marks scarring his skin where the stiff leather still rubbed.

Probably not the most polite thing to say, but the only word that could be used to describe what he could do – suck the magic out of other mageborn, drain them and make them impotent, helpless. Safe.

Like a sickness, ma'am. But it is my honour to serve.

That had been it.

It is my honour to serve. They all said that, the very words the Hollow King was said to have used when he knelt before Lucien Larelwynn, captive and alone. Before he died on the Godslayer blade. Some meant it more than others. But all the mageborn had that phrase drilled into them from childhood. So had Grace and all the Academy – although they did not suffer from the same terrible burden of power as their mageborn brethren, or the same obligations. *My honour to serve.* A mantra, a reminder, a promise, a curse.

By now Grace knew Kai hadn't told her the truth. Not the whole truth anyway. Being a Leech mageborn was more than that. She could read the pain, written all over his expression like letters on parchment. It hurt him. It was agony. Like drinking poison and trying to transmute it into something else through sheer force of will alone.

It hurt them both. The Gore she didn't care about. But Kai was her friend. Mageborn or not.

She tried to drag herself to her feet, her whole body aching, right down to the bones, like they had all been splintered and rammed back together. But that was nothing to the expression on Kai's face.

The colour drained away. He was grey and bloodless, his teeth gritting so hard she could see the lines of his jawbone through his golden-brown skin. The hollows beneath his eyes were bruises, and the tendons on his neck stood out like wires.

The Gore screamed, a high-pitched and helpless shriek that ripped through her head as if it had barbs.

Kai dropped him and he slammed onto the floor, unmoving.

For a moment Grace couldn't move either. She dragged in a breath, then another. 'Kai?' she said, desperately. 'Are you… are you okay?'

But the expression of agony didn't lift from his face. Kai pitched forward onto his knees, his hands coming up to hold his head. His eyes squeezed shut and he gasped out loud, a horrible, strangled sound. A glow engulfed his body, moving up through his skin, coalescing in his eyes.

Grace scrambled to his side, every movement an agony. 'Kai? Are you okay? Kai, talk to me.'

But he didn't, not a word. He was shaking all over, curling up into a ball like a child at her feet, eyes aglow, teeth clenched.

'Boss? You up there? You okay?' Ellyn and Daniel were at the bottom of the steps. Finally.

'I'm fine, I'm okay. Stand by, I'm sending him down. Secure him with a sigil and get him out of here.' She knew she ought to do that herself but she couldn't think of anything but Kai right now. Daniel would have to handle it.

She half-dragged, half-kicked the Gore's body to the top of the staircase and dumped him down, listening as he thumped and rolled down the steps to them. If he broke something on the way, so be it. She really didn't care right now. The more pain the better. If it was his neck, well, that would be just fine as well. She had more urgent matters to deal with.

'Kai, listen to me. Talk to me.' She dropped to her knees, pulled him into her arms and held him. 'Please, Kai.'

He was trembling from head to foot, tears silvering his face. A noise came from him and suddenly she realised he was trying to sob. This was the worst one yet. She'd seen him go through this before to a lesser extent. Sometimes he could just shrug it off. Sometimes.

But not this time.

They'd all heard the stories. Draining the magic from too powerful a mageborn could kill even the strongest Leech. Do it too often, do it carelessly, do it too quickly...

Hollow, they called it. Going hollow. Too much magic eating away inside them. The way the Hollow King and his followers had gone, mad with magic, a monster.

Not even a sigil would help Kai now. It would probably hasten the damage, locking it all away inside him with nowhere to go.

Magic was fickle. It was dangerous. Magic was a pool into which mageborn could dip but go too deep and it would swallow you whole. Lose control and it could destroy not only its host but everyone around them. The Magewar had been the worst of it, so they said, but Grace saw it all the time. Helene's magical command over water had drowned her, but she'd almost taken Grace with her. Her best friend. Her only friend before Daniel. And they had just been children. Before that life was a blank. Her life began in the Academy. Her life had begun with Helene's death.

Grace held the huge man against her, the man who was gentle as a child, who abhorred violence and hated to see pain in anyone, the man who had saved her life more often than she cared to remember. And in doing so, put himself through agony every single time.

This was her fault, all her fault. She'd promised to protect him. She'd promised to protect them all.

'I've got you, Kai. I promise. I've got you. It's going to be all right.'

She already knew she was lying.

Chapter Two

They crossed the Temple square and all but dragged Kai up the Royal Promenade. As they left the lower city, the streets became cleaner, the decrepit buildings giving way to golden sandstone and marble frontage. Kai woke up halfway there, screaming up at them, light spilling from his eyes. Grace had to use one of the sigils, knowing it would burn through before they made it. He wept until he passed out again.

Statues of dead kings and heroes gazed down impassively, heedless of the fate of one broken mageborn. Grace felt a surge of anger as they passed Lucien Larelwynn, the first king, centuries dead: he had defeated the mageborn, had made them his subjects, his slaves. He had not pitied the mageborn in life, and there was no pity in his stony stare now. How could there be? Stone didn't have pity. Neither did kings. At least his statue seemed to face them. It was better that than the people who turned their gaze away. Mageborn scared of the Academy, non-magic quotidians who didn't care about someone like Kai, or anyone from either group, too afraid of this wild man to get involved. The palace loomed over them, built on and in the hill overlooking the bay. The Healers' Halls were part of that complex, and it still took far too long to get there.

As they finally dragged Kai into the Hall of the Healers, the curtains spread out in the breeze like bridal veils. The high arched windows looked out over the red tiled roofs of the ragged city far below and the sound of the distant waves carried up here like music. It was a holy place, a sacred place, open to all and, like the palace, far removed from the squalor below. The wonder of the place lay in the people that worked there, of that Grace was sure, so patient, so giving. She appreciated their efficiency and professionalism, and the fact that they didn't even flinch when she presented them with an ailing, mageborn Leech from the Academy.

It had taken them too bloody long to get up here.

The healers loaded Kai onto a gurney and pushed it off to a corner room, leaving Grace and Daniel standing there by the doorway. Grace stared up at the ornately decorated ceiling, painted with scenes of imaginary rural bliss, a world away from where they were. Fictional scenes. Pretty lies.

'Are you sure you're feeling all right?' Daniel asked. He touched her shoulder oh-so-carefully. He'd been tentative with her since he helped her guide Kai out of the house.

'Yes.' When she glared at him he jerked his hand back and then tried to cover by running it through his black curls. But he didn't look any less concerned.

'What happened up there?'

She heaved a breath in and out, mainly to be sure she could still breathe normally. She had to keep doing it, just to remind herself that she could. Every so often panic would set in, tightening around her lungs like iron bands. But she could force her way through it. When she focused. When she didn't think about what might have been.

'He had me. The Gore. He was going to kill me. Kai stopped him.'

'And the rebound—'

'Yes.' She knew her reply was curt but also that Daniel would understand. He had to understand.

Ellyn arrived, her long white-blonde hair loose now, her leather jerkin unbuttoned. She looked far calmer than Grace would have in the circumstances.

'Handed the Gore over, boss,' she said blithely. 'Utter creep. He started sobbing as they took him down below, can you believe it? After what he did to those girls?'

Grace pursed her lips, still staring at the door to Kai's room. She didn't care about the Gore. Not any more.

'Did you see *him*?' Daniel asked. A little too interested. *Him*… the Lord of Thorns. He was a bit obsessed.

'They weren't letting me in there, were they?' Ellyn replied. 'Anyway, I don't want to get caught up in whatever the Lord of Thorns gets up to in his dungeon.' She gave an exaggerated shudder. 'Might as well ask if the Hollow King wants to come out to play. What did they say about Kai?'

When Grace didn't answer, Daniel spoke hesitantly. 'Nothing yet. Not to me anyway. Boss?'

'No. Not to me either.' And that just wouldn't do. She was Kai's squad leader after all. He didn't have anyone else, no more than she did. If she didn't stick up for him who would? 'Come on, let's find out.'

People folded back out of their way as they advanced. The healers weren't used to conflict and they certainly weren't used to leather-clad Academy officers marching through their halls as if they were on a mission. By the time someone even thought to protest, they were at the door through which the gurney carrying Kai had vanished.

'You can't go in there. What do you think you're doing?' The healer blocked their way, outraged. A little Valenti islander like Ellyn, narrow-framed and delicate. Grace was pretty sure she could break her in two if she wanted.

'I'm going to check on my friend,' Grace said.

The girl had large grey eyes and a slightly owlish, dark-skinned face. She looked Grace up and down for a moment but she didn't move.

'Your... your friend? The mageborn?' Her accent betrayed more about her than her looks, city-born but from parents who hadn't bothered to integrate.

'Officer Kai Albren, first class.'

Ellyn shook her head and muttered something in Valenti. Grace's knowledge of the tongue wasn't good enough to catch it but it didn't sound polite. The healer scowled at her.

'There's no need for that sort of language. You can't just walk in on him, that's all there is to it. He's fragile. He's hurting and there's nothing we can do. We've sent for... someone... to help him. A specialist. It won't be long.'

It was the way she paused, as if afraid to name the someone, whoever they were. *A specialist.* It set every alarm bell chiming in Grace's head, igniting the itch beneath her skin again.

'Who?' she asked, leaning in, as intimidating as she could be without actually threatening harm to this healer.

She saw the woman flinch back, swallow hard, and in that moment Grace knew – just knew – that her own reputation had come before her. And yet, the healer still didn't want to say anything.

'You'll... you'll have to wait, Officer Marchant. I'm going to have to insist...'

Grace didn't say another word, just flicked a brief hand signal to Ellyn and Daniel. Then she pushed by the healer, Ellyn catching the woman's arm before she could intervene. Daniel blocked anyone else from following, always effective when it came to something like this. Which left Grace with a clear path. The door opened with surprising ease.

Inside, Kai lay stretched out on a bed, twisting against the bonds pinning down his arms and legs. His neck and back were arched like a bow and he groaned, soft and broken. He slumped back down, sweat drenching his shirt and loose trousers. That was all he wore, apart from the ever-present collar. He looked strangely vulnerable there. They'd stripped him of his leathers and all his weapons of course, in some initial attempt to treat the fever ravaging his body. But it was no ordinary fever. All his belongings were discarded in the corner, a forlorn heap.

The special sigil buried in the collar glowed like embers in a fire.

'Kai?'

His head turned towards the sound of her voice and he tried to focus on her. He was awake, thank the divinities, but the effort it took him was palpable. His mouth tried to form her name but the next wave of pain silenced him, leaving him breathless. His eyes snapped wide open, eyes that spilled light down his cheeks like tears. Inhuman, mageborn, lost.

'Great divinities, what have they done to you?' She edged towards him, reaching out a hand she couldn't stop from shaking. He was Kai, her Kai. And he would never hurt her.

'I wouldn't touch him if I was you,' said a new voice, deep and warm, soothing, cultured. Instinct got the better of her. Still fuelled by adrenaline, forgetting where she was and thinking only of this new threat, she spun on her foot, instantly ready to attack whoever had just entered the room behind her. Knives leaped to her hands and she went low, the better to engage this unknown assailant.

'No, Grace,' Kai sobbed at her. The pain in his voice – and the sight before her – froze her.

A man stood just inside the door, tall, broad-shouldered and slim-hipped, clad entirely in black. Just a glance told her that every scrap of clothing was worth more than she'd probably ever earn in her whole lifetime, even if she took every bribe offered and extorted the rest. But she wasn't looking at the clothes, not for longer than the second it took to process the information. That would have been foolish in the extreme. She took everything in instantly: hair black as crow feathers, curling softly against the gold-kissed skin of his neck, features fashioned like one of the statues which lined the Royal Promenade. Most shocking, though, were his eyes, as black as obsidian, so dark they barely looked real. There was only one family with eyes like that and she'd never seen one of them quite so close up before. Why would someone like her be allowed anywhere near a royal Larelwynn?

The man gently closed the door and leaned back, crossing his arms over his chest: effectively blocking her escape and keeping any help out.

'You appear to be between me and my patient.'

His voice sent a shudder through her, deep and rippling with power. It was surprisingly soft, lyrical, almost kind. She hadn't expected that.

'Your patient.'

'Yes.' He took a step forward, and another, and impossibly, Grace found herself retreating, backing up towards Kai as if she could defend him still. But she couldn't. She knew that. 'My name is—'

She'd be an idiot not to recognise him – Bastien Larelwynn, the Lord of Thorns, first cousin to the king, and seneschal of the mageborn, the one who oversaw them, protected them and punished them, someone that no one wanted to cross. All his forebears had been the same, his ancestors stretching back in the royal line, a constant companion to the king of Rathlynn, the strong arm of the crown as well as the wielders of magic. The title came from his family home, Thorndale

Castle, and his crest, but most people cited his personality instead. From somewhere, Grace found her voice. 'I know who you are. I'm not letting you take him.'

He studied her for a moment, his head tilting to one side as if he could get a different view of her, as if she was a thing to be examined.

'*Letting* me?' That tilt again, the other way this time. Then his lips quirked up into a smile that begged to be punched off his starkly handsome face. 'How do you think you're going to stop me?'

If she attacked, she'd probably be held up on charges of treason. If she was lucky. The stories about him, about magic, about the days of homage that all law-abiding mageborn paid, about the things that went on in that dungeon of his… She'd have to be very lucky indeed.

But the mageborn sent to him for judgement were the worst of the worst. People like the Gore this morning. That was where he'd been headed, where Ellyn had delivered him. What happened to them Grace never asked, never wanted to know. No one did. They were never seen again. The Lord of Thorns dealt with the same people she hunted, but his was the final judgement.

But people like Kai…

He was meant to help people like Kai. That was what they said. Except… except… Kai was hollow now, mad with magic. And Grace knew that there was no coming back from that terrible brink.

Panic seized her like it never had before. She felt like a rat in the mouth of a terrier. She needed to get control of herself, and fast. She needed to think. 'He's one of mine, my squad, he's *our* mageborn. He's good, he's loyal. He does his days of homage, more than his share. He serves the Academy. His fealty is absolute. He's sworn. Look.'

She turned around to point out the sigil in the leather collar, and the Lord of Thorns was on her seconds later. The heel of one hand struck a nerve in her right arm and the knife in it fell from her suddenly numb grip. The other grabbed her left wrist, twisting it with a practised ease so it was behind her back and she was pinned against him. She couldn't move. She couldn't have dropped the second knife even if she tried. He held her against the hard warmth of his body, immobile and helpless. She could feel him breathing, every hitch of his chest. She could almost believe she could feel his heartbeat.

And his grip, while firm and implacable, wasn't painful at all.

'He's one of mine now.' His voice was a whisper against her hair, every syllable a threat. 'Stand down, Officer, or you'll regret it. Now and for the rest of your life. Not to mention your extremely short career. Understand?'

She nodded. Not like she had a choice.

He released her and she stumbled forward. She looked back at Bastien Larelwynn, hoping to see a flicker of... concern, or something, anything in his features, but he wasn't looking at her now. He was studying Kai's face. What he saw there, she couldn't say, but she recognised the grief reflected in the prince's eyes.

'What are you going to do with him?'

'What I do with all mageborn who go hollow. What I must do. Now, I need you to leave, Officer.'

Grace froze, staring at Kai, at the pain etched in his features, at the light spilling out of him, burning him up from the inside. He was in agony, lost. 'He's a good man,' she tried, one last time.

Kai tried to reach for her but the restraints held him back. His hand went wide and she slipped hers into his grip without thinking.

Bastien lurched forward in alarm, but paused when all she did was smooth Kai's sweat-drenched hair back from his face. He stilled beneath her touch, just for a moment. But his hand tightened on hers, in a crushing grip.

'Kai?' she whispered. 'Kai, are you all right? Talk to me.'

A hiss escaped his mouth and she could see his clenched teeth behind the taut lips. His hand tightened still further, grinding the bones in her palm against each other. She sucked in a breath of alarm, of pain. And that something in her, that wild instinctive response rose in her blood.

No, not here, not now. Not with *him* so close.

Her vision blurred, her breath catching in her throat. And a shadow moved past her. The fire inside her died, as Bastien Larelwynn stepped right up behind her, almost cradling her as he reached past her, for Kai.

The Lord of Thorns pressed his hand to Kai's forehead, his cool touch making Kai sink back again. His other arm wrapped around Grace's body, holding her safe. The air chilled, and something like an echo of Kai's power rippled through the air around them, just a faint memory of that vacuum, that ill wind which stole the power from the mageborn. Bastien drew in a breath and his chest moved against her back. She studied his long elegant fingers, his perfectly manicured nails, the veins beneath his skin. He wore a ring, a simple gold signet ring embossed with a circle of thorns. His skin seemed to glow as her eyesight swam back to normality.

Kai went limp, his glowing eyes closing, the light consuming him fading. Air rattled out of his throat and his hand slipped from hers.

Grace stared at him, waiting for him to move again, for his chest to lift, for his eyes to open. Nothing happened. Kai was gone.

She tried to step back but was blocked by the too-tall, languid frame of the Lord of Thorns. *Kai... Kai was...* Her strength went but he caught her before she could fall, holding her up in strong and sure arms.

Kai. Kai was dead. Her breath caught in her throat, choking her and a dark hole opened under her, sucking her down. Kai…

'You *really* shouldn't be here,' Bastien Larelwynn said again, his voice softer, calmer now. It eased her senses in an unexpected way, rippling through her, but steadying her, reminding her where she was. And who she was with. 'I know you only want to help your friend, but he's beyond your help now.'

Mortification spread through her. What was she doing, standing there, pressed up against him? What was she thinking? She didn't stand this close – this *intimately* – with anyone, and not with a member of the royal family. Especially not him.

Not a monster like Bastien Larelwynn.

'You *killed* him?'

The words came out before she could stop them. And it wasn't her imagination. The moment she said it the Lord of Thorns flinched and pulled away from her.

'I've killed a lot of people,' he said, all gentleness bleeding from his voice until it was cold again, cold as the winter winds. 'He's just mageborn, after all. You hunt them every day, don't you?'

Hunt them? Yes. Mageborn who broke the law, who threatened others. But not people like Kai. Never people like—

Sometimes they hunted ones who had gone hollow. Some were just evil, like the Gore, sick or perverted, bullies and thugs. But the ones who went hollow… they were always the worst. They didn't know what they did. They were empty inside. And when something was empty, something rushed in to fill it, something darker and emptier than anything else. When a mageborn went hollow, they were gone. That had caused the Magewar, all those years ago.

Bastien's voice hardened to steel. 'He had to be stopped. You know why you hunt the hollow. No one wants another Hollow King. Now, get out of here. And forget about him.'

Grace didn't pause. She was free of him and she had to take advantage of it. The first order she could obey.

But the second? Never.

Grace Marchant didn't run from anything or anyone. She prided herself on that. She never had and she never would.

She drew herself up to her full height, shook her red hair back from her face and began to walk away.

The king was a kind man, just and fair. They called him Marius the Good. He was blessed by the higher powers, beautiful in body, nature and spirit. But every light had to have a shadow and his shadow was Bastien, his cousin, the nightmare behind the throne.

'I'm sure they'll assign you someone else,' said the Lord of Thorns, standing over her dead friend.

Assign someone else? Another mageborn to take Kai's place? The very idea.

But they would. Of course they would.

She reached the door and wrenched it open, aware already that a sob was working its way up inside her, a sound threatening to be so violent and painful that she couldn't let him or anyone else hear it. She needed to get away. She needed to run. Kai was dead. It was her fault. He'd used his power one time too many and it had devoured him. Because he had needed to save her.

True, it could have happened at any time. True, the sigil set in the collar which helped earth his powers only put off the inevitable. The day of homage, paid by all mageborn to Bastien as representative of the king, secured the wild magic inside them, stopped it running out of control, as it had during the Magewar hundreds of years ago. Some went only once a year, but others needed to go more often. Like Kai. He'd made his way to the palace every other month now, it seemed, where he'd sworn to obey the king as he knelt before the Lord of Thorns. And Bastien Larelwynn had laid his hands on Kai's head and rummaged through his mind, doing whatever was necessary to ground the magic, make it manageable again.

But Kai had always been back on duty soon after. Always ready to use his gift in service. He had chosen this path, even if his choices were limited. He was only a mageborn.

But he had been hers. One of her squad. Her friend.

As Grace stood in the doorway, she glanced back. A part of her didn't want to, but she couldn't help herself. The Lord of Thorns stood over Kai's still, peaceful body. He'd taken off his collar and held it in his hands, staring at it, his head bowed.

'Rest well,' he murmured. 'You honoured us with your service and your fealty is cherished. The Larelwynns thank you. Return home to the light of the Maegen and be at peace.'

The urge to vomit at the hypocrisy of it all sent her blindly running from the Healers' Halls.

Chapter Three

Bastien hadn't expected anyone to be in the room with the stricken, hollow Academy officer. Certainly not the soldier's squad leader. He definitely hadn't expected her to try to defend poor doomed Kai Albren.

No one had stood up to him like that in… years. More years than he cared to remember. Not that he could remember too many years. The irony of the phrase struck him. Ten years, perhaps, since the accident had jolted his memories out of his head. He wasn't sure how much time had actually passed. It seemed longer. Marius had filled in his past for him, his cousin, his friend, his king. Simona and Lyssa occasionally let things drop. Despite the privilege of royalty, it wasn't a pretty picture. But that was true of most of his life.

As his marshal, Simona Milne was his right hand, and the voice of his conscience should he need it. Her hereditary title didn't belie her efficiency and determination. She was older than him by perhaps ten years, trained for her role like her father before her. He relied on her more than he cared to admit, especially to remember the things he couldn't. Her father had served his. He'd known her all his life. She was his shield at court.

He wondered what she would make of Grace Marchant. She'd probably tell him to steer clear at all costs. And now the mageborn was dead. The warrior woman was gone and he had been left on his own in a room with a corpse.

Where he belonged, perhaps.

That's certainly what the court would say. And half the city. Most of them wished he was the corpse.

'Your highness?' Merlyn, his sometime assistant, opened the door and peered inside. 'My apologies, but there's a messenger from the king requesting that you attend him.'

A flare of fear rushed through him, black and terrible, barely controllable. Bastien turned on him and Merlyn shrank back. He'd discovered Merlyn Hale about a year ago, a young man, gifted but thankfully not mageborn, so very clever, with an innate talent for healing. He understood the body, and the dead, and what they could tell the world about how they died. His family were upper crust, but couldn't be called noble. They'd made sure he had the best education possible and hoped he'd pull them all up the social ladder behind him. Bastien wasn't so sure.

'Thank you Merlyn. I'm finished here.'

Merlyn frowned as he looked past him at the body. 'And the patient, your highness?'

'Too far gone, unfortunately. Hollow. There was no containing it, no bringing him back. Have him taken to the morgue. We'll see what he can teach us. Then a burial with full honours.'

'But he's—'

Some instinct stopped Merlyn finishing that sentence. Or perhaps it was the glare Bastien shot his way.

'What?'

Merlyn swallowed and from somewhere he dredged up his courage. 'He's mageborn, your highness. There are laws.'

The law does not bend, and cannot break. That was what the Academy taught, wasn't it? Something like that.

Bastien knew all about the law. He just chose to ignore it. It was forbidden to bury mageborn in royal ground. Cremation was the only way. But Bastien wasn't in the mood. He pointed at Kai's body. 'Do you see a collar on that man's neck?'

Merlyn's gaze locked on the scrap of leather which Bastien still held in one hand. Then he dutifully averted his eyes. He studied the intricate tiling on the floor instead. 'Um... no?... your highness.'

The last two words were spoken hurriedly enough. The healer would probably go far, if he managed to survive the palace. He was ambitious. Even the Halls of the Healers played a role in the political games of the royal court. That was exactly why Bastien had decided to keep an eye on Merlyn. Of course, it might just mean that he got him killed even faster.

'Full honours. Of the highest order. Understand?'

Merlyn nodded and bowed his head, stepping back to allow Bastien to leave the room.

The messenger was waiting, somewhat impatiently, another pompous idiot who didn't realise the precarious nature of his newly exalted position. He'd learn. They all did.

He bowed in an overly exaggerated way. 'Your highness, if you would follow me? The king commands your presence.'

Follow him? Through the palace that had been his home all his life? Besides, he didn't like the tone.

'I think I know the way,' Bastien replied coolly and left him standing there.

*

The throne room should have been packed with dignitaries, visiting emissaries and those poor souls begging the king's favour. It was the middle of the week after all, and not even the hour of Vespers. But when Bastien entered, it was empty. The only sound was his echoing footsteps. He could almost hear his own heartbeat in the deep and heavy silence.

Crimson and gold curtains hung on either side of the windows, framing the raised dais where the thrones stood waiting. They were empty, which made him pause. It didn't take a genius to realise how wrong this was. He'd been summoned to an empty throne room, on a day and at a time when it should never have been empty.

A shiver darted down his spine as his instincts made him tense up.

They probably saved his life. Again.

The crossbow bolt passed right in front of his face, so close he could feel the wind it kicked up in its wake. It slammed into a portrait of his great-great-great-something-or-other, King Darien the Fair. From what Bastien could see it improved the picture, but he had other things on his mind.

'You missed,' he said, as calmly as possible. 'And it takes time to reload one of those. Does that mean it's my turn now?'

The stench of fear reached him, locating the assassin for him perfectly, and he smiled. There were four ways out of the throne room, only two publically known, one the servants were aware of and one only those of royal blood were allowed to know. The assassin was holed up by the servants' door, but he clearly didn't know it was there. He was fumbling frantically with the next bolt, trying to get it into place.

Worst assassin he had encountered in months.

Bastien stalked towards him. This was the second attack on him today, and he had been more concerned about the woman defending her mageborn friend than this amateur.

'So, who sent you?'

There was an audible click, an inhalation of relief and the slight rattle as the crossbow came up again. But too late.

Bastien grabbed the contraption and tore it free of the boy's grasp before he could fire. And that was when he realised what he was facing. Not a soldier, like the Academy officer, honed and ready to fight and kill. Nothing like Officer Grace Marchant. This was a boy, barely more than a child. And he was terrified.

Large, long-lashed grey eyes looked up at him from a gaunt face. His blond, dirty hair was stubble short and the clothes were plain, homespun and simple, the type they sold in the markets in the lower city. Half-Brindish from the look of him, pale and skinny. No palace brat this, not even a servant. He looked like he came from the streets. Maybe thirteen years old, maybe younger. But how in the world had he got in here and who had armed him?

The boy sobbed out a noise that was half a prayer, half despair as Bastien grabbed him by the scruff of the neck. Quotidian, not even sensitive enough to warrant a trip to the Academy for testing. There was no way he could have found his way in here by luck or by accident.

The boy raised his hands, shielding himself. As Bastien glimpsed his palms, burned and scarred, he found his feet rooted to the spot. The air shook, turning damp and chill.

'Forgive me, forgive me, forgive me.' The grey-eyed boy chanted the words over and over again. Bastien tried to push forward but something held him. A wave of power came through the air itself, through the floor beneath him and the stones around them, as if something was being sucked from them.

'What is this?' Bastien hissed.

'I have to. You don't understand. They said this was the way, the better way to do it, and I didn't believe them but…'

Water coalesced from the air, glistening on his skin, forming droplets. The tears from the boy's eyes flowed like streams and suddenly it all rose towards Bastien in a wave.

A Tide. The boy was a Tide.

Except... he couldn't be. He didn't feel mageborn. Bastien had seen none of the indications. Not until now. It was almost as if he'd just come into this power, as if he'd been completely quotidian one moment, and the next...

Bastien held up a hand before the water reached him, halting it with his will alone. As the magic in him boiled up, he saw the boy more clearly, just a boy, a child, hollow-cheeked and bloodless with terror. Hanging over him was a sheen of something else, a line invisible to the naked eye, filling him with someone else's power. It coalesced around his chest, where something hung, tucked beneath his drab clothes. It wasn't even that strong. Just... unexpected.

Bastien knew the work. It was his own. He remembered explaining it to Simona, who had looked at him like he was insane, both before and after she understood. *Take a jar, an ordinary jar...*

The marshal had not minced words with her verdict of the idea. Neither had the king. Bastien hadn't listened. And now...

'How is this possible?' the Lord of Thorns asked. 'Who sent you?'

He flicked his hand towards the tether. It held for a moment and, with a pop like a soap bubble, it snapped. The boy cried out and the vine of magic unravelled, all traces of it fragmenting and melting away. He clutched at his chest, pulling out a chain with a broken pendant of some kind on it. The magic he was so afraid to use was gone.

He sobbed in horror. 'They'll kill me. Please...'

Bastien loomed over him, a dark shadow of menace.

'Someone will, especially if you don't talk. And they'd have to reach you first. I'm already here.'

He couldn't make his voice kind or warm. It wasn't in him. He was well aware of the reputation he had among the poor of the city, and among most of the nobility as well. He just didn't care. Why should he? His spells had been used against him. His work had been… twisted.

'They said… They said I could help. It's my duty. The… the king is sick… dying… the queen is barren… and you… you…'

'And I am the heir presumptive.' Of course. It all made sense. Grab some pathetic, desperate boy from the street, fill his head full of duty and patriotism. It wasn't so different from what the Academy did every day. Bind him up with someone else's magic. Plant him in the right place at the right time and let things take their course. But who would do that? Who? 'Go on, say it.'

'You cannot take the throne. We can't have another Hollow King. They… they said you cannot…'

He'd heard all this before. It was hardly new. Everyone said it. Just not in his hearing. 'I'm sure they did. I'm an abomination.'

The boy's mouth dropped open. He looked like he was about to wet himself. 'You can't take the throne. Not you, nor your line…'

'Who did this to you?' Bastien's grip tightened to steel.

Running feet behind them, shouts of alarm as guards finally appeared in the empty throne room, and Bastien and his captive were surrounded. He held out the crossbow to the first one to approach without comment.

'Your highness, apologies, we were—'

'Where is the king?' he asked. He had no interest in their various excuses. So many people should have been here, the guards were the least of his worries. If they were elsewhere they had been ordered to be elsewhere.

Not you, nor your line...

'He took to his bed an hour ago. His physicians are with him. And the queen, of course.'

Where else would she be? Aurelie adored her husband. Everyone knew that. She made sure of it.

'I should go to him then. When I was summoned I assumed he was holding court. Take this...' He dragged the boy out of his corner like a squirming pup, and dropped him at the guard's feet. The boy just lay there, sobbing, his chest heaving in great racking silent sobs. There was no point in crying for help, no help going to come for him. Not now.

He knew it as well as everyone around him.

Not you, nor your line...

The echo of those words taunted Bastien. He couldn't summon up a feather's weight of pity with that simple phrase rebounding through his mind.

'Take him to the dungeon. Give him to Marshal Milne, under my authority, understand? I'll interrogate him myself.'

'Yes, your highness,' the guard stuttered and tried to bow, but Bastien had already turned away.

Intriguing that no one had told him the king was ill again. And that no one had thought to inform him that the throne room was empty. The messenger... ah, of course. The messenger hadn't said where the king was. He'd asked Bastien to accompany him, meaning he would lead the way.

Where would he have led him? Here? Or to the private chambers?

Bastien sighed, annoyed with himself now. If he had listened, if he had enquired, this might not have happened.

But that didn't explain why the boy was waiting here. He'd been set up. Perhaps they both had been. But by whom?

Ah, that was the question, wasn't it? There were so many options.

Enough. He needed to see the king now as commanded, or questions would be asked. It wasn't the sort of time to defy direct orders, after all. People would talk.

Though who was he fooling? They always talked.

He turned back. He should question the boy first, while he was still more terrified of the Lord of Thorns than anyone else.

He passed a group of servants, all laughing about some servant concern. As he came into view they fell into respectful silence and curtsied, one after the other, a sea of bobbing heads and downcast eyes. And when he had passed them, he heard the whispers starting, a wave of noise on the edge of hearing which set his teeth on edge. They vanished down the master staircase, towards the terraces and the kitchens below.

He couldn't get that phrase out of his mind. It mocked him, taunted him, like a nursery rhyme that he couldn't shake off.

Not you, nor your line…

His thoughts were interrupted by an explosion of noise. The shouts of the guards up ahead, the screams of the servants below.

Bastien sprinted to the end of the corridor, where it opened up to a balcony. The guards were clustered around the balustrade, staring down.

And he knew, knew with all the certainty in him, what he'd find.

The half-Brindish boy, would-be assassin of the Lord of Thorns himself, was sprawled on the paving stones of the terrace, two floors below, his limbs twisted, blood spreading around him in a glossy pool.

Not you, nor your line…

*

Marius was meant to be sleeping but the moment Bastien arrived, he levered himself up in the bed and tried to smile. He wasn't a vain man, Bastien knew that, but he pushed his dark brown hair out of his face and tried to look as if he hadn't been overcome with exhaustion yet again. Pain lined his face, made shadows under his eyes. He had that kind of refined beauty of the royal family, hard lines and delicate features, and a gaze that Bastien had always found compassionate.

The king looked small in the enormous bed raised like a throne in the room that Bastien always thought far too ornate to be restful. Gold scrolling decorated pillars and cornices. The crystal chandelier hanging from the ceiling rose blazed with light. Everything was sumptuous and rich, every surface gleaming. Velvet throws covered silk sheets, and Marius was childlike beneath them. Marius, who, for as long as Bastien could remember, had been the centre of his world. More brother than cousin.

'I didn't think you were coming,' Marius said, in that soft voice which made Bastien worry for him. A kind man, a good man, a man consumed by his role and the magic that bound him to the throne.

Bastien bowed, and the respect in the gesture wasn't in any way feigned. He had never bowed like that to Marius's father, or so Marius liked to tell him. King Leonis had found it amusing, as if his rebellious nephew was no more than a joke. Bastien somehow doubted the truth of that but it was the tale Marius always stuck to.

'I was delayed. My apologies, my king.' There was no way he was going to tell the king what had happened. He would deal with it himself. Marius had more than enough to worry about. 'Is the pain bad? Can I help?'

Marius sank back again, his hands shaking. 'It… it has been easier.'

Bastien knelt beside him and took his wrist. His pulse was racing and his skin felt cold. 'May I?'

'Please.' The king closed his eyes, and with his other hand touched the necklace hanging around his own neck, a small golden disc, like a coin. The royal warrant. Even looking at it made Bastien's heart ache because he knew what it was, what it could do, what it could make Bastien do. The pact between the royal Larelwynn family and all the mageborn in the kingdom dated back to the fall of the Hollow King. It bound them together, made them all safe. But there was a price. There was always a price, for both the mageborn and the king. Bastien himself was payment of that price. The pact Lucien Larelwynn had demanded of the Hollow King bound one member of his bloodline to control the mageborn, to keep them in check, and to keep everyone safe. But that much power was dangerous. The king needed to control him. That was why mageborn could never rule. Mastery of Bastien's magic, and by extension the mageborn themselves, resided within the golden disc that hung around his cousin's neck.

But Marius never used the warrant. In fact, though he wore it, the king made a point of hiding it from Bastien in an attempt to protect him. They were like brothers. In other circumstances, in another world, they would have been friends. They almost were. In the brief moments when they could forget who they were. What they were. And how they were bound together.

Bastien closed his eyes and let his magic draw the pain out of the king's body, the golden light inside him welling up and spilling out, skin warming where they touched.

'Better?' he asked, as Marius relaxed, the tension in his whole body melting away.

'Much better. Thank you, my dearest.'

Once more, Bastien sought out the source of the illness, but it was elusive. It always had been. If he didn't know it was impossible, he almost thought it was magic itself, or the source of it, the Maegen, eating away inside him. But the king had no magic other than the ability to command him, the Lord of Thorns, through the warrant. And Marius had never abused that.

'There's nothing you can do,' Marius said, his hand stroking Bastien's. 'I know you would if you could. Will I tell you a story instead?'

Bastien's throat closed as grief choked him. 'Please.'

When they were boys, they had listened to stories together, tales of their history, their family, their heritage. Tales of Lucien Larelwynn and the Hollow King. Tales of their ancestors' famous acts of heroism. Not that Bastien had any memories of these stories – not since the accident, when he was around eighteen. Even the details of that were gone and no one had ever filled in the gaps sufficiently. No one wanted to talk about it. He had to believe what Marius told him because, otherwise, who could he trust? He had completely lost his childhood – their childhoods. So Marius had taken it on himself to fill in all the gaps. Even when he had so many more important things to do. Even when he married. Even when he fell ill.

'What will it be? Do you remember when Kazelle Durin came to fight in the tournament of champions? He looked so terrifying we thought he was the Hollow King come again. He wasn't though. We were thirteen and you were so determined to sit at the front to best see the combat. So you and Hanna and I stole away from Simona. We even brought little Asher with us…'

Bastien sat back against the bed, on the floor, still holding the king's hand, listening to another chapter in his life that had been wiped away, and fought back tears. Marius had the kind of voice you could listen to forever, gentle and lilting, musical and arresting. At some point Marius's other hand reached across to rest on his head and Bastien sat so still, listening. He wove wonders with that voice. And soon, Bastien knew, it would be silent forever. Because he couldn't find the source of the illness, he couldn't make it go away. Whatever was killing his friend, his cousin, his king… he couldn't cure it.

No one could.

What good was magic anyway if it couldn't save someone like Marius?

Chapter Four

The dream was always the same. It began with fire and billowing waves of light. It encircled her, caressed her. She floated in a pool of liquid sunlight and phantom kisses teased her skin. It was bliss, this perfect peace, this serenity.

Then she heard the voice.

'Beloved,' he would murmur and that single word made her heart grow inside her, made the fire in her blood sing.

In that unfurling luminescence, she curled into his embrace as she had done a million times. But only ever here. No other lover had ever compared. Who could compare to a dream? His kiss brushed her throat as she let her head fall back to give him access. He paused against her leaping pulse to trace it, feel it, and she ran her hands along his broad shoulders, marvelling at the strength and the tenderness, the way they combined, embodied only in him. She drew in a ragged breath and buried her fingers in his long hair, pulling his mouth towards hers.

His kisses consumed her. His touch made her gasp into his mouth and the answering groan of desperation that forced its way out of him ran like electricity around her heart.

They moved as one, bodies entangled, filled with flames, burning with a radiance too bright for the mundane world. The ripples skimmed her skin and she filled with light, with him, with pure joy.

She cried out, and his mouth claimed the sound. The burst of raw energy that engulfed them both made the pool of light blaze anew. Brighter than the sun, brighter than the stars.

Slowly he guided her back, his hands still caressing her, soothing her, and when she could almost breathe again she opened her eyes to try to catch a glimpse of him.

His eyes were dark and endless. She recognised them at once.

Here, deep in her dream of the Maegen, the source of magic, where the power of everything from divinities to the mageborn originated, she stared directly into the eyes of Bastien Larelwynn.

*

The rec room reeked of sweat. As they jogged by her, the cadets paused and saluted before running on, so young and full of life. They made her feel ancient rather than a woman in her twenties.

'Get moving!' Dayne roared at them. He nodded to Grace, a grim gesture of respect and mutual grief. 'All right, Grace?' the sergeant at arms grunted.

All right? No. Definitely not all right. But she just nodded in return.

The three remaining members of their squad had been given the traditional twenty-four hours' leave, most of which Grace had spent asleep. She'd hardly eaten because any food made her want to throw up right now. Not long before midday, she'd found Ellyn in the baths, annoying the supervisors as only Ellyn could. They had been sparring for the last half an hour in the gym and now they sat, facing each other, drinking cheap wine in silence. It wasn't even lunchtime and Grace really didn't care. When Daniel arrived they barely looked at him, but he sat down with them at the low, plain table and poured himself a cup.

'They won't tell me when they're cremating him.' He slammed back the wine, which Grace already knew from bitter experience was a really bad idea. Daniel shuddered and then swore, as he wheezed. 'Where did you get this?'

'It was cheap,' said Ellyn and lifted her cup towards him in a salute. She didn't give any answer other than that. Cheap, yes, and with good reason.

'They're not going to release the ashes,' Grace told him bleakly. 'The Lord of Thorns has him.'

She hadn't told them everything that had happened in that room. She didn't dare. Prince Bastien Larelwynn had killed their friend and she had stood there and let it happen. She couldn't tell them that. They'd never forgive her. Even if he was a prince and she was a nothing guard from nowhere, with no past and with no future. She'd promised to look after them. All of them. And she had failed Kai already. It was eating her up inside. She couldn't fail them as well.

As for the dream... well, she couldn't tell anyone about her dreams. They were just dreams, she kept reminding herself. That was all. Stupid light and stupid fire and stupid lovers. And the darkness underneath.

Could she have stopped the Lord of Thorns? If she'd actually tried? He was a prince of the royal blood, powerful in every way. But it was more than that. High station and any kind of power didn't impress her. She came from the streets and she'd probably end up bleeding out on them. No member of the royal family could do what she had to do on a daily basis. But her physical reaction to him had shaken her to the core. His presence had stolen all sense from her, all strength from her. It all happened so quickly. She couldn't even get it straight in her mind any more.

It must have been magic. There was no other explanation. He was the Lord of Thorns, blood royal, seneschal of the mageborn. And now he was in her head.

Stupid, stupid, stupid. She poured more wine and gripped the plain earthenware cup in her hand.

'Slow down, boss,' Daniel said, the edge of concern in his voice irritating. 'Leave some for the rest of us.'

'You've got to catch up, Danny,' Ellyn told him. 'Serves you right for slacking.'

They were so at ease together. So comfortable. Whereas Grace felt like she was wearing someone else's skin. They bore their grief honestly.

She couldn't tell them what had happened, what she'd seen the Lord of Thorns do.

'There you are,' Craine said as she entered the room, her crutches clicking on the tiled floor. She looked as neat and perfectly turned out as always. Her uniform was pristine and her coppery hair was freshly trimmed, which meant her wife was back in town. 'A body's dropped. Down by Belport. You're up.'

'We're off duty,' Ellyn protested and waved the wine at her. The commander gave her a flat look.

'We're short-staffed, in case you hadn't noticed, de Bruyn. I have five experienced officers up at the palace for their day of homage who aren't back yet. And you've had time off. It's meant for recuperation, not getting blind drunk.'

'But boss—'

'You could be on the night shift if you want. I'll put you in charge of cleaning out the drunk tank, how about that?'

Daniel was the first to stand, his chair scraping back across the stone floor. 'We haven't had that much.'

'Speak for yourself,' Ellyn muttered, but she stopped arguing when threatened with the worst job in existence. Piss, shit and vomit had that effect, Kai always said. Grace smiled bitterly. Short-staffed indeed.

'We're a man down, Commander,' she said in low scornful tones. All the mageborn had to pay homage annually, although those sworn to the Academy usually went more frequently. And who did they report to? Bastien Larelwynn of course. He was everywhere today.

If Craine noticed her mood, she ignored it. 'I know. And if I could afford to give you all a longer break I'd do it. But I can't. They found her this morning near the docks. She's not from Rathlynn, or even the kingdom – Leanese by the looks of it, and all hell could break loose about that. The Watch has the place secure for now but that won't last. It's not their jurisdiction. Looks like someone got greedy with an illegal syphon, and a nasty one at that. Just sort it out.'

Grace felt her stomach twist. A syphon was a trade in magic, usually under duress, and usually not a great situation for the mageborn involved. They were often just kids, desperate and afraid. Her own history pointed that way. She'd been dumped on the Academy steps, magic burned out of her, stolen. She tried not to think about it too much. The syphon rings traded in magic, and the worst of them trafficked mageborn and killed them when they didn't perform. Or when someone got too nosy. The gangs ruled half the city, even if the royal family thought differently. Eastferry was their stronghold, and the docks were the dumping ground. Not even the Royal Guard were stupid enough to go there. Too many mageborn vanished into its labyrinthine lanes. Too many other people too.

'Without Kai, I don't know that we'll be able to track them.'

Magic responded to magic. Mageborn could sense each other. Hunting a syphon ring without a powerful mageborn was like looking for a needle in a giant pile of needles. And Grace wasn't looking forward to another expedition into Eastferry, even if she did have Daniel Parry – her secret weapon – at her back.

Craine fixed her with an all-too-knowing scowl. 'I'm sure you'll manage, Lieutenant. You usually do. The mageborn will be back from the palace soon enough. I swear, I think they take their own sweet time. We'll assign a new one to you when they become available.'

Like a piece of kit, a useful bit of equipment. Not a human being.

But what else could Grace say? Orders were orders.

'It's my honour to serve. Where's the location, Commander?'

*

The waterfront of Rathlynn was divided into two sections. One, Adensport, was beautiful. Tall ships from all over the world came in there, bearing emissaries and trade delegations, the great and noble of other countries, as well as Rathlynn's own children returning home. The seafront was lined with pretty cafes, and inns, various shops and ateliers. Little boats plied their trade between the larger ones and brightly costumed mageborn entertainers could be found on the quayside – Lyrics who spun song out of a breeze and Zephyrs who danced on the air. Emporiums sold goods from all over the world, riches and treasures more exotic than anything in Rathlynn.

The second, the other port, was best described as a shithole. Some joker had called it Belport. They were probably still laughing in their grave.

This was where everything else happened. Every underhand deal, every dodgy cargo, every stinking haul of fish, every knife in the dark was found in Belport. The taverns heaved all day long. That was where business was done, the locals would tell you, but Grace knew that the legal business done there was in the minority. That didn't bother her.

The dead body of a Leanese sailor did. A young woman. Perhaps nineteen.

There were burn marks on the woman's palms, and her eyes stared in horror at the sky overhead, like she couldn't believe this had happened. There was no obvious cause of death, and she wasn't wearing a collar like anyone mageborn in Rathlynn was forced to do. But the Leanese had a different marker for their mageborn: the tell-tale tattoo on her wrist hadn't quite burned away. She looked like a beautiful doll, copper-skinned and black-haired, and that endless, vacant gaze. The brightly coloured split skirt she wore splayed out around her body, too bright in the dank laneway.

'What ship was she from?'

Daniel shrugged, staring at the woman in morbid fascination. He couldn't take his eyes off her, like he was trying to look inside her head to find out her secrets.

Grace drew in a breath to centre herself. She needed to keep her cool. Especially now. 'Do you think you could be bothered to find out for me? You're meant to have contacts, aren't you?'

'Oh, right, sure. Yes boss.' And off he went like a hare through the crowd that had gathered around them now the Watch had gone. Ellyn was doing her best to shoo them back but not having a great deal of success. Everyone there had been drinking far more than they had, and for much longer.

'What did she die of then?' someone yelled. There were various suggestions, all of them obscene, so Grace ignored them.

She closed her eyes and tried to sense it, to reach out and feel whatever lingered on the air here. It wasn't easy. Kai could have done it in a second, whereas she had to scrabble for whatever echoes she could find.

But there it was, the trace of magic lingering like an invisible thread, a shimmering in the air which quickly translated to an itch under her skin.

'Lieutenant Marchant?'

She opened her eyes to find a man of medium build standing beside her. He had the familiar Rathlynnese golden tone to his skin, and his auburn hair was darker than her own red. Good-looking, in a very proper way. His kind never looked twice at someone like her. He was well dressed, clean-shaven, and clearly had no place here in Belport. His eyes were sharp and cunning, that sort of blue that turned up only in the oldest Rathlynnese families.

'Who are you?'

'I was sent to assist.'

She glanced at him again. He wasn't wearing a collar so he couldn't be a mageborn. She'd never seen him at the Academy. She'd remember. Where had Craine dug this one up?

'Assist me how?' Suspicion made the howling pain in her head sharpen.

'In your investigation. I'm a healer.'

Grace raised her eyebrows and looked pointedly at the body. 'I think she's a bit beyond your skills, healer. Unless you can raise the dead.'

He gave a snort of laughter which was almost human and shook his head. 'I'm not a Barrow, if that's what you mean. Or a Curer. And certainly not a Gore. Just a healer. The common or garden variety.'

Well, if he was here to help – whatever that help might entail – she might as well make use of him. She stepped closer to the body, circling it. Craine must have some idea what she was doing and it wasn't the first time a healer had helped on a case.

'Fine. What's your name, healer?'

'Merlyn Hale, Lieutenant. His highness Prince Bastien sent—'

She spun on one heel to face him. 'Excuse me, what?'

Hale shied back, the alarm in his eyes almost comical. 'The prince thought...'

'The Lord of Thorns? What interest does he have in this case?'

'He thought you could use my help.'

She scowled. Her? Need help? Oh, he thought that, did he? Why?

'I can do my job, Hale.'

'And I can do mine, Lieutenant. The prince wanted a report on this death.'

'Why *this* death in particular?' she asked. There was nothing obvious here, nothing special. Except for the burn marks. And the fact there was no other obvious cause of death. But maybe a healer could tell her more. Maybe.

Hale gave a tight-lipped smile which made his mouth even thinner. 'He didn't share that with me.'

I'll bet he didn't, Grace thought. Bastien Larelwynn didn't strike her as the sharing type.

'So what can you tell me?'

He pushed his auburn hair back before taking out a strip of fabric which he proceeded to wrap around his narrow features, covering his nose and mouth. Grace watched, bemused, as he crouched down and peered closer at the body.

'Leanese, obviously. And from her dress a sailor. Sixteen or seventeen.' Younger than Grace had thought, then. That shouldn't have distressed her, but somehow it did. 'She died quickly, very quickly. No sign of...' He actually blushed and coughed, like he couldn't say 'rape' in front of her. 'The marks on her hands need studying.' He reached out and pulled down the woman's lower eyelid with the tip of his gloved finger. 'She was... it looks like the life was just drained out of her.'

'Have you seen this before?'

'Once or twice. But there's usually more of a struggle. It takes time and this... this was extremely rapid. A syphon like this is... well, unheard of.'

'Definitely a syphon then?' That was what Craine had thought. But then, Craine knew this city better than anyone.

'Well yes, but... like I said, it would have been almost instantaneous. A syphon takes much longer to entirely drain a mageborn of their powers .' He picked up one hand and cradled it in his own as he studied the burn marks on it. 'There's a curious residue here.' He tilted the hand to and fro and something on it caught the light, some kind of oily sheen on the charred skin. 'Like she was holding something when it happened.'

Interesting. Grace didn't know why yet. But it was interesting. 'Can you find out what?'

'Perhaps, back in the palace anyway. Not here in the street.'

'You need to take the body?'

'Better that than just the hand, I suppose.'

She caught up with his words and froze, trying to work out if it was a joke or not. He didn't appear to be smiling. He was still staring into the face of the dead woman, still holding her tiny hand like it was a treasure.

'Grace?' Daniel called. He was back, slightly out of breath. 'Found the ship.' That was quick. He'd been lucky. Must have been one of the first ships he started with. 'Only Leanese in port. Captain Vayden is on his way. He's not happy.'

Grace muttered a curse and Hale looked up at her with a mild expression of shock on his polished features. Where he came from women clearly didn't swear at all. Or made sure no one heard them. Posh boy, then. Well, you usually had to be to become a healer. And to serve the Lord of Thorns.

Her headache pounded away behind her eyes. The sensation of magic in the air was still lingering, but it was fading now. She ought to be following it. Not standing here.

'Are you feeling well, Lieutenant?' Hale asked. Oh, he was too sharp for his own good, that one. She'd have to watch him.

'Fine. Stay with the body, Hale. Make the arrangements you need to but make sure I know what you're doing and where you're going with her. Danny, where's this captain?'

The captain stood by Ellyn, an older Leanese man, with sallow skin and dark eyes. He wore the same bright coloured clothes. It might as well have painted a target on him.

'Where is she, my Windtalker? What have you people done with her?'

Grace glanced at Daniel who grimaced and didn't make eye contact. 'I just asked if someone was missing. Didn't tell him anything. I thought—'

'You Rathlynnese are all the same. You cannot take her. They all told me, down on the wharf, how you are rounding up more and more of the blessed. She's a free woman. She doesn't serve your crown or any other crown. Just my ship.'

A Windtalker was what they called a Zephyr, Grace recalled, a mageborn who could control the air. Handy on a ship. Valuable even. The blessed was how they referred to mageborn in general. She had often wondered if it was a joke. Nothing about their lives seemed blessed.

'Damn,' she sighed. This was not about to go down well.

The captain sensed the darkness in her mood. Maybe he was more blessed than he let on too. The anger drained from his face, replaced by concern. 'Where is Losle?'

Why couldn't Daniel have told him? He was better with people than she was. Better at breaking their hearts, better at keeping them calm while he did it. 'I'm afraid I have bad news, Captain. Perhaps if we could talk somewhere quietly?'

He looked past her, saw Hale and then the body. The bright skirts stood out, their patterns unmistakable. She watched recognition and understanding creep across his face in stages.

The pain hit her in a wave, all at once, crashing through her mind, and she flinched back from him.

'No!' he shouted and surged forwards, reaching out for the woman. Grace and Daniel caught him before he could get to the crime scene and disrupt what little evidence they had. He dropped to his knees, wailing out his grief. 'My daughter! Losle, my little girl!'

That explained the reaction. Grief swamped Grace's senses but she held it off. They wouldn't get anything from him now, but Daniel was already at work. Not always the greatest for the tough side of the job, but this… he was made for this.

'Come away,' he said in that kind, gentle voice that always worked. He wasn't mageborn but his voice could be like magic. 'Come and sit down inside.'

'Daniel, it cannot be. Tell me. Who did this? What monster did this?'

'We'll find out. I swear, we'll find out.'

She watched them go, the grief and rage overwhelming the man. Daniel, being Daniel, would find out what she needed to know. He was already on first-name terms. But then her friend had grown up not far from here. He knew a lot of people. That was what made him so useful down this way. If he was a bit cagey about *how* he knew people, well, you could take the boy out of Eastferry…

He knew what to ask, but it was patently obvious that the captain hadn't killed his daughter. Or else he'd missed his calling on the stage. But Daniel should know better than to make promises like that.

A Zephyr, lying dead in a Belport alley, with burnt hands and all the magic ripped out of her. A girl, a daughter.

But this wasn't the work of a Leech. Or at least not the normal kind of Leech. And it wasn't a syphon, either.

'Hale?' Her new helper was peering into the girl's eyes as if they could tell him what had happened. She remembered the old story about the eyes of a victim capturing the face of the killer. If only that was true.

'Yes, Lieutenant?'

'You've studied the mageborn, yes?'

'As much as I can. It's a fascinating area of research, you know? The more we can understand about them—'

'What kind of a Leech could take all of someone's magic so quickly?'

'None of them. It takes time. Even the really powerful ones. There's only—'

He shut his mouth so quickly he almost bit his own tongue. Grace watched guilt make him squirm and didn't look away for a moment. He couldn't have been more obvious.

She'd only once seen a man syphon power from someone else in an instant, or as near to it as didn't matter. He had absorbed so much power that it should have taken hours, should have destroyed the Leech doing it. But he hadn't seemed affected. He had barely flinched. If anything he had seemed stronger.

Just sucked down all the magic running wild in Kai, and stood there, holding Grace off as if she was nothing at all. No threat, no danger, no one.

The ability to drain someone in moments. And he never wore a mageborn collar. Who would dare to put one on a prince?

'Don't say it,' Merlyn Hale hissed at her. 'He's blood royal. He's a prince, the Lord of Thorndale.'

The Lord of Thorns.

Of course he was. Because that was just her luck.

So she said it anyway. 'He might be. But he's also a suspect.'

Chapter Five

What do you remember?

Being here, being at the Academy, induction, training, working.

Before that.

There were some memories. Not many.

Sunlight filtering through long grass and a woman with red hair like her own, laughing, spinning her around. A pair of hands in hers, so strong, so gentle. And that song. That voice.

Flames came easily and the long grass burned.

'Never do it again, Gracie. Never ever. Promise me now. Never again.'

And she promised. Oh how she promised. But she hadn't kept the promise. She couldn't. That was her fault. It was all her fault.

Auntie bought her, body and soul, and Auntie burned the fire right out of her.

'You want to eat, you earn your keep.'

Each phrase punctuated by a slap.

'Just another mouth to feed.'

A punch.

'There's been a war, everyone's hungry.'

A kick.

'You're no use to me. Not any more. You're nothing. A liar. No one will ever believe you.'

Only they couldn't have brought her to Rathlynn and handed her over to Auntie. They were already dead. They had already burned.

*

Grace struggled out of her nightmare. It wasn't the first time that tangle of half-memories crawled through her dreams and she knew it wouldn't be the last, but it still left her gasping for breath, her eyes burning. Snatches of memory, echoes of a life she couldn't remember.

Most people would say Grace was better off now, without the magic inside her, that whoever or whatever had burned it out of her when she was a child had done her a favour, lifting the curse of a life lived as a mageborn, shunned from society. And maybe they were right. The flames she'd conjured as a child had taken her life from her, her family, her home. Even the brief snatches of memories she still clung to made that clear. No one ever said it to her face though. Not twice.

She dragged her aching body out of bed. The terrible wine had got her through yesterday and that wretched crime scene. It had kept her together enough to keep going until there was nothing else to do last night except sign off and collapse into the bunk.

When had she last actually slept? After Kai died? But that had been broken and terrible, twisted with grief. Before they'd caught the Gore? Years ago? Had she ever really slept?

She poured freezing water from the jug into the bowl on the nightstand and washed her face. It was a better way to wake herself up than screaming.

Less antisocial too.

Daniel walked by the door, singing at the top of his voice. Off-key. Because he always was. Livvie and Sana were giggling in the room next door. Colville yelled something about the showers being freezing this morning and Ingard called him a wimp, laughing at him. Some choice words followed. Sounds of the Academy. Sounds of her life, her home, her family, for want of a better word. She closed her eyes, listening, comforted. This place had saved her. She owed the Academy everything.

Her dress uniform hung in the cupboard. That's what she ought to be wearing today given where she planned to go. Eventually. She stripped off the oversized shirt, pulled on a tunic, ignoring the scars scattered over her skin – she'd had them so long they'd become an intrinsic part of her – and looked at the blue and gold jacket on its hanger. The only hanger she owned. The only one she needed. It wasn't even a good one, just a twisted piece of metal on a lump of wood.

Kai had given it to her. He'd probably made it himself. He did things like that. Or used to.

No, it wasn't a time for her dress uniform. One day she might even find a time when it felt appropriate. But not today.

Instead, she put on her regular leather armour. It felt safer. The jerkin fitted snugly over her shirt and her belt sat tight around her waist, the sigils already replaced on it. She settled the leather strap of her baldric over her shoulder and sheathed her various weapons. Leather bracers slid onto her arms, like shields from her wrists up to her elbows. She studied her outfit, wondering if she could put on anything more and still move in comfort. Armour was figurative as well as literal. Because she had never felt quite so terrified in her life.

It wasn't just the reputation of the Lord of Thorns. It wasn't just the things he did, the *thing* she had seen him do. And it wasn't even the idea of confronting a member of the royal family, albeit the one they all wished had never been born.

She could still recall the feeling of him in the room with her, the sensation of his body against hers, the quiet strength, the implicit threat of him. It was familiar. And not... not unwelcome.

And he had sent Merlyn Hale to help her. Sure. *Help.*

But while she still planned on going to the palace to see the healer and discover what he had found in the Zephyr's body, she was also determined to interview the one person known to have the innate magic that could do such a thing.

She paused at Craine's office, waiting for the others.

'Something I can help you with, Lieutenant?' The commander sat at her desk, surrounded by files, spectacles perched on her hawk-like nose.

That woman didn't miss a trick.

'My report from last night.'

'Yes? Want to fill in the bit you left out?'

Not. A. Trick.

Grace stepped inside the office and pulled the door closed behind her. There were seed cakes in a box on the desk.

'Your wife's home?' she asked.

Craine glanced down at the cakes and smiled. Just for a moment. 'For a while. She has another trip coming up though.' Then her eyes found Grace's again and all was business once more. 'Your report, Marchant.'

'There's one suspect. I didn't want to put it down. But... one Leech who I think could have done it. He's already trying to interfere with the case.'

'Is he now?' Craine glanced down at the file open in front of her. 'I suppose the Lord of Thorns sending his man down to aid you might look that way, yes.'

So she knew about that too. Of course she did.

'Any thoughts?'

Craine raised her eyebrows. 'Well it's nice to see the traffic go in the other direction for once. He's continually co-opting my people.' Grace didn't smile. She wasn't sure if Craine wanted her to or not. It almost sounded like a joke. And yet somehow it didn't. 'Tread carefully, Lieutenant.'

'Well, that was the idea, ma'am.'

Craine rolled her head to one shoulder, then the other, with an audible series of cracks. She looked tired. Exhausted, if Grace was pressed. Not that she'd say it to Craine's face. It was good that her wife was back. Maybe Lara could make her take some time off, or at least go home at night.

'You might want to look at some of the case files. We've had a number of similar reports. No one's followed up on them. No one as high profile as a captain's daughter from Leane, it seems.'

Grace's stomach turned inside her. She took a step towards the desk and took the top file. Two months ago, a girl from Eastferry. Who gave a shit about a girl from Eastferry? No one, that was who. No one but her and Craine.

'Same signs? The burns on the hands?'

'Same signs. Never seen them before. Not until I started looking anyway.'

Grace curled her hands up into fists, hiding them behind her back.

'Commander? Have you been here all night?'

Craine laughed bitterly. 'Last night and many more, Lieutenant.'

'But...' She looked at the cake again.

Craine shook her head. 'It's my honour to serve. Lara understands that. Sometimes it's easier.'

She glanced at the crutches leaning against the desk, just within reach. Craine didn't get out much, not because of the pain involved in moving about since she broke her back and both her legs in the line of duty, but because she was a workaholic. She'd survived the last Great War and countless days on patrol, and still she pushed herself with every ounce of strength she had. And she expected as much from those who worked for her.

'Now, you have an investigation to follow up on. I'll go through these reports and have them for you when you get back. Take Sergeant Childers along with you until we get a new mageborn assigned. He's reliable and he knows the city. And pick up some new sigils from Atelier Zavi before you go. You might need them.'

'It's my honour to serve,' Grace said. Because that was what you always had to say.

'Grace,' Craine said. 'Take some cake. I swear that woman is trying to butter me up, or fatten me up, for something. I suppose I'll find out what this evening.'

*

The Atelier mageborn forged sigils and weapons, and any manner of things. At the Academy this role was filled by Atelier Zavi Millan and there was not a single craftsman in all the kingdom as skilled as he was.

Grace loved to watch him work, the mixture of artist, metallurgist and mageborn making her head spin. He let her sit by his forge and watch in silence. It felt so much like the home she couldn't remember, one of the only places she had felt safe when she first arrived in the city. When she grew up it was still her place of comfort – that and the garden – and he still let her stay and watch him work.

That was all. Watch in silence. Until today.

'That Gore was a bad one,' he said, without looking up from his work. His old hands were deft and strong, twisting gold wire into delicate patterns, tracing light through them to activate the spell.

'Very bad,' she agreed, not sure why he was breaking their tradition of working in silence. He was someone she respected, so she wasn't about to ask. *Take the win*, Ellyn would say. Of all the mageborn, Zavi had always been there. He knew about Grace's past, as much as anyone did. He knew what she was, or rather what she might have been. Like called to like. 'We brought him straight to the palace, to the dungeons there.'

'To the Lord of Thorns, eh?' He spat to one side, away from his work, to ward off evil.

'I met him. When Kai died.'

'Did you?' He didn't sound surprised, not really. And he was waiting for more. She could tell.

'He's... he's not what I expected.'

Do I tell him that he killed Kai, she wondered. How on earth was she to explain that? Or that she'd let him? Kai and Zavi were both mageborn, both Academy-sworn. And the mageborn stuck together. Even when their magic had been stolen along with their memories. Grace wasn't mageborn now, but she had been once. Not that she could remember. She had lost that ability along with her memories of life before the Academy. But something lingered still and the mageborn knew it. They might not be blood relatives but Academy was family.

'Bastien's father was strange too,' Zavi said. He finished the sigil and started another, working as he spoke. 'Tall, same colouring, all contrasts and sharpness. Unearthly. So much magic in him. All kinds. Not just the one like most of us mageborn. Too many to count.'

'How did his father die?'

'Led the mageborn troops in the battle of Howe's pass at the end of the Great War. Like a huge black crow he was, up in front of them all. The king had held him back until then. King Leonis, Marius's father, that is. Afraid he'd lose control, or so they said. Unleashing someone… something, like the Lord of Thorns… well, the old king didn't make that choice lightly. Tlachtlyans didn't stand a chance. It ended the war, but still… He died that day. A lot of the mageborn did. The life of the Lord of Thorns always ends badly. And so do the lives of those who follow him.'

This one would too, she supposed. The fact Bastien had already etched himself into her thoughts and crept into her dreams so completely already just made ignoring him all the more difficult.

He was a royal prince, and if Marius died without naming another heir, destined for kingship. But that was impossible. He was mageborn. Maybe the whole kingdom would end up badly then.

'Zavi, when the king dies—'

'Divinities prevent it.'

'Yes, of course. But when he does, will Bast— will the Lord of Thorns really be king? A mageborn king? I can't imagine it.'

Nothing in their world allowed that. And yet, it seemed to be inevitable now.

'There's no one else, is there? Unless the queen conceives and that's a bit difficult when they don't share a bed.'

'But she… I mean… if she had a lover…'

There were tests for that, of course. Magical and medical. But tests could be cheated. Results could be faked.

'None but a Larelwynn can sit on our throne,' said Zavi solemnly. 'That's the way it works since Lucien Larelwynn's time. His bargain with the mageborn, the pact he made… Every Larelwynn king needs someone to hold up his end of the pact, and that person has always been the Lord of Thorns. I don't know what happens if it's the same man. The Lord of Thorns as the king? Maybe it all falls apart. Or maybe not. If she conceives… well, there's only Marius and Bastien to do the deed anyway. Bastien's child could pass as Marius's, don't you think?'

Grace froze, thinking of the beautiful, golden-haired queen entwined with Bastien Larelwynn, his hands on her skin, his mouth on her mouth. The image flared violently in her mind and she stared into the bright flames. They grew and danced before her, heating her face.

Zavi hissed between his teeth and opened a vent, letting the excess heat escape. He gave her a look, a warning. Maybe. She'd never shared her fears about her magic with him. Nor with any of them. Except Kai. Her magic was gone. Everyone said so. So it couldn't have been her who raised the flames. And that was what she would keep telling anyone who asked. She had to.

Zavi turned back to his work, the new sigil, and it glowed brighter than ever before.

'Here,' he said and tossed it to her. 'A special one, just for you. For luck. There's a bit of you in there anyway.'

She caught it out of the air and closed her hand tightly around it. It should have been hot, she realised, given how brightly it had glowed. But the metal was cool in her hand. You never turned down a gift from Zavi. You never knew when you'd need it.

It was strong, powerful. More than the usual ones. She could feel that right away. And coming from him, directly from him, made for her, with her and all she might face, in mind, it was more precious than any other one. She needed to keep it safe. With great care, she threaded it onto the thong she wore around her neck.

'Thank you, Atelier.'

He snorted. 'Keep it in case you run into your Lord of Thorns again. You may need it.'

Your Lord of Thorns. The thought made her shudder.

'A mageborn king. That'll change things, won't it?'

'We can only hope.' He rubbed his neck, his hand on the collar, pulling at it just a little to adjust it. *We?* Mageborn, he meant. All of them. But he looked directly at her when he said *we.* It made her shiver, although she hid it as best she could, squeezing the sigil he had just given her in her fist.

'Not everyone likes change.' She sighed. Many people didn't want Bastien as king, she knew that. It was fine to have mageborn living in the city, working alongside you, doing the tasks that you didn't want to, but ruling? No. It wasn't just his reputation, or the stories that spread like wildfire about him. Assassins came out of the shadows all the time. Some came from other lands. But most were closer to home. The Royal Guard were brutal. So was he. Some of the mageborn might want him to rule, in the hopes that their lives might get better with one of their own on the throne. But few others felt that way. 'They're probably going to toss me out on my arse rather than let me see him anyway.' She tried to make it funny. A joke.

'I'd like to see them try, Grace,' Zavi chuckled, more out of loyalty to her than anyone else, she suspected. 'And if he has any sense, he'll hear you out.'

She couldn't admit that the thought made something twist inside her, or that for a moment, when she'd pictured him making love to the queen, the woman's hair had been the same shade of red as her own, instead of gold.

*

The Leanese ship was gone. The captain must have shipped out at the first possible opportunity. Grace didn't blame him, but it would have been easier to follow up on things if he was still here. Someone on his crew might have seen something and, while Ellyn, Daniel and Childers had spent the evening taking statements, they hadn't brought her anything. Bright sunlight spilled across the docks and the breeze made the spars on the ships sing like wind chimes. Seagulls reeled around, shrieking like demons, which told her the daily catch wasn't far off shore now. Soon the fishing fleet would descend and all would be swallowed up in the barely orchestrated chaos of the mart.

For now, it was almost peaceful. Or as peaceful as it got.

The pie shop on the corner of Fletcher's Alley was open. It was little more than a hatch in a wall which led into a kitchen but all of Belport knew it. Academy officers too. There was no actual way of knowing what went into the fillings but by the seraphs they tasted divine. Grace wasn't sure what magic Alyss used to make them. It had to be something.

But Alyss wasn't there this morning. Stef, her father, leaned on the counter and stared at the water in the harbour.

'Where's Alyss?' Grace asked as she slid a coin over and Stef handed her a pie.

'Out.'

Grace frowned. 'Really?' She couldn't imagine the cheerful, chatty Alyss doing anything other than this. 'Where?'

'Up in the palace,' Stef grumbled. Alyss's sweet nature must have come from her mother.

The pie was good, but not that good. It was just a pie. Grace glanced down at the crisp pastry which seemed a bit tougher than usual too.

Lesser, somehow. Stef could make pies, no doubt about it, but not like his daughter.

'Did she get a job in the kitchens?' she asked. Divinities knew, she was a good enough cook, although Grace wasn't sure common street pies would be regular fare up there.

'Goddess knows. It was an offer she couldn't refuse, if you get my drift.'

Ah, that kind of job. Her day of homage, vassalage, duty.

'Want me to look in on her? I'm heading that way.'

Stef shook his head. 'She'll come back when she can. When they're done with her. Just some test of her skills for the Lord of Thorns, so they said. It might take a few days.'

A few days? The day of homage was meant to be just that: a day. Usually no more than a few hours. How long did it take to get up there, kneel in front of the Lord of Thorns and make a promise? What was he up to?

'Has that been happening a lot?' she asked after she swallowed down a lumpy mouthful. Definitely wasn't one of Alyss's. It was only ever meant to be one day. It seemed to get longer and longer. Fewer mageborn in the city, some said, though where they'd gone she didn't know. Larks, the stories called them, those who had flown far away from Rathlynn.

'Too often. Davy Fisher only got back after the guts of a week and his mam said he just slept for days. Hasn't eaten either. Exhausted, poor kid. Drained. And they had to send for a Curer to treat his—'

Then he seemed to remember that he was talking to an Academy officer and shut up.

Drained. She really didn't like the sound of that. And what did the Curer have to treat? She was going to have to call in on the Fishers.

'It's all going to shit, isn't it?' Stef muttered. 'A mageborn king, eh? Who would have thought it? The Lord of Thorns on the throne...'

With the king ailing, and only a mageborn heir, the whole kingdom was racked with unrest. If Bastien stepped aside, as many said he should, other families would vie for the crown. They weren't Larelwynns though. No one knew what would happen to the pact controlling the mageborn without one of the royal line on the throne. And if Bastien Larelwynn took the crown, no one knew what would happen at all. Could he do both? Magic was fickle, dangerous. Those who wielded it doubly so, or so the old saying went. Perhaps it was better, some people whispered, if the mageborn ran away, if they left the kingdom of Larelwynn completely.

The Hollow King had made a pact with the first Larelwynn king to save his skin, and save his mageborn people. He'd given up everything for it, including his life. No one wanted another Magewar, not like that. They'd barely survived the war with Tlachtlya and that had been mundane enough. People were scared. The neighbouring kingdoms were already getting belligerent. All along the borders, life was becoming dangerous.

Who was going to notice if a Leanese stranger got jumped in an alley and drained of magic somehow? A girl who wore too-bright skirts and stood out in Belport? Who was going to notice any of the others Craine had discovered? And who was going to notice if Davy Fisher didn't recover, or Alyss the Pie-Maker never came back?

'Boss!' Ellyn waved at her across the quay and pointed up towards the Healers' Halls. 'We want to get a move on. Danny's still down in the Rowan. We're going to have to drag him out of the place. Is that one of Alyss's pies?'

It wasn't. It really wasn't. Grace handed her the remains of it anyway.

The kids playing by the old well in the quayside had gone silent. They'd been almost as loud as the seagulls when she'd arrived.

A group of men filled the quayside, a few mounted, most on foot. They were armoured, with red tabards, the mark of royal blood and Royal Guard.

Stef's expression turned even more glum. Instincts made her look at the gathered men. Royal Guards weren't supposed to operate outside the palace. When they did it was usually trouble. The Watch dealt with crime in the city if it wasn't magical, which was the remit of the Academy. The Royal Guard looked after the blood royal. That was about it. Threats, wars, politics, that kind of thing. They were the strong arm of the king.

'What are they doing here?' Grace muttered.

Throwing their weight around from the look of it. Two of them were harassing the fishmonger's boys while the rest laughed. All but one. On the magnificent sable charger nearest to them, a tall, handsome man watched absently, as if distracted by other things. The messenger with him handed over scrolls which he read carefully, commenting occasionally in reply. Clearly he was a noble, possibly some scion of the blood royal himself, to judge from his bearing, and his flawless features. He had thick blond hair, like gold, and his blue eyes were cold like ice. He ought to have been attractive, but he wasn't. He chilled her to the bone.

And that was when Grace felt it. Magic where there should have been none. She wasn't sure what it was, exactly, or where it came from, but the air shivered.

One of the boys, the younger one, went down on his arse as if his legs had just been swept out from under him. The bucket of iced water he'd been carrying went up in the air, flipped over and came down in a shower, soaking him. He cried out in shock and was answered with a roar of male laughter.

Divinities, she hated that sound.

Ellyn moved forward but Grace brought up a hand to stop her. She scanned the crowd quickly. Not one of them was collared. They all appeared to be Rathlynnese at first glance and there were no other markers of magic on them.

But one of them was, without a shadow of a doubt, mageborn. It was the only explanation for what she had just seen.

'Make ready to move out,' the noble called and they shuffled back into lines.

Grace stepped into their path, blocking them.

'Is there a problem here?' The eyes of the noble alighted on her, on her uniform and her gaze, and, to her disgust, he smirked. The only word for that ugly expression on so handsome a face.

Something cold and clawed slid down Grace's back. Irritation followed it.

'Get out of our way,' the man said when she didn't immediately answer.

'We don't want trouble here,' Stef called. 'I'm sure they're just on their way, about their own business, Officer Marchant. You know how it is. High spirits and all.'

High spirits. You could get away with so much because of 'high spirits' if you had the right name, or the right uniform, or the right friends. Or at least you could with some people. Not with her.

'Problem, boss?' Ellyn asked lightly, as she joined Grace, hands resting on her sword hilt.

'Oooh, there's two of them now. The little one's for me, lads. Who wants to tackle the firebrand?'

Grace's eyes flicked up to the nobleman again. Funny word that. Nobleman. She'd never seen much of anything noble about any of them.

And then, the unauthorised mageborn among them made his final mistake.

A gust of wind came from nowhere, sweeping dust and dirt into Ellyn's face, and her friend stepped back shielding her eyes. And Grace spotted him.

A bald, scarred man smirked a moment too early, like he knew what was about to happen.

Grace moved, leaping forward, her hand already on a sigil which flared into light as she drew it. Her expert touch ignited it.

The unfairness of Kai's fate blazed through her. That this fucker should flaunt his magic without fear of repercussions while Kai died to protect Rathlynn from rogues… that the uniform of the Royal Guards should protect him when the uniform of the Academy made Kai disposable? No. Not on her watch.

She grabbed him by the neck and brought him down with the sigil unfurling around his throat before he'd hit the ground. There was a brief, panicked surge of wind around her and then the spell worked, containing him. He didn't even know what was happening.

Which was odd. His confusion was written all over his face. What sort of mageborn didn't know about sigils and what they could do?

Grace looked up into a sea of blades, bristling all around her. But she didn't care as she snarled the words of the Academy at him. 'In the name of the crown I arrest you and charge you with the crime of being an unregistered and unsworn mageborn. You will submit to examination and yield up your magic for the greater good. In the name of the king.'

An eerie silence fell over the quay. A moment like a bubble which, when it burst, could go either way. Spars rattled overhead, the waves whispered against the slip and the seagulls reeled and cried high overhead.

The noble in charge of this rabble of guards cleared his throat.

'There must be some mistake, Officer.' He even had the tone of a general. This... this wasn't good. Still, Grace held her ground. Truth and justice. That was all that mattered.

'Sigils only react to those with magic. He isn't collared, so he isn't a vassal of the crown.'

'But he is sworn to the crown. He's a guard of the blood royal.'

'He used magic in public, General, without a collar to regulate it. That's against the law. I have to take him in.' She fought to keep her own voice steady. There was something here that didn't feel entirely right, something she was missing or didn't understand. It was not a good feeling.

'Lord Kane,' the man she'd subdued cried out in shock and genuine fear. 'Lord Kane, please...'

The general – Lord Kane, it appeared, and Grace filed the name away for future reference – didn't like being named right about now, that was certain from his scowl.

'*The law does not bend, and cannot break*,' he intoned in his perfectly modulated voice. The first precept of the Academy, the first law Grace had ever learned. 'You must do your duty then, Officer. Stand back, men, and do not interfere.'

They didn't like it but they didn't dare disobey him. More likely, she suspected, from fear rather than respect. They sheathed weapons and withdrew back into their ranks while she hauled the mageborn guard up onto his feet.

Kane turned his horse's head, signalled to the other riders who had watched from a distance and gave a curt signal that they were leaving.

As he passed, Grace's captive tried to fling himself towards his commander. She barely stopped him ending up under the hooves of the charger. But he managed to break free of her. 'Please my lord, it's a mistake. It has to be. I'm not a mageborn, my lord. You know that. Please!'

He clawed at the stirrups and Lord Kane drew back an arm and struck him across the face. The man spun around, knocked senseless, and fell in a heap on the wet stones.

'I had one rule, Griggs,' Kane spat at him. 'You all agreed to that when you chose to follow me. You swore to obey and you have squandered that chance on cheap amusement.'

The troop moved off noiselessly, chastened.

The sigil around Griggs's neck glimmered, still active. But the sense of magic from him seemed less powerful now, less repulsive than when he'd been part of that group. Grace watched them go uneasily.

'What in all the seven hells was that about?' Ellyn asked.

'I'm not mageborn,' the guard mumbled as they hauled him up. He wouldn't shut up about it now. 'I'm not mageborn.' He repeated it all the way back to the Academy where Craine looked him once over and told Childers to lock him up until he could be properly tested. He wasn't anything dangerous like a Gore or a Barrow. Probably just a nascent Zephyr, although one with a bully's sense of humour.

'I'm not mageborn. It's a mistake.' Grace could still hear him saying it as he was led away. 'They did this. They did this to me.'

'Glories, some people will try anything,' Ellyn muttered. 'Like we'd be able to frame him. We should go and find Danny.'

Grace rolled her shoulders and tried to shake off the feeling that she was missing something. He wasn't anything special. It was just… strange that a mageborn who had managed to hide so long, and so well he'd entered the Royal Guard, should betray himself in so stupid a way. But then, men were stupid sometimes.

Like Daniel. Ellyn was right. They ought to go and get him.

'Who's the love of his life this week?' she asked.

When things went wrong Daniel usually threw himself into a brief, destructive romance with someone entirely inappropriate. Losing Kai definitely counted as things going wrong.

'Oh divinities,' Ellyn sighed. 'Blake has a new harper down at the Rowan. He's damned cute. Danny's down there. I bet you a beer he won't have moved.'

*

The bar of the Rowan was almost empty, which was a pity since the young man in the corner, bent over his harp, sang with the most beautiful voice Grace had ever heard. It didn't take a glimpse of the collar around his neck to recognise him as a Lyric. But there was talent there too, not just magic. He was skilled. His hands moved in a delicate dance over the strings and the harmonies sent shivers of unexpected pleasure through her. He was also beautiful, golden-haired, golden-skinned and gracious, like some kind of spirit given human form.

Daniel, meanwhile, sat with his back to the bar, listening with rapt attention. If Grace walked right up to him this very second and kissed him on the lips, he probably wouldn't even notice.

'You see what I mean?' Ellyn said.

'He's good.'

'I'm not much for music but he's great to look at. Anyway, not him. Danny.'

Some deep-seated loyalty made her say it. 'Danny's not so bad.'

Ellyn gave her an arch look. 'Yeah, well… Danny's Danny. Want to see if I can pull the stool out from under him before he sees me?'

'That's your plan?'

'I'm improvising.'

Grace laughed. They were sometimes too alike. 'Go for it.'

But before Ellyn could move, the harper finished the song and Daniel was up on his feet, heading towards him. He still hadn't noticed them. All he could see was the pretty musician with a magical voice.

'Before they get to awkward flirting,' she told Ellyn, 'we should probably break them up.'

As they approached, Daniel was talking quietly, leaning in towards the harper's indulgent smile.

'—at the Larks' Rest in three days' time. Leeland had to change his schedule so Kurt says—'

It didn't sound like the type of line that would woo someone like that. Maybe Daniel wasn't the flirt he thought he was after all.

'Are you talent-scouting for your brother's bar now?' Ellyn asked slyly, coming up behind him. She glanced at the harpist. 'I don't know, mate. This one's a lot nicer. You'd be trading down.'

Daniel leaped back, his eyes wide in alarm. 'Ellyn? What are you doing here?'

'Looking for you. We're meant to be working, remember?'

'I was just… I mean, yes, of course we are, but I just—'

Ellyn snorted a laugh. 'Oh I can see what you were *just*.'

'And you are?' Grace asked the Lyric, her best officer of the Academy face on full display.

He smiled easily, not in the least bit uncomfortable with their arrival. Cocky little shit, wasn't he?

'Misha Harper, Lieutenant. Danny has told me so much about you.' He held out his hand, unafraid, and she shook it, impressed already. She didn't particularly want to be, because Daniel was a disaster when it came to relationships, and she didn't want to spend the next few weeks reining him in and the few after that picking up the pieces when it inevitably all fell apart. But this felt different. This felt... good.

'I hope he hasn't,' she replied and Misha laughed gently.

'All good, I promise. He's afraid you might not approve.' He slid his fingertips under the delicately patterned leather collar, the expert tooling an effort to make it less like a necessity and more like a fashion choice. The sigil in it glimmered. It was also a challenge and a teasing gesture she couldn't miss.

'That's not what I meant,' Daniel spluttered. 'I just... I didn't...'

The harper reached out for Daniel's hand. Ellyn smirked, Grace smiled and Daniel turned puce and forgot to breathe.

'I don't have any reason to disapprove,' Grace replied. Let him infer a *yet* if he wanted to. It would be a warning and she meant it. 'Harper? Did the name or the profession come first?'

His soft laugh told her she was never getting an answer to that. 'A bit of both, Lieutenant.'

Oh, he was a charmer. She'd have to watch him. She'd also thought they were the only ones to call him Danny, apart from his brother. 'I'll get the full story another day, perhaps. But we need to get to work. Duty calls, *Danny*.'

Misha grinned at him as Daniel tried to stammer out an apology. 'I told you it would be fine. But she's right. Duty and honour, Danny. I'll do as you ask and sort out everything with Kurt. Don't worry. It'll be fine.'

And he pulled Daniel towards him, planting a very visible kiss on his lips.

'Fine,' Daniel echoed as they parted. He looked slightly dazed.

Ellyn extracted him from the harper, linked arms with him and led him out of the bar, while Misha settled down to play again.

'*Fine?*' she mimicked him perfectly, her voice drifting and soft. '*Fine?*'

'I just… I mean, I met him and I… he was in the bar and… and then he said come to hear him play…'

'Wow, coherent,' Ellyn teased. 'Well done that man. I didn't know Lyrics were meant to addle the brain too. Did you, Grace? Is he half woodsiren or something?'

Grace shrugged. 'Can woodsirens come into the city? Are they even real?' Daniel squirmed. She couldn't help herself. He was normally so self-assured. 'What about a Charm? Maybe he's just a really good Charm and we all think he played beautifully because he wants us to.'

'No, he's just… I just… I like him, Grace. I really like him. A lot.'

'*No? Really?*'

Ellyn couldn't take it any more. She roared laughing.

Grace finally relented. 'It's *fine*, Danny. He seems nice. And he clearly likes you too. A lot. Now, your love life aside, we have work to do. We're already late.'

It wouldn't last. Daniel's relationships never did. Unsuitable wasn't the word for it. And the Academy didn't look kindly on relationships between its officers and mageborn. It muddied the waters, Craine said. But she turned a blind eye too. Everyone did. Because when you got down to it, what did it matter? Grace didn't care who he slept with. She just didn't want him getting hurt.

'Late for what?'

'Interrogating the Lord of Thorns.'

*

The palace was built on and into the hill overlooking Rathlynn. While the towers and spires went up into the sky, the kings had also tunnelled down into the heart of the earth. The complex was huge. Grace was pretty sure only the royal family of Larelwynn knew just how big it was. The rumour went that the deepest cells in the dungeons never saw natural light. Or so the people of Rathlynn liked to say, late at night, with a shiver behind the words.

As they descended the stone steps to the morgue, daylight faded behind them. The stairs curved so it was impossible to see ahead but there were torches at relevant points, just enough so that there was light to navigate by. The air got colder, leeching the heat from their bodies. That was the reason Grace suppressed a shiver as they reached the next floor, and that was what she would continue to tell herself, or anyone else who asked.

The narrow staircase opened out into a wide hall, lined with tapestries for warmth, and lit by candles. There was a window, of sorts, at the far end, covered with iron bars and yet still glazed with ancient, rippled glass. It let in only a dim, smoky light.

'Morgue's this way,' Ellyn said, turning abruptly left, away from the window.

Grace knew the way. She also knew what lay in the other direction. Bastien Larelwynn's domain, and she'd have to go there later. She'd have to interview him. A shiver crawled down the line of her spine. It was almost like that sensation of being watched, but when she glanced back, there was no one there.

Merlyn Hale didn't look up as they entered the barrel-vaulted room. Lamps illuminated it, the unnatural, clear brightness signalling right away that magic powered them. The air shimmered with it, like the hum of static, setting Grace's teeth on edge from the moment she walked in.

'Hale?'

He was bent over his desk, studying his notes, but the sound of his name snapped him out of his thoughts.

'Oh Lieutenant, there you are. I've been…' He glanced at Daniel and Ellyn. 'Yes, I was hoping to talk to you. The corpse…'

'Losle Vayden, from Leane, the victim. We spoke to her grieving father, remember?'

He gave her a confused look, as if she was talking nonsense. Perhaps he didn't see the girl as a person. Losle was only a mageborn after all, even if she didn't wear a collar.

'The victim…' he began again slowly, finally getting Grace's cue. 'The victim was drained of magic so quickly her whole system appears to have gone into shock. It wasn't removed so much as ripped out of her.'

He crossed to the mortuary slab and uncovered the Leanese woman's face and torso. The chest had been cut open and Grace stiffened in shock.

Behind her Daniel slapped his hand over his mouth, gave a muffled groan and turned away abruptly.

'If you're going to throw up, Officer, there's a bucket in the corner by the door,' Hale said, calmly. 'Then take it outside. Now, if you take a look here…' He pointed into the chest cavity as Daniel lost his breakfast and probably last night's dinner too, sprinting to the bucket by the door and only just making it.

'Ellyn, help him outside, will you?' Grace asked, keeping her voice calm and even. Something in her ruffled a little. It was almost as if Hale was setting out to upset them, possibly for his own amusement, but possibly for some other reason. She glanced up at the auburn-haired man to see his smirk still turned on Daniel. 'Maybe take him up to get some fresh air. I can let you know if there's anything pertinent later on. Please continue, healer.'

Ellyn nodded at her, just once, clearly picking up on her tone, and then seized Daniel by the armpit, hauling him and the bucket up. 'Come on Danny. Let's get you out of here.'

Grace didn't allow the amusement inside her to show on her face. First the new boyfriend and now this. Ellyn was not going to let Daniel live today down in a hurry. But this wasn't a place for levity and Hale made Grace uncomfortable in a way she couldn't quite define. He was too clever by half to begin with. And there were different kinds of teasing.

'Please continue, Hale.'

'If you are quite sure you don't need a moment?'

She thought of the bodies the Gore had left behind. If this healer wanted to shock her, he would have to do a better job than this.

'I don't have unlimited time. I have other things to attend to.' Like interviewing the Lord of Thorns. Not an enticing prospect. Definitely not. 'Get on with it. What have you found?'

'She was in extremely good health. Her magic wasn't having any detrimental effect on her physical wellbeing. Quite often we can trace the effects on the internal organs as a kind of scarring. But not here. Remarkable.'

Again, Grace tried not to wince. *Quite often.* How many mageborn had he opened up like this to examine? And who had supplied them?

Oh, but she was fairly sure she knew the answer to that.

'What killed her?'

'The rapid extraction of magic. And I mean, rapid. This was no ordinary syphon or Leech. It would have only taken minutes.

And for any normal Leech that should have meant an overload and certain death.'

She thought of Kai, of the light within him, brimming over, burning him from inside. She tightened her fists until her nails dug into the palms of her hands and let him continue.

'And then there's this.' Hale lifted one of the young woman's hands in his long fingers and turned it over to display the palms. They were blackened, burned. 'One mark on the palm of each hand. The skin is burned in a perfect circle, right through the outer layers and into deeper tissue, the muscles themselves. Almost to the bone.'

'What could have caused that?'

He paused, as if deliberating what he should tell her. 'I have no idea.'

He sounded offended by the thought. Grace narrowed her eyes and wondered if he was lying. It was possible. She didn't know him enough to trust him on this.

'You've never seen this before? Nothing like it at all?'

Because she had. More than once. In the files Craine had given her. Once again, she forced herself to ignore the itch in her palms. It wasn't the same as that. For one thing she was still breathing.

'I've seen it. I just have no idea how it happened. There was a body—'

'*A victim,*' she corrected him coolly, lifting her chin and giving him a hard stare.

'A… a victim then… there was one a few weeks ago.'

'Do you often make such studies of the dead, Hale?'

'I do my duty, Lieutenant. As all must. It is my honour to serve.'

'That's not an answer.'

His eyes widened as they turned on her. 'Am *I* under investigation now?'

She smiled, a sweet smile tinged with acid. He looked outraged, but also a little more concerned. Better. It took the smug superiority out of him.

'I do my duty, healer. As all must. It is my honour to serve.'

A long silence followed. She waited for him to fold. She wasn't disappointed.

'Perhaps one or two corpses – I mean...' he winced and swallowed hard. '*Victims* a month. The study is vital to our work as healers, you know? We learn so much from the dead. Not just mageborn. And not all victims of others either. The diseased, those who met an accident or a timely death as well. It's important to understand. It will help, in the long run, the greater work of healing.'

Wonderful. He was an equal opportunities butcher of the deceased.

'And mageborn?'

'To study why they are born, how the magic affects them, their links to the Maegen...'

The word almost made her take a step back from him. She'd never heard anyone say it so lightly. Something lit up in his eyes, interest at her reaction. She didn't like it. The need to cover herself was instinctive and immediate.

'The... *what?*'

'The Maegen. The source of power. Have you never asked one of them about it? They feel it, inside themselves, like sap in a tree. Some even dream of it. It's a spiritual thing for them.'

Them... Mageborn were others to him. Something to be examined, studied, dissected. Chilly fingers of instinct played at the back of her neck. She knew the Maegen, knew it intimately. She remembered the dreams, the light, that shifting light like the reflection of water or the bubbling of lava...

She pushed the thoughts away in case they betrayed her. Hale might not notice her reaction. But others here could.

'Where is the Lord of Thorns?'

Merlyn Hale glanced at her, his eyes very blue beneath the fall of his auburn hair. He chewed on his narrow lower lip for a moment. 'A word to the wise, Lieutenant. Don't call him that. He hates it.'

'And why is that?'

'It's not exactly complimentary, is it?' There had been a Lord of Thorns ever since Lucien Larelwynn's brother took the title, passed down through the generations. But they never ruled. They were the seneschals of the mageborn and thus mageborn themselves. They all died young, in violence and despair. Being the Lord of Thorns wasn't so much a title as a curse. 'Don't push it, Lieutenant. He isn't patient.'

'Well,' she smiled her blandest smile. 'I wouldn't want to upset him, would I?'

Chapter Six

Bastien's head pounded. Aurelie had thrown a party and insisted he attend. He'd wanted to leave early but the wine had gone to his head and he'd spent a large portion of the remaining time there trying to disentangle himself from her. She loved to flirt, the queen did. And there were not many people she could flirt with comfortably. He had been forced to excuse himself and he knew she'd be pouting for days that he hadn't stayed. And that half the court would be talking about it. He'd end up the villain in this. She would see to that.

Asher laughed at him when he complained.

'No one else would turn her down, old friend.'

Maybe not. But she was still the queen. She was Marius's wife and, at some point, someone would get the wrong idea.

He hadn't slept well, and couldn't stop thinking about the boy assassin on the terrace below the balcony from which he'd thrown himself, his blood pooling around him in a glossy sheet. Whether he really had thrown himself off, as the guards swore had happened, or if he'd been helped along the way… well, that was another matter.

Would they lie to him?

It was hard to say. He knew they feared him. But he wasn't so much of a fool to think there was nothing they feared more.

Rathlynn was a dangerous place and the palace the beating heart of that terror if you got on the wrong side of the wrong person. The city was just a microcosm of the country. There were enemies at every turn. The war with Tlachtlya might have ended twenty years ago, but that didn't mean it was forgotten. Any weakness would be seized upon at any level.

And the weakness now was in the crown itself. In the king.

His cousin was dying and Bastien was the heir presumptive. A mageborn heir. An impossible thing.

People would die to stop him succeeding Marius. People would definitely kill.

Hale had taken the body to try to find out anything of use but Bastien didn't think there was anything to find. He doubted he himself would find anything either. A fanatic, perhaps a useful pawn in a much larger game. A game of kings and queens, royal dynasties and bloodlines. The boy had no place in it. He'd been doomed from the moment he'd agreed, or been coerced into action.

But who had given him that power? Who had tethered him to a Tide? The process was still dangerous, almost impossible to stabilise. It could kill them both. Bastien knew that. He had created it. And because of that he hadn't shared it with more than a few people yet. He'd mentioned it to the king. Marius had been… well… appalled didn't even cover it.

The door to his office opened and he didn't bother to look up.

'What is it, Simona?' he growled.

A discreet cough made him pause and lift his eyes. 'Simona wasn't around. I let myself in, your highness.'

The woman from the Healers' Halls stood there, the one who had tried to save her mageborn friend. The officer from the Academy with the auburn hair like fire and the attitude to match. She stood there, slender and elegant, with a scowl on her face which did nothing to mar the looks she clearly didn't care to think about. Bastien usually read people with ease. Not this time.

'It is usual to knock.'

A smile played across her lips and she folded her arms in front of her chest. 'I knocked a few times. I don't think you were listening.'

It wasn't that she was irritating. Although perhaps that was part of it. Distracting. Yes, that was the word. She distracted him. Everything about her. He studied her for a long moment and she didn't flinch under his dark gaze. She didn't look away either. Most people couldn't hold his stare for long. Their attention shifted, darted elsewhere, but she just stared back at him, unrepentant. Intriguing.

'Perhaps I wasn't. I lose myself in my work sometimes. What can I do for you, Lieutenant Marchant?'

If it surprised her that he knew her name, she was good enough to keep it hidden. Because why shouldn't he have learned her name? He hadn't had anyone stand up to him as completely as she had in years. It didn't matter that it hadn't done her any good.

'I have some questions for you. About a murder. And Merlyn Hale.'

'I sent him down to have a look.' Another death so quickly was a concern. Especially as it was a mageborn. *Burns to the hands*, Hale had said, *drained of magic, a hyper-accelerated syphon… worrying signs*. Almost as worrying as the boy assassin with magic he shouldn't have had.

'Why?'

He smiled, a slow warning smile. 'Perhaps I wanted to get him out of the Healers' Halls to see what the real world was like. Or perhaps I thought he could help.'

'Or perhaps you wanted him to cover your tracks.'

Oh, so that was what she thought. Well, she wouldn't be the first. As a member of the blood royal, and a mageborn to boot, it was natural that suspicion fell on him. He'd heard such things all his life. Absentmindedly, he reached up and touched the golden torc around his neck. Not a leather collar for him. Oh no.

Lieutenant Marchant's eyes followed the movement.

'That wouldn't have been very smart, would it? Given he obviously told you I sent him right away.'

'And how do you know that?'

'I told him to.'

'And has he reported back to you yet?'

Bastien shook his head and stood up. 'Not more than the basics. He brought the body back here and is examining it now. A Leanese woman, a Zephyr, completely drained of magic.' He didn't mention the burn marks. Neither did she.

'I know. I spoke to him.' Of course she had. He gazed at her dispassionately. Was she questioning him? Interesting.

'Do you have any other suspicions? Aside from me, I mean.'

She gave a laugh, a bright sound he hadn't expected from her. 'And why would I suspect you, your highness?'

'Well, you'd be a fool not to. I'm the strongest Leech in the country, among other things. The mageborn report here, to me, for their day of homage. And any who transgress are sent to me as well. But I hardly need to go sneaking around the docks late at night attacking young Leanese girls and stealing their magic.'

Grace thought about it and then nodded slowly. 'You have ample opportunities, don't you? You don't have to hunt them in the city. They're brought right to you. There are people missing, you know.

People who came to pay their day of homage, and haven't made it home. Or if they have, it's days later and they can't say what happened.'

Bastien frowned, suddenly uncomfortable. That couldn't be right, could it? He'd have to check with Hale. Something was wrong with that story. 'I'll look into that. You have my word.'

She didn't look convinced. Not that he could blame her. Her reasoning was sound, even if the information leading her to these conclusions was limited. But the accusation stung. She glared at him and somehow he felt the need to explain. He'd never felt that with anyone but Marius and it unnerved him.

'Do you know how my magic works, Lieutenant? I don't need to take magic from others. It's not like a hunger or an addiction. It's just a thing I can do. I don't *need* to do it. Or at least, not physically.'

She tilted her head to one side, considering this.

'Psychologically?'

It was quite the question.

He fought to suppress his smile. 'Do I have a psychological need to drain magic from others?'

'Yes. Kai… my friend, the mageborn you…' And for the first time her voice shook. She'd tried to stop him, tried to help her friend. She'd been defending him, even though a prince had ordered her out of the way. Had they been more than friends, he wondered. Lovers? They would have made a handsome couple together.

And unexpectedly he felt something he hadn't felt in years. Something he barely recognised any more. It felt almost like a surge of jealousy.

'Officer Kai Albren, first class. A Leech. His file was impressive. Everyone spoke highly of him.'

'You haven't answered my question, your highness.'

'Bastien,' he said.

She frowned, confused by this tack. It shouldn't have amused him as much as it did. But just to see her wrong-footed, just for a moment, was endearing.

'*Bastien?*'

'My name. Rather than "your highness". It's quicker.' It wasn't. The way she said it took exactly the same amount of time. But still… the way she frowned made it worthwhile.

She gave a little laugh then, barely more than a breath. 'I would have thought you would prefer the title. Isn't it a sign of respect?'

'That rather depends how you say it, doesn't it?'

'Right then, *Bastien.*' Oh yes, it entirely depended on how you said it. Marchant raised her eyebrows. And she waited.

It was his turn to laugh. 'I still haven't answered your question. When I take magic from another mageborn, I do it to help. Your friend Kai was dying. He would have died screaming in agony. As the power inside him grew wild and ungovernable, it would have tried to… possess him, for want of a better word. And such power is dangerous.'

If Albren hadn't been strapped down, he would have tried to kill her. Just because she was there. He might have loved her with all his heart and it would still have happened. Because she was right there, right in front of him. Because of the ghost of magic he could sense in her. Bastien had seen it before. But how could he tell her that? She wouldn't believe him anyway.

'So you were trying to help him? By stealing his magic and taking his life?'

If only it was as simple as that. 'Have you ever heard of the Hollow King?'

'It's a legend. An old story.' She said it dismissively, impatient to get on with her questions rather than answer his. Of course she'd heard of him. You couldn't live in Rathlynn without hearing about him. But Bastien wasn't going to be rushed.

'It's so much more than that. He's the reason why mageborn must swear to serve the crown, and never to aspire to wear it.'

Which left him in a predicament, didn't it? The torc suddenly felt very heavy. He could feel her eyes on it again.

'You're mageborn,' she said, an accusation with which he was all too familiar.

'Yes.' There was no point in denying it. The whole kingdom knew. It was his purpose in life. To be mageborn – and to control the rest of them.

'And King Marius's heir.'

'So they tell me.'

'Who tells you?'

'The king. His wife. His ministers. The whole court. Oh, and all the people trying to kill me.'

'A daily event, is it?'

She had no idea.

'More or less, my dear lieutenant. One of the perils of life in the court. I've lived my whole life with the knowledge of it. The Hollow King devoured the mageborn of this country, plunging them into his madness. Unchecked they would have killed everyone. They say he tore the Maegen itself out of its pool and took it all into himself, gave himself up to the shadows in its depths. If he couldn't have magic, he took that quintessence that makes us human, that drives life itself. He rampaged through the kingdom and destroyed his own bloodline, consumed by darkest magic. He burned my ancestral home, made desolation out of the valley of the roses and called it Thorndale. My ancestor, Lucien Larelwynn, was the one to finally kill him. He forced him to agree to the pact and then he ran him through. You can't make a deal like that without blood, after all. There must always be blood. We still have his sword, Godslayer. It hangs over the throne. A cautionary reminder. Do you know the rest of the story?'

She shook her head, not because she didn't know it. Everyone knew it. But rather because, like everyone else in Rathlynn, Grace Marchant didn't really believe it. 'It's just a story. I'm trying to trace a killer. And the girl wasn't the first victim either. You know that, don't you?'

He knew. But he wasn't finished.

'The Hollow King cursed us. All of us. He cursed my ancestor, and his family, and all descended from him. The Maegen is fickle, and powerful, and dangerous. We see it as light, but there is darkness as well. Beneath the waters of the pool, the Deep Dark waits for us all. The Hollow King knew that. He used that. That was what destroyed him, after all, and he passed that doom on to us as well. He cursed us with magic and ensured that for every Larelwynn king there's a Lord of Thorns. Even if it's made of gold, it's still a collar.'

Her gaze flickered down to the torc and then back to his face.

'And you wear it so you can't become another Hollow King.'

She was quick.

'I wear it to remind myself that it's always a possibility. I have no desire to hunt down unfortunate mageborn who are doing nothing but trying to live their lives. No more than you do, I presume. My role is to help them, guide them and be the touchstone that anchors their power, stops them losing control. Like your friend did. That's part of what the day of homage is. I bring them balance, and peace. I still the darkness that can rise unbidden through the Maegen and destroy them. I draw it out of them, subdue it if I must, and send them on their way. I work to make that easier for them, to find ways to make the pact easier on us all. My role is to protect them and that is my paramount desire.'

He closed his eyes, breathing out slowly. It was more than he had admitted to anyone in years. When he opened them again Grace was studying him carefully. Waiting. Her patience unnerved him. He'd have to watch that.

Time for honesty then. Not about everything, but about his intentions perhaps. 'I sent Hale because I thought he could help you. I am willing to come with you, should you so wish. You have no mageborn working with you since Officer Albren's demise. That puts you at a disadvantage. We should rectify that.'

He couldn't have put her more off balance if he'd swept her into his arms and kissed her. The temptation to compare the two was unexpectedly strong. He forced himself to shake the thought away.

'You... want to work with me...'

'If you will have me, Lieutenant.'

She glared at him, eyes narrow, suspicion in the depths of them as she tried to figure out if he was joking or mocking her. He could hardly blame her.

'I don't need you.'

He lifted his chin just a little, a gesture to remind her of his status, but that didn't seem to have the desired effect. 'And what if I insist?'

'As the royal heir? Or as the Lord of Thorns?'

She spat out the words and he took them like the blows they were. It didn't matter. He'd heard far worse.

'Something is afoot in this city. Something dark and evil, and someone is trying to make it look like I am part of it. Not to mention trying to kill me.' Admittedly that could be any number of people but he decided not to go into that for now. 'I would like to know who it is. And why. I think you are the person to help me discover it. Who is using my people? Who is using my work?'

'Your work?'

'Yes. Certain aspects of this case are... familiar to me. I'm not at liberty to tell you more.'

She gave a brief, dismissive laugh. 'Of course you aren't.'

'I serve the king. As you do. So yes, Lieutenant Marchant, as the royal heir and as the Lord of Thorns, I insist.'

'Well then...' She scowled. 'It's my honour to serve.'

She didn't sound like it though.

Chapter Seven

What could she do? He just stood there and invited himself onto her team as if it was some kind of holiday adventure or a hobby to pass the idle hours. Lecturing her on ancient history and old legends. All the time, smirking at her with that too bloody handsome face of his. And every second she stood in his presence, the instinct to get the hell away as soon as possible was growing stronger. Or to do something else. Something reckless and insane.

'Fine,' she said. But it wasn't fine. Not *Danny and Misha* fine. It was just a word that everyone used when they were trapped into a situation that they knew was going to be a disaster but there was nothing they could do about that.

She needed to get out now. The glow inside her, the one she kept buried deep in the pit of her stomach, was stirring like a seed after winter, just standing that close to him, and she needed to smother it as soon as possible.

'Should I come with you now?' he asked.

'No.' Damn it, there had to be a way out of this. 'I'll have to clear this with my superiors and you'll have to…'

'Clear it with mine?' He laughed softly. 'I don't think my cousin will mind.'

'But my commander might.'

'And who does your commander report to? Let me see… Come on, Lieutenant, we can find out together.' He swept towards her and the only way out was through the door ahead of him, with the Lord of Thorns following right on her heels like her shadow. There was no escaping him, not down here in his domain.

She rounded on him, finding him just a little too close for her comfort. 'Back up,' she snapped and to her surprise he did. He drew himself back a step or two so that suddenly it felt like she could breathe again, and think.

Having him on board might be a good idea. She could keep an eye on him, wait for him to slip up. And if he wasn't the killer… if it really wasn't him, he'd certainly open doors around here. And terrify people into answering her questions. If he didn't terrify them into complete silence first. It could go either way.

Running footsteps made her turn and Hale appeared. 'Oh thank the divine, there you are, the king is looking for you.'

'What does he want?' Bastien asked.

'No… not you, your highness. Her. Lieutenant Marchant.'

Her stomach dropped down somewhere around her ankles. 'Me?'

'I don't know any other Lieutenant Marchant around here, do you?' Bastien said with a laugh. 'Come with me, I'll show you the way.'

'But why does the king—'

Bastien linked his arm with hers and she was too stunned to shake him off. 'He probably doesn't. Not personally, anyway. He doesn't do much of anything these days. It's going to be the queen.'

The way he said it made it sound like a death sentence. No love lost there, clearly. But the little Grace knew about Queen Aurelie was that the foreign queen was well liked in Rathlynn, and in the realm in general. To many she was the perfect queen, the darling of the nobility, kind to the common people, and generous to her various charitable causes. Her devotion to the king was legendary.

'Do you know her well?'

'Aurelie? She's not the sort of person you *know*.'

*

Daniel and Ellyn were waiting for her in the courtyard above the Lord of Thorns' domain, but there wasn't any way they could come with her, not into the most secure parts of the palace. Grace caught little more than a brief glance at their surprised faces as she passed them. Bastien led the way. He moved like he owned the place. Which he pretty much did, or would one day. He had lived here all his life. They passed extravagant tapestries in greens and golds, depicting Larelwynn's long-dead forebears battling endless enemies. Lucien Larelwynn and the Hollow King faced each other on the walls of Thorndale Castle. His son, Anders the Great, knelt before the Little Goddess and founded the Temple in her honour. The three sisters of King Riah cut off their hair in mourning at his funeral. There were portraits too, face after face staring down at Grace. The same eyes, the same nose, the same high cheekbones so sharp you could cut yourself on them.

But she didn't have to look far to see those features anyway. She watched him from behind, the broad shoulders, the slim hips, the long legs. Everything about him screamed his pedigree.

She needed to look anywhere else than at him. Anywhere.

Their footsteps echoed through the high halls as they passed over intricate mosaics and painted tiles of white and azure blue. It was overwhelming, the beauty in here, especially when Grace thought of the austerity of the Academy where she'd grown up. Or the poverty and violence she saw every day in the city below.

And yet, Bastien barely glanced around him as he walked. He didn't even seem to notice the magnificence all around him. But there was nothing comforting here, nothing anyone could possibly call homely. She thought of Craine's watchful eye, of the laughter ringing out through the mess hall, of blankets shared and boots handed down, borrowed clothes, the water of the baths, snatches of song and dirty jokes, and a hug when it was needed most.

Had anyone ever done anything as vaguely human as hugging Bastien Larelwynn? She couldn't picture it. When she tried to imagine it her brain just wouldn't create the image. Had anyone held him when he cried? Had he ever cried?

Grace didn't expect the surge of pity she felt for him. She certainly didn't want to feel it. If anything she should be feeling pity for herself right now.

Divinities, she wished she'd worn the stupid dress uniform now.

They climbed a sweeping staircase, Bastien's hand brushing lightly along the marble bannister. At the top, at the far end of a long corridor more sumptuous than the last, they stopped in front of a huge set of double doors, painted a brilliant white with the carvings highlighted in gold.

'Ready?' he asked and before she could answer, he pushed the doors open.

There were at least a hundred people on the other side. They wore court finery and more jewels than Grace had ever seen. They were beautiful. More than beautiful.

It was like a glimpse into the realm of the divinities themselves.

Her mouth went completely dry.

'Lieutenant?' Bastien said, so quietly, so gently that she couldn't believe for a moment that it was him.

'I shouldn't be here,' she whispered.

'Yet here you are. Ready?'

'If I say no, what happens?'

He smiled at her, a normal, human smile, and she wanted to believe in it, in him. She wanted it more than anything. 'It still happens.'

Of course it did. This was so far beyond her petty control that she might as well try to put reins on a cloud.

Grace swallowed down her terror, lifted her chin and straightened her spine. It wasn't going to be worse than facing down a riot, was it? Or an inquisition to detect mageborn? Or capturing the Gore? She'd been through all of those things.

And survived.

She walked through the crowd, which parted – more she guessed for Bastien's benefit than for hers.

The far end of the room was bathed in light, all kinds of colours which shifted and moved. She squinted at it and then realised it came through five long narrow stained-glass windows surrounding the thrones, which captured swirls of bright jewel colours. Two thrones, one much bigger than the other, and both of them occupied. The man – the king, she corrected herself immediately – was slender and pale, almost wan. He had the same dark hair as Bastien, neatly cut to his jaw, and his skin was the colour of marble. It looked stretched over the bones underneath. Rumours of his illness were not an exaggeration, that was for sure. In fact, they probably didn't do it justice. In full health he would have been handsome and there was still something about him, something delicate and enticing. The same high cheekbones as Bastien, too, but here the cheeks below were hollow. Similar eyes too, although his were a deep brown rather than the intense darkness of his cousin's. He wasn't as tall, or as broad. He sat very still watching her.

She sensed that he missed nothing.

The queen sat beside but slightly behind him, on a smaller throne, though it was still clearly a throne. She wore a golden circlet and a gown of brilliant white. Golden hair, as fine as silken threads, was styled around her face, accentuating her slender neck and delicate shoulders. And she really was beautiful.

The pale blue eyes scanned across Grace, taking in everything, but then moving on, lingering past her shoulder. On Bastien no doubt. Queen Aurelie had already dismissed her with a single glance. Grace tightened her jaw and tried not to clench her teeth. She looked up instead, past them. The sword hung in front of the central window, above the king's throne: Larelwynn's weapon, the Godslayer. It caught the light, reflected the colours, but there was something dark and dangerous about its edge. Like an aura of shadows. It felt cold, as if it sucked in light and heat, and everything good in the world.

As Grace reached the foot of the raised dais, she bowed. It wasn't the bow of a courtier, but it was the best she could do.

'Lieutenant Marchant,' said King Marius. 'We are most pleased to receive you.'

'Your majesty sent for me. I am honoured to obey.' The fact she had no idea why she was here or what he wanted had to go unspoken. She was out of her depth and struggling to keep up.

'My cousin informs me that he wants to work with you to solve this mystery. Will you have him?'

Oh. Bastien had already asked. Grace squirmed inside as she tried to think of a way to answer. Would she have him? She didn't have a bloody choice, did she? What did they expect her to do?

She could name Bastien as a suspect right here in front of everyone. She could refuse his help and leave. She could even tell them that they should not be interfering in an investigation. That they had no right.

Except they did. They had every right. She served the crown.

He wasn't wearing it but he might as well have been.

'Your majesty does me too high an honour.'

The queen laughed, a pretty, girlish sound, covering her mouth as she did so. Then she leaned forward and laid a hand on her husband's arm. 'You misunderstand, Lieutenant,' she said.

Misunderstand? It wasn't an honour. Grace understood that well enough. What else was she misunderstanding right now?

'Forgive me, your majesty. I… I'm… how may I serve you?'

The king lifted his arm, which forced his wife's touch away. Great, Grace thought, here's the point where he orders me taken away in chains or something. And where was Bastien bloody Larelwynn in all this, standing behind her like a statue. So far she hadn't been able to shut him up but now, when he could have been the one to speak for her, he was silent.

'Serve me by finding out who is doing this, and make sure my heir does not get himself killed.'

'Your majesty,' she replied weakly. That was that, then.

'Bastien, you'll need to learn how to take orders,' said the queen. She was smiling again, smiling at Bastien. It wasn't a pretty smile, not when you looked into her eyes at the same time. 'I'm not sure that's possible for our Lord of Thorns.'

Laughter rang around the court. Nasty, petty laughter. They really hated him, didn't they? Grace stood there, feeling ice clutching at her insides, imagining facing this day in, day out, in what was meant to be his home.

'Hush,' said King Marius and the laughter died away instantly. 'Cousin, my wife makes a point. Can you obey this officer?'

Bastien stepped forward, beside her, and to Grace's surprise he bowed his head. It shouldn't have been a surprise. He was bowing to his king, and though the gesture was small he did it with the utmost respect.

'I can and I will, your majesty.'

A ripple of shock flowed around the room. Why did they need to do this here, in front of all these people? Why make him humble himself like this?

The king had never struck her as cruel.

Not that she knew him. Not really. None of them did, except perhaps Bastien.

'Very well.' Marius turned his attention back to Grace and she half wished he hadn't. 'Come here, Lieutenant.' He beckoned her, his thin hand like a skeleton's. She didn't want to move but what else could she do?

She stepped up onto the dais and approached the throne. Not too close. She wasn't suicidal. The Royal Guard were already bristling all around her and she was armed. One wrong move and someone would have an arrow in her back before she could explain.

'Kneel,' he said and his voice was kindly enough.

Grace obeyed, dropping to her knees.

'You serve the crown already, and with distinction I am told. One of our finest officers. In recognition of that, and to give our cousin something to think about, I am awarding you a royal warrant.'

He leaned forward, taking something from around his neck, and then that same something fell heavy against her chest. For a moment she thought it was a collar encircling her throat, about to tighten, and the sheer sense of panic made her head whirl. But it wasn't. A heavy medallion on a golden chain nestled against her chest, clinking against the sigil Zavi had given her. It bore the mark of the Larelwynns and it was clearly worth a small fortune.

'Your majesty, I…'

She looked up and instantly wished that she hadn't. The emaciated face of the king gazed down at her, his dark brown eyes seeing into her soul as clearly as Bastien's did. A family trait then.

He leaned forward, embraced her, and Grace froze in shock. All around her she could hear shocked mutterings, but Marius just held her close and she couldn't pull away. For someone who looked so frail, he was strong. As he held her, he whispered in her ear.

'Keep him alive. Whatever else, I charge you, protect him. That is my primary command. He must live. To protect the mageborn. That's what we forgot. Not just control. Protect. That was the deal we made, the Larelwynns, right at the start. Give the warrant to no one else. Keep it safe. It is just for you.'

He released her and she had to fight to stay upright. Marius had just broken every rule about engaging with royalty, especially for a commoner like her. He'd just ignored all protocol. Which, as he was the king, she supposed he was allowed to do. But still…

Keep him alive. A royal command. How was she meant to do that?

'I hereby name Grace Marchant a captain of the Academy, and adjunct to the Royal Guard in honour of her years of dedicated service to the crown. Let all honour her, respect her and aid her in her duty.'

Marius fixed Bastien with a terrible stare and just for a moment Grace was sure his eyes glowed with a golden light. 'And cousin, you *will* obey her.'

Bastien winced suddenly, his shoulders tightening, his body flinching as if in response to an expected blow. His mouth opened and a dazed look passed over his beautiful features, a shimmering of something beneath his skin. He looked so shocked, so betrayed, tears glistening in his eyes. The eyes he couldn't tear away from the king.

The instincts inside Grace that had saved her so many times flared into life as she sensed magic. It surrounded him, bound him, and Bastien was helpless before it. The collar, she realised. The torc he wore was still a collar.

Bastien had thought he'd been so clever, volunteering to help investigate. And Marius the Good had called his bluff.

The king smiled weakly and waved his hand at some functionary or other, who raised a voice like the ringing of a bell. 'Their majesties will retire. The court will disband. Divinities be with the king. Long may he reign.'

'Divinities be with the king.' Every voice there echoed the words as the royal party left, the king visibly aided by his attendants. 'Long may he reign.'

Grace stood in the middle of a storm about to explode, with a golden pendant hanging around her neck, and beside her, the mageborn prince bound to obey her.

And all she could think of was how was she supposed to do her job now?

'Captain?' someone whispered. Bastien, she realised. It was Bastien. 'Captain? We should leave.'

Captain. She was a captain now.

Could he do that?

Of course he could. He was the king.

Just like he could order her to protect Bastien. Just like he could make Bastien – but that had been magic. She knew it. The king had used magic.

'Grace,' Bastien said more urgently. It seemed to snap her out of whatever enchantment had its claws into her.

'What?'

'We have to go. I can explain.'

She gave him a glare, the hottest, most furious one she had in her arsenal. 'Oh I very much doubt that but I'm willing to hear you try.'

Walking at a brisk pace through the halls and corridors while courtiers whirled around her, trying to engage her in conversation, was not something Grace had ever expected to have to do. Bastien followed, silent and dour. Not one of them tried to engage him.

Grace almost made it to the grand staircase before he said a word.

'Captain Marchant.' His voice sounded different. So different. Gentle, soft, broken…

'That explanation?'

'He's trying… I think he's trying to protect me.'

Keep him alive…

Well of course the king was trying to protect his cousin. He had as much as told her to do it. Commanded her. Bribed her with a promotion. But why her? Why did he have to pick on her? There were any number of Royal Guards, trained bodyguards, people far more qualified than she was.

'This makes no sense.'

She lifted the medallion from her chest. It was small, no bigger than a coin, but much thicker. The king's coin. Solid gold. Enough to get her knifed even in the less shady parts of Rathlynn.

Bastien's voice came out in a rush. 'I need to talk to him.' So much for helping her. But he was better off here. Safer. While she sorted out this mess with Craine.

'You do that. I need to get back to the Academy.'

Not to mention that she needed to tell her commander about her sudden rise in rank.

'And in the meantime?'

'In the meantime what?'

'What do you want me to do?'

Divinities, *orders*. He wanted orders. How would she go about ordering a prince around?

'Just… just stay out of trouble. You'll be safe here, won't you? It's a palace. You're a prince. Just… If you need me you know where I am. I'll come back tomorrow.'

She stalked away, heading for the doors and a last taste of freedom.

Chapter Eight

As Grace walked away, Bastien felt the tug of some ethereal connection dragging at him, trying to draw him after her. The spell, he presumed. Marius's spell and the warrant, which was an older magic by far. That had to be it. The fact that it felt like the power of the Maegen calling him was something he tried to push away from his conscious mind.

'That was unexpected,' Asher said, approaching from down the corridor. He wasn't in uniform. Perhaps it was his day off. Bastien glanced at his childhood friend. 'Is she meant to just leave you like that? If she was one of my captains I'd—'

The thought of it made something dark and terrible flare up inside him. The words were out of his mouth before he had a chance to consider what he said. 'She's not,' Bastien snapped. 'Yours, I mean.'

Asher raised his eyebrows but otherwise kept his face as smooth and polished as a statue. The consummate courtier, that was Asher Kane. He'd learned from generations of his family. But he still had to get a dig in when it came to Bastien. He always would.

'And now you are hers.' A tiny smile pulled at the corner of his expressive lips. 'Her charge, I mean. Is she meant to abandon you like that?'

Asher clearly couldn't resist it. He always did love to tease. He was never going to let this go, of that Bastien was sure.

'I suppose she thinks I'm safe here. Is there something you wanted?'

'A drink, I think. Come on Bastien, let's go and see if we can dent your family wine cellar.'

Why not? He and Asher hadn't been able to just slip away and drink like friends in months. They'd barely been able to talk. There was always a function or a duty, there was always the queen and her various courtiers. There was always something.

And the spectre of Hanna hanging over them all the time.

Fifteen years ago they had been inseparable. And then he'd fallen in love with Hanna, Asher's sister. Both families had encouraged it.

Except for Bastien's own sister, Celeste.

No, Celeste had not been pleased at all.

They'd told him he tried to stop her, but the fall down the stairs had robbed his memories from him. And his own sister, who loved to sing and dance barefoot, who told tall tales of gods and monsters, had been sent away to the Temple to serve. Where she couldn't hurt anyone again. They couldn't stop the rumours though. And Hanna was still gone.

After the funeral, Asher hadn't spoken to him in years. No more than the necessary politeness to a prince of the realm, the deference owed, the perfunctory and distant courtesy bred into him by generations of duty. He'd joined the army, volunteered for ambassadorial missions, anything to get away. It was only when he took up his duties here with the Royal Guards that they had started to repair a friendship. Less than three years.

It would be good to just spend some time together, somewhere quiet. Away from the court, and difficult newly minted captains who confused him more than he could say.

'Aren't you on duty?'

'Not until the morning.'

'And the hangover won't be a problem?'

'What hangover? You can magic it away, can't you?'

He laughed. They used to do that. All the time. 'No.'

'What good are you then?'

By the time Bastien thought of a good enough answer to that they were installed in a corner of the cellars, three bottles of wine down and talking about something else entirely.

And that was when the summons came. The page had raced down to the cellar and now stood in front of them, amid the empty bottles scattered on the floor, terrified and appalled. The prince and the general, drunk as lords, sitting on upturned barrels, draining another bottle... how must they have looked to him? And then he said the worst thing Bastien could imagine: Aurelie wanted to see them. Both of them. Right away.

The urgency in the summons made him careless. He just agreed and followed Asher. As they reached the private quarters assigned to Aurelie, Asher stopped him and pulled a small silver hip flask from his belt.

'Liquid courage,' he said with a grin. 'Knock it back.'

He did and instantly regretted it. The liquor was sweet and strong. It burned down his throat and set a fire in his stomach. There was something eerily familiar about it. As if he had tasted it before. In another life.

'What is it?'

'Oh, that's one we brought in from the far south of Barranth. Costs a fortune. Enjoy it. I'll send you a bottle. They aren't as big as the ones we already finished though so be warned.'

Be warned? Any more of the stuff and he wouldn't be able to feel his legs any longer. Let alone deal with Aurelie. Bastien made a mental note not to be too generous with his own measures of it if the bottle actually arrived. The doors opened and music spilled out around him. The room beyond was the queen's private sitting room. It was empty, apart from a man playing a mandolin by the window, his eyes somewhat glazed, and a delicately patterned cream leather collar around his neck. A Lyric. He didn't pay any attention to the open door, but looked in adoration at the slender, golden-haired woman who lay back on the velvet-covered chaise.

'Oh there you are!' Aurelie beckoned them in, ignoring the musician. 'Come in and close the door.'

'Your serene majesty,' said Asher. 'You honour us. Your every wish is our pleasure. Isn't that right, Bastien?'

He was teasing. He had to be. Talking to her like that. But the queen just laughed, delighted with the statement.

Aurelie pushed herself up from her seat, languid and fluid as a dancer. She was a beautiful woman, the most beautiful in the greater kingdoms, or so everyone said. And married to his cousin. Everything about her was elegant, polished, the epitome of style and refinement…

But why, when he looked at her flowing hair, her elegant form and her exquisite face, did he picture instead a scrappy red-head in battered leather?

He shook his head and the world seemed to pulse and spin around him. The drink in his stomach swirled and boiled.

Something was wrong. Terribly wrong.

Aurelie took both his hands, but he could barely feel it. His skin felt numb and his senses twisted. When she drew him forward he followed, dazed and bewildered.

'We haven't talked in too long, Bastien,' she murmured, her musical voice playing on his ears. He couldn't find any words right now. 'Not just you and I. Alone.' Aurelie glanced at Asher as Bastien sat down on the chaise she had just vacated. 'Did he drink it? All of it?'

He shook his head, trying to clear it. But nothing worked. What was she saying? It didn't make sense.

'I see you tested it on the Lyric first,' Asher replied. He didn't look happy about whatever she had done.

Aurelie gave him an arch look. 'I had to make sure it wouldn't do any permanent harm, didn't I? Marius would never forgive me.'

And she laughed. She actually laughed.

Asher didn't. He grabbed the musician by the arm, jerking him from his seat, the music jarring off-key. The man just smiled at him and leaned in to kiss him, full on the lips. For a moment Asher did nothing. Then he pulled back, a cruel smile on his face.

'Maybe he has some uses.'

'You can take him off my hands,' Aurelie told him. 'For a while. I might want him back. Later.'

Asher glanced down at Bastien. There was no trace of friendship left on his face. Nothing. Not even the lie. 'Really?'

'Waste not, want not,' she replied. 'Don't mark him. I like him. He's pretty.'

'You like musicians too much.'

'I like to be a muse, don't I, my darling?' She trailed her hands over the mandolin player's bare back and the man arched to meet her touch.

'He won't even remember you in the morning, Aurelie. That's what it does. It might make them willing but it wipes away the memories. They've used it for generations, the Larelwynns. And they guard it closely. It was not exactly easy to get hold of. If the marshal knew...'

She laughed, waving him away. 'Well, that's just what makes it so special. Isn't it? It's new every time.'

'My queen,' the musician murmured. 'My beloved.'

She teased him a little longer. Then shoved him back into Asher's arms. 'Now you go and be nice to Lord Kane. Show him how much we value him.'

'Aurelie…' There was a warning tone in Asher's voice. Even Bastien could recognise that. Even though he didn't recognise much else at the moment. The seat was soft and the room was warm. His mind was swimming in some kind of syrup. He needed air. He needed to get out of there.

Bastien tried to lever himself off the chair but his legs were like lead. 'I should… I should go…'

Aurelie peeled herself away from her lover… or lovers… and peered at Bastien. 'I don't think you're going anywhere,' she said. 'You didn't give him enough, Asher. Poor Bastien. Close your eyes, my Lord of Thorns. I'll get to you in a moment. It'll get there eventually. It always does.'

He didn't want to. Didn't mean to. But the world turned hazy and vague. The warm golden light of the Maegen spilled in through the cracks in the edges of his consciousness. He was lost, drowning in it. It had never felt so strong, or… or he had never felt so weak. So vulnerable to it.

He slipped into the light, and into the darkness beneath it.

*

His body ached, longed. He floated in the pool of the Maegen, swallowed whole by it, his world subsumed in its light. It flowed through him and enveloped him. He breathed it in, and it drank him down.

Floating, lost, he reached out for her, for the lover who had always been here for him, to help him, comfort him, hold him. Arms encircled him, and her body pressed close. Her mouth searched for his, kissing, teasing. Desire and need swept through him, terrible, insatiable yearning.

'Don't worry,' he heard her say. 'I'm here. I will take care of you. Of everything. You don't need to remember. Let go, sweetheart. Let me be the one to command now.' A cool glass lifted to his mouth, replacing her lips, her kisses. The liquid inside was treacly and honeyed. 'Drink it, Bastien. Drink it and forget. You know you want to. Just a little more. It'll help.'

The light shimmered and broke. He saw shadows moving up from beneath him, hungry, cruel.

'Bastien?' a different voice, blurred by concern, sleep and exhaustion.

Her hands were calloused and firm, strong. Not the soft, pampered hands that touched him now. Her hands held weapons, were weapons. And her hair... her hair was the colour of fire. She was fire.

'Grace...'

Panic made him push back, staggering to his feet. The world was distorted and glowing, the light of the Maegen everywhere, winnowing through everything. What he was seeing was only half real. The light squirmed against him, or maybe that was the woman he peeled off himself, pushing her back from him.

'What... what are you doing?' Aurelie's seductive tones transformed to anger and alarm. 'Stop. I command you to stop. Asher! Asher!'

The door crashed open and the light blazed beyond it. Asher was a silhouette of shadow, a hole in the world.

'Run,' Grace whispered, from somewhere deep inside his consciousness, deep within the light of the Maegen. He was sure now. It was Grace. He knew her voice and he needed to find her. The Maegen tugged at him but he struggled free. He didn't want to give in, not like this. Not to... Aurelie... it was Aurelie. Not Grace.

He had to find her. He needed her.

'If you need me you know where I am.' That was what she had said.

He saw a room, a narrow, bare room, with a simple bed and a tiny window overlooking an alleyway. He saw her lying there, her hair like scarlet flames spilling over a pillow. She shifted fitfully, her brow furrowing as his dream touched hers. As the Maegen reached out for her, she reached for him.

He needed help. She was too far away, in the Academy, across the city. Simona… Simona would know what to do, how to get there…

'Bastien, find her.' He heard Grace's voice as clearly as if she was beside him. *'Find Simona and come here. Come to where it's safe.'*

*

He threw himself forwards, out of the door, down the hallway beyond, heedless of the shouts of alarm, the angry curses. Asher followed him, the general, Aurelie's man, not his friend. Perhaps he never had been. He knew he needed to leave, that he couldn't stay there. He had to find Grace. Not… not… the other woman… the other…

More memories bled away as he hauled himself forwards, clinging to the wall. People folded out of his way, expressing shock and alarm, but he pushed himself onwards. Let them stare. He was a monster. But he needed people around him, the more the better. Because as long as he was in public, in a crowd, they couldn't come and take him back to that room. They couldn't… Asher and Aurelie… They…

What had they been doing?

There was music. There was a man playing music. There was a drink that burned like fire inside him. There was light…

Voices he knew.

'He won't remember. Not now. Just leave him. Come away…' The voices were hushed, conspiratorial. They stopped following him. He carried on. He'd make it if he had to crawl and that was starting to feel like a distinct possibility.

He finally fell into Simona's office, heart pounding as if it would burst, chest contracting, his body drenched with sweat.

The marshal surged out of her chair, eyes wide. 'Your highness, what happened?'

He barely managed to hold himself up against the doorframe, his legs sagging beneath him, his shoulders heaving as he forced the words out.

'Please, Simona. I have to go to the Academy. To Grace.'

'Grace? Grace Marchant?'

'Please… please…'

He'd never begged for anything in his life. Not that he could remember. But…

There was so much he couldn't remember. Years of his life. All his childhood…

He won't remember. Not now. Just leave him.

And they were right. He couldn't remember. Not really. Scattered images. A girl… a woman… lying on a bed, bathed in golden light even though it was night time. Her red hair spilling around her like blood. Her face, her hands, her voice…

'Take me to Grace.'

'Your highness, we should wait for morning. The city at night isn't—'

'This cannot wait. There was a drink… I think I tasted it before but… I can't… Simona, I can't remember…' He frowned, trying to bring back those fading memories. What else had he forgotten? How many times had this happened? His memories were all he had. He knew that. If they were gone, if they were draining away…

Simona seized him, shook him, her expression suddenly frantic. 'What drink? Bastien? What did they give you?'

'It was sweet,' he said and stopped. He couldn't recall. The memories were sliding away like rain on a window pane. 'Sweet and sharp…'

She turned away, dragging out keys and unlocking a cabinet behind her, swearing violently as she did so.

'Simona!' he snapped and she turned sharply, her expression full of anger and dismay. Whatever she had found, or not found, she wasn't happy.

If you need me, you know where I am.

'I need her. Grace. We have to go now.'

Chapter Nine

Craine took the news without flinching. Someone must have already sent word.

'What does it mean, *adjunct to the Royal Guard*?' Grace asked.

'It means he's seconding you to the palace. To mind his cousin, a man who has had more assassination attempts in the last few years than...' She shuffled through the papers and then sighed. 'Than anyone in the history of the city, it seems. Stay here tonight, and go back in the morning. That's time enough.'

'And my team, ma'am.'

Craine gave an exasperated noise and pushed herself up from the desk. She slotted her crutches under her arms and crossed the room to stand in front of Grace. 'You want to take them with you? In there?'

'Yes. I'll need someone at my back, won't I? I'm not finished investigating him. Just because I get a promotion and a role babysitting him doesn't mean he's innocent. He killed Kai, after all. I... I watched him do it.'

Craine drew in a shaky breath and let it out again. She reached out a gnarled hand, more used to the sword than this sort of interaction, and placed it against Grace's cheek. It was the most human gesture she'd ever seen from her commander. It shocked her into silence.

'*Grace*, Kai was dying from the moment you brought him out of that house and you know it. If Larelwynn did *anything…*' there was a warning in the emphasis, Grace knew that '…it was to hasten the inevitable. It was a mercy.'

Mercy. Right. Grace had looked into Bastien's face. There wasn't a scrap of mercy in him.

But she swallowed hard and nodded. Because what else could she do?

He's blood royal, she reminded herself, and you belong to the crown, yesterday, now and forever.

'As you say, Commander Craine.'

Craine studied her for a moment or two longer and then seemed satisfied with what she saw. 'Good. If the king himself has assigned you to protect Bastien Larelwynn, there must be a reason. That means it isn't a job just anyone could do. Which means… he must be in terrible danger.'

That was true. But from whom?

The dark and endless eyes of the Lord of Thorns came to her mind's eye. The way he'd stared at her, the way his very presence had drunk her in until she couldn't think straight. Who could be a threat to him of all people? Who would dare?

'Yes, Commander.' Grace whispered the words, because she couldn't find her voice properly. All she could think of was the way he'd felt against her, and the disdain in his voice.

In all the years she had served, through all the monsters she had faced and all the deadly situations in which she had found herself, she had never felt herself so much at risk than with him looming over her. Who exactly needed protecting?

'Keep your temper, Grace. And watch your mouth.' Craine glanced towards the door of the office and leaned in. 'He's dangerous,' she whispered. 'We all know that. Only a fool would think otherwise. But if someone else is out to hurt him, they must be even more dangerous. I'll talk to Lara, see what she can tell me. Think of it as all those days of homage you owe, all run together.'

Grace straightened, a stab of fear running through her. Craine knew her past, knew she'd been born a Flint but that the power was gone. But what else did she know? What else did she suspect?

'I've never... I've never done a day of homage in my life.'

Craine shook her head as if Grace was the densest new recruit she had ever encountered. 'I'm sure he's fully aware of that too. I mean it, Grace. Those with nothing to hide have nothing to fear. But... if you *do* have something to hide... Keep your head.'

Easier said than done. People who crossed the royal family had a habit of losing their heads, and other vital body parts. Especially people who annoyed them more than once.

She highly doubted that Bastien Larelwynn was in any way different.

'I still want Daniel and Ellyn with me.'

'Fine. I'll see to it. Dismissed.' Grace turned to go but Craine cleared her throat. 'You'll want to take those files of yours with you.'

'Files, ma'am?'

Craine nodded to a pile on the desk. 'Your outstanding case files. The other dead mageborn. I don't like work unfinished, Grace. You know that. And you should do some follow-up interviews. A few of those files mention alms taken from the Temple. Mother Miranda might be of help. I think you should ask some questions and see what you can find out. It's on your way, after all. Take Childers with you. He's good on the streets and did some work with the Temple wards last month. They'll talk to him. You can send him back to me afterwards. I'm short-staffed enough, especially if you're absconding with de Bruyn and Parry.'

'Yes ma'am.' She scooped them up, puzzled but keen to get back to her own quarters and out of the office. A crowd had gathered outside, her colleagues all eager for a good peer at her. Her former colleagues.

All the Academy was buzzing. Like it or not, they all knew. Childers was on the desk, and he even managed to look slightly less bored about it than usual.

'Heading up in the world, are we?' he asked.

'Not by choice, mate. And it looks like you're coming with me. What happened with that mageborn Royal Guard I brought in? Griggs?'

'Oh him,' Childers groaned. 'We had to let him go in the end. Just as well. Divinities, he never shut up moaning. Then the sigil came off about an hour after you left. Must have been a fluke.'

'A fluke?'

'That's what Craine said. Andley tested him and everything turned up negative. As solidly quotidian as you and me, Grace.'

That couldn't have been right. Grace frowned as she pulled the report book to her, and there it was set out in Craine's neat script. But she'd seen what Griggs had done. She'd felt the magic flowing through him as he'd tormented that poor boy for the amusement of his mates. She could still taste it like ozone at the back of her throat.

But she couldn't say that. Couldn't tell them because that would mean admitting to those in authority over her that she had more than a passing affinity with the mageborn, which would of course lead to the question – was she still mageborn herself?

She still dreamed of the Maegen. And of her lover in that golden light. That lover who reminded her so strongly of the Lord of Thorns. No quotidian dreamed like that.

She wasn't collared. It hadn't been deemed necessary when she came here. There was no magic left in her. Once it had started to rekindle… well, she had guarded that secret. She didn't want to be collared. Some of the mageborn might say it protected them, helped them channel and control the way they used magic, kept them from being lost in its depths, swept away in the stream, or pulled down into the Deep Dark beneath.

But if that was true, why did so many run? Why did people actively flee Rathlynn instead of doing their duty and submitting?

Why was it even *called* submitting?

Those with nothing to hide have nothing to fear, said the law. Grace wasn't sure about that one either any more.

She shut herself in her room and opened the files, flicking through them. Losle Vayden, the Leanese victim from the docks, and several others. The earliest was ten years ago. They all had burns on the palms of their hands, and the magic drained completely from them. They were all young, fit and healthy. And dead, very very dead.

How was she going to investigate this? True, Bastien had wanted to help her. That was what he said. But from the palace, not the city. Which already put her at a disadvantage. He was going to get in her way. She knew it. Just by being there.

It was tough enough getting answers when you came from the Academy. Grace had contacts. They all did. But were any of them going to talk to her when she was accompanied by a prince of the realm, one who inspired more fear than anyone else?

She curled her hand into a fist and slammed it down on the little desk as anger at the situation burst through her.

Right in front of her eyes, the candle stub sparked, flickered, and then burst into flame.

She reached out before she thought about it and wrapped her hand around it, squeezing until it went out. It didn't burn. It ought to hurt. But it didn't.

'Grace?' Daniel stood in the doorway, staring at her. Her breath caught in her throat. She snatched her hand back. He couldn't have seen. Her body would have blocked him. She forced herself to relax just a little, just enough. 'You okay?'

'Yes. Fine. Everything's fine, Danny.'

'What happened back there, at the palace? What did he do?'

She almost laughed. Her heart was thrumming away inside her chest like a bird's and she couldn't quite get her breath. What if he had seen her hold the flame? What if…? But it was Daniel. She'd known him all her life.

All the life she could remember anyway…

'The king made me Bastien Larelwynn's keeper. But that's okay because Bastien himself wants to be the mageborn on our squad, or maybe wants us as his pet Academy officers or…' She sagged forward, and Daniel caught her shoulders. Before she knew what was happening he was essentially holding her up.

'Sit down,' he told her. 'Come on. When did you last just sit down and take a breath?'

'I don't know.' But she did what he said anyway. They sat side by side on the low bed, and Grace tried to calm her breathing. She leaned forward, and the warrant coin dangled down in front of her. It clinked off Zavi's sigil.

'Is that…?' he asked, hypnotised by the gleaming warrant.

'Yes. The king's coin. I think he… he used magic. Did you know that he has magic?' She didn't call Marius mageborn. She couldn't. That would be a step too far.

'The warrant's magic. It enforces the vow of fealty, to hold the Lord of Thorns as seneschal, ties them together somehow. It's part of the pact. We learned this, Grace, remember?'

The Larelwynn pact. Lucien Larelwynn's deal with the mageborn made after the defeat of the Hollow King. If they swore fealty to him, he would protect them. But only so long as they served.

'When we first came here, yeah. You, me and Helene. I remember.'

Helene would have known. Helene always remembered facts like that. But Helene was dead. Helene's own powers had betrayed her. They'd almost taken Grace with her. She hadn't been able to save her friend. Magic wasn't made to save.

Helene and Daniel had been the first people at the Academy to befriend her, when they were just cadets. She'd been sweet and gentle, a Tide who didn't want to be a Tide. And her magic made sure of that in the end. It turned on her.

'A king has to control the mageborn. Or someone with…'

'The king's warrant, yes, I know.'

Grace picked up the coin again, held it in her hand, weighed it and felt the soft buttery metal warm against her skin. Damn. Damn, damn, damn.

'Are you sure you're okay?' Daniel asked again. His hand touched her forehead and she didn't even think to flinch back. Not from him. 'Goddess, you're burning up.'

She pulled away. 'I'm fine.'

'Have a shower. Get some sleep. I'll get the medic to look in on you.'

'I said I'm fine.' She didn't feel feverish. Just warm, and she knew of old that was never a good thing. A shower – an icy cold shower – was an excellent idea. 'But a shower sounds good. I'll do that. Don't worry, Danny. We'll work through this.'

'Ellyn and I will be with you all the way. Promise.'

She stood up and then ruffled his hair. He was like a brother to her, always had been. He and Ellyn were closer than family. 'I know, kiddo. And I'll look after you. Promise.'

She'd look after all of them. That was what she did.

The shower helped, barely. It was stone cold and left her shivering and miserable. But the fire inside her was gone and that was all that mattered.

She curled up in bed under a pile of blankets and tried to make herself go to sleep. The golden coin around her neck felt like it weighed more than anything else in the world. It tied them together, a magical tether. She'd worn it while she showered. She hadn't dared to take it off. Despite the freezing water, it still felt warm.

It nestled against her like an echo of Bastien's touch.

*

This dream wasn't the same. The light was there, the deep and endless pool. Its reflection bathed her skin and sparkled with energy. But she stood on the edge, in the cottage garden in the heart of the Academy, and where the well should have been the pool of Maegen glowed like the setting sun.

The shape under the surface was a dark mark, lost, drowning…

She could sense Bastien, drifting, his mind dissolving in the light, his consciousness bleeding away until all that was left was raw power, desperate desire…

And fear.

Divinities, she could taste his fear like her own, metallic and harsh at the back of her throat.

'Don't worry,' Grace heard a woman's voice say. 'I'm here. I will take care of you. Of everything. You don't need to remember. Let go, sweetheart. Let me be the one to command now.'

She recognised the voice right away. Aurelie. The queen.

He didn't know what he was doing. She had to reach him. She reached out her hand and plunged it into the glowing pool, trying to grab him and pull him out.

There was a drink. Grace could almost taste it, sweet and sickly, like the light itself given form. Like acid in his mind. '...Drink and forget...'

'Bastien?'

'Grace...'

His eyes flickered open. He didn't even seem to see her, or know where he was. He stared up at her through the light of the pool, helpless and confused. The misery in his voice was a spear in her chest.

She plunged into the pool, feeling the glowing water of magic rush over her. Their fingers brushed against each other. But magic was greedy, dragging at him, pulling him from her. His eyes were open, staring at her in desperation. Inside them desire ran wild. Such dark desire.

'Bastien!' She couldn't pull him clear. She was too weak.

But she had to. She simply had to.

She saw the room as if from a great height. He was sitting on some sort of long low seat, his expression confused, dazed. The golden-haired queen nestled in beside him, holding his face so she could kiss and caress him. Bastien's hands closed on her body, trailed down her bare arms. The queen laughed, a deep and throaty laugh of lust and triumph.

Need swept through the Maegen, a terrible, desperate need. A longing for something he could never have, something he had always been denied. Aurelie offered it to him now. Offered him everything.

Except what she offered was not real.

Grace couldn't help him, not when she wasn't there. She should never have left him alone. She should have known he'd end up in trouble. Marius had tried to warn her. He'd told her to keep him safe. She should never have left. But the palace, the place he lived, the place where he was guarded, his home *should have been safe. She'd been so naïve.*

'Run,' she told him. But where could he run to?

She wasn't there, but his marshal, Simona Milne, was.

Simona… Simona would know what to do, how to get there.

It was his thought. She was sure of it. Bastien was still there, still able to think and reason. Even now. He had to be.

She plunged deeper, winding herself around him, her mouth to his ear and her lips brushing his skin. He had to hear her. He had to.

'Bastien, find her. Find Simona and come here. Come to where it's safe.'

The light of the Maegen dragged him from her. The light faded. The dream went with it and the magic flowing through her petered out. Exhaustion crashed over her and everything went dark.

*

A violent banging jolted her out of sleep in the small hours.

'Just a moment. Just…'

The candle flame jumped into life again. Grace hissed with frustration but the door was closed. No one else had seen it. She was safe.

This couldn't be happening. She wasn't mageborn, not really. Just a repressed power, something that gave her an edge and let her be the best at her job. It let her sense the other mageborn, but she couldn't actually do anything.

Until now.

But the dreams were magic. The Maegen was the source of magic and she had dreamed of it. And he was always there when she did. Bastien Larelwynn…

'Boss, open up. It's important.' Ellyn's voice. She sounded scared. 'They just turned up asking for you.'

Grace wrenched the door open. Ellyn was in a nightgown, her hair a silvery plait down her back. And she didn't just sound scared. She looked it, too.

'What is it?'

'From the palace. From—'

Dark figures lurched into view at the end of the corridor. Grace's hands went for weapons she wasn't wearing. Her fingertips glowed with heat. She folded her hands behind her back, trying to hide them.

'Down here,' she heard Daniel say. 'It's just down here.'

A man was draped between Daniel and a woman Grace didn't recognise. She was tall, her black hair scraped back from a strong face. Tiny silver studs glittered along the curve of her ears and there was a ring in the side of her nose. She was older than any of them, and looked hard as nails.

'Is that her?' she asked bluntly when she clapped eyes on Grace.

'Yes, Lieutenant – I mean *Captain* Marchant.'

And suddenly Grace recognised the wilted mess of a human being slung between them. He was drenched in sweat and barely moving, his head lolling down and his long dark hair plastered like oil over his face. But that wasn't the worst of it. His skin was pale and sickly, gleaming like mother-of-pearl instead of gold. And he didn't appear to be conscious.

'Bastien? What happened?'

'We need… to put him down somewhere…' Daniel grunted. 'He's bloody heavy.'

'You should have tried getting him this far,' the woman snapped. 'Thank the goddess there was a carriage ready.'

'In here,' Grace said. 'Put him on the bed.'

The two of them obeyed and the woman settled him, crossing his hands over his stomach. His head lolled to one side and the torc looked very bright in the candlelight.

'What happened to him?' Grace asked again. 'And who are you?'

'Simona Milne,' the woman replied, still gazing at him. 'He came to me about an hour ago, sick and delirious. There was some sort of party, though why he went, I don't know. Something Lord Kane cooked up, no doubt to please the queen.' She paused as if she had said too much. 'The prince's position is delicate. With the king ill, many people are jockeying for favour. And power.'

'You think they gave him something.'

'I think… I think they tried. There is a drink the Larelwynns use from time to time. A precious, dangerous drink. It steals memories. It makes people… malleable. I think this was why the king gave you the warrant, Captain. To protect him from situations like this.'

'You haven't told me what *this* is.'

'I serve the king… and the prince… but mainly the king. It is my honour to serve.'

My honour to serve.

'I've heard that before,' Grace murmured as she stared at Bastien, at the sheen of sweat on his skin. Images from her dream resurfaced and she shuddered. What had happened to him? What had they done, or tried to do? 'Simona, tell me what happened, in the king's name. For his sake.'

Simona's face crumpled and she sank down to sit on the edge of the bed, her head in her hands. 'Only a Larelwynn can sit on the throne. Only their blood is acceptable. The pact demands it. When Lucien Larelwynn defeated the Hollow King, that was the price. A Larelwynn on the throne, and a way to control the Maegen, to channel it, to protect the mageborn. But it has to be one of them. Marius calls it their curse as much as their blessing. What started off as protection soon became control. And now…' She sighed. 'The queen wants a child to maintain her power and Marius has not provided. Perhaps she can't conceive. I don't know. It'll never happen if they don't share a bed.'

And the realisation had already swept over Grace. 'And Bastien is his cousin. So he has Larelwynn blood too.'

The images from her dream, the desire, the overwhelming need, the golden-haired woman... Grace's stomach twisted. What had they done to him? How much of his mind was still intact?

'He left before anything happened,' Simona said. 'Before she could—'

Grace fought the urge to snarl. 'Rape him.'

Simona didn't flinch. Perhaps she'd worked at the palace for too long, seen too much. 'That's a strong word, Captain.'

It left Grace disgusted. Why did she have the feeling that this wasn't the first time Simona had dealt with something like this on behalf of her king? Hushed it up. Papered over the cracks. She knew all about this drink, after all. How many times had he been given it?

'It's a legal word too.'

The marshal didn't flinch though. If anything her expression grew harder. 'He's your responsibility, not mine. The king has given you his warrant. It cannot be removed except by you or the king himself. He bid you protect him.'

Protect him. Not just his life. There was so much to protect. Bastien was far more vulnerable than he thought.

'Doesn't anyone test for poison in that palace of yours?'

Simona smiled briefly, her expression still bleak. 'But it wasn't a poison, was it? He'd know it of old if it didn't work quite so well. Memories are malleable. Gaps can be explained. A childhood accident, something like that. That's the easy part. He's too trusting by far. Always was. And when it comes from a so-called friendly hand… He didn't see it coming and neither did I. My mistake.'

One for which Bastien was paying. Grace narrowed her eyes but Simona ignored her. If she truly felt guilt, she had a funny way of showing it. What was she? Bastien's keeper? Until now…

'I should go back. There will be questions. I can take care of things until morning. Bring him back when it wears off. I'll tell them he's helping you with your enquiries. When he's back to himself, he'll find that hilarious.'

If he was ever himself again.

Grace couldn't seem to make herself move. Bastien Larelwynn lay in her bed, unconscious, burning with fever, and the woman who had brought him was about to go.

'Wait, what do I do?'

'Look after him. I don't need to do your job as well as my own.' Simona swept out of the tiny room, past Daniel and Ellyn who stood back, as shocked as Grace was. 'Someone show me the way out of this labyrinth,' she yelled after a moment and Ellyn hurried after her.

Grace was left looking at Daniel in despair.

'He's sick.' Daniel said it as if it was meant to be helpful. It really wasn't. Hadn't he been listening?

'I'm aware of that. Get me some cold water and cloths and… Divinities, I don't know. Go and wake the medic on duty.'

Chapter Ten

A cool cloth pressed to his forehead. His skin was on fire, and the magic inside him whirled out of control, tearing through him and devouring as it went. Punishing him. The Maegen was an inferno and he was lost.

A voice spoke, murmuring soft and gentle words which soothed his mind. The cloth went away and then came back, refreshed with iced water. That touch, that delicate touch, was the only anchor he had in the world. When he opened his eyes all he saw was fire.

Was he lost then? Lost to the tormentors and the accursed, to be burned away and left a charred corpse?

But her hands, her voice, her gentle care… no, that couldn't have come from anywhere but the Maegen. It was part of his dreams, his only comfort. She sang. He knew the tune but couldn't place it. A nursery rhyme or a fisherman's song. Something he knew from so long ago it was buried in those vanished childhood memories.

'It's okay,' she said to him and he wanted to believe her. But he couldn't.

But when she tried to move away, he grabbed her wrist and held onto her. He couldn't let her go. He knew he was gripping her too tightly, heard her gasp of discomfort, felt the jerk where she was about to fight back but restrained herself. Her bones bowed beneath his grip, grinding against each other.

He couldn't let her go. Not this one. Not Grace.

'Shush, I won't leave, I promise. I'm just getting more water.' She forced the words out through clenched teeth.

Bastien had to make himself release her. He tried to sit up, tried to focus on her, but all he saw was the same fire, the candlelight behind her illuminating her red hair. She was beautiful, like one of the divinities incarnate. She was everything. She wasn't from his nightmare any more. He wasn't there. Not now.

He was here. With her.

'Grace?' he said. It was Grace. But it was also the Maegen. It flamed inside her. He could see it beneath her skin, leaping and dancing, calling to him. She had rescued him. In his nightmare, it was her voice guiding him, giving him the strength to... to... what? When he tried to remember there was just endless darkness. And the soft wicked laugh he ought to know.

'I'm here,' she assured him. 'You're safe, Bastien. I promise. Just... just rest.'

His body betrayed him and he slumped back down into the edge of his twisted nightmares.

She brought the cloth back, damp and cool once more, and laid it on his forehead. Then she slipped her hand under his head and lifted it up, so gently, so carefully. The cup touched his lips.

'Drink it, just a little. It'll help.'

He tried to do as she said. Whatever the drink was, it tasted sweet and he gagged without meaning to. A golden-haired woman laughed in the depths of his mind.

Aurelie... Aurelie laughed.

Drink it, Bastien. Drink it and forget. You know you want to. Just a little. It'll help.

He choked, cool water splattering everywhere.

But Grace just cleaned his face and made calming sounds, her voice the balm he needed. She was the balm he needed.

Without thinking he pushed himself up and caught her in his arms. His lips found hers. He didn't mean to. Even as he did it he knew it was a stupid idea, a disaster, but he couldn't seem to stop. She was cool against him, her lips so soft, her mouth so warm. She melted into his embrace and all he could think of was her touch, her kiss, her warmth.

'Stop,' she mumbled against his mouth. She pushed him back and he released her, because he had to. Not because he wanted to, but because he had already overstepped the mark. The wash of shame only served to steal what little strength he still had. He slumped back onto the pillow and gazed up at her.

'I'm sorry,' he tried to say. The words were no more than a breath. 'I'm sorry for everything.'

His eyes closed before he knew it, and her hand brushed the side of his face in a gentle caress.

'You have nothing to be sorry for,' Grace told him. 'It's okay. You're safe here. Go to sleep.'

Kindness undid him, just as it did with Marius. He couldn't help but obey.

*

Thin sunlight woke him, stabbing into his eyes like knives. His head pounded and his stomach felt like it had been hollowed out with a dull blade. Bastien tried to move and every muscle protested but he forced himself onwards.

There was a puddle of bedlinen on the floor beside the bed and, in it, Grace slept fitfully, her red hair spilling across the borrowed pillow.

He tried to get up without waking her, but the moment he shifted more than an inch towards the edge of the bed she moved, twisting around and coming up to face him, wide awake.

They stared at each other for a long moment. She had the eyes of a hunter. Quick, alert, dangerous. He could stare at them all day. Copper brown, almost golden, a hawk.

'You're awake,' she said.

She got up and began folding the bedclothes, piling them neatly on the narrow desk, then placing the thin pillow on top. He watched her, even though he knew it was a terrible idea. The nightshirt she wore was a normal shirt, oversized, and old, threadbare in places, transparent.

Divinities, he shouldn't be looking.

'I'm sorry,' he said again.

'I know. You were ill. Can you explain what happened?'

What happened? Well, that was the question, wasn't it? He'd kissed her. She'd responded. But… he'd been delirious and she had told him to stop. Before that… before that he couldn't remember.

'I…' He raked his hand through his hair, trying to push its length back out of his eyes and formulate an answer. 'I thought I'd be all right at the palace. When Marius gave you his warrant and… assigned me to you… I just went for a drink.'

She gave him a cool look. 'Oh, a drink, how lovely.'

'Asher just wanted to catch up,' he said and then sighed, trying to pull his recollections back into order. They fragmented even as he reached for them. 'There was wine and I… I couldn't be rude. Asher – he's general of the Royal Guard, I've known him all my life. And then Aurelie… the queen… They gave me something. Something else. I think.' It was blurry and confused, a maelstrom of laughter and misery. Bastien remembered someone kissing him, his clothes being too tight, his head pounding… Simona shouting…

'*Something else…*' The smile faded from her eyes. It wasn't a story of him being stupid and over-privileged now.

'Grace, it's not the first time. It doesn't matter. They think it's funny. Because I'm…'

Her jaw firmed. 'It doesn't sound funny. You're telling me they drugged you. As a joke. And it's not the first time. I'm adjunct to the Royal Guard from now on. Your safety is my responsibility. And this Asher…?'

'Lord Asher Kane, General of the Royal Guard. But really—'

Her look told him he was far too trusting.

'I think I may have met him,' she murmured darkly. 'I'll move to the palace today. It won't happen again.'

The relief almost made him collapse again, though he tried not to show it. He couldn't. 'I'll arrange quarters for you.'

'And for Daniel Parry and Ellyn de Bruyn. They're coming with me.'

Ah. That made sense. She wanted her team with her. She wanted people she trusted close to her, to help her. 'I'll see to it.'

'And Bastien, you have to promise to tell me, in future, anything that might harm you, endanger you, or threaten you. If anyone hands you drinks or invites you to parties, I need to know. I need to be there. Do you understand?'

He nodded, confused for a moment. It sounded more weighted than the words implied. 'I understand,' he said, even though he wasn't sure he did.

Another scrap of memory raced across his mind. Simona. He'd collapsed in her office. He'd told her to bring him here. Because Grace had told him… that made no sense. He pushed it away.

'The king told me to protect you, so that's what I will do. In the meantime I also have other duties, duties to the city and its people. I mean to continue doing those.'

This was more manageable, firmer ground. This was something practical that he could lend his aid to. He stood up, a gesture of solidarity. 'I'll help you.'

The sheet slid away and that was when he realised he was naked. Grace's eyes grew wide, like a startled deer, and she swallowed, her throat moving as if trying to find words somewhere inside her. Bastien blushed and grabbed the sheet again, wrapping it around himself as she turned away.

'I'm sure you will,' she said, calmly, as if nothing had happened.

He felt like a fifteen year old again. A fool. Flustered and making an idiot of himself at every turn.

'My clothes?' He couldn't have sounded more pathetic if he tried.

'Were drenched in sweat. Ellyn took them to the laundry. The medic said to keep you cool. He said it was… just a fever. He's seen it before.'

Everyone who worked the seedier parts of Rathlynn had seen something like it before, of that he was sure. It wasn't exactly sophisticated. Just effective. Just a fever indeed. What had they given him?

A little silver flask. A sweet and sickly drink…

Grace thought she could protect him from whatever Asher and Aurelie had in store for him? He couldn't even protect himself. Divinities, this was never going to work. What had Marius been thinking?

'I'm going to need clothes,' he said wearily, feeling his vulnerability. 'And to bathe.'

Grace just nodded. 'I'll find them. And… well, there are communal baths.'

She waited, seeing his reaction. He kept his face impassive even though inside his stomach churned. 'They'll have to do.' What choice did he have?

'I'll find you a robe and Daniel can show you... Will you be all right if you're not with me?'

'I will. And I would appreciate the robe.'

She smiled as she looked him up and down. 'I think the whole Academy would be better off if you had something on, your highness. Seeing the heir to the throne here will be startling enough. The heir to the throne in your state of undress might finish off the whole Academy.'

*

Even with the robe on, everyone stared. Daniel prattled on, which appeared to be his default setting, as they made their way down under the halls of the Academy and every face they passed turned to look at him. Bastien knew he ought to be used to it. It had happened all his life for one reason or another. Somehow it felt more invasive now.

He didn't recognise any particular one of the mageborn Academy members, even though he knew he should, from their days of homage. Mostly they were young, just cadets. He recognised the shiny looks on their faces, eager to please, full of duty and honour and the desire to serve. It made him feel jaded to his core.

The steps down led to a vaulted steam-filled room with deep pools fed by natural springs and heated by a hypocaust system, hot air under the floors piped through the whole area from a boiler below. He'd studied it once, his tutors keen on encouraging his interest in engineering at the time.

When his ancestors had taken the city and founded the Academy, they had taken the same care designing the building to house their gamekeepers that they had taken with the palace. More, perhaps, because it wasn't sprawled on top of a rocky outcrop and didn't burrow into the depths of the earth like a rat. It was neat and regimented, efficient. He found himself admiring the building, the way it ran like a well-oiled machine. Everything had its place and its role. Everything and everyone. There was a comfort to that.

Daniel Parry showed him to a secluded corner pool and stood back, almost like a courtier. He'd fit in well in the palace if he kept that up.

'Thank you,' Bastien said, slipping off the robe and handing it to him. Daniel's eyes widened, but he took it without protest and Bastien slid into the water, letting it soothe his tired and aching muscles.

The bathing pool was deep, coming up to his waist when he stood, to his neck when he sat on the little step-like seat built into the side. He could stretch out his legs through the milky water and let the steam rise around him. Tilting his head back he let it rest on the curve built into the edge. Everything perfectly designed.

He closed his eyes and leaned back, inhaling the scent that came from the vents, the mix of lavender and tea tree. Behind his closed eyelids he could see the light, the Maegen so very close, a dream away. It warmed him, soothed him.

'Right so, I'll just…' Daniel's voice tailed off. 'I'll wait here then.'

'I'll let you know if I need anything,' Bastien told him.

The Maegen surrounded him, suffusing the water. In the deepest part of the pool he could feel it pulsing, breathing, a living thing. He knew it was a risk, especially given where he was. He just couldn't help himself. He needed it. Now more than ever.

It didn't take long for an interruption to come. If anything it was entirely predictable.

'Are you… are you him?' It was a girl's voice, young and breathless. Bastien cracked open one eye. She was standing on the edge of the bath opposite him and Daniel was making choked noises behind him. Not noises of alarm. He was desperately trying to warn her off.

Long mousy brown hair hung down almost to the small of her back and she wore the simple uniform of a cadet. She couldn't have been more than fourteen. A plain leather band encircled her throat, the sigil in it dark but still shiny. There was a group gathered behind her, still some distance back. They must have put her up to it. Or bullied her into it. They were collared too.

'And who do you think I am?' he asked in a low drawl. Privately he thanked the divinities for the water's depth, and for whatever minerals they put in it that made it cloudy. He was far too naked for this conversation.

'The… the Lord of Thorns?'

Goddess, he hated that name, that mocking title used to terrify people and make him the monster. It wasn't their fault. It was all they heard of him. *Be good or the Lord of Thorns will come for you. Behave, or we'll give you to the Lord of Thorns.* It made him as much of a fairy tale villain as the Hollow King. He couldn't shake it off, no matter how he tried. All he could do was own it.

They were mageborn, all of them, staring at him, at the gold torc around his neck, at his dark eyes. They looked terrified, but also… desperate. Even here.

'Yes,' he said in reply.

The girl stepped back to her friends, and some of them reached out to her, touching her, and he felt a surge of magic in the air, like ozone tingling against him. She was strong, but they made her stronger.

Interesting. A Leech, just like him, but with others willing to share magic with her, rather than forcing her to take it.

He tilted his head to one side, watching them while Daniel told them to bugger off and find someone else to hassle. But that wasn't going to happen. They were young, idealistic. And stubborn. All the Academy were stubborn.

The girl edged closer, leaving the others, coming towards him alone like a frightened animal. Every instinct should have told her to run, but she didn't.

'They said you were sick,' the girl said, when she was aglow with transferred magic energy.

'I was.'

She knelt down at the edge beside him and spread her hands out on either side, bowing her head.

'Lord Prince, you're mageborn like us. If you need magic, we offer it. It… it's our honour to serve. We offer fealty and homage.'

Bastien turned in the water, facing her, and studied the girl carefully. She would be beautiful one day, and powerful too if the Academy didn't break her, or drain her, or if her heart, so full of giving, didn't betray her.

Lord Prince…

Something stung his eyes but he didn't have it in him to name it.

'What's your name?' he asked.

'Carla, Lord Prince.'

'Carla,' he said. 'I thank you. But it isn't your day of homage yet.'

'But… but Lord Prince…'

'You've done this before?' Of course they had. All the mageborn did to an extent. And he was sure now he had seen some of them at the palace on their days of homage, their faces illuminated.

'We help each other. It's our way. It always has been.'

Of course it was. They had to survive somehow and sharing their magic was often the only way. 'But I am not part of your way, sweet child. I'm a Larelwynn. I can't be.'

She looked so bewildered, as if he wasn't speaking the same language. 'Lord Prince... you're *our* prince.' The emphasis on the word was subtle, but there.

'And my cousin is *our* king,' he told her. He laid his hand on her head and gently sent out a wave of power, a soft surge of warmth and acceptance which swirled through her, making the power within her sing as it flowed back to those it had come from. A Tide, a Lyric, a Charm, and a Flint. A number of each. Strong and young, full of idealism and some rebellious thoughts. He trailed along with the magic, touching the minds of each one and blessing them, his magic – the other side of it – strengthening each of them. The Maegen flowed through him, the deepest part of the pool filling him to bless them.

A shout of anger broke through the spell.

'What in all the seven hells do you think you're doing, Larelwynn?' Grace had arrived.

Chapter Eleven

Grace paused in her search through the pile of discarded shirts and tunics, her head swimming as the golden hues of the Maegen settled around her. The warmth spread through the air and her skin prickled.

It had never happened while she was awake before. Not even in a daydream. It had to be because he was so close, because he was here in her home, because... because he had kissed her...

A voice cut through the reverie, urgent and out of breath.

'Grace? You'd better get down to the baths. I think there's a lynch mob gathering.'

Childers stood opposite her in the laundry. The problem was she hadn't heard him coming, or even noticed him until he spoke. She'd been that far gone.

Enough was enough.

Damn it, she knew she shouldn't have left him. She'd thought Daniel could manage babysitting him for a trip to the baths at least. She was an idiot.

She tried not to run, but the thought of what could happen, both to him and everyone at the Academy if this went sideways, was too much. She ended up sprinting.

He looked like a god rising from the waters, just like she had seen him in the Maegen. It ran down his body in rivulets and light blossomed in his hands. Water caught its glow and reflected the ripples of the pool up onto the vaulted ceiling. He laid his palm on the head of the girl kneeling on the bath edge and her eyes went wide, the pupils blown out to pools of darkness, her mouth opening in an 'o' of surprise.

It swept over Grace like a tsunami, almost taking her to her knees as she tried to keep moving. Fire boiled at the base of her spine, her hands ached and her skin tightened over her bones. It was like something akin to physical desire. She wanted him, needed him, and felt that need to the vital core of her being. Every nerve came to light and the torches on either side of the door blazed even brighter.

From somewhere she found her voice. It didn't even sound like her voice. It was a voice full of rage and fire, a voice that couldn't believe what she was seeing. What was he doing?

'What in all the seven hells do you think you're doing, Larelwynn?'

He looked over his shoulder, his wet hair spilling down his back like oil, his eyes shining with a light that should not have been there. It was like the light that had killed Kai, and it brimmed on his black eyelashes like tears of gold. He smiled, just a little, a soft apologetic smile, as if he had been expecting her. There was no remorse there, though. Not an iota of regret.

The light faded and then he was just a man, standing waist-deep in the milky water of the baths.

'There you are, Captain,' he said. The tiredness in his voice made her pause, and her anger transformed to concern. But Bastien, being Bastien, had to go and ruin it immediately. 'Good. Did you find my clothes?'

Like a servant. Like she was there to fetch and carry for him. Like she had no actual value at all aside from what she could do for him. Anger came back, sweeping away concern.

'Get out of here,' she yelled at the mageborn students, who scattered rapidly at her voice, clearly shaken but still in awe of him. Not so much, however, that it affected their survival instincts. 'Get out now! And you, you utter bastard, get out of the water and put that fucking robe on. Danny, what the hell were you thinking letting them in here?'

Daniel, *thinking*. That was a joke.

'I just… I didn't do anything… they just…'

'I don't care what they *just*, Danny. What did he do to them? What did you let him do?' She bore down on him like an avenging spirit and he stood there, shocked. But before she could reach him, Bastien stepped between them, still pulling the robe back into place.

'If you're angry with anyone, it's me, Captain Marchant. Channel it properly.'

He glanced past her, drawing her attention to the candles which were now bubbling pools of wax. That, finally, brought Grace up short. She dragged her gaze back to him and all the strength seemed to go out of her.

He knew.

He'd probably always known. He was the seneschal of the mageborn. Of course he knew. But now he knew for sure.

'Would you be so good as to leave us alone, Officer Parry?' he said in the softest voice imaginable. 'And see that we are not disturbed.'

'You're not in charge here,' she told him, but her voice sounded unaccountably weak.

'Of course not, Captain.' Bastien took the bundle of clothes from her and headed for the changing rooms so quickly all she could do was follow him.

'What did you just do?'

He undid the robe again and through a heroic act of sheer self-preservation she turned her back on him. A soft chuckle echoed around the small tiled room and she cursed him inwardly. The sound did things it shouldn't do to her insides.

He towelled his hair and body dry using the scratchy towels from the changing room without comment or complaint, and then pulled on his clothes with silent efficiency.

'Would you care to sit down?' he asked.

Sure, in a damp changing room that needed cleaning. It stank of old sweat with an undercurrent of mould. That was just perfect.

'I would *care* to have an explanation.'

'There's a garden here, isn't there? Why don't we go outside?'

'Are you putting this off?' She almost wished he was.

'Not at all. Tell me what you need, Captain. I am yours to command.'

There was an edge to the way he said it and she winced before turning back to face him. When she did, she almost wished she hadn't.

The dark and brooding Lord of Thorns was back, a contrast in gilded skin, black hair, clothes and eyes, and that shock of gold around his throat, his only adornment.

What did she need? She needed him to stop being so bloody distracting. And so arrogant. And so... so... himself. She needed space.

And she needed him to kiss her again, like he had last night.

Of course, he'd been delirious and drugged. She should never have responded but the temptation had been too great, and she herself had been half asleep tending him. It was all a horrific mistake and as soon as she could get to see the king she'd tell him that.

As soon as she could get to see the king, that was laughable. Like the king was going to listen to her. Like he'd even deign to see her again.

A king did whatever a king wanted. And the same could be said for a prince.

'Let's go somewhere private,' she said, making her voice calm and even. How she achieved that miracle she didn't know. Even as she said it and saw the teasing edge of his crooked smile she knew that it was a bad idea. 'We need to talk. *Just* talk.'

She shouldn't be responding to him like this, but ever since she had met him her body didn't seem to be doing what it was told. That had to stop. How was she supposed to do her job and—

Ah, but her job wasn't entirely her job any more. It was looking after him. Keeping him alive.

'Just talk,' Bastien assured her.

*

The cottage garden behind the kitchen was the only place she could think of. If that was because he had asked about a garden, or because it had been in her dream, Grace wasn't sure. But it was private.

It wasn't much. Vegetables, herbs, a few stray flowers, some chickens scratching around in the corner. The square beds were as regimented as the Academy, everything in its place, and, thanks to the talents of a few young Loams recently arrived here, the garden bloomed with abundance.

There was definitely no glowing pool of light in the centre.

Bastien sat on the low, ramshackle bench across from the kitchen window, ignoring the bucket of sand full of poorly rolled cigarette ends and the sorry pile of empty beer bottles under it, with all the diplomatic skills she would expect from a prince. He closed his eyes. Beyond the high walls the sounds of the city filtered through, but it sounded far off, distant. It had always been her escape, hers and many others. Here there was birdsong and a breeze. You could barely even hear the cook yelling blue murder at the unfortunate scullery boy in the rooms behind them.

Grace tried to make herself relax, but she couldn't sit still. She shifted around, crossing and uncrossing her arms, and she finally managed to stand at ease, even though she wasn't really at ease at all. She just waited there, in front of him, trying to figure out how to broach this.

He beat her to it.

'How did you hide yourself for so long, Grace?'

She could argue. She could deny everything, play innocent or ignorant. It had worked all the other times the suspicion had reared its head.

'I don't know what you mean…' She didn't even sound convincing to herself. Not this time around.

He just sat there, as patient as stone. Waiting. She folded her arms, defiant.

'You're a Flint. But something happened, when you were a child, I presume. Before the Academy.'

'I don't remember life before the Academy.'

He gave a little sound of understanding, a brief 'hah' and lifted his head in a nod of understanding. 'Memories can be difficult, I know. I can help with that.'

She shied back from him, even though he hadn't moved. 'You're not touching me again.'

He laughed. Actually laughed. And suddenly he was on his feet, moving faster than she could have anticipated. An instant later, she was in his arms, her body pressed to his, far too intimately, and his lips were only a whisper away from hers.

She could kiss him. Just lean forward a little and kiss him. Like he had kissed her last night. That weird, feverish kiss that should never have happened.

Like they had kissed in the Maegen, so many times. He had been her lover in the light, so tender and so careful of her, bringing her such joy. No earthly lover had ever compared. She knew him better than anyone else. More intimately. Completely.

'Really?' he said.

Something snapped inside her, that spell he wove over her, the madness that seemed to infect her just being close to him. It melted away, and anger flooded in to replace it. Anger she could work with. Anger was good. Anger was strength.

She twisted in his grip, dropping her weight, and kicked hard into his ankle. Startled, Bastien released her and she leaped back from him, landing in a crouch, her knives already in her hands.

'Don't try that again,' she snarled.

Bastien shook off any pain or humiliation. Perhaps the Lord of Thorns didn't feel either. 'You certainly have the temperament of every Flint I've ever met,' he said ruefully. 'It's a wonder no one else ever realised.'

'*I* didn't even realise.' He gave her a single look which branded her a liar. She straightened, but kept the knives to hand. 'I didn't. Not at first. Look, I was mageborn. And something happened when I was a child which took it from me. A syphon or something. I was burned out completely when I got here. Craine knows. They all knew. I was tested and found… empty. It was only recently that I…' She sighed, surprised how difficult this was to admit. Because she had never admitted it before to anyone, apart from Kai. 'It started to come back. Like an instinct, a feeling, and then… just a little. Kai helped. Whenever I needed him to.'

'You let him drain you?'

He made it sound illicit, like something to be ashamed of. She scowled. 'It wasn't like that. He helped, that's all. He was my friend. We're Academy. We look out for each other here.'

'Oh Grace,' Bastien whispered. It was a sound of deep remorse, and terrible understanding.

The wave of horror that had been hanging over her for days finally crashed down on her. Her shoulders sagged as she admitted her darkest fear. 'Did I kill him? Was it my fault?'

'What?'

She pressed on. She had to know now. And Bastien could tell her, even if no one else could. 'Was it my fault? If he syphoned power from me, and then he—'

'No. It doesn't work like that. I promise. We aren't just batteries, Grace, absorbing power and overloading. Sometimes, like any mageborn, it's just too much to house inside us. Sometimes it's just our time. The Maegen... it has a life of its own. It wants to escape the pool. It wants to be used.'

'But you don't just leech magic, do you? You did something else. With those students.'

And as quickly as that, he seemed to close himself off from her. 'It was nothing.'

She'd walked in and seen him there, felt the surge of magic, the raw power swirling in the air all around them. It was not nothing. She'd thought he was draining them, that he was stealing all their magic as hers had been stolen. And in that instant, all she knew was rage.

They were just cadets. Little more than children. And she'd lost it.

Now... now she wasn't so sure. She didn't like the feeling. She needed answers.

'I felt it too, Bastien. Remember? It made the Flint in me stronger… the torches, the candles… I thought… I'm sorry. I was wrong. You weren't leeching their magic. But what were you doing?'

He sat down again, his hands folded in his lap, his head bowed. 'I was just helping them. Securing their powers, strengthening them, keeping them safe. That's what I'm meant to do. The Maegen flows through me, more readily than through anyone else. I can send it either way. I'm not really a Leech, or… not just a Leech. I… I manipulate the Maegen itself. That's what the day of homage is, a way of securing the powers of the mageborn, stopping them becoming overwhelmed, as your friend was.'

She recalled him standing over Kai's body, the strange gentleness as he stroked her dying friend's face and drew the magic devouring him out of him.

'You didn't kill Kai, did you?'

'I released him.'

And she'd cursed him, hated him. When he had finally set Kai free.

'Does it hurt?' she asked.

He didn't answer for a moment. He looked stricken, then bowed his head, staring at the ground.

'Every time.'

Like a sickness, ma'am. But it is my honour to serve. That was what Kai had said. And he was right. It infected everything. Grace stared at the Lord of Thorns, not able to think of a single response.

As if uncomfortable with the line the conversation had taken, he seemed to shake himself off and turned away. 'All right, I promise. I won't touch you without permission. Never again. As you command. It's not like I haven't had the experience and it isn't one I relish.'

For a moment she thought he meant touching her. But then she realised. Being touched without permission... maybe he did remember... or at least he knew, in theory, what had happened.

Her stomach twisted again and she sheathed the knives. His promise would have to do. She still wasn't sure if she believed him, and it didn't really matter. He sounded like he meant it. Remorse stained his eyes. He might be struggling with what happened to him last night. Perhaps this was his way.

But he knew her secret now. He was the worst person who could have found out.

'And if I'm a...' She couldn't even say it. Not out loud. It was too much. Too dangerous. 'Bastien, what... what do I do?'

He paused for a moment, considering. Then said the impossible. 'Nothing. Say nothing, do nothing. Unless you want a collar around your neck too.'

'But—'

Duty said otherwise. Protocol and directives. If it was anyone else, she would be honour-bound to report it. And if she looked, if she dared to actually look through the regulations she had once memorised so assiduously, she was certain she'd find one telling her she had to turn herself in. But she hadn't dared to look. She didn't want to remember.

'No buts, Captain. I'll protect you.'

She couldn't help the smile, a broken wavering expression. 'That's my job, Bastien. I'm meant to protect you.'

'Then we protect each other. It seems only fair. Deal?' He held out his hand and she stared at it. An awkward moment passed and a bird flew out of the apple trees at the rear of the garden, distracting her. When she looked back, his hands were folded in his lap again and his head was bowed. He got to his feet, every movement elegant. 'We should go. I will be needed back at the palace.'

'Bastien,' she said firmly, pulling his attention back to her. She offered her own hand this time and Bastien stared at it. 'It's a deal.'

He stood, towering over her, his shadow falling and encircling her. But she didn't feel the cold, not now. 'It's a deal,' he said and slipped his hand into hers.

His skin felt so cool and inviting against hers, his hand strong and yet gentle. She remembered it holding her, effortlessly. Magic pulsed inside her, in time with her heart. Or maybe in time with his.

She didn't mean to let go quite so quickly. 'All right,' she said, trying to mask it. Knowing he wasn't fooled for an instant. 'Back to the palace. But... but first, I need to interview someone. Can we make a stop on the way?'

The light of intrigue entered his dark eyes. It looked a lot like hope.

Chapter Twelve

The Great Temple of the Little Goddess, far older than the palace or the Academy, sat in the very centre of Rathlynn. Far older than anything else in the city. The thought of it played havoc with Grace's imagination. The round building stood on a labyrinth of catacombs that interconnected with countless other subterranean paths, because the Rathlynnese colonised everything, above and below. It was topped with a golden dome and the round arches encircling it led into the cool interior. The windows had been added later, a mosaic of blue and white glass, tiny mullioned panes the size of duck eggs.

Four galleries stretched out to each compass point, leading to towers where the novices, sisters and servants of the Temple lived. In the quadrants between, the gardens spilled life everywhere, lush with fruit and flowers, all the bounties of the Little Goddess.

She brought life to every garden.

So too, Grace thought as they lingered in the cool shade of a reception room, just beyond one of those gardens, did the number of Loams who she had already spotted living here, tending the plants, turning the soil, singing soft and magical songs.

It was a legally acceptable thing, of course, fosterage at the Temple, a viable alternative to the Academy. Certainly better than the streets. Kids went missing all the time, mageborn kids most frequently. She thought of the file in her pack, the ones whose bodies had been found with their hands burned.

Bastien paced back and forth, unable to settle. The long black cloak made him look like a crow.

'How may we be of service, Officers?' The voice of a woman floated softly into the room, followed by the woman herself. Daniel and Childers were already bowing. Ellyn took one look and dropped to her knees.

'Mother,' she gasped. 'You honour us.'

Grace winced, but she bowed too, while the Mother of the Temple laid her hand on Ellyn's head. Grace hadn't really expected her to come herself. She stood, tall and stately, robed in her customary green. Long chestnut hair, threaded with strands of silver, was piled on top of her head and tumbled in graceful curls around her face. She was younger than Grace had imagined, in her middle years, but still beautiful. For some reason Grace had always thought that the woman would be ancient. But she wasn't. The same age as Craine perhaps.

Then Mother Miranda noticed Bastien. She smiled, the smile of a much younger woman by far.

'Your highness? We weren't expecting you today. Do you wish to visit her? She's… not having the best day, I'm afraid.'

'Not today, madam. You are too kind.' He smiled, but it didn't make it all the way to his eyes, Grace noticed. Whoever he was being invited to visit, he clearly didn't want Miranda to know whether he actually wanted to or not. 'I'm simply assisting the Academy with their investigation. I'm sure you'll want to do the same.'

'But of course, my dear. Tell me, Captain, how can I help?'

She was the most powerful woman in the city, next to the queen. Settling herself on the bench overlooking the garden, Miranda beckoned to Grace as if she was an old friend.

Grace's spine stiffened in alarm. Her mind had a frozen image buried in it, a woman sitting like that, overlooking a ramshackle and pathetic garden, which had more buckets of stagnant water and broken bottles in it than fountains and verdant foliage. Something in the back of her mind clawed at her memories, the dark, forgotten part of her life. She closed her hands into tight fists to stop them shaking.

'Ma'am,' she began and the others all looked at her in confusion. You didn't address her like that. Of course you didn't. What was she doing? 'Mother…' That didn't feel right either.

Miranda smiled. 'There's no need to be afraid, Captain. Come, sit down.' She gently patted the bench beside her.

Grace shook herself, telling herself to focus, to fight this unknown fear and do her job.

'It is regarding a series of murders. Mageborn left with burns on their hands. Commander Craine sent us to ask for your help.'

'Dear me, the poor things. Do you know their families? We can send some financial aid, or counsellors. We can always make space here if needed.'

'Only one,' she said. 'A sailor who was a Zephyr.'

Miranda bowed her head and said a prayer. 'And the others?'

'I have descriptions, some drawings. If you recognise them, if they ever came here, or if you know of any mageborn who came for healing with burns on their hands…'

'Show me. We will help in any way we can. Let me call some of our wards and see if they can identify them. Children, you know, have the most remarkable memories.'

The words seemed to echo through Grace's head for a moment, rebounding back and forth. *Children… memories…* She swallowed hard and tried to make herself breathe.

Grace took the files from her pack, while Miranda sent an attendant off to call her wards. Moments later the courtyard was full of children of all ages. Ellyn, Daniel and Childers set about showing them the pictures and talking to them but it quickly became clear that this was going nowhere.

Bastien watched from the corner, a dark shadow, and Grace glanced his way only when Miranda approached him. She put her hand on his arm and he pulled back as politely as he could. If it offended her, she gave no sign.

'The queen sent word,' she said. 'They were worried when you left so suddenly. Are you feeling better?'

'Yes,' he replied, his voice cold. 'I'm fine. Now… Miranda… how is she?'

'She's… she's been better. Not a good day today but you could see her if you want. You know we will always make accommodations for you, Bastien.'

'In return for what?'

She shook her head, smiling. 'Your company, nothing more arduous than that.'

He looked up and his eyes met Grace's. His face fell to perfect stillness. 'Thank you for helping them. But if there's nothing else we really should get back to the palace.'

*

With the dregs of the market clearing up in King's Square, they diverted along Grand Way, the wide white-stoned street which led towards the palace and the Royal Promenade. Grace kept her eyes on the junctions and the rooftops. Something niggled away at the back of her brain, something that didn't feel right. As they passed under the shadow of the watch house, she felt a chill and her shoulders tightened.

'Captain,' Bastien said, his voice no more than a whisper of a warning.

The explosion from the left blew out the timbered colonnade. Grace threw herself back, reaching for Bastien, but Daniel was already on him, pushing him towards the ground.

'No! Get to cover!' Grace yelled. She hauled Bastien up and headed for the other side of the road but as she did so, a group of armed men and women descended on them. They wore grey clothes, their faces wrapped with scarves, hiding their identities.

From overhead, arrows rained down. It seemed to be just one archer but his aim was good and he was fast. Worse, the arrows were aided by the wind itself, a Zephyr behind them, no doubt. Zigzagging back towards the square, Grace heard the crash of weapons as Childers and Ellyn engaged. She and Daniel formed up around the prince. Bastien had drawn the sword he'd borrowed from the Academy armoury. He had to know how to use it. That was the type of thing posh boys like him learned from childhood, wasn't it?

But she'd bet he couldn't use it the way they did.

Ellyn wielded her swords like a dancer. They spun around her as she pirouetted, her pale hair flying out like a veil. Two of the swords-men tried to engage her, one going down in a tangled heap almost immediately. The other held on, barely.

Childers hacked at his opponents, an older, more brutal school of fighting than the Valenti islander. He fought dirty and hard, just like always, a style – if you could call it a style – learned on the streets of Rathlynn.

They dived into the colonnade on the far side of the square, snatching a moment's cover. Grace shoved the prince unceremoniously behind her. At the far end was a lane leading towards narrower streets and more cover. They could make that. She pointed at it and Daniel nodded.

'There are more mageborn among them,' Bastien told her.

Was that what she was feeling? Beyond her normal instincts, beyond years of reading the city and its streets.

'What kind?'

He tilted his head to one side, cat-like. 'Zephyr… probably the archer. And a Charm, I think or a Shade. And a Flint. A strong one or that explosion wouldn't have been more than a puff of smoke.'

Grace swore under her breath. Three mageborn was three too many, especially with a Charm and a Flint. A Charm could persuade anyone of anything. A Shade would be even worse. Maybe there were more. The swordsmen had scattered.

'Reinforcements will be on the way,' Daniel said, but he didn't look convinced. They weren't even far from the Academy, and the Temple bells were ringing in alarm. This much mageborn activity was bound to attract attention, not to mention the fight happening all around them. Arrows came raining down again, forcing Ellyn and Childers to cease pursuit and take cover on the far side of the road.

Ellyn sprinted towards them, but a wall of flames rose in front of her and she shied back. Childers broke right, down another laneway leading towards the docks. He'd circle back to them, she knew that. It was protocol. But she didn't like this. They were splitting up and that wasn't good. Almost like they were being corralled.

'Grace,' Daniel yelled. 'Grace, where are you?'

'Daniel?' She couldn't see him. Or Bastien. They'd been right behind her a second ago. They couldn't have gone. But she couldn't see them now. The lane ahead was dark with shadows. Had he gone ahead of her? Damn it. This couldn't be happening.

Grace rounded the corner and it felt like running into a brick wall. She fell back, sprawling on the ground, dazed as a man loomed from the shadows. Mageborn, definitely, a Brawn, and bigger than Kai, like a bear standing over her, magic enhancing his strength. She reached for her sword but he stood on the blade before she could lift it.

'Stay down, Academy,' he said. 'Stay out of the way. It'll be over soon.'

'What'll be over?'

'We just want him. Nothing was said about you. Just...' But his voice trailed off as he looked at her. 'Well now, that changes things.'

He wasn't wearing a collar but that wasn't a surprise. He wasn't the only one using magic either. For a brief moment she thought with a burst of hope that it might be Bastien. The shadows were darkening, thickening like fog around them.

The Brawn reached down and, before she could gather her wits, grabbed her by the throat, lifting her up off the ground.

'Found it!' he shouted and he shook her for good measure as she choked in his grip and failed to kick her way free.

Another man coalesced out of the shadows. No question that he was mageborn. A Shade. The shadows danced around him.

They dragged her out to the centre of the square, where the arrows were scattered about.

'Tell the Lord of Thorns to surrender,' the Shade said in a flat voice. She hadn't seen a Shade in years, not one with abilities like this. He left the world feeling cold and desperate, draining it of life and laughter, darkening everything. His touch was fear itself. Grace desperately pushed away the descriptions from the texts in the Academy, all the horrors they could inflict, and tried to dredge up the sections on their weaknesses. Her mind was blank. The fear that just being near him brought out froze her mind. This wasn't happening. Couldn't be happening. Shades, like Gores and Barrows, were the stuff of nightmare.

The brute dropped her but the shadows moved like snakes, twisting around her, pinning her arms to her side, tightening around her chest. The Shade had her now. All her weapons and sigils were useless.

'Grace!' Bastien yelled from wherever Daniel had made him take cover.

'There you are,' the Shade laughed. 'Come out, my lord, or we'll have her make you come out.'

'I'm doing nothing for you. Don't listen to them, Bastien.'

The vine of shadows tightened around her throat and the end reared up like a snake and plunged into her mouth. She gasped for air, her vision darkening.

'You don't need her,' Bastien shouted. Why wasn't Daniel shutting him up? 'The warrant commands me. Take it and let her go. I'll cooperate. I swear.'

She would have cursed him for telling them if she could have found the air to curse. What kind of idiot was he, telling them his weakness? She struggled, trying to tear herself free, the fire inside her trying to build. It was useless. It would never be strong enough. This was not how she wanted to go out, helpless, exposed, used as bait.

'Take the warrant,' the Shade ordered his Brawn. The two of them worked as a pair, but there was no doubt who was in command. 'Give it to me.'

The Brawn grinned at her as he flicked open her shirt. There was nothing she could do to stop him. Shadows crammed into her mouth, forced their way down her throat, even as they crushed it from the outside. Burning tears filled her eyes, frustration and rage making them boil.

His meaty hand closed over the warrant. And he seemed to freeze, all at once, his grin turning brittle and stretching too wide. His eyes grew round in panic, bulged. He tried to jerk back from her, whether to pull the warrant free or simply get away she didn't know.

And then he burst into flames. He went up like a great torch in front of her. He didn't scream or try to run. He didn't even move. He couldn't. Flames devoured him, eating away at his skin, the fat and muscle underneath melting, the bones charring until they turned to ash. The stench filled her nostrils.

At some point, he fell. Or crumbled.

The warrant dropped back against her chest where it hung still. She could feel the icy weight of it through her jerkin, so cold it even sucked the warmth from her skin.

The Shade staggered back, appalled and horrified, but he didn't release her. He wasn't a fool. As a captive, she was all the insurance he had left.

'What are you?' His voice was stricken.

'Dev!' another of the conspirators yelled to him from overhead, the archer, wherever he was. But the warning came too late.

Bastien Larelwynn attacked in a blur of movement. The sword he'd borrowed from the Academy had never moved like that since its forging. Zavi and the weapons master would have wept to see the skill, deadly beauty enshrined in every movement.

It lasted only seconds. Whoever had trained him had taught him not to show off or mess around, an approach of which she approved. He took the Shade's head off with one blow.

The shadows crushing Grace vanished and before she could fall Bastien caught her. He dragged her to the shelter of the arcade on the edge of the market square.

'Did you… did you do that?' she asked, her voice broken and hurt. 'No.'

Then something even worse occurred to her. 'Did I?'

'Grace,' he smoothed back her hair from her face, looking down on her like she was something precious. No, that couldn't be right. 'You aren't strong enough for that.'

'No… no I'm not…' She tried to heave in a breath, but it hurt. Everything hurt. 'You knew it would kill him. You knew.'

'I guessed. It protects itself. And you. Can you move? Here,' he moved as if to touch her forehead. She felt the magic rise in him. Her hand snapped up to catch his wrist, holding him away.

'No. No magic,' she barked and pulled herself free.

'I can help.'

'I'm sure you can. But no magic.' Her legs felt like jelly and she couldn't seem to make herself breathe properly, not really, although it was easing. She'd recover. She knew she would. When she got to her feet she almost went down again.

'I'll carry you.'

'If you carry me *anywhere* in front of my squad, I'll make you wish you'd never been born.'

As it was, he had to help her. Daniel dragged both of them the rest of the way into the lane. Childers had found them and Ellyn limped behind him. 'Just a scratch,' she said. 'One of the arrows. I'm fine.'

Grace nodded, accepting it. 'We need to get to Eastferry, along the docks.'

'You want to go through the dodgiest part of the city?' Childers growled.

'Do you have a better idea?'

'We stay put. The Temple's sanctuary. They won't—'

Fire blasted up the side of the wall beside them, licking the eaves. 'Really? Won't they? We won't make it back there.'

'Can you see him?' Bastien asked. 'Any of them? The mageborn? They're going to come after us.'

'How do you know?' Daniel asked.

'Because they're trying to kill me.'

'Popular hobby, is it?'

Bastien gave his crooked smile. 'Very.'

Grace shook off their nonsense. Who had sent them? Why? So many questions and they didn't have a moment to ask them, let alone wait for an answer. 'This way. Stay close. With me, all of you.'

The narrow lane took them under an arcade of crafters' shops and out of the range of the archer.

As they ducked out of the far end, into the open plaza between them and Eastferry, Childers gave a shout of warning. The arrow took him in the neck a second later. He collapsed, blood pumping from the wound.

'Do something,' Ellyn yelled, pulling him back under cover. He gurgled something, grabbing at her jacket, and then he went still. Ellyn's face crumpled and she held him for a moment.

Without pause, Bastien leaned down and pulled the arrow free, ignoring Ellyn's cry of outrage. Daniel stepped between them as she surged up but Bastien didn't seem to notice. He held the arrow close, whispering over it, and then hurled it into the air. It flew from his hands as if he had fired it from a longbow himself.

There was a distant cry, a noise of pain and betrayal.

'Come on,' he said and strode out across the plaza. 'Before the Flint finds us.'

'What did you do?'

'I sent his arrow back to him, with interest. I doubt he's dead but he won't be a problem for a while. The other one though...'

How had he done that? How was it even possible?

The fire was spreading, leaping from building to building, the Flint whipping it up to try to trap them. This area was a tinder box. He'd see the whole city burn if it meant it got them too, of that Grace had no doubt.

Eastferry wasn't far. There were places to hide. They could make it. If they moved now.

'With me,' she told them. 'Stay close and keep moving.'

'We need to raise the alarm,' Ellyn said.

'I think you can consider it raised, Ellyn. Move quickly and quietly. Now.'

They moved as one, in a rush, pitching downhill into Eastferry, the one place most of the guards didn't go, because why would they? The whole of Eastferry was gangland, and the best place in the city if you needed to vanish. Grace nodded to Daniel to take the lead.

'Danny? Is Kurt still top dog?'

He grimaced. 'Better hope so. Just stay behind me and shut up, okay? He hasn't forgiven you for the last time.'

'Hood up, your highness,' said Ellyn. 'Or they're going to eat you alive.'

*

The moment they entered, Misha Harper was up on his feet, running towards Daniel. 'There you are! I thought... I mean... I was afraid...'

Daniel just held him close and Grace decided to look the other way, into the depths of the Larks' Rest, the seediest of seedy bars in Eastferry.

Kurt's place hadn't changed. Never had, and probably never would. It was the same sticky-floored haunt of misery it always was. The girls looked jaded, the barman looked belligerent and the customers, such as they were, studied their pints and didn't make eye contact at all. Uniforms had that effect, especially here. Kurt sat in his usual booth at the back, his legs splayed wide, his arms behind his head. He probably had at least one knife hidden behind him. Grace would have been disappointed if he hadn't.

'Hello Duchess,' he said, fixing her with his trademark leer. 'Been a while.'

'Hello Kurt,' she replied. She was tempted to add 'not long enough' but she needed him on side.

He gave Bastien a long assessing look but when Bastien didn't react at all he turned his attention back on her. 'So, what've you dragged my baby brother into this time, Duchess?'

Duchess. Because her name was Grace and duchesses were 'your grace'. Because he'd called her that from the first moment she met him, when he'd dumped Daniel at the Academy, even though he wasn't much older himself. Goddess forbid he ever just called her by her name.

'She's a captain now, Kurt,' Daniel interrupted. Like that was going to impress him.

'Captain? Well, aren't you on the up? Company you're keeping, I hear.'

So, he *had* heard. Which meant he had a good idea who Bastien really was. Damn.

'We're just passing through, Kurt. We don't want any trouble.'

He unfurled his arms, and pushed himself up to stand. He had always towered over her. 'Looks like you brought it though. They're hunting rogue mageborn, as I heard it. But they don't sound too rogue to me. More like… the ones doing the hunting.'

'Is there a price on our heads?' Daniel asked. Misha flinched when he said it, the colour draining from his handsome face, his mouth opening in shock. Grace pushed down the urge to slap him and tell him to grow up.

Kurt shrugged. 'Some of you. Not you, Danny-boy. I think they're treating you as just collateral damage. Shame they don't know who you are. I'll have to see to that.'

Little brother to one of the sharpest gang leaders in Rathlynn, that was who Daniel was. They didn't speak of it. He didn't acknowledge it and Kurt had never asked anything of him. Not yet anyway. Grace was pretty sure it was just a matter of time. When the time came, when the score was big enough, when Kurt had nowhere else to turn…

Maybe he just wanted to protect his brother. Maybe. That was his line anyway.

'Please don't,' Daniel said but Kurt just grinned at him.

'And you?' He finally fixed his attention on Bastien again. Grace had known it was coming.

Bastien met his gaze without flinching. 'Just trying to get home.'

A slow, knowing smile spread over Kurt's face. 'Are you now? Well, that might be worth a favour someday.'

Bastien gave a terse nod. 'Many things are.' His reply was cool and Grace wished he'd just shut up. He didn't know how to talk to someone like Kurt Parry. Many of the ones who got it wrong ended up in the harbour with their throats cut.

Not that she thought even Kurt would have the nerve to do that to the Lord of Thorns.

They glared at each other, neither one willing to give an inch. Grace had seen enough pissing matches in her life to know they never ended well. Whatever masculine face-off was going on between them made her cringe. Daniel moved off to the side of the room with Misha, talking to him with quiet urgency, reassuring the harper or at least trying to. It didn't seem to be going terribly well. Ellyn was already at the bar, ordering the strongest liquor they had. That's when Grace noticed her hands, shaking and fidgeting, her breath short and sudden.

She joined her. 'Ellyn?'

'Sorry boss. Sorry...' She knotted fingers together, trying to stop them betraying her. It was far too late. 'I just... I've known him for years.'

Grace pulled her into a hug. They'd only just lost Kai, and now Childers too.

'It's okay. Have a drink. Just not too much. I need you ready to go whenever...' She glanced over her shoulder at the two men. 'Whenever they're finished.'

'We need to lie low, boss,' she said. 'At least until nightfall.'

'You can wait upstairs,' said Kurt, approaching them. 'No one will bother you. Or find you. Just don't drink me out of house and home, Ellyn.'

Ellyn smiled brightly, all shock and grief suddenly masked. She, too, knew better than to show any weakness to him. Only Daniel could get away with that.

'I doubt you have enough booze at the best of times, mate. Not drinkable, anyway.'

Kurt laughed. 'Get them whatever they want, Halyk. Do you want food? Scarlet makes a mean omelette.'

'Ooh, prostitute omelette,' Ellyn cooed. 'You're spoiling us.'

'Your loss. Snob.'

Considering Ellyn had grown up in the same sort of tenement as the Parrys, 'snob' was a stretch. They continued bickering good-naturedly. It was soothing somehow, especially for Ellyn.

Grace felt Bastien move towards her rather than saw him. It was just the sense of him, the way she felt his presence. Like a shadow. Like a glow.

'Shouldn't we be on the move?' he asked.

'Not yet. We're exposed out there. Eastferry will keep us safe for a few hours. We'll set off again after dark.'

'After dark?' He shook his head. She wasn't having this argument with him. He could just bloody well do what she said for once.

'Go upstairs. I'll find some food and something to drink.'

'Yes.' He paused only for a second, and then went on, apparently in complete sincerity. 'I believe Ellyn was recommending some kind of omelette?'

She scowled at him. 'Very funny.'

He smiled back at her outrage. 'It was, wasn't it? All right, I'll go upstairs and stay out of trouble. That's what you really want to say, isn't it?'

*

They waited. Word came through that the riot had been put down by the city guard with the usual stolid efficiency. The reports of mageborn among the attackers had started rumours though, nasty rumours.

They're always dangerous. They can't be trusted. There's a reason they need to be controlled. Everyone knows that. They'd wipe us out if they could. They tried. The Hollow King almost succeeded. No one could let that happen again.

There was no mention of Bastien. So there was that small mercy. The fewer people who knew he was outside the palace the better. But it wouldn't be long before someone blabbed. He'd been seen at the Academy. Besides, he tended to attract attention.

So far Grace had deflected four of the regular girls from going up to the room 'just to check if your friend needs anything'. It was draining.

When she went to check on him herself, he appeared to be asleep sitting up on the moth-eaten bed, his back against the wall, facing the window.

'Oh sorry,' said a voice behind her. 'I didn't know that there was someone here. He asked for some wine.'

A woman stood in the doorway, a jug in one hand and two glasses in the other. She was hard-faced and the dress she wore was almost falling off her, dipping down so low over one shoulder it nearly exposed her breast.

'No I didn't,' Bastien said, the suddenness of his voice almost making Grace jump. Not so asleep then. Only long experience meant she stayed still and kept her attention firmly fixed on the woman at the door. Her skin was flushed, a light sheen of sweat making it glisten. Like she was too hot. Like she was feverish.

The woman dropped the jug and the glasses which shattered, red wine boiling as it splattered across the wooden floorboards.

'Get out of the way,' she snarled at Grace, who didn't move. 'I don't want you. It's just him. He's a monster.'

'He's just a man.'

'That's what he wants you to believe. We know the truth. The Hollow King is coming!'

Behind her Bastien Larelwynn surged to his feet. 'What did you say?'

Flames roared from the Flint towards Grace, and she staggered back, throwing her arms up in front of her face as if they would protect her.

But the fire didn't touch her.

'Stand down,' she heard Bastien yell. 'I can help you.'

'You're lying. You are made of lies. You'll steal the life and the light out of all of us. You'll drain the whole city if you can. You can't become king. Not you, nor your line.'

His voice grew strangely gentle, quiet and calm. But cold. So cold. 'They've filled your mind with deception,' he said, the tone almost singsong. Like he was trying to charm her. Did he have that power? Was he a Lyric or a Charm as well as a Leech? Was that even possible?

The fire grew brighter, a wall of it moving towards Grace, hemming her in. The floorboards burned and the flames reached for her, like hands. Grace opened her mouth to scream, but as it touched her, there was no pain. Just a gentle warmth. Her hands shook as she reached out. It didn't burn.

'Bastien,' she called out. She could almost see him through the fire, a dark figure, tall and thin as a shadow, staring at her in horror.

And at that moment the woman made a dive for him.

But the Lord of Thorns was faster. The Flint flung herself towards him, fire blazing from her hands. Grace felt it, felt the power and the desperation which drove her. And the man in black caught her with one hand. The woman screamed and Grace screamed with her. Somewhere inside she was just a child. A terrified child.

Grace's knife flashed in her hand as if she could leap through the fire and attack him, and Bastien flinched back, but he didn't let go. Something dark unleashed itself from inside him, that terrible sucking vacuum. The woman shrieked and tried to wriggle free.

The flames died down, and the Flint fell still in his grip.

Empty.

He lowered her gently to the charred floorboards.

'Are you hurt?' he asked, without looking at the woman. 'Are you burned?'

It took a moment before Grace realised he was talking to her.

She was shaking, that was certain. She felt like all the strength had been drained out of her and filled with flames instead. 'I'm not hurt. I don't think she wanted to hurt me.'

'No,' he said, staring at the suddenly small-looking body. 'Just me. I'm a monster, remember?'

Four mageborn sent after him, powerful and terrible, hunting him to the most unsavoury dive in the worst part of town. And yet here he was, still standing.

'She isn't dead?'

'Not quite. But she'll never raise a flame again. There's that at least.'

The way he said it chilled her. Grace glanced at him, his fine-boned face and dark eyes. The strain was evident in the line of his mouth, and she could read exhaustion in his gaze.

'You've taken her power from her?'

'Would you rather I let her burn you? This whole building?'

'The building might have been an improvement. But she didn't burn me. She used it to drive me back so she could get to you. Don't you see that?'

He looked at her then and Grace wished she'd just shut up entirely. 'If you hadn't come up here...'

She shifted her stance uncomfortably. The thought of him just draining the power out of that woman made her on edge, nervous, and she couldn't say why. At least he hadn't just killed her.

Because she knew, the Flint hadn't tried to kill her. Grace had stared into the fire and she'd seen... what?

A little girl, with red-gold hair.

Something in the back of her mind shuddered and she lurched back. The lance of pain that struck would have taken her to her knees if she hadn't been standing near him. She couldn't fall, couldn't let herself show weakness. Not in front of him.

But the feel of the flames against her skin came back, the fire that touched but didn't burn her, and her blood sang at its touch, and at the memory. Her vision swam and she reached up to hold her head.

'Are you hurt?' Bastien asked. He tried to catch her in case she fell and she shied away from him, almost falling anyway in the process. 'Take it easy, Captain. Slowly. Breathe.'

'Don't tell me what—'

She sat down abruptly on the edge of the bed and her head finally cleared. Whether his power would have an effect on her or not, she couldn't let him touch her.

Breathing definitely helped though. As did the calmness of his voice.

Get a grip, Grace, she told herself firmly. Get your act together and stand up, soldier.

It took all she had to do it.

'We need to leave,' she said.

'We can't leave her here.'

'We aren't taking her with us. Let Kurt mind her. Promise him money. He likes money. You can send for her later. Right now, I need to get you to safety. That's what I came up to tell you. The city's quietened down again but they're blaming mageborn terrorists.'

She glanced down at the unconscious Flint.

'They weren't terrorists. They were assassins.'

'I heard. What did she mean about the Hollow King, Bastien?'

He looked troubled, his brow creasing as he frowned. 'I don't know. But I need to find out.' Then he looked up, his eyes darker than ever, a shadow beneath them. 'You didn't burn, Grace. You're getting stronger.'

She tried to shrug, tried to make it nothing. It wasn't.

'I'll be fine,' she replied.

'I can help. Not now, maybe. Not so soon after…' he glanced down again. 'But I can help.'

If only she could trust him. But after what she had just seen? No. She couldn't do that.

'I'll be fine. Let's get moving.'

Chapter Thirteen

As the sun set over Rathlynn, Bastien found himself following his ragged group of erstwhile protectors out of the dregs of the city and up to the main gate of the palace complex. The walls of yellow stone curved inwards to the Lion gate, the azure blue tiles set with golden lions blazing in the light.

All along the main approach to the gates, figures gazed down on him, the Larelwynns of the past, all his ancestors. They all had his own face, or aspects of it. His nose, his jawline, his eyes... His heritage, his history was everywhere, but he didn't feel part of it. He never had.

Home. Or at least its public face. There were other ways in. Few people knew them and, though it was tempting to just sneak inside by another way, people clearly needed to know that the Lord of Thorns was back.

He heard the shout go up as he walked forwards.

'Captain, let me go first,' he said. For once, Grace listened to him. The Royal Guards flocked forwards, and for the first time since they left the Temple Bastien felt able to breathe again.

'Your highness,' the overly handsome man who had been promoted above his ability to lead a group of veterans gushed at him. 'The king has been so worried. He has been asking for you.'

'Thank you, Lieutenant...?' he fished for a name.

'Lieutenant Neren, your highness. Of the Camford Nerens.' Bastien had no idea who they were but he nodded as if he did. 'We can take it from here, Captain. You can stand down.'

Grace didn't move. There was something dark and dangerous in her eyes. Of course a lieutenant shouldn't be ordering around a captain, even if he was Royal Guard, of the Camford Nerens.

'Captain Marchant carries the king's warrant and is assigned to my personal protection, seconded to the Royal Guard. We should probably talk to General Kane, don't you think? You could go and make sure someone has prepared rooms for her and her people. In my apartments.'

Neren went white, a mixture of anger, humiliation and fear. It almost made Bastien laugh, but that wouldn't have been becoming, and would have compounded the problem. He didn't need another enemy just now. But he didn't like the way the boy talked down to Grace, or the way his squad looked at Ellyn and Daniel. They'd lost people today. Childers was dead. So Bastien sent Neren to make sure accommodation had been arranged for the Academy officers he thought so far below him and smiled softly to himself when he thought no one could see.

That said, he was pretty sure that Grace noticed. She saw everything.

Except perhaps her own potential. The fire in her was growing stronger. And the need to reach out and touch her, or taste her, was growing too. He could feel her power, humming just beneath her skin, warm and inviting.

He'd moved too fast. He'd made fun of her. That had been a mistake. It didn't matter that he'd been trying to protect himself, to push her away because he couldn't deal with what might have happened to him the previous night. Nothing helped with that.

And now... now... he had to face Asher Kane.

Asher was in his office, lounging back in his chair, drinking from a mug that Bastien firmly hoped didn't contain anything alcoholic. Or worse. When he saw them, a ghost of annoyance crossed his face for a moment. Just a moment. Then he smiled, too knowingly. He got to his feet, putting down the mug. As their eyes met, Bastien suppressed a shudder.

'Your highness, you're back. How's the head?'

So that was how it was going to be? Dismiss everything as drunkenness? He kept his voice calm. He didn't know how.

'We had some problems on the way.'

Had Asher ordered the attack? Had Aurelie? Would they do such a thing? It didn't seem possible. And yet… he knew where that drink had come from, who had handed it to him.

'So I heard.' Asher looked past Bastien then, and nodded at Grace. 'Problems, eh?' He grinned, that irritating all-too-knowing grin that had got them in trouble all their lives. 'Well done, Captain.'

Grace's expression didn't change. Bastien tried to remember what he'd told her about Asher, what he might have said. If you looked in her eyes, Bastien could see she didn't trust him. How did she do that?

'It was not without casualties, sir.' She spoke curtly, carefully.

Asher nodded and his expression grew more solemn. Bastien breathed a sigh of relief. He'd been worried there would be a confrontation. But Grace was better than that. And Asher was more the diplomat than he gave him credit for.

'My condolences. Their names will be written with honour. You have credentials for me?'

Grace undid the top of her leather jerkin, and Bastien found himself unaccountably warm all of a sudden. He caught a glint of gold hanging in her cleavage, the coin, the warrant which tied him to her, and that sigil she held so dear, the intricate workmanship of a master Atelier. She reached inside the jerkin and pulled out a small envelope which she handed over.

Asher's eyes hadn't missed any of that. He raised an eyebrow and Bastien knew, just knew, that Aurelie would be hearing all about this later.

And if Aurelie saw Grace as a threat...

Asher unfolded it, reading carefully. Then he folded it back up and put it on his desk. 'Commander Craine speaks very highly of you. Welcome. You will report only to me, or to his majesty.'

Not to me, Bastien noticed. Trust Asher to try and leapfrog him in the process.

'Technically I outrank you both,' he reminded them.

They gave him a look which made Bastien suspect they'd either forgotten he was there or that he had said something deeply foolish. From by the door he distinctly heard Daniel Parry snicker.

Wonderful. This was just the nightmare he'd been worried about.

'Of course you do, your highness,' Asher said smoothly. 'There's also Marshal Milne. I believe you met. She, too, has a special dispensation from the king himself. Actually from his father, and his father before him, carried down through her line. Such is the way of things. The royal family of Larelwynn works by generations. Now, Parry and de Bruyn...'

They snapped to attention so hard Bastien almost heard the crack; if he looked at them he was pretty sure he'd see them vibrating. They weren't stupid. Asher was probably the highest-ranking military officer of any kind they'd ever seen, never mind had address them. 'Good, good. You report directly to Captain Marchant as usual. No deviation. What the three of you must understand is that the chain of command is more important here than anywhere else. It is paramount. Too many people within these walls think they have every right to hurl orders around, and they will try to take advantage of your relative naivety.'

'With respect sir, we are not naïve.' Grace, prickly as ever. Bastien should have warned Asher. It would have been fairer. But far less satisfying.

'And with all *due* respect, Captain, I have been here a lot longer than you. Watch your back. You're here to work with and protect the prince, at the king's command. Your people are here to support you. Don't be drawn into politics and dramas. You will need to…' he gave their rough day uniforms a dismissive look… 'attend court functions and dress accordingly. Attire will be provided.'

'Attire?' Ellyn said nervously. 'What sort of attire?'

'Dresses and such, de Bruyn.'

'I don't think Parry wears dresses,' Bastien interjected but no one smiled. Well, Ellyn almost did. She covered remarkably well.

Asher just scowled at him. 'We are finished here. My thanks for your time and patience, your highness. Captain, officers, you are dismissed.'

'Thank you, General,' said Grace, giving him a neat bow. 'Just one small comment.' She smiled so sweetly, but it didn't make it to her eyes. 'I hold the king's warrant. I report only to him. But my thanks for your advice.'

It was almost worth being there to see the look on Asher's face.

*

Bastien's apartments occupied an entire tower. It was bigger than the Academy and the security was second to none. There were only a few access points. On the top two floors were a study and his private chambers. There were reception rooms, kitchens, a guards' room and a way down to the dungeons. Marshal Simona Milne lived here too, apparently, but she was nowhere to be seen.

'Your royal highness, we have been beside ourselves with concern.' The voice came from the stairs and footsteps followed, heralded by the glow of a candle.

'This is Lyssa,' Bastien said as a small, neat woman with white hair and all the bearing of a noblewoman appeared. 'She'll take care of you. I have… I have things to do.' And like that he was gone, up that same flight of curling stairs from which the woman had appeared, leaving them in the path of a veritable whirlwind.

'I'm Lady Lyssa Arenden of Valencourt. My late husband was master of ceremonies in the royal court of Larelwynn for many a year. Prince Bastien, bless him, found me a position here after his death. You can call me Lyssa. Now, rooms, and a chance to refresh yourselves perhaps. I'll have someone go and draw baths. You look half dead, you poor loves.'

'There are other servants here?' Grace asked and then felt foolish. Of course there were servants. She just didn't think they would be serving her.

'We run a small household here. His royal highness dislikes company at the best of times and we are so removed from the main palace here. It's very… peaceful. Yes, peaceful. What else? Have you eaten?'

Grace thought back to the prostitute omelettes and the rest of the dubious fare Kurt had provided. 'Not for some time, but we…'

'Oh well, we'll have to see to that. And some wine perhaps?'

The housekeeper fussed around them like a mother hen and showed them first to the rooms set aside for Ellyn and Daniel. They were neat, functional, and far more spacious than either of them were used to. Ellyn's overlooked the sea and she stood there, staring out the window for the longest moments, as if she couldn't believe it.

'Get some rest,' Grace told the two of them. 'We'll regroup in the morning. Ellyn? You okay?'

Jessica Thorne

Ellyn glanced back, tears silvering her eyes. 'Sure boss.'

Sometimes when the job got too much, when terrible things happened, it wasn't until you were safe that you could let yourself feel anything. Grace knew that as well as anyone. And Ellyn didn't like to share her feelings. None of them did. It was too dangerous.

'The bath's in there, pet,' said Lyssa in a curiously gentle voice. She couldn't know what had happened, not in any detail, but she knew something had. She was intuitive. Grace felt respect blossom for this woman, who was kind when she didn't need to be to people who weren't that important. Ellyn was just a guard, after all. A no one. All of them were. That didn't seem to matter to Lyssa.

'I'm here if she needs us, boss,' said Daniel from the opposite doorway. What else could she do? Daniel would keep an eye on her, Grace knew that too, and now the day was catching up with her. She felt dead on her feet, like a Barrow had raised her. Everything took more effort than it should.

Grace's room was a whole new level of surprise.

They climbed to the third floor above the great hall – furnished at great expense by the Duke of Anlieu, Bastien's something something ancestor two hundred years ago, a vast dining room, far too big for one man, that looked unused – and the long corridor opened up to a landing with a stained-glass window. Moonlight streamed through it, and gave the impression of a shifting world viewed through the fires and smoke of a bonfire.

It was a man, wreathed in flames. He was beautiful, strong and powerful, and his eyes were golden. They glowed as the light poured through them. Black thorns wound around his hands as if binding him.

Grace couldn't help but stare.

'The Hollow King window,' said Lyssa. 'A work of art, three hundred years old. King Anders commissioned it.'

'It's… it's gorgeous.'

And unnerving. Grace couldn't shake the feeling that she was being watched. Worse, it made her skin itch in that old familiar way, as if something was crawling underneath it.

Don't be scared, Gracie. It'll be all right.

The voice was an echo, a memory she couldn't quite grab of a smiling woman with golden eyes and a tumble of shining red hair just like her own. It was something from her nightmares, from a world she didn't remember, a world that had gone away. It was a memory of sunlight and waving corn, of a wide blue sky and somewhere she could never have been. Before the stone walls, and the grey clouds, before the darkness.

Grace shuddered. She was exhausted, that was all.

'Come along, child. You look half dead. You need warmth and rest.' Lyssa opened the door to the left. 'I'm just over there.' She pointed across the corridor to the second of the four doors. 'If you need anything, just knock. You bathe and I'll bring up the refreshments should you want them.' She lit the candle inside the door and left Grace standing there, her jaw hanging open.

Realistically, in a building this large, it was not a big room. But it was still bigger than any chamber Grace had ever had to herself. The bed was four times the size of her bunk in the Academy and covered with freshly laundered sheets, lush blankets and a heap of pillows. Drapes hung around it, richly embroidered, the décor of a gentlewoman's apartments. In a small adjoining room she found the full bath, the water warm, fragrant steam rising from it. She lit another candle in the bedroom, placed the one she carried in a holder in the bathroom, and stripped off as quickly as she could.

There was no wasting this. It would be a crime. She kicked her filthy clothes out the door and closed it behind her. Her body ached, she longed to sleep but the lure was far too strong.

She stepped into the water, her skin blushing as she did so. Sinking down into it was a luxury she couldn't define. A gift unexpected. The bath wasn't big enough to stretch out so she sat with her knees bent up against her chest, marvelling at this.

She found a bar of rich and creamy soap, scented with sandalwood and orange, and began to wash herself. Normally she'd have to scrub and scrub to work up any kind of lather, but this was like cream in solid form. She washed her hair, wondering when was the last time she'd had anything more than a cold shower or a plunge in the communal baths. Her fingers worried at her scalp and she combed through the tangles until the strands fell wetly and loosely through them.

Finally she felt truly clean, cleaner than she had in years. Perhaps ever. No one had a bath like this in the lower echelons of the capital.

Eventually, she made herself stand and grabbed the nearby towel, soft and fluffy and made of wonder. When she wrapped herself in it and stepped out into the bedroom again, intent on finding her bags and digging out a shirt to sleep in, she found the tray left on the table, the bedlinen turned down and a nightgown there, waiting for her.

Clearly Lyssa had been busy.

Waste not want not, as she had always been taught. Still, it seemed like sacrilege to touch the sleek, soft material which hugged her like a second skin. And when she sat on the bed, it dipped softly beneath her, too deeply, too welcoming.

She put the nightgown aside, found the old shirt from her gear and made a nest on the floor at the foot of the bed instead. True, she did use the blankets and one of the pillows. She wasn't a fool.

Larelwynn's tower made noises in the night, sighing with the breeze, creaking and groaning as it settled. She heard footsteps, voices and singing. But not enough to fully wake her. Instinct told her to be aware, but there was nothing she or her unconscious mind would consider an actual threat, not yet.

She knew when Lyssa made her way to her own bed. She heard others moving around, the servants and guards, she presumed. But there was nothing to concern her as she slept.

In the barracks at the Academy the ability to sleep restfully and still be alert in an instant if necessary had served her well. It was a skill she had always had. One thing she felt sure of as she lay there in near sleep, yet not entirely lost to her dreams, was that this tower was not as she expected. And she was sure that it was not as empty as it seemed.

As she drifted off she was sure she heard singing from overhead, a lullaby, in a strange lyrical voice. A girl's voice. And then she heard a laugh, deep and melodious. His laugh.

She'd know it anywhere.

Oh, she thought, he has a lover installed here. Of course he does.

It shouldn't have been the disappointment that it was. He was a noble and they were all the same, weren't they? No wonder he'd been so keen to go up to his own quarters, away from her. She had just been an amusement, a distraction. That was all she had ever been. She should have known.

Chapter Fourteen

Morning brought a whole new set of problems. It always did.

'The queen wants to see you,' Lyssa said the moment she appeared. Bastien was sitting at the dining table with Ellyn and Daniel, both of whom looked more uncomfortable than she'd ever seen them. Daniel, of course, was tucking into an overloaded plate of every conceivable option of fried pork while Ellyn just pushed a pile of bread pieces around her plate, occasionally picking one up to shred it a bit more.

'The queen?' Grace asked.

'She sent word this morning,' Lyssa went on. 'She wishes to welcome you to the palace and to ensure that you know that you are most welcome here. She does you great honour, Captain.'

Sure she does. I saw the look on her face when the king gave me his warrant. If she could have scratched my eyes out right then and there she would have. I'd be an idiot to think she wished me well.

'When?'

'She wants us to come to dinner,' Bastien said in a voice that sounded like they'd been invited to an execution.

'Dinner.' That wasn't what Grace had been expecting.

'A formal dinner. Not private. There'll be twenty or more guests. She wants to intimidate you.'

Of course she did. And how charming of him to put it so bluntly. But at least a dinner with a group meant he was less liable to be drugged. And she would be there.

'I'm not easily intimidated.'

'You'll need a gown,' Daniel said, unhelpfully.

That hadn't even occurred to her. What on earth was she going to wear to a formal dinner? The look of panic must have showed on her face. Bastien grinned and she wanted to slap him.

'Lyssa, please see to that if you will,' he said as if he was doing no more than asking for the laundry to be changed. 'Tonight. And in the meantime I believe we have work today.'

We do. Or at least I do and he'd promised to help. She still wasn't sure why, but that hardly mattered. Not to mention they needed to work out who had tried to have Bastien killed, who had completely derailed their journey back here, who had sent that Flint to track him down.

'Of course. Ellyn, Daniel?'

'At least have something to eat first,' said Daniel, through a mouth overstuffed with food.

Grace gave him her most innocent look. 'I'm not sure I can, Danny. You seem to have eaten it all.'

Ellyn laughed and Lyssa tutted before indicating a sideboard behind her, full of everything Grace could conceivably want and some things she didn't even have a name for. There was no sign of the usual runny porridge, cold congealed eggs, or bread fried in lard.

It was only when she had eaten that Bastien spoke again. 'Will you join me, Captain Marchant? The prisoner has been brought in. She spoke of the Hollow King?' he reminded her.

Ellyn cleared her throat. 'It's a legend. The king who went insane with magic, who started the Magewar. Lucien Larelwynn defeated him, forced him to agree to the pact and killed him. An old story.'

'It's so much more than that. He's the reason we have the laws we have. The reason why mageborn must swear to serve the crown, and never aspire to wear it.'

Which left him in a predicament, didn't it? Grace looked, directly at him. '*You're* mageborn.'

'Yes.'

'And King Marius's heir.'

He just nodded.

'And… that's the problem, isn't it?' Daniel asked. 'Your… your highness… and that's why they're trying to kill you?'

Bastien raised an eyebrow. 'Yes, I rather think it is.'

'But they were…' Grace frowned and shook her head. 'Who sent them?'

Bastien pinched the bridge of his nose. 'That's what I need to find out. We need to interrogate the girl.'

Oh. Grace didn't like this tack, or where it was possibly heading. 'I… I don't torture people.'

'Neither do I.' No, he probably had people for things like that. People like Hale…

The doubt must have shown in her expression because he smiled again. It warmed his eyes, suited his face, made him seem less cold and hostile. More like a living, breathing human being.

'Oh, you've heard those stories too, have you? I'd love to know how they get started. No, I don't torture people, I don't experiment on mageborn and I don't murder them.'

Ellyn spoke before Grace got a chance. 'Did you… Kai…' she tried to say. 'Did you…' She couldn't quite get the words out. She turned her gaze to Grace in desperate panic. She didn't know what to say.

Bastien shifted in his seat. 'Your friend was dying. The magic inside him would have taken hold. He would have fed on the energies in Grace, and you, and on everyone in the Healers' Halls and…'

It had almost happened to Helene. Grace suppressed a shiver as the old memories flared up inside her. Her friend's eyes had glowed – like Kai's, like Bastien's sometimes did – and the water had crept over her skin like a living thing. And where Grace touched her, it had tried to consume her too, glowing specks dancing in the depths, its touch so cold it froze her. She shook her head, driving the ghosts of the past away. They weren't talking about Helene or Kai. This was the long shadow of something so much worse.

The Magewar was three hundred years ago. It all ended when Lucien Larelwynn destroyed the Hollow King and freed the land from his tyranny, when he drove his sword through him and cut out his heart to burn it on the altar of the powers. Or whatever variation of his bleak fate you chose to believe. When the Larelwynns became the royal family and this land became Larelwynn. The pact with the mageborn had been the last defence for humanity, a way to stop the magic from running wild again. But sometimes it still went wild. It was always a risk.

'Kai would never…' Grace choked on the words and fell silent. Because he could have. There had been a change in him before he died. His grip had tightened, his eyes had burned with unholy light. She had barely recognised him. If she was honest.

'Perhaps,' Bastien said and it was an unexpected kindness. 'He was a Leech. He might have managed to transmute it in the end. But it would have left him broken. He would have wished for death.'

'You don't know him,' she growled at him. 'He would never have…' And then she remembered who she was talking to. No one knew more about the pact and the mageborn than he did. He was the seneschal, overseeing them all. He took their homage and maintained their magical equilibrium. He was a Larelwynn. That history was part of him. His family were the heroes. Instincts made her shut the hell up. Let him believe what he wanted. Kai was better than that.

She pushed away what she had seen in him.

'Perhaps,' Bastien said again. And he stood up, leaving the table. After she had composed herself again she watched him. He was beautiful, if you could use that word about a man like him. Like a sculpture, like something from the temple or the tapestries. Like Lucien Larelwynn himself was meant to be. She'd seen a thousand depictions of him, for as long as she could remember. Dark hair, dark eyes, the sword raised over his head while the Hollow King knelt before him, defeated.

She probably shouldn't be sitting while he was standing. Wasn't that royal etiquette? She got to her feet again, and the others did the same, following her lead. They all stood at ease, hands behind their back.

'So you want to interrogate the Flint,' she said at last. 'To find out who sent her.'

'Yes. I think she'll be more cooperative now. Or at least I hope so. She's a victim too. Bought, sold, used. I hoped you might help.'

'Help you do *what* to her?'

'Damn it, Grace,' he snapped and turned on her. 'I'm not a barbarian. I want you to talk to her. You have experience interviewing victims as well as tracking their attackers. She wears a collar, or used to. She was sworn to the crown as we are. Whoever recruited her and sent her here… that's who I want to go after. Not some sad little Flint who will never raise so much as a spark again.'

'You took her powers? All of them?' Daniel asked, startled.

Even Kai couldn't do that. He could mute them for a while. To take someone's powers, that took a strong ability, stronger than anyone she'd ever heard of. Grace narrowed her eyes, studying him again. *A sad little Flint, indeed.*

'Like I said,' he replied. 'She's done. And she's young enough to live a perfectly normal life somewhere far away from the capital, where no one knows her. She can say she's a widow and find a new home. Does that meet with your approval?'

Daniel didn't let up. Suspicion darkened his gaze. 'You've done this before.'

Mageborn were missing from the city. Mageborn vanished for days on end when they came here to pay homage to the king, through Bastien as seneschal. Oh, he'd done this before. Daniel might need to ask, but Grace didn't. What worried her right now was how often and to whom? And were they willing?

'Many times. Even by request. Now, will you do as I ask?'

Grace lifted her chin and looked him in the eye. If he was telling the truth – and she had no reason to believe otherwise – he could help the girl, even though she'd been sent to kill him. And somehow Grace wanted to believe him.

They'd been attacked as soon as they left the Temple, as soon as they had asked questions about the dead kids. Bastien had been the target, sure, but he hadn't been the one to die. That had been Childers, one of her people. And they had all been targets. So maybe… maybe the assassination attempt hadn't simply been aimed at Bastien.

Besides which, the assassins had been mageborn. And that made investigating it her job. It always had been.

'I'll talk to her.'

*

It was a cell, Grace supposed, though not like any cell you'd see elsewhere in Rathlynn. But then this wasn't the royal dungeons, this was the base of Bastien Larelwynn's tower. Less a cell and more a small, comfortably furnished bedroom with no windows and highly effective security.

The Flint sat on the edge of the bed. Her red-rimmed eyes showed she'd been crying and her pallor made her look ill. She held her hands clasped before her and even that couldn't stop them shaking. Daniel and Ellyn took up position outside the cell. When Grace entered, the Flint stood up, ready to fight, argue or plead her case, but when Bastien followed, she almost threw herself back into the corner.

'Please... please... don't let him hurt me.' She dropped to her knees, sobbing once again.

Grace's stomach tightened, but she didn't say anything. Bastien didn't need to torture anyone. His reputation did that for him.

'Perhaps I should wait outside,' he said in that soft, calm voice. He didn't even need to make it threatening.

'Thank you,' Grace replied. 'That might be best.'

But still he paused for a moment. 'If you should need me...'

She cut him off with a look. Need him? Why on earth would she need him? And if it was a threat aimed at the girl, it wasn't exactly helpful.

He closed the door gently behind him. She didn't hear the lock slide home.

'What's your name?' Grace asked.

'Sylvie, Sylvie Lexin.' And suddenly, as if naming herself released her tongue, she was talking, quickly, desperately. 'They said... they said it was just a simple job. Just kill him, they said. They didn't tell us who he was... I would never have... if I'd known...'

Who hadn't told her? That was what Grace was here to find out. But rush it and Sylvie would panic. She was already panicking. She had a lot to panic about. Threats weren't going to get anywhere here. There was an art to this and Craine had taught her well.

'Do you often do jobs like that?'

The woman buried her face in her hands and sobbed again. She was younger than Grace had thought, thinner too. Desperate. Slowly, carefully, Grace reached out and helped her back onto the bed. She picked up one of the luxuriously soft blankets and wrapped it around her shoulders. Bastien had said Sylvie was as much a victim as a perpetrator here. Perhaps more so. What choice did she even have?

What choice did any of them have?

'Were you very young when you found out?' She didn't need to elaborate on what Sylvie had found out. They both knew.

'Five. Maybe six. I don't know. It was fun at first, lighting candles. The house was draughty but I could heat it. My mam worked long hours as a seamstress and she'd make tea but it would go cold. So when she came back I'd heat it up for her.'

They'd been poor then. Desperately poor. Like so many of the people of Rathlynn. Grace knew this story well. She knew what happened next.

'When did they find you?'

She shrugged. 'Not long after. Took me one day from outside when I was minding my baby sister. Slapped a collar around my neck and said I belonged to them now.'

'Did you ever see your family again?'

Sylvie bit her lip and looked away. 'A couple of times. Mam died last year. Two of my sisters as well. Fever.'

In a freezing house, starving. It happened a lot, especially in the winter. 'I'm sorry.'

'Why? You don't wear a collar. Neither does he.'

And perhaps that was the point.

'Not all collars are visible, Sylvie. Who sent you after him?'

The miserable girl sucked in a series of breaths and for a moment Grace thought she might answer, but instead she asked a question.

'What's he going to do with me?'

'Answer the question and he'll let you go.'

Sylvie looked up, viciousness entering her eyes, and the little-girl-lost act promptly fell away. 'You believe that? Divinities, you're stupider than you look.'

It always ended up like this. Grace didn't want it to be true, but it was. The mask slipped. Street rats could bite. 'Sylvie…'

'He's from the guards, from the palace. Don't know his name. Dev dealt with that.' She paused and then gave a bitter laugh. The Shade Bastien had killed.

'Was it just the prince they were after?'

'The prince,' Sylvie scoffed. 'Sure. Just him. We weren't expecting anyone to help the Lord of Thorns. Sidekick, are you? Sleeping with him? Does it get you off knowing what he is? What he does to people like me?'

People like her… Grace's heart plummeted inside her but she kept her expression neutral. And as for the insults… well, she'd heard far worse.

'Can you describe the man?'

Sylvie didn't even pause. 'He's got blue eyes. And a mole in the shape of a crown. And six fingers on one hand.' The mockery in her voice made it clear he had nothing of the sort. 'And a massive, massive—'

'Enough!' Grace snapped. 'If that's the way it is, fine. I can't help you. I'll tell him that.'

She started towards the door but Sylvie leaped to her feet.

'No wait, please.'

'We've nothing left to discuss. I'll let him know.'

'Please…'

'Then answer the question.'

'I… I can draw him.'

*

The picture was good. When Sylvie had finished it depicted a man, in his forties maybe, older than Grace and Bastien anyway, with a strong jaw but nothing else to distinguish him. Grace took it and her stomach twisted as she looked at it. The face of a bully, of a coward. She knew him. Then, because she couldn't do anything else, she handed it over to the Lord of Thorns.

'What… what about me?' Sylvie yelled through the door. 'You said I could leave.'

'Let her go,' said Bastien, still looking at the drawing. He didn't seem able to tear his gaze from it. Simona came to join them, her expression dubious.

'Do you know him?' Grace asked.

He looked at her then, his face a frown. 'Yes. He works for Asher Kane.'

A few steps away from the king then. Which meant the order could have come directly from Bastien's cousin. Or his wife. Or Kane himself. A smile quirked at his lips as he watched her work it out.

'You're sure, Bastien?' Simona asked.

'Yes.' He swallowed suddenly, as if trying to clear something from his throat.

'Are you sure you want to let her go?' Simona went on, not quite sure of his intent, perhaps feeling that this was a terrible idea. Grace had to agree.

But instead of answering he took a coin bag from a pocket somewhere and held it out.

'Open the door.'

Simona did as instructed. Sylvie burst out of the cell but staggered to a halt when she saw him in the corridor. The next second her eyes lit on the purse which dangled from his fingers.

He shook it to get her attention. 'Listen to me. You'll leave Rathlynn. Take this, get as far away from here as you can and don't come back.' He reached out and she flinched back, but there was nowhere to go but back in the cell.

She hesitated and then snatched the purse from his hand. Grace drew a knife before she realised she was already too late. Sylvie's hand closed on his and she smiled triumphantly, a vicious, terrible smile. Her eyes slid closed and she threw back her head.

'No!' Grace yelled, as she felt the Flint's power unfurl.

A rush of warmth, an ache of loss and despair shimmered through the air around them and dissipated. Sylvie shuddered from head to toe. Her jaw dropped open wide.

'What did you do to me?'

Grace grabbed her shoulder, pulling her back from him, but it was like moving smoke. The woman didn't resist, didn't fight, just stood in shock.

'What did you do? Where's my fire?' she screamed.

Bastien hadn't moved. If anything he stared at her in pity. 'It's gone, Sylvie.' Simple as that. Grace shifted uncomfortably on her feet. 'It won't come back either.'

But Sylvie just clutched the purse. 'What will I do?' she wailed.

'Whatever you want,' Bastien replied. 'If you need help to find somewhere I can help. But don't come back to Rathlynn, understand?'

She threw herself towards him, nails like claws, screaming. Grace blocked her this time, throwing her back against the wall where she slid down to the ground, sobbing and shaking, devastated.

Bastien watched for a moment, clearly uncomfortable. 'We should go,' he said at last. 'Have someone escort her out.'

Daniel and Ellyn nodded and dragged her to her feet.

'You're the monster,' the girl snarled at him, snot and tears gleaming in the half-light. 'You're worse than the Hollow King. You're cursed, Larelwynn. You're all cursed.'

He stopped in his retreat, flinched, his shoulders tightening under the black silk of his shirt. He was beautiful and he was in pain. Grace recognised it when she saw it in another. Even in him.

His voice when he spoke didn't sound like a prince, or a lord. 'Sylvie, that's the first thing you've said which I know to be true.'

Daniel and Ellyn accompanied her out, with Simona leading the way. Which left Grace alone with Bastien in the corridor outside the cell.

'You said you'd help her?'

'I did. I've set her free. Even if she can't see that.'

'Do you think she'll leave Rathlynn?' she asked at last.

Bastien shook his head. 'I hope so. Whoever sent her won't take kindly to her failure. Or her loss of power.'

She recalled the flinch and the way his shoulders had tightened. 'You took her magic from her. Completely. When she tried to use it, it wasn't… it was like a void… an emptiness… drawing on you…'

He gazed at her for a moment, as if she was a puzzle to be solved, and then slowly nodded. 'You felt that then?'

Warning bells were ringing in the back of her mind. She shouldn't have said anything. But the feeling… it had been so familiar… She busied herself re-sheathing her weapons.

'I… I felt it.' Her face heated as he turned to look at her, his expression thoughtful. 'It felt like her power was trying to tear itself out of you.' He watched her like he could see right into the heart of her. It made her squirm. It also made her want to tell him everything.

And she knew, as surely as she knew herself, that was a really bad idea.

Bastien's dark eyes gentled, the lines around them smoothing out until he looked like someone her own age. Which he was. She kept thinking he was older, but he wasn't. Maybe a year or two, but no more than that. Not even thirty yet.

'Do you want to explain why that is?'

'You don't know?' She didn't believe that, not for a moment.

'May I?' he asked. She wasn't sure what he meant but something made her nod. Madness perhaps. Or stupidity.

He brushed his fingertips along the line of her jaw and she found herself leaning in towards him. No, this was a terrible idea. She knew that. She just didn't seem to be able to move away. His touch was strong but gentle, like velvet wrapped around steel. He made her body do strange and bewildering things. With her breath caught in her throat, her face tipped up towards his, she was helpless. And she couldn't have that.

'I think I know, Captain Marchant.'

His kiss on her lips was a complete surprise, gentle, curious, intoxicating. His hand curled behind her head, cupping her skull, his fingers buried in her hair. She could escape in a moment, logic told her that. Her skill, her training, her physical strength... it all told her she could, and really should, pull herself free.

But her mind didn't seem to be in charge any more.

He was the one to pull back, staring into her eyes. 'Grace, don't forget why we're here.'

It was like being doused in cold water. She jerked away from him, twisting free and knocking his hands aside in a deft move.

'You said you wouldn't touch me again,' she told him, but Bastien just smiled.

'Never without your say-so,' he said. 'That I swear. But I asked permission, didn't I? And one day, my dear captain, you're going to tell me what happened to you. I'll find out anyway.'

He left her standing there, retreating before she gather any thoughts of a reply. Grace just stood there as he vanished up the staircase back to his study and his tower.

Chapter Fifteen

Bastien wasn't sure why he'd kissed her, why the urge to do so appeared whenever he looked at her. Devilment perhaps. The need to see a crack in that shell. And because he had wanted to. So badly.

She was a beautiful woman, whether she saw it or not. Her hair felt like silk between his fingers and her lips parted for him as if she longed for him just as much.

So why did he feel the need to push her away as well? To tease her to the point of anger, so she'd tell him to leave her alone with venom. Or draw knives on him.

Protecting her? Or protecting himself?

He hadn't felt this way about a woman in years. Not in his conscious memory. Not since Hanna.

This was ridiculous. He barely knew Grace. She was just a glorified guard and enough trouble for him already. And there was something she wasn't telling him, something about her, about her past, about her background. She tensed up whenever her childhood was mentioned. He could relate to that at least. Much of his own youth was a mystery. An accident. Celeste had gone for Hanna, enraged about something, and he'd stepped between them. His sister had never known her own strength and she'd sent him flying down the stairs. By the time he woke up it was too late. Hanna was dead. And Celeste was taken away.

Everything was hushed up. Marius and Simona had explained it all. What would his sister say about Grace? He really was playing with fire.

She was too distracting. Had been from the very first.

The people he cared for got hurt. Always. He couldn't afford to have any sort of feelings for anyone. He knew that deep down in the heart of him.

Work harder, Bastien. Find a way to shut out this woman. If he truly wanted to protect her, the biggest danger was being anywhere near him. Just like everyone else in his life, his mother, his sister, Hanna…

Simona would agree, wouldn't she? The marshal would tell him he was being a fool and remind him of all that was at stake.

But Simona was nowhere to be found. She must still be with Daniel and Ellyn, seeing the former Flint off the grounds of the palace and arranging for her to be sent far, far away. Grace was right, this wasn't the first time. It was costing more every year, but he still kept on doing it. It didn't really matter where they went. They had enough coin and a future.

The wave of pain struck him unexpectedly, like briars curling through his veins. He gasped and grabbed the bannister to hold himself upright. Sylvie's power wanted out. Grace hadn't been wrong about that. It would tear its way free if he didn't do something.

She was beside him in seconds and reached out to catch him. She'd followed him. He hadn't even heard her come up the stairs but now she was here, almost holding him up.

Grace.

Alone together for a moment at the turn of the winding steps, he stared into her eyes and she stared back. She gazed into his soul, into the heart of him, and he didn't know what she found there but he didn't like the reaction. There was something in her, something that leaped and danced and fought, something bright and terrible. He knew it. He recognised it. Even if she did not.

'You should rest.' Her voice was gentle, not the strident voice of the fighter, the protector. Caring.

'Yes.' He wanted sleep more dearly than he had ever wanted anything. He wanted peace. But he wasn't going to be afforded that luxury in this or any other lifetime. He knew that.

Grace pursed her lips as if making a decision, not one she relished. She slipped one hand under his elbow, the other on the back of his upper arm. 'Come on.'

He ought to protest, but he didn't seem to have the power to fight her. She made him climb the remaining steps, out into the comfort of the upper floor. Deep carpets softened their footsteps. The tapestries protected them from the chill, brightening the world.

'Captain Marchant…'

'Grace,' she said.

He sighed, giving in to the inevitable. 'Grace, I just need to rest. I'll be fine.' They'd made it as far as the door to the study. He wasn't going to be able to get any further.

'Of course you will, your highness. But I need to know if you're hurt. Sit down.'

He didn't have the strength to stop her. She all but pushed him into the nearest chair. It was wooden and hard, carved from a whole oak about two hundred years ago by a master Atelier sworn to his ancestors. The man's work was legendary now, sought after and coveted. It was worth more than she could possibly earn in her lifetime serving the Academy. No one had sat on it for centuries. Lyssa would have a fit.

It wasn't even comfortable.

Grace Marchant sank to her knees in front of him, still gazing up into his face with those eyes that saw far too much. Where his eyes were dark, hers were almost golden. Where his hair was the colour of night, hers was fire. Everything about them was a contrast. And yet something inside him reached for her.

And he sensed something in her reach back. Every time they came close to each other.

A mystery. A wonder.

That was why he couldn't help himself. That was why he kept trying to connect with her, and to drive her away at the same time. This was dangerous. For both of them.

'Grace,' he whispered.

'I know. You're fine. Where does it hurt?'

He laughed, a short and bitter laugh. He couldn't help himself. 'Everywhere?'

A smile ghosted over her lips. Such beautiful lips. He had kissed those lips. It had been like touching heaven.

A shiver ran through him and he felt the light inside him build uncomfortably again. The wires of agony twisted further, tightening on each other. The light was running out of control. It shouldn't have been this fast.

'You look like Kai did,' she said, concern making her voice shake. 'What can I do?'

'I need a jar.'

She looked so confused it was almost comical. Or would have been if the situation weren't so serious. 'A jar?'

'Hale will be able to help you.'

She shook her head. 'Hale's not here. I don't need help finding a jar… your highness.'

'A special kind of jar.' The pain made him speak through gritted teeth. 'In my study. There's sealing wax and red string too. But the jar is what matters. They're round, like globes.'

'Don't try to get up,' she told him, the tone of command very clear. Not that he would have obeyed her if he needed to move. But still, when she left, he stayed seated as directed.

It was definitely not because he feared he lacked the strength to move right at the moment, let alone stand. His vision swam and he forced himself to focus on his breath, to control his pulse, and force down the rising surge of power inside him. It was wild, out of control, and like a cresting wave it would swamp him in an instant if it had the chance.

Magic. He hated it. He needed it. He had no choice but to subdue it and transmute it. Not if he wanted to live.

A moment later she was back, quicker than he expected, so she saw him bent forward, his head in his hands.

'Are you going to throw up? Do you have concussion?'

He looked up through the black shadows of his hair and saw her freeze, the jar in her hand stuffed with a ball of the red string and a block of blood-red wax.

'No. I'm fine. Did Hale help?'

Grace set the jar down carefully on the floor in front of him and removed the contents. Oh, she really did think he needed something to throw up into.

'I don't know where he is. I found them inside, with the others.'

She looked like she wanted to ask more, if he did this regularly. Throwing up into jars. Sure. His favourite pastime.

'It's not what you think,' he replied and took the jar in his hands, lifting it to his lap, picking up the thread and wax from where she'd placed them on the floor, and staring down into it. He ought to send her away. This was not something he shared with others, not something he wanted an audience to see. But he didn't have the time or the strength to say anything.

Perhaps he didn't want to. Stupid man.

For a moment the magic in him resisted. It always did.

He needed it, coveted it, but it hated him. Of course it did. He was the thief, the one who tore it from its home and trapped it. If he could transmute it, or tame it, he did. But in this case... in times like this...

He wrapped his will around the seething mass of light. His chest constricted, burning with the effort. It hurt. Powers above, it hurt every single time and he never got used to it. He sucked in another breath, thin and cold in his lungs.

He closed his eyes tightly and, behind the lids, the light glowed even brighter.

Hands touched his shoulders, soothing. Her hands. Her gentle caress. So much for his royal dignity.

And the magic twisted inside him, suddenly compliant. It purred through him and tumbled from his eyes like tears, flowing into the jar. He could no longer see. All was the light of raw magic. It burned like acid, etching lines of agony down his cheeks. He couldn't help it. A sob escaped him.

And Grace pressed her fingers to the place between his shoulder blades, the pressure releasing the tension, the touch sparking something else inside him. That need. The one he really didn't want to acknowledge.

Was she watching all of this? Studying him? Pitying him?

The last of the glowing power inside him fell away, swirling in the round confines of the jar. He held it carefully.

'The lid,' he said, his voice harsh and broken. She scooped it up and handed it to him. He fitted it expertly and then set to work with the string, binding it as his mind ran through a ritual he knew better than his own names and heritage.

'Wax,' he barked and she gave him that too.

'I'll get a candle to melt it.'

'No need.' He snapped his finger and a small flame appeared in the air. Grace flinched. The wax dripped like blood, covering the string. The pool took only a moment to begin to harden. The signet ring on his finger was all it took to complete the ritual, its imprint forming the seal in more ways than one. The sigil, a circle of thorns closing the trap. Shadows clung to it, making the thorns black as night in the imprint.

Finally he could breathe again.

He still hurt, everywhere, as if he'd been crushed in a vice. Only her touch had brought comfort, but now she withdrew. She circled him again with awe on her face that could not be denied.

Not horror.

She knelt in front of him. When she spoke, her voice was hushed with wonder. 'There's more magic in you than I've ever sensed. More than should be possible. More than should even be safe.'

'I… I'm sorry.' He didn't know what else to say. He couldn't help it.

'Are you… are you all right? Can I fetch you anything else? Should I get the healer?'

The tenderness was too much, as if she had seen his need and pitied him. He didn't need her pity.

And he didn't deserve to have anyone look at him like that.

'No. But… thank you.'

'Do you want me to take it? Put it with the others?'

He should have said no, that he could do it himself.

'Please.'

She took the jar from him, and paused. He knew what she was feeling – the warmth, the way it moved, the purring sensation that rippled through the skin against the glass. He knew it intimately. His fingers itched to touch it again. That was the risk. The need, the addiction. Like his need for her.

Grace didn't move. She just stood there staring into the light.

'Bastien, show me your hands,' she said at last.

'My hands?'

She gave an impatient snort. He almost laughed. No one but Grace would make such an unladylike noise to a prince of the realm.

Abruptly, she turned away from him and went back into the study. She came back out without the jar, hunkered down in front of him and took his wrists in her hands, turning his palms upwards. Her touch was so gentle but his skin shivered with sensation at the contact.

Not his palms though.

They were red and raw. Burned. Marks spread from the centre of the palms, out like an explosion. They would heal in time.

'It happens,' he told her. 'I have a salve. Hale makes it for me. It's just in there on the—'

But she interrupted him. 'Does it happen every time? Doesn't it hurt?'

'Yes, but not as much as… as the light inside.'

'Bastien… I've seen burns like this before.' So had he. He'd read the reports. Hale had told him what he found. He had examined bodies with those burns, not least the Leanese girl. But he had never put it together.

'I know of no one else who can transmute power as I do.'

'I didn't say they could transmute it. But they might have tried. I saw them on the Leanese Zephyr, Losle. And the others. The file describes them. They were on the hands of all the dead mageborn.'

His hands shook in hers. He pulled them away and she released him without a struggle. He couldn't bring himself to look into her face so he stared at her hands instead. She still held them out, her fingers curling slightly over the palms. The palms marked with faint white scars. Scars which, apart from the colour, didn't look too dissimilar to the red starburst burns on his own.

'Where did you get them?' he asked.

For once she didn't recoil and try to change the subject. She stared at her hands and then dragged her gaze up to meet his.

'I don't know. I don't remember. I told you, I don't remember anything before coming to the Academy.'

'Not even who you are?'

'I know who I am,' she told him solemnly. 'I'm Captain Grace Marchant.'

'Who you were, then?'

She tried to smile. It wavered on her face. 'No. Just... just the name Grace. Just flashes of memory, my mother calling me Gracie, her red hair. I... I could be a long lost princess for all I know.'

She tried to laugh at her joke but he didn't join her so she fell silent.

He forced himself to speak into the silence. 'I don't think we're missing any princesses unfortunately. Not to my knowledge.'

'No, of course not,' she smiled as she spoke. Not the smile he expected. Gentle and just a little sad.

'Do you wish you were?'

She laughed then, a brief, dismissive laugh. 'Every orphan in the Academy wishes they were a long lost royal. It's what all the old stories revolve around. Sometimes it's all that keeps them going. I know what I am, Bastien. Don't worry about it.'

All the same, he felt like he'd said something terrible, that he'd somehow trampled on her dreams.

'Thank you, Captain,' he said softly.

'For what?'

'For helping. For being here.'

'I'm doing my job, remember? Besides, according to our king I have to be here. And according to our queen we have to go to dinner tonight, isn't that right?'

He nodded. 'And preparation for that takes time, I am afraid. Lyssa will help you. She knows everything.'

'And I know nothing.' There was an undercurrent to the words. He almost missed it. She got to her feet, straightening and standing in that semi-formal way she did with her hands folded into the small of her back and her eyes fixed on some vague distance behind his head. Like that, the intimacy was gone. The soldier was back.

Bastien swallowed hard and pushed himself up off the priceless seat. 'Well then, we should be getting on. I'll send Lyssa to you shortly.'

He left her standing there, and headed for the study and sanctuary. She created havoc in his life. Just as he did in hers. He closed the door behind him and leaned on it, tilting back his head and closing his eyes. All around the walls of the study little jars of magic flickered, throwing their light up onto the ceiling, washing around him like water. She'd seen all of this, he realised, seen this and she didn't seem to care. The jar she'd brought in sat in the centre of his desk. The light inside it moved slowly, like a young rose, its petals unfolding. He sank into his chair and fumbled in the drawer until he found the pot of sweet-smelling salve Merlyn Hale made for him. He rubbed it into his hands as if the action was a ritual, a soothing, calming rite to banish the last traces of the magic from his skin.

The burns were the price of transmuting the magic and trapping it. A price he was willing to pay. What if other people were trying to do the same thing? With the jars, magic could be transferred. It could heal or harm. It could be put to terrible uses. And it could be stolen from the weakest to feed the strong.

To his knowledge only two people could syphon and transmute magic, store it like this. He was one, his sister the other. He'd tried to make it work, tried to teach Hanna, or so Celeste had told him. If she was to be believed. She'd said he was besotted. He didn't know. Another lost memory…

What if he was wrong? What if this had happened to Grace as a child?

And yet he had never met her before this week. He had never touched her before, even though that was all he wanted to do now. Touch her, kiss her, love her.

'I will find out what happened to you, Grace. I promise.'

Chapter Sixteen

It felt good to punch something. Even an inanimate object like the punch bag in the guards' rec room, which was nothing more than a storeroom off the kitchen when you got down to it, two floors above Bastien's study. Simona had taken one look at her and suggested a workout. But at least she hadn't looked at her like she'd wandered in from a bar and thrown up on the floor.

Such a look from a man who'd just poured a jar full of magic out of his eyes. Who let it burn his skin but didn't feel it.

Like that was normal. Any of that.

Grace punched the bag again, imagining it was him, imagining it bore his superior, snide look, his too bloody handsome face, that perfect nose which she was breaking, his freakish black eyes which she was turning into actual black eyes.

The feeling of his muscles under her hands, the tightness uncoiling, the strength in him, the warmth, the magic, that kiss…

Damn it, she had to stop picturing that. Touching him. Why had she even done it? What had she been thinking? And why had she allowed him to kiss her?

But he'd been in pain, lost and helpless. And she'd wanted… to make it better. Just for once. As she had for Kai.

Grief, pain and that humiliating rejection made the next punch stronger than ever and something else coiled behind it. It came from inside her, deep and endless, burning.

The bag flew from the hook and slammed back against the wall with a thundering crash.

'Woah!' yelled Daniel, dodging aside as he entered the room looking for her. 'Careful. You could kill someone with that jab.'

'Sorry,' she said and wiped sweat from her eyes. 'Here, I'll…'

He was already lifting it for her. But it was weighted and too much for anyone to lift alone. She grabbed the end and helped haul it up.

'Look,' he gasped. 'How did that happen?'

Grace almost dropped it. A round mark, black as soot, a burn in the leather. Right where she'd punched it.

She cursed under her breath. But she couldn't let him see that she recognised it.

Damn it, she hadn't lost control like this in years. Bastien Larelwynn was a disaster for her to be around.

She thought of him in pain, the desperation on his face.

No, not that. She didn't want to think of that.

'It must have hit something,' she said, aware even as she said it how feeble an excuse it was. Daniel shrugged. He didn't care and didn't seem to realise what he was seeing. And Grace found herself breathing a sigh of relief. 'It'll scrub out,' she said.

'Please, if that's the worst mark it ever gets it's not the end of the world. Just hang it the other way around. No one will bother. So, you're not wearing that to this command dinner with the queen, are you?'

She glanced down at her sweat-drenched workout clothes and gave him a withering look.

'Yeah, I hear it's all the rage.'

'Well, the prince is going to love it, I'm sure. They all will. The Academy will be delighted that you're representing us all. Craine will probably give you a commendation, just for this.'

Sarcasm didn't suit Daniel, she decided. The prince wasn't going to love anything about the way she looked at the moment, an angry, sweaty savage who just wanted to damage something.

She wanted to believe that might account for his behaviour, that she was just an embarrassment, that being near her shamed him. But she didn't. Not really. He was a prince and she expected it of him. She was a... a what? A glorified guard. For all the talk of the Academy, they were still just orphans and street kids. They still carried the taint of magic around them whether they wielded it like Kai or not. They chased monsters and everyone knew if you got too close to the monsters you became just like them.

And the Lord of Thorns wanted to find out what had happened to her. Like she had never tried.

Grace flexed her fingers and stared at them, at the scars that had been part of her life for as long as she could remember. She'd never wanted to be special. She'd never envied the mageborn. What was there to envy? It was a short life of servitude and danger. But of course that wasn't so different from her own.

She had found her own people – Helene, then Kai – and now they were all gone. She'd known that she'd lose people, of course, that it would happen. It happened to all of them in the Academy, mageborn or not. She still had Daniel and Ellyn, but for how long? When you chased monsters they tended to notice. They chased you back. Grace remembered the Gore's face, maniacal with glee as he'd tormented her. He hadn't been the first and he would not have been the last, even if she'd stayed in her normal life at the Academy. He still wouldn't be. Perhaps now she was in more danger than ever and not just from Bastien.

Rathlynn was a dangerous place to be. The death rate was high. The streets were not kind. Even accidental death and disease had a habit of catching Academy officers faster than most. City life. Illness could quickly become an epidemic. You could be knifed in the back going for a drink after a shift, just for looking the wrong way.

But standing anywhere near Bastien Larelwynn was probably the most dangerous place in the world to be. It had been for Childers.

Daniel was still there, watching her, waiting.

'What is it?' she asked, forcing herself to be patient. He thought something was funny.

'Lyssa's looking for you.'

Oh. Great.

'I'll… fine. I'll be there directly. Tell her…' But while Grace was faffing around here, nothing was happening in their investigation. 'No, don't. I'll tell her. I want you to go and find Hale. Ask him about the marks on the hands. Find out if anyone has come in to the Healers' Halls with similar burns for treatment.'

'Sure boss,' he said. Always happy to help. That was Daniel. If he was any perkier and more eager to please, he'd probably be a puppy. 'Is it a lead?'

'I hope so. We need one.' She wasn't terribly confident about it. 'This case is getting swallowed up in…' she waved her arms around her '… all this. I don't like it. We were meant to find out who killed that Leanese girl and all the others. The mageborn who were syphoned. Send a message to Craine and tell her to bring in Arlon Griggs, that soldier Ellyn and I brought in, the one who was using magic but not mageborn. He's involved with the assassination attempt on Bastien, the one that killed Childers, and he was one of ours.'

She paused, raking her fingers along her scalp. She could turn most of it over to Craine and another squad, even though it galled her to do so. She wanted to finish it. She needed to. And she needed information. More than she could gather herself. She couldn't shake the feeling that the two were tied.

'And Danny, get word to Kurt. See if there's anything he can find out for us. Off the record. Any rumour, any stories, understand? Anything about the attack on us, and about the kids with burns on their hands. Anything. Tell him I need it.'

His face fell a bit at that order. He dreaded dealing with his brother, with his old life. Grace understood and hated getting him to do it, but she still would when it was necessary. Kurt might answer her. He might not. He'd never deny Daniel.

'He'll want something for it.' The warning in his voice was clear, and for a moment he wasn't just 'Danny' any more. She could hear the hint of Parry in his voice, the echo of his brother. Kurt would want something from her. A favour. It was never a good idea to owe anything to the devious bastard.

Of course he would want something. She'd be shocked otherwise. But what choice did she have? And she'd only owe him if he delivered.

'Sure, but tell him I decide what it's worth, not him. And tell him if he wastes my time, the prince and I will pay him a visit he won't forget.'

Bastien would probably be horrified that Grace was using him to threaten the criminal underworld of Rathlynn. Or maybe not. He didn't seem averse to terrifying Sylvie the would-be assassin to find out who had sent her. Or using Grace to do the threatening.

Which brought her mind back to the sketch. Bastien had recognised him, Arlon Griggs, who worked for Lord Asher Kane. She recognised him too. The not-mageborn guard from the quays.

'And find out if Kurt knows Griggs. But careful. I don't want to spook anyone. Take Ellyn with you. She knows what Griggs looks like. And Kurt likes her.'

'She doesn't like him.'

'Remember that. I don't want her stabbing him. Your mother would never forgive me. I mean, I know he gets handsy but Ellyn doesn't hold with that and I don't blame her.'

Daniel just grinned at her, relieved that talk had turned a little lighter. 'Stop putting it off, Grace. Go play at being a noble. Date with a prince and all that.'

'It's not a date.' She cut in too quickly, too sharply, and Daniel's grin grew even wider. Damn it, she was never going to live this down. It was going to be all over the Academy by the time they finally got out of this nightmare and back to normal. She could picture it now, the laughter in the mess hall and the training room, the jokes, the constant teasing she'd be subjected to – good-natured, sure, but still… That time Grace went on a… *not-a-date* with the Lord of Thorns. That time she was dolled up like some kind of freak and paraded around in front of the highest echelon of nobility Rathlynn had to offer. That time—

'We won't wait up,' Daniel told her, waving her off.

'Tell Misha I said hello,' she snapped after him and had the satisfaction of seeing him turn scarlet again. 'Maybe you could interrogate him as well. He'd probably enjoy that.'

*

'Turn around,' said Lyssa. Grace did so reluctantly. The dress felt wrong. Her hair felt wrong. So did the tiny slippers on her feet instead of her boots. Everything felt wrong.

Lyssa darted forward and pulled at her hair again, teasing a few locks loose from the sophisticated and unnatural style into which she had spent an age sculpting it.

'Now,' she said, with an air of satisfaction. 'Look.'

Grace didn't recognise the woman in the mirror. She wasn't wearing enough clothing for one thing. Her neck was long and elegant. Her shoulders were bare and there was a bosom that was on the verge of heaving in a ridiculous way. The embroidered green fabric flattered her skin and hair in ways she had never considered possible. She didn't look like herself. The Academy uniform was always dark and drab, the colour of shadows, moss and mud. This shone. And so did she.

'I don't know…'

'You don't need to know,' Lyssa said. 'You just need to wear it and smile.'

Grace glared at her instead but that didn't seem to have any effect at all. Lyssa carried on, fussing and adjusting the outfit that belonged on someone else. As if it needed adjusting. Well… maybe pulling up…

'This is a terrible idea.'

'The queen invited you herself. Well, not *herself*, but her master of entertainments sent the invitation and she's never sent an invitation like that to us before. Not even to the prince.'

'She's never invited Bastien?'

'Not to a dinner party like this. Oh, she wants his company at times, of course…' She stopped, as if aware she had said too much. To recover, she fixed Grace with a schooling look. 'She's the queen consort, child. She doesn't invite. She commands. As queen she outranks him, barely. She clings to that. And she's Tlachtlyan originally, of course. They're obsessed with formality and protocol.'

Grace grinned, falling back on the one reserve that had always kept her sane in the past. She dragged her gaze away from the horror in the mirror and down to the diminutive woman fussing like a grandmother over her.

'Obsessed? Really? Who would ever be obsessed with protocol?'

But Lyssa wouldn't have recognised sarcasm if it danced naked in front of her. Oh, she'd be shocked and appalled, but she wouldn't have recognised it. Or if she did, you'd never have known.

'Don't make that face, Captain. It's common.'

'So am I. Always have been.'

Lyssa shook her head and gave a sigh of exasperation. 'Well I suppose you're as good as you will ever be. Just try not to speak. Now, how's your curtsey?'

Grace thought about that. Then she bowed, a formal, military bow of the deepest respect that was definitely not a curtsey and was never going to be. Lyssa openly scowled at her this time.

'Don't make that face,' Grace parroted back at her. 'It's common.'

To her surprise, Lyssa laughed, a broad, delighted laugh that almost seemed too big for her. 'Well, you'll have to do. You'll shake them up, at least, and his highness will be there to guide you. And protect you. Just keep your wits about you.'

'Thank you,' Grace said solemnly, meaning it, and Lyssa flushed.

'Not at all, child. You're beautiful. It's an honour.'

It stole every smart-mouthed reply from her. Not one had ever called her beautiful before. Not like that.

It's my honour to serve. The formal words echoed through her mind. Was that what she was doing?

A discreet knock on the door made them both turn.

'That'll be him,' said Grace, shaking off the shock that had silenced her.

'A prince doesn't just come calling at a lady's chamber door,' Lyssa told her. Grace swallowed down the urge to shout that she wasn't a lady either – she was worried poor Lyssa might actually collapse. 'He will receive you downstairs. You aren't even late yet.' As if that was something to be expected rather than avoided. Trained to be punctual all her life, Grace smiled at the thought.

But when Lyssa opened the door, Bastien was standing there, looking darkly handsome and mysterious as ever.

'Is she ready?' he asked and Lyssa opened the door wide with a knowing look on her face. Now who was grinning?

Bastien looked like he had been about to say something else but his voice had suddenly stopped working and his mouth hung open as if he'd taken a blow to the head.

'I'm ready,' Grace said.

He stared at her as she came towards him, and then seemed to shake himself back into this world from somewhere else. Years of diplomacy, decades of training and instruction, and maybe a deep-seated survival instinct finally made him react. His bow put hers to shame.

And as he moved Grace found her own breath stopped up in her throat, her heart crashing against the inside of her ribs.

He wore black, of course, because he always did. But it was the black of raven feathers, the black of the deepest night. It was smooth and glossy, and it hugged his body in ways that didn't seem so much formal as sinful. The Little Goddess would hide her eyes.

The other divinities, however…

Yes, the others would be looking as much as possible.

Grace forced herself to breathe. She shouldn't be reacting to him like this. It wasn't safe or sane. But she was. She couldn't deny it any longer. Safe and sane remained to be seen.

She thought again of the woman's voice she was sure she had heard. No one had mentioned anyone else living here. She hadn't seen anyone. And yet she couldn't shake the memory. She hadn't imagined it. She knew that. She just wished that she had.

'Shall we?' he asked. Grace watched him swallow, the movement of his Adam's apple in his throat almost hypnotic.

'Shall we what?' she asked.

'Go.' He held out his arm and she stared at him.

Touching him would be a really bad idea. Every instinct in her told her that while at the same time they screamed at her to do it.

She folded her hands behind her back, then realised that doing that made her chest more obvious. Instead she tried to cross them in front of her.

'Here,' said an exasperated Lyssa, and she draped a silken shawl around her shoulders. It was the same emerald as the gown that clung to her, embroidered with shimmers of gold. Tendrils that glittered and shone wound around her shoulders and upper arms like vines. Lyssa fussed and adjusted it so that it draped around her front, and either end trailed down her back like wings.

'You'll be late. Too late for politeness. Get a move on, both of you,' she said at last when neither of them seemed inclined to do anything but stand there.

'You're beautiful,' Bastien said as they stepped out into the hallway beyond his tower. The tone was not what she'd expected. It sounded like wonder.

'I'm… I'm just a…' Just an officer of the Academy. Just no one. That was what Grace wanted to say. It felt disloyal, somehow. To be here, like this, when the Academy had given her everything. Men had told her she was beautiful before, once or twice. They had never sounded like that when they said it.

What was she doing? This wasn't some sort of fairy tale. She had to remember that. She had to focus.

'Why are we doing this, Bastien?'

'Because we have no choice.'

She gave him *that* look. 'Come on, there's always a choice. I mean, we might not like the repercussions but there is always a choice.'

That same brief smile flickered over his lips. It made a rush of heat flood her body and she hurriedly looked away, studying the portraits they passed, the carpet under their feet, anything else.

'Well then,' he said, a dark chuckle entering his voice. 'We're going because I want to look in the face of someone who might be behind the assassination attempts. And you're coming because you're astute, quick and now, apparently, the perfect distraction.'

'I hope I'm more than that.' She shivered, uncomfortably. 'I wish there was somewhere to keep a weapon in this thing.'

He looked her up and down in a glance. 'There really isn't, is there?'

The way he said it made her skin flush red. Damn him. He knew it too. And then she realised that he found it funny. Of course he did.

'No,' she told him coolly. 'Just as well I don't need one.'

'I'm sure you don't. We're going to a dinner party, not a gang fight.'

Were they? She wasn't so sure.

'Besides,' Bastien went on. 'There will be knives on the table. And I can't wait to see the damage you can to do with a spoon.'

She would have laughed but they turned into the corridor and there were guards flanking the door at the far end. Before she knew what was happening, Bastien had entwined his arm with hers and was leading her effortlessly onwards.

Into the den of the she-wolf.

Chapter Seventeen

The doors opened before they even approached them. The guards didn't move, their attention fixed in the middle distance. Not that it meant anything. Tempted to throw something at them and see if they reacted, Grace pursed her lips. That would be the test. It was easy to zone out on guard duty. She remembered Craine telling her that a guard lost in their own thoughts was as useless as a mace to an archer.

What she saw next drove all thoughts of guards and procedure from her head.

Overhead, in the vast space beneath the vaulted golden ceiling, illuminated by the evening sun streaming through panes of coloured glass, half a dozen figures twirled and danced on thin air. Grace tilted back her head, staring, her mouth open at the aerial ballet. Music filled the room, delicate and beautiful, and at first she couldn't see the source. But she could feel it. There was a shiver in the air, the touch of magic creeping all over her skin. She looked around, to find a young dark-skinned Lyric spinning music with his hands. He stared into nothingness, entirely enraptured by his art: she had to admit, he was a master. Other musicians accompanied him, on mandolins, violas and flutes, each one making music with magic. Or perhaps the other way around. The dancers were mageborn too, she realised, Zephyrs, using their magic to lift themselves and move like elementals.

They all wore collars. The sigils in them glowed faintly. They all had a dull sheen to their eyes. Something was wrong. Terribly wrong. Every instinct told her that. Magical and mundane.

In the middle of the room, as the Lyrics made music and the Zephyrs swirled through the air, a group of people sat at an elaborately set table, ignoring both dancers and the music, ignoring everything except each other. They laughed and drank the rich red wine from crystal cut glasses. The food heaped on the table was enough to feed areas like Eastferry or Belport for a week.

'Bastien, you're here!' the queen said in an overly loud voice. Her face was flushed and her eyes shining. She'd clearly been enjoying the wine. Hopefully just the wine. 'You're late.'

Bastien just bowed. 'Apologies, your serene highness. We must have misjudged the time.'

They hadn't. The invitation had been specific. If anything they were early, in spite of Lyssa's fears. But Grace didn't dare to argue. She bowed, and the queen smiled in bemusement. She probably should have curtsied like Lyssa wanted but that was just not happening.

If the queen took it as an insult, so be it. Grace hadn't liked her the first time she'd seen her. She hadn't learned anything to change her mind since. Far from it.

'Captain Marchant, how different you look. Doesn't she look different, my darlings?'

All eyes turned on her and Grace struggled to hold herself still and not back away, or, worse still, flee from their presence.

Different. What a word to use. Different didn't mean good. Not to people like this.

The world suddenly felt very dangerous indeed.

Someone laughed, a nasty underhanded laugh. Grace couldn't help it any longer. She flinched back. She didn't belong here. She should never have come. She looked ridiculous in this dress. She had scars and callouses. If only she'd just refused, or at least worn her uniform. If only she had her sword. Or even her knives. All she had was the warrant and Zavi's sigil hanging around her neck.

A hand caught hers, a strong and gentle grip, his fingers threading in between hers. Just for a moment. Bastien squeezed, and the breath suddenly flooded back into her lungs. Her spine straightened.

She couldn't run. More than that, she wouldn't.

Yes, she looked different. She glanced around her and slowly dragged her gaze back to the queen. Different from her. She looked strong and capable. She looked like she did something every day rather than waft around a palace. Good.

'Come and sit down,' Bastien said on a breath. He crossed to the table and pulled out the nearest chair for her. As she sat and he pushed it in, he leaned in close by her ear. 'Don't listen to them, to anything they say. You are magnificent. They are nothing next to you. Look at them, really look at them, drunk and stupid, inbred fools with no taste. Remember that.'

She looked up the length of the table, directly at the queen. Aurelie's sapphire eyes locked on her, and the practised smile slid from her face. It was a challenge. Both of them knew it.

Bastien pulled out his own chair ready to sit.

'Come here, Prince Bastien,' the queen said, her voice suddenly sharp. He froze, staring at her, suspicion writ large across his face. 'Sit by me. Lord Kane, please change places with the prince.'

A shocked silence fell over the riotous table. All eyes turned to the man sitting by the queen's side. His handsome face had frozen, hiding a rush of anger behind the mask of a diplomat. The general was her favourite. Or used to be.

'Your serene highness, I go at your command but with every regret.' As Bastien reached the seat Asher offered no bow to the prince. He stepped back, waiting, his mouth a hard line. 'Your highness.'

'Lord Kane, my thanks for your sacrifice.'

Kane looked down the length of the table at Grace and his expression turned predatory. 'At least I am blessed with your charming companion. I didn't think you were the kind to share.'

Grace picked up one of the knives. It was heavy, silver, and sharp. The balance wasn't bad either. She smiled her coldest, most calculating smile, and looked up to meet Lord Kane's eyes. She tried to ignore the grin that Bastien couldn't hide.

Before Kane could join her, a flurry of servants arrived, whisking away the food already on the table and instead serving fragrant roast meat and delicately seasoned vegetables. Grace waited, watching the way they moved, the careful, determined way they worked, unobtrusive, never once making eye contact.

'Lamb again,' Kane sighed. Grace started and turned to look at him, seated beside her as if he had never been anywhere else. She looked back at the slab of meat on the plate in front of her, more food than she'd normally see in a week, sometimes longer. Beans, cheap cuts of unidentified meats and dubious sausages were more her usual fare.

She cut off a mouthful and ate it, savouring the rich flavour and the strange things it did to her taste buds. It was like nothing she'd ever eaten before. The pleasure must have shown on her face – how could it not? When she opened her eyes, Kane was watching her in amusement.

'Should I leave the two of you alone?' he asked. She just stared at him and he lifted his wine glass up in salute. 'You're quite the talk of the court, you know, Captain. Everyone wants to know all about you. And here you are, beside me.'

'Here I am,' she agreed. Not that she was planning on agreeing to anything else. At the far end of the table, sitting next to the queen herself, Bastien looked like a dark cloud. He hadn't touched his food or the wine. That was good at least. Aurelie couldn't drug him if he didn't. Grace met his gaze and tried to smile but Bastien didn't react. He was watching them both with an unwavering gaze. The queen was speaking to him, her hands moving like fluttering birds.

'Have you known Bastien very long?' Grace asked, absentmindedly.

'*Bastien*, is it? He doesn't let just anyone call him by name. But I suppose that gives you a lot of leeway.'

For a moment she thought Kane was indicating her chest with the nonchalant flick of his hand. Then she realised it was the coin, the king's warrant which she wore in lieu of jewellery. Lyssa hadn't been too happy about that, but Grace didn't feel comfortable taking it off. The sigil hung alongside it, just in case. Because she had never felt more unprotected than she did now.

'That's what he said to call him,' she replied as blandly as she could while at the same time resisting the urge to pull the silken shawl a bit more firmly around her. It wasn't much of a shield but it was all she had. That and her own determination. 'But you haven't answered my question.'

He downed his wine and waved the glass in the air to have it refilled. 'All my life, I suppose. You can't live here without knowing the family and Bastien is the most notorious of them. His father was the same. When he rode off into battle no one ever knew what was going to happen next. Completely unpredictable. But then, that won the Great War, didn't it?'

Did it? Grace didn't have a clue. Bastien's father the war hero wasn't something that people really mentioned. Not where she came from. Except for Zavi.

Too many of the Academy had died in the Great War. That was why the current contingent were so young.

'How did he die?'

'Up to his neck in dead Tlachtlyans, I believe. His mageborn powers meant he could deal out death like no one else. Add his military training and complete lack of morals… well…'

He downed the wine and held out the glass. The boy with the decanter hurried forwards to fill it again. Grace figured he had just taken up residence behind Asher Kane's seat.

Up at the head of the table, Aurelie was leaning against Bastien, one long pale arm draped over his shoulder. He couldn't have looked more uncomfortable if he tried.

'What age was he? Bastien, I mean.'

'When the old man died? I don't know. I was three and Celeste was about ten, I think, so… seven, maybe eight?'

'Celeste?'

'His sister. Didn't anyone tell you about his sister? Beautiful girl. Went completely insane. Dangerously so. Sent off to the Temple…'

She'd heard the rumours about what happened, of course. Another person who had been taken from Bastien. His sister in the temple. Locked away because she lost her mind.

'And their mother?' Grace hardly dared ask.

'She died when Bastien was born.' Of course she had. Grace felt like a fool for asking. Everyone left him. Everyone. Or, to be precise, was taken away from him. 'Lyssa Arenden raised them. Poor old Lady Lyssa. Can you imagine? A house full of Bastien and Celeste as children?'

'It… it can't have been easy.'

'Easy? Two mageborn of their pedigree and power? No. Definitely not easy. To be honest, they probably should have been separated far earlier. Bastien alone would try the divinities themselves. Marius used to tell us all kinds of stories about the things his mageborn cousins got up to. Goddess, we laughed. Well, we laughed then. It became… less funny over time.'

'Less funny how?' She wasn't sure she wanted to know the answer but Asher Kane hardly flinched.

'Has no one told you that they killed my big sister yet? The rumour mill is really slowing down around here.'

'They?' Her voice almost broke as she said it.

Asher grinned wolfishly and drained his wine glass. 'Celeste then. Poor old crazy Celeste. Not happy about my sister Hanna shacking up with Bastien. Like a grown woman didn't know her own mind? My sister understood exactly what she was doing and Bastien wasn't complaining. Don't know if it was jealousy or the age gap, but oh Celeste didn't approve. All those years ago.'

But Bastien had just been a boy then, surely. What had a grown woman been doing with him? It must have shown on Grace's face.

'Oh, don't be like that. It would have been a wonderful match.' He called for more wine again and drained that too. There would be none left at this rate. 'Nobility always do things differently. Bastien was besotted. King Leonis would have bent eventually and accepted it.' He lifted his glass in salute towards the head of the table, where Bastien was. 'Not Celeste though. Crazy bitch.'

Hanna Kane… Grace hadn't heard that story in years. Not since most of the family had been carried off by some plague or other. Everyone said they were cursed. Pieces clicked into place. Asher was the younger brother by ten years of the eldest daughter of the Kane family, rich and influential, the society darling, who had died in the palace. No one knew how or why… but clearly her brother had a theory. Bastien and Celeste? But why hadn't they been charged? She frowned as she realised exactly why, disgusted at her own naïvety. They had been children, sure. But more than that, they were Larelwynns, that was why.

She'd been even younger when she was dumped at the Academy. Only she couldn't remember anything before that. The Academy had become her home, the people there her family. People like Craine and Childers. Like Daniel and Ellyn. Like Kai.

If she hadn't ended up there, with those people around her, what would she have become? A bitter drunk like Asher Kane? Or a lost soul like Bastien Larelwynn? Or a corpse like Hanna…

Grace didn't want to push too hard, not yet. But how much wine had Kane already drunk? He was talking, already saying much more than he should. But she needed her attention off the distant past and on the here and now. She needed to distract him.

Turning towards him she drew the shawl slowly off her shoulders and his eyes plunged into her cleavage. He licked his lips and she had to suppress a shudder.

'Do you know a man called Arlon Griggs?' she asked suddenly, artlessly, or so she hoped, watching his response with interest.

He paused, just a hair's breadth too long, and stared down into the wine. He wasn't drunk enough yet. Damn. 'Of course. You met him too. You arrested him on false charges.'

She straightened in her seat, cursing inwardly. 'They were not false charges.'

His cold smile didn't reach his eyes. 'No? And yet they released him shortly afterwards. Of course, he didn't have a lot of options when you hauled him out in front of the troops and accused him of being a mageborn.'

Interesting. Could be a deflection of course. It could be an outright lie, but one they should be able to check easily enough.

'What else does he do?' she asked.

'Now? Oh, he does very little now. He's dead.'

She bit back a curse. 'Dead?'

'Took his own life. The disgrace, you understand. And his young wife left a widow. It's a tragedy.'

Was Asher trying to stoke her guilt? If so he was trying the wrong tactic.

'And when did this tragedy take place?'

'Yesterday.' He put down the glass and began to tear into his food again, stuffing his face with the lamb.

Grace looked away, slightly sickened by the sight, just in time to see the queen consort all but climbing into Bastien's lap. Aurelie ran her fingers through his hair, fussing at him, and he sat there like a statue, staring into nothing.

This wasn't right. He looked dazed. Was he getting through this by zoning out completely, or had someone managed to slip him something after all? Grace looked down at her own cup and deliberately tipped it over with her fingertips.

'Oh no, what a shame. More wine over here,' Asher called without hesitating.

The music played on and the dancers pirouetted overhead. People around her ate too much and drank too much and laughed too loudly. She had little idea who most of them were. Royal favourites, no doubt, scions of the great houses of the kingdom of Larelwynn, Rathlynn's noble sons and daughters. The young, the rich, and the inbred.

Grace thrust the plate and the drink away from her. She needed to get Bastien out of here, that was clear, but she had to be careful. The queen was not going to give up her prize easily. Grace pushed back her chair, ready to leave the table, when another woman entered the room and clapped her hands.

The music stopped, and the dancers floated down to the ground. The servants turned abruptly and left the room, followed by the entertainers, although some of them lingered by the doors, watching. A strange hush fell over the room, pregnant with expectation. Bastien frowned, confused, and Grace's feelings of concern deepened. The woman standing inside the door was not a stranger.

They'd seen her in the Temple, interviewed her, been attacked as soon as they left. She wasn't in her robes now though. She wore a satin gown and her hair was as elaborately arranged as anyone's there.

'Mother Miranda?' Grace murmured.

But she didn't look like the Mother of the Temple now. She looked like someone else... someone...

Memories stirred. Painful, terrible memories. Dreams of fire and pain, of misery and desperation. Memories Grace had pushed deep down and thought lost.

Strength deserted her. She slumped back into her chair, staring.

'Ah, our last entertainment,' said the queen in delight. 'And our final course, as promised.' She jumped up from her seat and held out her hands like a child expecting a present for her birthday. 'Mother Miranda, what have you brought us?'

'Gems from across the city, your serene highness,' said Miranda. That voice. It jerked Grace upright as if a wire had hooked into the top of her head. She knew the voice. It haunted her nightmares. It taunted her. Why hadn't she recognised it before? 'Fire, wind, earth, water, song, and the flesh itself. All the wonders. All there to taste and enjoy. To make you giddy with delight. The Little Goddess provides.'

Memories she couldn't quite grasp twisted in her mind. They slid from her fingers like ice.

She looked for Bastien, and found him still sitting in his seat, staring at Mother Miranda, confused and appalled. This was wrong, so very wrong. What was she doing here?

They needed to go. She knew that. They needed to get the hell out of here and never come back. Panic rose up inside her.

'First a demonstration,' said the woman from the Temple. 'Asher, if you will.'

Asher Kane nodded and made for the doors. He was gone only a moment. When he returned, the guards came with him, dragging a chained, collared and sigiled man. He looked as dazed as the musicians, but far more dangerous.

'No,' Grace hissed between her teeth. Her eyes met Bastien's, locked onto them as she tried to warn him. She made to get up but he raised a hand, stopping her. What was going on? Did he know about this?

It was the Gore, the one that had caused Kai's death. He was meant to be rotting in a dungeon under the palace, his powers stripped away. Grace was never going to forget that face, even though now it was thin and gaunt, those vicious little eyes a million miles away.

'We know some mageborn cannot be controlled. We are fortunate to have Academy officers like Captain Marchant here to track them down and capture them, removing them from the general population whom they threaten.'

There was a light smattering of applause as all eyes turned briefly on her. Grace felt horribly complicit. In what, she couldn't say. But she didn't like the feeling.

'What then?' Miranda went on. 'In the Temple we try to offer sympathy and comfort to their victims and their families. But that is all we can do. What happens when they are captured?'

'Bastien removes their magic,' Aurelie answered, in bored tones. Perhaps this was all taking too long for her. Perhaps she simply wanted to get on to her entertainment, the final course as she said. The thought of what that could be sent chills down Grace's spine.

And then the Gore fixed his gaze on her, tilted his head to one side as if trying to recognise her. He looked so puzzled, she knew he had been broken. In body and mind.

She refused to feel sorry for him. She knew what he was. But this… no one deserved this.

Asher had joined Aurelie and he hushed her gently. He really doted on her. Grace doubted the feeling was returned. Not in the same way.

'Yes,' said Miranda. 'His highness performs his duties with admirable dedication. But he is only one man. Even his powers don't stretch that far. And so… Behold.'

From her neck she lifted one of the many necklaces that hung there. Suspended from the chain was a small glass globe. It looked like nothing more than a keepsake holder, into which one might put dried flowers or a lock of hair.

One of her assistants handed her another globe. When she touched the two together, both began to glow with a faint, throbbing white light. She offered the larger one to the Gore.

Bastien surged to his feet, reaching an understanding that was beyond Grace's capabilities.

'You can't do this,' he shouted, much to the shock of everyone around him. 'Where did you—'

Miranda held up one elegant hand, her long nails glinting in the red light. Grace flinched, an unknown instinct or memory firing like an explosion in her brain. A punch. A kick.

There's been a war. Everybody's hungry.

'I think you know that, your highness. Why, this is your work, isn't it? And what I offer completes it.'

'It isn't safe,' he went on. 'For either party.' Grace pushed her chair back and stood quietly, trying to make her way to his side. This felt dangerous. She couldn't say why. But her instincts were rarely wrong.

'Bastien,' Mother Miranda said with an admonishing tone, one friend to another. Like equals. 'No progress is without risks.'

She touched the necklace to the globe in the Gore's hands. Both of them blossomed with light, vibrant and terrible, red like blood, like the bodies he turned inside out. It pulsed more strongly than before.

The Gore gave a soft groan and fell, caught by his guards, but the jar was still held firm in his hands. His fingers were clenched around it, fixed, as if rigor mortis has set in.

'Now,' Miranda purred. 'He is no threat to anyone, but his power on the other hand…' She held up the necklace. 'Lord Asher, if you will.'

'Asher, don't,' Bastien murmured but the general didn't spare him so much as a glance.

Miranda smiled as Asher Kane joined her and bowed so she could slip the chain over his head. As the pendant touched his chest, he drew in a shaky, uneven breath. His eyes widened. Grace was sure she saw his pupils dilate with pleasure.

Bastien was still on his feet. But he didn't try to stop anyone.

'You, come here,' Miranda snapped at one of the musicians who still lingered by the doorway. Startled and uncertain, he blushed and tried to back away. When he did, two guards seized him and thrust him forward. 'No need to be shy, dear. Hold still. This will only take a moment. Here Asher, break his arm.'

'What? No!' The musician tried to pull away. 'No, mistress please. You… you can't. This is my livelihood. Please…'

Asher smiled. 'Wrong place, wrong time,' he murmured. 'Again.'

And he reached out, pressing his hand on the man's arm. It only took a touch. There was a terrible crunch and the musician howled in agony. A jagged bone tore its way through his golden-brown skin and blood splattered up into his face.

'Now heal him,' Aurelie snarled.

Asher rolled his eyes. 'Really?'

'He's mine,' she told him. 'I told you not to mark him. He's my favourite… mandolin player.'

As if aware she had said too much, she sank back into her seat, her face ugly with suppressed rage.

Behind them someone snickered. The queen's head snapped around looking for the source of the noise. But every face was a mask.

Asher grabbed the man's arm again, dragging him up and shaking him like a dog to get him to cooperate. For a moment nothing happened, and then, in front of everyone, the bone began to reknit itself, pushing back into the musician's skin, which crawled back over the wound. In theory any Gore could do this, Grace knew that. They commanded the body and the blood. She'd seen one who could fix internal bleeding, broken bones, perforated lungs… anything. But mostly that particular magic lent itself to cruelty. They made excellent torturers.

The musician's sobs died off. He blinked, staring up into Asher's face. The general smirked, just for a moment.

And the mandolin player screamed, tearing himself free. He ran for the doors.

But he never made it. As he reached the threshold, Asher made one simple gesture with his hand, a quick circle with his wrist, practised and sure.

The musician's head turned. With a sickening crack, his neck snapped and he fell.

Aurelie screamed. She lunged forward, then seemed to remember herself and stopped. She gasped out a sob, then another. But suddenly the grief stopped as she regained control of herself. Then she rounded on Asher like a fury.

'What did you do that for?'

But Asher just looked unrepentant. 'You know I never liked him. Or his whiny voice. Besides, we didn't need him telling tales.' He lifted the little orb, still glowing. 'I can see many practical application of this, Mother Miranda. Not just healing. Torture too. Assassination. Combat.'

The Gore made a noise suddenly, a strangled sob. His body arched and he convulsed. Foam flecked with blood bubbled from his mouth. Miranda's face froze and she ran to his side, snapping at the guards to get back. She checked his pulse, peeled back his eyelids, and cursed. She looked up with a look of rage on her face, her eyes searching the watching crowd for one man.

Grace felt a surge of magic and Bastien clenched his hands to fists at his side, his eyes tightly closed.

'What are you doing?' she whispered.

'Putting a stop to this.'

'Bastien, you're killing him.'

He didn't reply. The Gore arched up, twisting against those holding him down, and an agonised groan wrenched its way out of his mouth.

Then he fell down as if a string had snapped. The light in the twin orbs faded.

'Well, applications that last for a little while.' Aurelie gave Kane a smug glance. They didn't even look at Bastien. They hadn't realised what he'd done. 'There are better things to do with magic. Come, everyone, let us celebrate. Get them out of here,' she told the guards. 'Miranda, this is meant to be a party. Not a failed demonstration of your experiments.'

Mother Miranda hid a scowl behind her flawless face and clapped her hands again. Globes of light appeared around her, little orbs like the jars in Bastien's study. They bobbed across the room, dancing in the light, the flickering flames inside them casting wild shadows everywhere. The queen squealed in delight, her beloved mandolin player soon forgotten, and jumped up to catch one. The others all joined in, leaping up from their seats and lurching around after the bobbing orbs.

Bastien grabbed Grace's arm. 'We have to go.'

Grace didn't even have the strength to fight him, allowing him to pull her after him. But before they reached the door, he glanced back and stopped, his hand releasing her abruptly. Bastien stared past her, dismay making his eyes huge, and Grace turned, slowly, reluctantly. Kane stood right behind her, towering over her, holding an orb in his hands. It glowed with a green light and Kane smiled, his eyes reflecting it. The expression on his face was even more frightening than the orb.

'Take it,' he said. There was no trace of drunkenness to him now. Not the kind that came from wine. He thrust the orb towards her. 'Why not join us, Captain? Take it and drink.'

'Yes, drink it,' said the queen. She still moved like a dancer, graceful and elegant, but whether that was innate or stolen it was impossible to tell. She locked eyes with Grace, lifted the orb to her own perfect mouth and light flowed into her, illuminating the veins in her skin from inside. 'Drink down the magic. We can all share in it. Command him, Captain Marchant. Make him share. You can do that now. Come on, Bastien. Don't be greedy. You aren't the only one any more.'

'Where… where did it come from?' Grace asked. 'The magic, where did you get it?'

'Oh, she brings it, silly captain,' crooned the queen. Her eyes glowed now, purple like the light that had been in the now empty orb. She fumbled with it, dropped it, the glass shattering on the tiled floors. 'We pay handsomely. And Mother Miranda provides. The Temple of the Little Goddess always provides.'

She laughed, and wriggled her fingers. The pieces flew up, whirling around her head like a crown made of shards.

'Drink,' said Kane. He held the orb out to her and Grace felt her fingers itch to take it. It called to her and she wanted it. Just from looking at it. She could feel the lure of the Maegen. 'Fire at your fingertips. Fire in your blood. Grace Marchant, the Lord of Thorns can never offer you this.'

Fire? The last thing she needed was more fire. But all around her, the chosen nobles, the favourites of the queen, were dancing around like drunks, making fire, fanning it with a wind made of nothing, swirling the wine around like ink in the air. One of the men seized a hunk of lamb and bit it until it started to spout fresh blood and shake in his hands.

Grace retched, staggering backwards. Kane laughed at her and drank down the fire in the orb, the stolen magic of a Flint, just like her. How they had done this, how they were doing it, she didn't know. She didn't want to know.

Bastien caught her in his arms. 'Grace, stay with me,' he said and this time she nodded. She knotted her fingers with his and they backed towards the doors.

'Spoilsport,' the queen cried out. 'Another, oh give me another, Mother Miranda. Make me a Lyric for a moment or two. Please. I'll give you anything.'

'No need, your serene highness. I have all you want,' Mother Miranda laughed and held out another orb, this one filled with gold which Aurelie snatched greedily. The failed experiment and Bastien were clearly forgotten. Magic could do that to the unwary, make them forget. Zavi liked to say it fed on memories. What would they remember about tonight? Not a murder... two murders... or more.

'Now, Grace,' Bastien said. On the other side of the room a beautiful young woman wound her hands together and dragged the air out of the lungs of her companion. He went down on his knees, gasping, clawing at his own throat. She laughed as she smothered him.

They turned on each other as if it was all a game, tearing into each other, laughing at the pain and death.

Miranda blocked their way. 'Leaving?'

'This is an abomination,' Bastien snarled at her, but she just smiled.

'Because it's what you do? Come, Bastien. We have no need for secrets, you and I. You enjoyed ending that Gore. Just as she enjoyed hunting him. We're not so different, the three of us. I know you of old, remember? I can help you remember. Join me. You know you want to. Use your magic as it was meant to be used. Control these fools. Rule them.'

'Hard to rule the dead,' he replied, disgust seething from every word.

But Miranda's smile didn't fade. 'Not if you bring them back from the Deep Dark. Not if you reach down there. You can do that, can't you? I know you can. You told me once. Remember?'

Bastien just stared at her as if she was talking nonsense. 'I... I never...'

'No? Then who taught me this?' she asked.

One of the courtiers was already on the ground, blood pooling from his chest. She stretched out her hand and his wound closed, his chest heaved and his eyes opened.

'What have you done?' Bastien growled.

Miranda's smile grew even wider, wolf-like. 'Remember…'

Grace recoiled, but Bastien didn't seem able to move, staring at the woman.

'Divinities,' Grace growled. 'Are you mad? Move.'

'He's tempted,' said Mother Miranda. And she smiled at Grace. 'He always has been. That's the danger of being mageborn, isn't it, Bastien? I know that better than anyone. Of being the Lord of Thorns. Tell her.'

'It's… it's always a temptation,' he said, his voice pained and broken. It didn't sound like his voice at all. The words seemed pulled from him. A compulsion? How was she casting a compulsion on him?

Miranda reached out her free hand and touched his face, drew him towards her. Magic coiled around him, cold and terrible. How strong was she? Grace's skin prickled with the proximity. Miranda didn't seem to even notice she was there now.

'So deliciously powerful,' she whispered, as if describing a favourite meal. Bastien's eyes fluttered closed and he wilted, his knees beginning to give out. 'You always were so powerful. Oh sweet Bastien, if only you were malleable like this all the time. Think of what we could do together.'

Grace moved without thinking. She grabbed Bastien's arms.

'Bastien.' It was a voice of command, of the warrant. She felt it heat against her skin, her power and its power entwining. 'Bastien, come with me now.'

He jerked back from the woman, and turned to Grace in horror.

Miranda laughed, releasing him. 'You always were headstrong, Grace. Take him, then. Command him and teach him to obey. He hates that, but he can be made biddable. I'm sure you'll manage. I'll find him again. I always do. Just remember, you both belong to me.'

I remember her, Grace thought. I remember. Her voice, her laugh, the mockery, the hatred buried beneath it. I remember.

She stumbled but forced herself up and onwards, dragging Bastien with her. Out into the corridor, down the stairs and back up again until she reached his tower, his home, his sanctuary. They fell in through the door, Grace managing to get back up on her feet to slam it shut. The hall where they had eaten that same morning was empty, silent, and dark.

She slumped down against the door, a sob finding its way out of her lungs. Her hair spilled everywhere, the dress, the beautiful silken dress was torn and soot-stained. Blood splashed across her chest, or perhaps it was wine. She didn't know. She didn't care.

'Grace,' Bastien whispered, his voice hoarse. He was still sprawled on the ground, his shoulders shaking.

'It's okay, we're safe now. We're safe here. Aren't we?'

'Yes. Safe. Here.'

'Who let her in?'

'Mother Miranda? She... she's Mother of the Temple. You met her before. Interviewed her. She's a Leech, powerful but—'

'I know,' Grace said. 'I remember now. She's the one.'

Bastien shook his head, confused. 'The one what?'

'The one who stole my magic.'

Chapter Eighteen

Her hands were shaking. He hadn't thought anything could make Grace tremble, but here they were. Bastien tried to pull himself together and felt the edges crumbling.

He'd been so tempted. A moment longer and he would have given Miranda anything. Where the surge in her power had come from he didn't know, didn't want to know… but he could guess. What had she done?

And what had she done to Grace?

'Grace?'

She didn't answer. Grace sat with her back to the door, that gorgeous red hair spilling down from the elaborate style into which Lyssa had fashioned it over her bare shoulders.

'Grace, please.' He knelt before her and took her hands in his, stilling them. 'What do you remember? Please, tell me.'

Something seemed to snap her out of it. She looked up at him, and he saw her wind that iron control over herself. 'It… it doesn't matter. What the hell happened back there? What were they doing?'

He grimaced. 'What the rich have always done. Entertaining themselves at the expense of the poor.'

'They're using magic? For… for fun?'

'It's an addiction,' he replied. But Grace didn't look convinced. If anything her disgust deepened.

'Did you supply them? Did you take it from those kids with a syphon?'

He recoiled. 'No!'

'Did she?'

He shook his head. 'I don't know. But I don't... I don't think she has reason to. If she wants...'

'Why not?'

'She has a ready supply.' He couldn't explain, not easily. Not with words. There were no words for what he had to confess. 'Come with me. I'll show you. I'll show you everything.'

He'd never promised so much to anyone. He'd never dared to.

There was no one he trusted enough.

But now, he was trusting her, willing to tell her every last secret. He couldn't bear for her to keep looking at him like that. But perhaps... perhaps, when he showed her, it would be even worse.

It was a risk. But it was one he would have to take.

He'd never met anyone who every instinct begged him to trust until now.

'Fine. But no more secrets. Tell me everything.'

Everything. The thought of it made his stomach turn, but still, he nodded.

Grace slid her hand into his and let him pull her back to her feet. She raked her other hand through her hair, trying to get it back into some sense of normality. Her eyes glittered but she wound that steel around herself and he couldn't help but gaze at her in wonder.

The stairs seemed even longer than usual. There was no sign of her team, Lyssa or any of his servants. He led her past the study, past her bedroom, under the watchful eyes of the Hollow King window and finally up to his own apartment. If she hesitated when he opened the door it was only for a moment.

Grace made her own decisions. He understood that. She went where she would, walked the path she wanted to walk. He wished he could be like that. Like her. He wished he was half as strong.

His rooms. No one else came in here. No one at all. It was his world. His place. His sanctuary. What was he doing bringing her in here? If he wanted to keep his place of safety to himself, he was going about it the wrong way. He knew that. It just didn't seem to matter any more.

The first room they entered was the sitting room. He liked to read here some evenings. When he had time. He worked in the study, but here he could relax.

He kept the mirror covered. That was just common sense. And if he needed to look, needed to talk, all he had to do was uncover it.

The soft cream cloth slid off and he held onto it, winding it between his fingers.

It wasn't big. Just the kind to hang on the wall at the right height to reflect his face. Luckily Grace was much the same height as him. Around the edge, set into the frame, were enamel medallions containing images of the divinities, and others showing the different powers of the mageborn. It was old. He didn't even know how old. And precious. More precious than anyone knew, because it was one of a pair.

Grace peered at it, then turned her head, looking at his chairs and the bookshelf behind her. When she looked back at the mirror, she tilted her head to one side. Her reflection wasn't there. It never was. Neither was the reflection of his room.

'Celeste?' he said softly.

It took a few moments but his sister wasn't always the most cooperative. She never had been. Headstrong, Marius's father, their uncle, had called her. Never in an approving tone.

She was still beautiful. Always beautiful. Like their mother had been, or so he was told. The only portrait he had of his sister didn't capture the madness.

But Celeste's face did.

'Hello Bastien,' she said. He almost breathed a sigh of relief. She was pale and hollow-eyed, but her voice was relatively calm today. A good day. 'There were mice in the walls again. They danced and sang for me, like the stars did once. And... who are you?'

'Celeste, this is—'

But Grace held up her hand. 'I'm Grace.'

Celeste studied her in that way she had, as if she saw things in Grace's face that no one else could see. She probably could, Bastien thought. There was very little she couldn't do.

His sister looked past the captain, seeking him out. When she saw him she smiled, that brilliant, beautiful smile that contained all the joy in the world.

'Bastien, you have a friend.'

Did he? He looked to Grace in a moment of panic, but she was still looking at the mirror and his sister, locked away on the other side of the city.

Using magic as if she had done so all her life. Talking to his insane sister as if it was the most normal thing in the world.

'Yes. He does. Where are you, Celeste?'

Celeste laughed, that high, giddy laugh which he knew meant she was on the edge, that any moment now she would tip over.

'I'm in the arms of the Little Goddess, in the little house, in the little room where I have been for longer than there has been a kingdom of Larelwynn. But we were gods once. We danced with the stars, we danced in the sun, in the pool of light. And in the darkness too. The deep darkness. They make you forget and forget and forget, but I remember. I remember everything. It sings to me. I want to dance again, Bastien, but Mother Miranda says it isn't time yet. When will it be time again?'

Bastien stepped up close to the mirror, pressed his hand to the glass, and Celeste did the same. She closed her eyes and he felt the ripple of power coming through. So much power.

'Have you had your treatment today?'

Her voice came into painful clarity. 'I'm not crazy, Bastien.'

The rush of pain made him close his eyes. 'I know, sweetheart.'

'There was a fire. I didn't start it. And then a flood. That wasn't me either.' It was never her. Except it was. Or most of it was. And it wasn't her fault. She had no concept of control, not any more.

'It's okay, Celeste.'

'There are so many jars, Bastien. Every day. She says it's for my own good.'

'It is.'

'She said *you* said I had to do it.'

'I did. It's important. It helps, doesn't it?'

She nodded but choked on a sob as she did so. 'But it hurts. I don't like it. I don't want to…'

'I know.'

'Sometimes I say no. Sometimes I can't help myself. And sometimes… sometimes… They said you were here. But you didn't come to see me. No one comes to see me. They lie to you, Bastien. They lie to you all the time. I remember. When will I see you?'

'Soon, sweetheart. Soon.'

'Bring your friend.' She grinned at Grace. It wasn't a comforting expression. There was something feral and dangerous about it. 'I want to play with her.'

He hid the bitter disappointment, reminding himself once again that Celeste could not help herself.

'No playing.' He kept his tone firm but patient. 'And do what they tell you. They're looking after you. Remember that.'

'I'll tell you a secret, Grace,' she hissed suddenly, and pressed her fingers to her lips. 'Just between us. Are you listening?' Grace must have nodded. She was clearly too horrified to find words. Celeste smiled, satisfied. She leaned in close again, whispering like a child. 'I'm the Little Goddess.'

It broke his heart to hear her. Every time.

'Stay safe,' Bastien told her. 'I'll come soon. I promise.'

His sister didn't answer, not even to acknowledge the promise. Instead something seemed to pass over her face, a strangely distant fae look, and she danced away.

Bastien resisted the urge to call her back. She was gone for the time. Off in her own world of wonders and horrors. That was where she spent most of her time. Far too dangerous to be allowed out of that room. Far too dangerous to be let do what she wanted. If the Maegen was a pool in him, it was a tidal wave in Celeste.

Grace stood there in silence, watching him. Watching them both. Carefully, he put the cloth back on the mirror, making sure it was secure, and then murmured the few words that would mute the connection. Not sever it. It never severed it. He wouldn't have it any other way.

He forced his breath to be even again, forced his shaky equilibrium back onto a balanced plane. It was hard. So hard. Celeste was a whirlwind. She always had been.

'So there you have it. My secret.'

'Your sister.' Grace put her hand on his shoulder. He hadn't even heard her move. But her touch grounded him, made him feel whole again. 'Your older sister.'

'Yes.'

'Wouldn't that make her the heir presumptive?'

'It would have. Once. But Marius changed the law. He named me. Because she was… She's mageborn too. But more than just that. She's… she's everything. All the powers, all rolled into one.'

'Like you,' Grace said quietly. Like him. If only she was like him. If only being like him was her problem.

'Yes, like me. But she can't control it. She… she's insane. Dangerous. She can't help it and she doesn't mean to be. There's so much magic in her. It spills out. It hurts people.'

'People like Hanna Kane?'

He recoiled. She'd heard. Of course she'd heard. Asher probably delighted in telling her his theory. 'Yes.'

'So they keep her locked up.'

'Yes.'

'And do *what* with her?'

'You asked where they got the magic. That's where. Celeste. I created the method of removing magic for her and her alone. The fact that I have to use it too is secondary. Her connection to the Maegen is wild and unpredictable. It burns through her and when it isn't controlled, terrible things happen. It's rare for me. It's daily for her. So they syphon magic from her. Miranda...'

'Miranda uses it for entertainment.'

'That was never the idea. We thought... healing, or irrigation... or...' Damn it, his voice was breaking as he tried to force the words out. He was an idiot, a fool. Miranda had assured him that they'd make good use of Celeste's excess powers. He'd showed her how to store magic in the jars. Now Asher and the queen would use them to do whatever they wanted.

'So they lock her up and milk her like some kind of livestock. That's where all the magic tonight came from. 'The bitterness in Grace's voice made him turn into her arms, to look down into her face and recognise the outrage there, the anger. 'And you're all right with that?'

No. No of course he wasn't. What did that have to do with anything?

Technically it wasn't his choice. He didn't actually have a say. He just tried to make it bearable. And failed.

'It was never meant to be like that. I did it for her, to help her. And others. To share mageborn power, so that their days of homage were fewer, so that they didn't have to serve. I tried to help them all.'

Her sigh was a balm to every sense. She whispered his name and she wrapped her arms around him, pulling him close to her. Grace, so near, so strong, so beautiful, was everything.

'Of course you did,' she said. 'I'm sorry, Bastien. I'm so sorry.'

It meant everything. One moment of understanding.

He wanted to hold her, to kiss her, to run his hands through her hair. But he couldn't seem to move.

'You said you remembered her. Mother Miranda.'

The shadow passed over her perfect features, darkening those golden eyes to amber. 'She wasn't called that. She was Auntie then. And we weren't in a temple or a convent or anywhere like that. It was a dive, probably a whorehouse, down by the docks. I've never been able to find it again. There were kids there. So many kids. She's moved up in the world. She must have thought your sister was a gift from the divinities.'

Yes. He could imagine that now. Miranda, salivating at the thought of all that power, easily accessible, ready for the taking.

'Your hands…'

'Burns, like those dead mageborn. Like yours. Like your sister's, I presume.'

'It's a side effect sometimes. The orbs overheat. I thought I'd solved it.'

'Not really.'

'And before that?'

'There is no before that.'

But how had Miranda used that method on Grace as a child? Had she always known how to do it? When he tried to think about it his brain throbbed. The memories weren't there for him either. But for her… maybe… Grace's memories. They could answer so many questions.

'There is. I can find it.'

She almost flinched, but held herself firm. She didn't pull away and for that he was grateful. Stupidly grateful. Her hands traced erotic patterns on his back, the touch so light and delicate, setting his senses alight. His magic unfolded inside him, blossoming like a rose in the walled garden, there for her and her alone. She could do anything right now, command anything of him and he'd do it. He'd kill for her. He'd die for her. The Maegen rose within him, eager to show itself, eager for her.

'No,' she said, and brushed the backs of her fingers down the side of his face. Bastien shuddered, leaning into her touch, and when he opened his eyes he saw her smile.

'Grace,' he whispered. She silenced him with a kiss.

'Bastien,' she murmured, her lips against his. 'No magic. I don't want anyone to ever use magic on me again. But... You can touch me. If you want. I won't order you or anything like that, but if you want...'

She didn't need to say it. There was nothing else he wanted. But he smiled nonetheless, unaccountably grateful for that mercy. For her.

His kiss was tentative, and she responded as if she didn't quite believe him. Bastien didn't quite believe it himself. But he wanted this, wanted her. This closeness, this tenderness. This comfort.

It was a kind of madness. He knew that. But it was a madness worth embracing.

She slid her hands under his shirt and he shivered, his breath catching in his throat. He groaned and deepened the kiss, as if unable to tear his mouth away from hers. She was air, and light, and water. She was everything he needed to survive.

For now. Just for these moments.

His hands unlaced the back of her dress and he helped her step out of it, holding her as if she was the most precious thing in the world.

'Are you sure?' he asked, his voice low and husky.

'Yes,' she told him. 'Divinities, yes.'

She gasped as his mouth closed over her nipple and something inside him simply gave way. His fingers traced whorls and spirals on her skin and he felt the magic inside her unfolding to reach for him, in response to him. There were old scars on her body, along the line of her ribs, on her arms, a nasty one across her hip. He traced his fingertips over each one and she started to pull back. Was she ashamed of them? Of the things that marked her as strong, powerful, a survivor.

'Please,' he murmured and she relaxed again. His lips followed where he touched while she shuddered and cried out. He gathered her against him and she wrapped one leg around his, pushing as close as she could.

Her hands, her mouth, her body… all he could think about was Grace, the darkness she sensed in him, and the light she illuminated in response. Her kisses scourged questions from his mind. She drove her fingers into his hair and pulled him against her.

'Please,' she whispered, urgently. 'Please, Bastien. Please.'

No one had ever said that to him before, not that way.

As he sank into her, body and soul, he promised her everything, even if he couldn't say the words out loud.

Chapter Nineteen

Grace woke in his bed, his body still pressed against hers, their limbs loosely entwined, the light of the Maegen still shimmering in the forefront of her dreaming mind. For a moment, for the first time she could remember, she felt content, sated. Golden light enveloped her and she was at peace.

She wasn't sure what she'd expected. For Bastien to be gone, probably. Not fast asleep, his long limbs loosely cast around her. She eased her way out of the bed, hoping not to wake him. Their clothes were discarded on the floor. Not that it was a lot of help. She couldn't get back into that gown by herself even if she wanted to. And she wasn't about to do a walk of shame back down to her own room when Daniel, Ellyn or, goddess forbid, Lyssa could catch her.

Divinities, what had she been thinking?

Well, she hadn't. Had she?

She looked back at him, at the peace in his face. He looked different, younger. Not the troubled man she had come to know. Long coal-black eyelashes brushed his skin, and his mouth was slightly parted as he slept.

The things that mouth had done last night.

And the rest of him. He didn't need to be mageborn to work magic, it seemed. He just needed to be… Bastien.

She sat on the edge of the mattress, surprised to discover that she didn't actually regret a single thing. When she got back to her feet and turned around she realised he was awake and watching her, his dark eyes staring at her, waiting for something.

'Hello,' she said.

'Good morning. Are you leaving?'

She swallowed hard. Did he want her to? Was he expecting her to just go now? 'No.'

Well, this was awkward. What had she expected anyway? She'd heard Celeste's voice the first night she'd been here – it must have been Celeste – and she'd thought the worst of him then. She'd just assumed… And now here she was. Like an idiot. He was a prince. She was a…

Bastien rolled onto his back, stretching out his arms and then folding them back behind his head, watching her all the while. He was sculpted like one of those statues. She had explored his body last night in every way and found it like the man in her dreams in every detail. He was perfect. It scared her how perfect.

'I haven't got anything to wear,' she said.

He started to smile, a gentle, fond smile that looked good on him. Not like anything she'd seen on him before. It gentled the hard lines of his face.

'Maybe that was my evil plan?'

Her own smile teased her lips. 'Devious in the extreme. I suppose I could wrap that thing around me. It has about a million yards of fabric to it.'

He was ready with some witty retort, the delight in the thought of saying it brightening his eyes. But a sudden pounding on the door made her turn. Bastien was up out of the bed in an instant.

'There are clothes in the wardrobe,' he said urgently, flirtation forgotten. 'Put something on.' Then he raised his voice and her gentle lover was gone. It was the voice of a prince. The voice of the Lord of Thorns. 'What is it? There had better be a good excuse for this.'

'Your highness.' The voice was uncharacteristically hesitant. Ellyn, Grace realised, but Ellyn sounding so unlike herself that it sent a shiver of alarm right through her. 'Your royal highness... the Royal Guard are here, looking for you. And... um... and Captain Marchant.'

Grace's stomach sank. They knew where she was then. But whatever this was, it was more important than her fragile reputation. She glanced at Bastien and realised she couldn't read his expression. It was completely blank. She pulled on one of his shirts and grabbed another. Sleek, pitch black, silken, it whispered as it slid through her fingers into his. He nodded and started to put it on.

'Spit it out, Ellyn,' Grace said through the door. 'What do they want?'

'They're downstairs. We didn't let them up.'

This really wasn't good. Why did she keep putting it off? Grace marched to the door and jerked it open. Her friend's pale face greeted her, Daniel at the end of the corridor, guarding the stairs just in case.

Even with the shirt on, she felt very exposed. It only skirted her thighs. 'What is it?'

Ellyn looked past her, her eyes fixing on Bastien who had somehow already managed to clothe himself immaculately, all in black, and was buttoning the jacket over the shirt she'd only just handed him.

'Your highness, they say King Marius is dying.'

Bastien was a statue, standing there, looking past both of them, his face a mask as the enormity of it swept over them all.

'Right,' he said at last. 'I see. Grace, can you—'

'I'll dress right away. Don't go anywhere without me.'

The warrant hung around her neck, impossibly heavy. She closed her hand around it and saw him frown. Damn. She hadn't meant it like that. She didn't trust the Royal Guards. She didn't trust anyone here to look after him. Except her team.

But he just nodded.

Daniel's eyes went wide as she sprinted by him but thankfully there was no one on the lower floor either. She slammed the door to her room and immediately started pulling on her trousers and leather jerkin. Her knife belt hugged her hips, reassuringly familiar. She pulled her mess of red hair back and tied it out of the way, then rammed her feet into her boots.

She eyed the sword for a moment and then decided not to take a chance. She might insult someone. In fact she was sure she would. It didn't matter now.

Only Bastien mattered.

She slung the baldric over her body and secured it, the sword hanging against her leg. The rest of her weapons and armour followed. To hell with what anyone else thought.

When she opened the door Bastien was waiting, flanked by Daniel and Ellyn. They were fully armed too. Good.

The torc shone around Bastien's neck, his only adornment, and he looked every inch the royalty he was. Heir presumptive. Heir to the king. The king who was dying.

Oh goddess, Grace thought. I slept with the man who could be king today.

The sick feeling returned.

Bastien's eyes swept up her body, the body he now knew better than anyone else, the body that had sighed and cried out for him just hours before. She was still wearing his shirt, she realised, and the warrant stood out as brightly against its sable hue as his torc did.

'Ready?' he asked.

She just nodded. If he was ready for this, so was she. Ready to defend him. Just as she had promised Marius.

But he couldn't be king, could he? He was mageborn. He was possibly the most powerful mageborn she had ever encountered. And more than that, he seemed able to wield more than one power, not to mention give it and take it away. She had never known anyone who could do that. No one except Bastien and now his sister.

But Marius had no other heir. And Marius wanted this. Celeste was insane, the power consuming her mind. And Bastien… Bastien was all they had left of the royal line.

They passed through the increasingly ornate hallways, past the hangings depicting the defeat of the Hollow King and a thousand other Larelwynn victories. Each scene felt designed to show them the enormity of what faced them, the weight of duty that would fall on him. It felt like a death march.

The elaborately decorated doors to the king's private chambers opened as they approached and Aurelie and her attendants emerged, Asher Kane among them. They all looked wretched, like day old drunks. You could put it down to grief, but Grace had seen them the night before, drinking down magic and careening around the room like maniacs.

'What are *they* doing here?' Aurelie snapped at Bastien. 'You were sent for. Not your pets.'

Pets. Charming.

Grace kept her face completely still. It didn't do to show a slighted queen the contempt you felt for her. She recalled the way the queen consort had almost crawled into Bastien's lap last night at dinner, the way she'd run her hand over his skin and… well… tried to do all that Grace had later actually done. She swallowed hard and hoped it didn't show on her face. Queens like Aurelie were not exactly forgiving.

'I'm here to see my cousin,' Bastien replied blandly. Then he looked past the queen, directly at Kane. 'The queen consort is overwrought with grief. Perhaps you might take her to her chambers and fetch her some refreshments.'

It wasn't a request. Everyone in the room gazed from one to the other, and Grace could almost feel the balance of power swinging.

The king was dying. The queen had no power without him.

'Tread carefully, Bastien,' she all but growled. Her eyes burned with unshed tears. But it wasn't grief for her dying husband, Grace knew that. Lost power was much more of a tragedy to her.

'Or?' he said in a voice as cool as a winter wind.

Then, before the whole court, Aurelie curtsied to Bastien and left, sweeping from the antechamber before another word was said, her hangers-on following. Asher Kane was last to go.

'Your highness,' he said, the consummate diplomat again. But Grace couldn't forget the cruelty she had seen in him last night. 'She's overwrought.'

'I'm sure she is.' Bastien folded his arms in front of his chest, waiting.

'But she has many who love her. Many who doubt the wisdom of a mageborn king. Who would not look kindly on…' He spread his own arms wide, indicating Bastien and the rest of them. 'Well, you know how things are.'

If it was a threat or a warning, Grace couldn't tell. She didn't like the sound of it either way. Bastien, however, appeared unmoved. He'd taken on that same cold statue-like quality that had made her fear him.

He fixed Asher with one of those looks, the kind that said he wasn't angry, just disappointed. The kind that made you want to curl up and slink away.

'Asher? You were my friend once, remember? When you and I were friends?'

'You remember things differently to me, Bastien. I *remember* my sister. I *remember* what happened.'

When she died. When Celeste killed her. When…

'It was an accident.'

'So everyone said.'

'Celeste didn't mean to…'

Asher glared at Bastien as if he was mad. 'No, of course, your highness. *Celeste* didn't mean to. She never does. Neither do you. But these things still happen, don't they? You can't take the throne. Not you, nor your line.'

Bastien's jaw fell open, his face going white. Asher took it in, with a cruel smile.

Then he bowed – so curt it could only be taken as an insult – and strode after the queen.

'Well,' Daniel murmured. 'That was—'

'Shut up, Daniel,' Grace said quietly. She wasn't sure what she had just witnessed but there was no need to rub it in when Bastien was standing right there.

Luckily Daniel caught her line of thinking. 'Shutting up, boss.'

'Fan out, trust no one, secure the entrances.' They moved without hesitation as she and Bastien entered the chamber. Around them, the Royal Guards fell back, manning the door. Inside, in a huge raised bed, Marius looked very small, like a child asleep, and Simona sat by his side. When they entered, she got to her feet and bowed to Bastien.

'Your royal highness,' she said. 'It's good that you're here. Give me a moment if you will.'

At Bastien's nod, she bent down to the king and whispered gently in his ear. Marius stirred, his body shivering as he did so, and he gazed past her, to Bastien. With enormous effort, he reached out a hand and Bastien shuddered, forcing himself forward. When he reached the bedside, he knelt, but Marius wrapped his hand around his and pulled him close.

Grace drew herself up to attention, tried not to listen and scanned the room. Simona was doing the same thing, trying to ignore their hushed conversation, trying to give them the space they so desperately needed.

But Bastien's voice rose in pain.

'I can't, Marius.'

'You must. There is no one else. It is time. But not here. You have to leave. It isn't safe. She will guard you and Simona will guide you.'

'You don't... you don't know what will happen...'

The king laughed fondly. 'Neither do you. None of us do.'

'Marius, there must be another you can name.'

'My wife asked me the same thing.' He began to cough painfully, each one racking his body. Blood flecked the snow-white pillow beside his face. When he fell still again, Simona offered him a drink, but he waved her away. 'She doesn't understand what it means, Bastien. This power, this magic. Our curse. She isn't a Larelwynn. She is drunk on power. Please Bastien. You are all there is. Protection, not control. Celeste is too far gone. You *must* do this for me. Then at last the curse can end.'

'You are the king.'

'And you will be.'

'Marius, this is madness. I can't. I'm... you *know* what I am.'

'My love, I know that better than anyone, even you.' He pulled Bastien's face close to his and kissed his cheek. 'You're my blood, my proclaimed heir, the line of my line. No one can deny it. But first… Do as Simona tells you. Every word of it, mind.'

'Please…' Bastien whispered, but from the tone he already knew that it was useless.

'Divinities be with the king,' Marius whispered, and closed his eyes. 'Long may he reign.'

Bastien stumbled back, tears streaking his face, his hands shaking. Simona laid her hand on the king's forehead, and then his neck.

'He's just sleeping,' she said, her voice loud for the benefit of the guards no doubt eavesdropping on everything. 'Still with us, thank all the glories. Do you want to stay, your highness? Sit with him? He would like that, I'm sure.' Bastien nodded, helpless before her commanding tones. 'Good. It will be done, your highness. Close the doors,' she told the Royal Guards directly. 'Take yourselves outside and hold them against any incomers. No matter who they are. I will call when it is time.'

She waited until her orders were carried out, leaving only herself, Bastien, Grace, Ellyn and Daniel with the king. Grace watched the guards leave and thought they were highly armed for attending a dying king. Once the doors closed, Simona turned back to them. And then, in that instant, her serene demeanour transformed.

'Quickly, there isn't much time. Captain Marchant, you have to get him out of here. The moment those doors open again they mean to kill us all and lock him up.'

Bastien looked up at Simona, startled. 'What?'

'The queen isn't going to let you succeed her husband, Bastien. Not without bloodshed. Marius knows this. She has those guards in her employ and half the nobles on her side. Perhaps more. We need to get you to safety. This is Marius's last wish. He would not see you enslaved to that harpy. You must leave Rathlynn. Now.'

'But Marius…'

'Do as I say and we can protect you. There are many who will fight for you, but not if Aurelie has you in chains. Or worse, in her thrall. She can make you obey, do whatever she wants, and you know it. She just needs that warrant. Why do you think Marius gave it to Captain Marchant? To keep you from his wife.'

'I would never serve her,' Bastien interjected. 'You know…'

'You wouldn't even know, pet. That drink, that potion. You'd forget.'

'How do you…'

But the shame in her face answered him. 'I know. I've always known. This is my burden to bear. My shame. I gave it to you, on his father's command, when he was a boy. And I'd do it again for him, if he commanded it. Do you understand?'

For a moment Grace thought he'd lash out, scream, but he looked at Marius again and his face fell. The despair was complete. It even swamped the betrayal in his eyes.

'All his stories… were any of them true?' But he looked back to Marius and shook his head. 'I can't just leave him, Simona. I can't just—'

'You have to, you foolish boy.'

'And what about Celeste?'

'We don't have time to go for Celeste. I'll find a way to get her out. I'll send her to you. I swear it, my Lord Prince. Captain, if you will?'

Grace joined her, trying to keep her equilibrium. 'You have a plan in place?'

'Of course,' Simona assured her. 'There's a secret passage. Marius was always a canny man.'

'He isn't dead yet,' Bastien growled but Simona just waved his anger away. She didn't have time for niceties.

'It will lead you to the dungeons and from there to the crypts. You can access the lower city from there. Bastien knows the way.'

'The Rats' Path.' The pain in his voice made it grate but Grace had to ignore that now, ignore the urge to comfort him, to tell him it would be all right. She couldn't promise that. No one could.

'A royal secret,' Simona said. 'We never thought you'd need it. But we are where we are.' She pulled him into her arms and he didn't fight her. She dragged his head down, kissing his forehead like a grandmother. 'There are things you'll need to attend to on the way. The storeroom and…' When Bastien frowned, guilt spread over her face. 'I'm sorry, love. So sorry. We tried to stop them but they had your work.'

'My… my work?'

He stepped back, confusion bleeding into something else, something horrified and full of rage. 'What… what do you mean?'

'You can still fix it. There's time. The storerooms… they aren't empty.' She glanced at Grace and then leaned in, whispering to Bastien. His face froze and then went ghostly with shock. Grace frowned, concern for him making her reach out, but Simona was already pushing him forwards, towards the doorway. He stumbled away from her. 'Go to Thorndale. I'll send word as soon as it is safe to return. Now, go.' She thrust a roll of papers at Grace. 'Permits and identities, maps and some contacts who will help. There are horses waiting for you at the Academy. They're well supplied and Craine knows everything. Her wife works for me, Lara Kellen. It's all arranged. She'll have all you'll need ready and waiting for you. Lara will meet you beyond the Main Gate.'

The Academy, and Craine. Grace almost felt a rush of relief. Craine would know what to do. They'd be safe there, if only for a while. And

Thorndale? That was Bastien's family home, wasn't it? A fortress in a vast forest estate miles from the city, somewhere in the mountains, far to the north. They just had to get there. Across open and potentially hostile land. With assassins coming after them, if not an entire army. Easy.

Still Bastien hesitated. He looked back at his cousin. 'Tell him… tell him I didn't want this. I didn't want any of this.'

'He knows, pet,' said Simona. 'Divinities protect and defend you, he knows.'

They stepped through the hidden door which slid shut behind them, plunging them into a strange half-light, illumination coming through cracks and vents, lines of light which made the world around them eerie and unknown. Grace led the way, the other two following Bastien. Silently, they made their way down through the secret pathways of the palace. All the time Grace was painfully aware that Bastien didn't say another word. She didn't want to ask what Simona had told him, but clearly it had affected him.

When they reached the lower levels of the palace, deep inside the tunnels, Grace checked the map.

'This way,' Bastien said, heading off in completely the wrong direction.

'No it isn't,' she told him. But he didn't even hesitate, just walked away into the darkness, his head down in determination. Grace glanced at the other two. Daniel opened his mouth to speak but Ellyn slapped his shoulder gently, silencing him.

'Bastien, stop,' Grace called.

He was already almost out of sight, his clothes and hair blending in with the shadows completely. Damn it, where was he off to? She strode after him, heedless of the darkness.

'Bastien, wait.'

He didn't pause but with a snap of his fingers a row of torches sprang into life, illuminating the way ahead.

'There's something I need to do, Grace. It cannot wait.'

Grace nodded back to the other two who followed at a discreet distance. She could always rely on them for that.

Something he needed to do…

Like escape before Aurelie seized control of his kingdom, drugged him, stole his memories and his freedom without him even knowing it was gone. That would be something.

Three more flights of dark uneven steps downwards, with Bastien lighting torches as they approached and putting them out behind them, apparently without thought.

'Can he do that?' Ellyn asked.

'Clearly he can,' Grace replied. What was wrong with him? What had Simona told him? Grief and anger didn't account for this, not all of it. She could sense betrayal and outrage coming off him in waves. This was something else.

'How… how many things *can* he do?' Daniel said. 'We've seen him leech, and he killed that archer by sending the arrow back, and—'

'And he has excellent hearing,' Bastien finished for him.

The look on Daniel's face said if he could have made the ground swallow him up, he would have. But Daniel wasn't a Loam. Bastien could probably do it though.

Grace took pity on her old friend. 'He's asking a fair question. Most mageborn just have one skill. You on the other hand…'

The question lingered on and she realised Bastien had finally stopped at a nondescript door in the wall. 'Me, on the other hand, I have many skills. I'm not like other mageborn. I'm blood royal. I can do many things, like my sister.'

But he wasn't crazy, or at least she hoped he wasn't.

Wherever they were going, they had reached their destination. He didn't look happy about it though.

His hand rested on the handle of the door, but he didn't turn it. He just stood there, waiting, his eyes closed.

'Bastien? What's in there?'

He inhaled deeply and ran his hand over the lock. She heard the bolts turning, and the door swung open without even being pushed.

'I want you to understand,' he said. 'I never meant for this to happen. I was trying to help Celeste. And countless others. I was only ever trying to help. *This* was never meant to happen.'

Light spilled out into the hallway, flickering, dancing light, different colours, different intensities. Grace stepped past Bastien into a room shelved from floor to ceiling the whole way around. On each shelf, small round jars glowed with the light of magic extracted from mageborn. Like those in his study. But so many more of them. Countless jars, bound and sealed and full of light. It moved, glowing petals of it blossoming as she watched, alive. Countless flowers of magic, trapped behind glass.

She glanced at Bastien but he just stood there, his eyes downcast and his mouth a hard line. But there was a flicker of something like relief in his eyes. Had he expected something worse? Behind him her team were staring in wonder. They didn't even know what they were looking at. But she did.

'Goddess, how much magic is stored here?' she asked him.

'A decade's worth at least. Those I've helped, those I've removed magic from when they asked. Those who didn't ask and cursed me for it. Those I syphoned because they were just too dangerous. Like you saw. Homage day offerings.'

Like I saw. I saw far too much. The burns on his hands. And now this.

There were so many; far too many to take with them.

'What do you want us to do with them?' Ellyn asked.

'We can't leave it all here. Not with Aurelie and Miranda… doing what they're doing…'

Daniel stepped inside, looking around in wonder. He didn't even make eye contact with Grace, just stared. 'Are you aware of what this is worth?' he asked.

'You sound like your brother,' Ellyn muttered. 'Once a Parry, always a Parry.'

'Well, Kurt would be right too.' He turned on Bastien. 'And where are the mageborn who kindly *donated* it?'

'Danny,' Grace said, unsure about the tone that had entered his voice. 'Enough.'

'Damn it, Grace. Can you imagine what could be done with all this?'

She could. That was the problem. 'Reel it in, Danny. He's right. We can't leave it here.' Not given what she'd seen at that so-called banquet. With this much magic at her disposal, there would be nothing stopping Aurelie taking over the kingdom. If Bastien ran now and left this behind, he'd never come back. The queen would make sure of that. 'So what do we do?'

'I'll do it. You might want to step outside. I don't want you to get in the way.' Or become collateral damage. Still she hesitated. His voice gentled suddenly. 'Please Grace. I have to do this.'

'Isn't it dangerous? Where will it all go?'

He hesitated and a shadow of regret passed through his dark and endless eyes. 'Into me,' he whispered.

Surely, that wasn't going to work. Too much magic in his system and he would be overwhelmed, just as he almost had been before. The

Maegen would swallow him whole. She turned to tell him exactly that, but he caught her hands in his and all the argument seemed to fade inside her. His face said it all. There was no other way.

'Too much power inside you...' She'd seen him almost collapse from it the last time. She'd seen the magic tearing its way out of him. Not to mention the agony and madness that had claimed Kai.

'I'll just have to manage.'

'Let me help.' She almost didn't recognise her voice as she said it. It certainly didn't sound like the type of thing she'd say. It wasn't the type of thing anyone sane would say.

If it was anyone else she would have said he looked horrified. 'Absolutely not. It will drink your memories, destroy your mind. I can't have that. I will not allow it. I could lose you.'

He wouldn't allow it? Of course he wouldn't. But if that was what he thought...

'Bastien, I want to help.'

He rested his hands on her shoulders, fixed her with his endless gaze. The light flickered, reflected in the darkness there, different colours, different shades, all the magic in the world. It was like staring into endless space.

'I know you do. And I thank you for it. But I'll need you, all of you, if we're going to reach Thorndale safely. And get Celeste out of the Temple. And...' He groaned. 'And everything else. Please, Grace. Trust me. I can do this. I just... I just need to be careful.'

'But that much power—'

'I can do it. It's just a case of not losing control.'

Easier said than done. She wanted to argue, but he clearly wasn't going to move unless they cooperated.

'Can't you just hide it down here? Seal the door or something?' Daniel asked. 'Can't you just…'

'So you can tip off Kurt?' Ellyn snapped. Daniel gave her an affronted look but she rolled her eyes.

'Destroy it, remove it, do whatever you need to, your highness. But we need to move.'

'Step outside, all of you,' the Lord of Thorns said. There was no doubting the tone of voice, or who was speaking. A king in waiting. 'Close the door.'

Grace couldn't do that. It felt like abandoning him in there. She was the last to leave. She clung to its edge, holding it ajar, listening to Ellyn and Daniel bickering quietly. She'd have to get to the bottom of that, too. What had Ellyn meant about Kurt? What did the Parrys want with raw magic?

A commodity, maybe. Or worse, a tool. She didn't want to think of someone like Kurt Parry with that much magic at their command.

Bastien took up his position in the centre of the circular room and slowly spread his arms wide. Grace stared as the air around him seemed to shimmer and tremble. Inside the jars, magic unfurled, drawn to his innate power, flowers reaching for the sun. The door shook beside her and she had to grab hold of it to keep it from slamming.

Inside her that long-suppressed magic shook itself awake again. That thing in her that Bastien recognised and that drew her to him. Like the magic all around them. Yearning for him.

Bastien threw back his head and every jar in the room shattered. Glass sprayed towards him but the magic was faster. It burst from the jars, the soft rose petals of light transforming to a blinding tangle of briars. It struck him like shining thorns, piercing his body in hundreds of places, each blow making him jerk like a fish on a hook. The glass shards hung in the air, glittering in the light. Bastien clenched his teeth, his eyes screwed shut and his fingers splayed wide. A cry wrenched itself from him, a smothered scream, but he didn't move, his body rigid in agony.

Grace wanted to help him. She desperately needed to, but she didn't know what to do. He hung there, frozen, like the shards around him as magic burrowed into his skin, sinking down inside him to nest there, like some sort of parasite.

Abruptly, the glass shards dropped from the air, shattering on the tiled floor. And Bastien shuddered for a moment before falling down heavily onto his knees, his shoulders slumped, his head bowed. Broken like every jar in the secret room.

For a moment she didn't dare move. But the smell alerted her first. Burning, the reek of charred wood.

'Grace!' Daniel shouted and the whole force of his lithe body slammed into her. She went down, but he grabbed her, pulling her back from the room.

Her handprint remained behind, a black and smoking imprint, burned into the wood on the outside of the door.

Chapter Twenty

'I can explain,' Grace stammered, without the first idea of how she was going to do that. The corridor stretched out endlessly into the dark on either side of them and her handprint was seared into the wooden door, little lines of fire still crawling around the edges. She couldn't tear her eyes off this damning, undeniable evidence of what she was.

Daniel exchanged a look with Ellyn, a patented *this should be good* look, and they both frowned at her.

'We know,' Daniel said quietly. 'We've always known. Come on, Grace, no one else has known you as long as us apart from Craine and Zavi. No one could do everything you do without some form of magic in them. It isn't gone, is it? Not entirely. Sometimes it comes out. We know that.'

'I… what?' she spluttered, trying to come up with an excuse, an explanation, anything.

'You really can't lie to save your life, can you?' Ellyn said. 'Seriously, I don't know how you got away with it for so long. Get up, the two of you.' And then she looked past them, to Bastien. 'Is he…? Is he okay?'

That shook some sense back into Grace.

Bastien had dropped to his knees, saturated with more magic than anyone should have been able to bear. Blood royal or not, he'd have to have the control of a god to contain it all. And gods weren't known for their control. Neither were the Larelwynns, if truth be told.

The backlash had made her betray her secrets to her oldest friends. The fact they'd already known didn't help. The black handprint still smoked on the wood of the door.

What if he went hollow? What if they lost him altogether and unleashed a monster like the Hollow King on the city?

She scrambled back into the room and over to his side, almost afraid to touch him.

'Bastien?' she whispered. His eyes were closed and he was still as stone, as if afraid to move in case he shattered. 'Bastien, we have to go.'

He opened his eyes and they were filled with golden light. She felt, rather than saw, them focus on her.

'Grace?' His voice was distant, faint. Like the voice of a dreamer. He remembered her. Thank the divinities he still remembered her. 'You are… the most beautiful thing in my life.'

She sucked in a breath and stared at him, not able to reply. No one had ever said anything like that to her. Never. Either his life was desolate or… or he saw her in a way far different from anyone else. She couldn't doubt that he meant it. But that he said it out loud, now, terrified her.

'Are you hurt?' she asked. 'Are you in pain?'

He shook his head absentmindedly. 'It isn't safe here. She'll know. She'll feel it.'

'Who?'

He frowned again, searching for the name, and Grace felt a mounting horror. 'I… I don't…' he said.

She pressed her hands to his shoulders, trying to ground him, to make him focus. 'It's okay, Bastien. Take a moment. Remember.'

He nodded, his hands wrapping around hers. The effort on his face was palpable.

The words came out in a rush of relief. 'Celeste. She always knows. And if she knows, so will Miranda, and the queen. There's more, Grace... so much more...'

So much more... she didn't like the sound of that. 'What?' she asked. 'What else?'

Light began to spill from his eyes like tears, the way the power had seeped out of Kai before he died. Damn it, this wasn't good. Even Bastien couldn't manage this for long. It would eat him up, hollow him out and then... then they'd see the Hollow King again. She knew it.

'There's more. The next room... I can feel them now... they're in there.'

More magic jars? No... it would destroy him.

'You've done enough. Come on now. Come with me. Let's get out of here.'

He winced, baring his teeth in a grimace. 'I can't leave them. Marius would... he'd never forgive me. And it will help. It will help me. I have to do this, Grace. I have to. It's all my fault...'

She helped him to his feet and they staggered out into the corridor again, Daniel and Ellyn trying to help. The next door was as nondescript as the last.

It hid something so much worse.

Bastien passed his hand over the lock and it didn't so much unlock as melt in the wood, dripping molten metal onto the stone floor. Daniel kicked the door open and the three of them stood there behind the magic-drenched prince, mouths gaping as beyond it they saw row upon row of cot-like beds, most of them occupied by a sleeping figure. Not just sleeping. They lay so still, stretched out on their backs, open eyes staring at the rugged stone ceiling, like so many corpses. Each one wore a simple leather collar. The sigils set in them glowed softly, as did the glass jars each one held, cradled in limp hands against their chests, illuminating the room like so many fireflies.

'Oh divinities,' Ellyn whispered. 'What is this place?'

Grace knew what she was looking at. She knew it without checking, without counting the number – which was far greater than she had thought – without looking at their faces or searching for the likes of Alyss, or any of the ones absent from the Academy.

'What… what happened here?' she asked.

'They're the ones missing, aren't they?' Daniel said in as cold a voice as she had ever heard him use. 'The ones doing homage who didn't get home? Did *you* do this to them? Did you…?'

Bastien tilted his head to one side as if studying him. Like a cat looking at its prey. His eyes, transformed from the black of night to glowing gold gave him the aura of something divine and, as the elders were so fond of saying, the divine isn't something that understands humans as anything more than tools or playthings. What were these people then?

'They are tethered, their magic going elsewhere, feeding others.' Bastien's voice reverberated with the magic in him, and the anger and grief behind it. It sounded like at any moment it would shatter. Or he would.

The Royal Guards, Grace realised. The ones manning the borders, and the naval ships. And the nobles who were in the queen's favour. The ones that served Aurelie. Divinities, what was she doing? But how could Aurelie do something like this? Kidnap people perhaps, command them to the palace in Bastien's name, sure. But this? Just lock them away and hope no one noticed?

But someone had noticed. She had.

'Bastien?' she whispered.

'It's my fault. I should never have told them… I shouldn't have…' He pressed his hands to either side of his head, his face crumpling up in despair.

Some of them had been here for weeks…

This is what Simona had told him back in the king's chamber. He hadn't known. Grace was sure of that. Or at least, she wanted to believe that. The Bastien she knew would never have gone along with this.

She pressed her hand to his back, right between his shoulder blades. He was trembling, rage and pain undoing him. Slowly she circled him, trying not to look at the rows of sleeping bodies. She focused on him, and gently, carefully, took his hands in hers and pulled them away from his face. 'Can you stop it? Can you set them free?'

At that moment, a voice rang out across the room, full of outrage and officious fury. 'What are you doing here?' And she knew it. Knew it at once. It explained far more than Bastien ever could. 'You can't be in here.'

Merlyn Hale stood at the doorway, still dressed as a healer in spite of all the new evidence of his true vocation, rows of empty jars in a trolley in front of him. Restocking or something horribly mundane like that. Changing over the vessels storing stolen magic. Checking the connections perhaps. Making sure none of them burned out. Like it was a normal part of his day.

Oh, he had studied the mageborn all right. He'd studied them, and dissected them, and experimented on them. He'd ushered them away from Bastien and down here. And now he was their keeper.

And if they did burn out, if the syphon killed them and left them dead and drained, those terrible burns on their hands, what then? Dump them in an alleyway in some dead-end part of the city perhaps?

Grace turned, knives in her hands ready to throw. But she didn't get the chance.

Bastien turned at the same moment and the blood drained from Hale's thin face. 'Your… your highness…'

He moved to slam the door but Bastien was quicker. The heavy oak ripped off the frame and then shattered into splinters that hung in the air like arrows poised to fire, all pointing at his assistant.

'*Hale*,' he whispered, and the voice hardly sounded like his. It reverberated with magic, and untold anger. It barely sounded human. '*What is the meaning of this?*'

'Your highness, I… I was only… I had orders. And the work… You understand… the research…'

The splinters hummed in fury. Bastien scowled and Grace remembered why others feared him so much, why even she had at first. And why, perhaps, she still should. '*The research…*' he murmured. '*You kept them. You locked them up here.*'

Hale staggered back, terrified, and turned as if to run, but in that moment the splinters released, thousands of them, great and small. They sliced through the air and struck him everywhere, throwing him back against the wall behind with a sickening crunch. He slid down, leaving a smear of blood behind him.

'*There isn't time*,' Bastien said, his voice like ice, echoing strangely with his power. '*Or I'd have made it last longer.*'

He took a step forward and his knees almost gave way. Grace caught him, holding him up. 'Bastien, are you…'

For a moment he didn't know her. She saw his confusion all over his face as the light spilled down his face like tears.

'*They agreed*,' he murmured. '*But not to this. It was one day. Homage is just one day. That was the pact, the agreement. All those years ago. One day, to come to me, and kneel, and swear service. To secure their power and keep them safe. That was all. Not... this...'*

Grace didn't know what to say to that. There was agreement and agreement, wasn't there? It was hard to disagree when surrounded by armed guards or facing the most notorious man in the kingdom, second only to the king himself and the one most likely to succeed him on the throne.

Except he wasn't now, was he? No matter what Simona said. They wouldn't be running if there was any chance Bastien could actually become king. Did he know that? Did he realise? Or with all that power winnowing through him and this nightmare in front of him, did he even care?

She followed him as he walked forward, reaching the first cot and laying his hands on either side of the young man's head.

'What are you doing?' Grace asked. She could feel the air moving, the tingle of magic scraping over her skin. Without a word, Bastien reached out and touched her hand. It was the briefest contact before he turned to the next bed and mirrored the same action.

Grace blinked. The world around her shifted and blurred. And then she could see threads of light, everywhere, like a spider web, each one grounded in one of the sleepers. It vanished into their chests, right into the solar plexus. Except for the man Bastien had already touched, and the one he held now. The thread unravelled as she watched, uncoiling and releasing him.

'Where... where am I?' The voice was groggy, exhausted. She turned to find the first man starting to sit up. He looked around, his expression bewildered.

Ellyn was first to him, professional instincts taking over. 'Take it easy. We're here to help.'

He stared at her and then reached his hand up to his throat, where the collar still hugged him, the light in the sigil fading.

'My… my Lord Prince?' said someone else, the second man, a bit older and thicker-set, his accent showing his rural background.

Bastien moved on, and all the while those who awoke gazed at him groggily, waiting for a response while he continued to work, cutting off the threads tethering them to whoever was benefitting from their magic. At the same time Grace could feel him shoring up their powers, whatever they might be, anchoring them deep inside each mageborn, and strengthening them, draining himself of all the stored magic a little at a time. The jars they held were abandoned on the cots, empty again. Grace wished she had time to smash every single one.

By the time he reached the last mageborn, he had lost that glow, the golden hues fading until he was just Bastien again. His shoulders sagged a little and he hung his head. Exhausted, drained. Grace pressed her hand to his back again and a surge of warmth spread through her. He straightened and looked directly at her for the first time since he had flooded his body with stolen magic.

He tried to smile but it didn't extend beyond the corners of his mouth. The weight of sorrow in his eyes flooded her and she pressed her hand more firmly against him, hoping it would give him some small comfort. He was listening to something, something she couldn't hear.

'Take a moment,' she told him.

'We don't have a moment,' he replied. 'Do we?'

He was right. Damn it he was right. From far above them, reverberating through the stone, rebounding down the stairwells and the tunnels, the sound came of the palace bells ringing. All the bells, every one, ringing out the life of a king, ringing for his death, ringing in the reign of a new monarch.

Grace hesitated for only a moment. Then she dropped to her knees. With a rush of sound, she realised the others did likewise and Bastien stood in front of them. He had never looked so lost.

'Please, don't,' he whispered, his voice suddenly hoarse.

'Divinities be with the king,' said Ellyn, in a firm, loud voice and the others took up the cry. 'Long may he reign.'

'I can't. You know I can't. We have to leave.' He seized Grace by the shoulders and drew her back up to her feet. 'We have to get them out of here, and quickly.'

'We have to get you to safety,' she told him but he shook his head.

'There is nowhere safe. The mageborn, that's what's important. These people. We have to get them clear of the palace and out of the city, or they are never getting out.'

'Bastien, if you take the throne, if you stand against her—'

He touched the warrant hanging around her neck, a cautious, glancing brush of his fingers. 'She'll find a way to control me. She'll wipe out everything there is of me and start again. I won't even know it. It's too much of a risk, Grace. Too much of a liability. With that, or with you, with something else. They'll never stop. Not with the power I can offer them. No, Simona was right, Marius was right. If they can control me, they can control all the mageborn. That's how it works, Lucien Larelwynn's pact. She won't just be content to rule as a queen. Her ambition goes beyond that now. Hers and Miranda's… We have to run.'

He was panicking. She knew he was. The problem was, she believed him. His affinity with the other mageborn, their devotion to him… it was dangerous.

'And your people?' Daniel asked. His voice came out harder than Grace had ever heard it sound. 'The others. Who aren't mageborn. What about them?'

'My people…' and he sighed. The struggle marred his face for a moment and then he pulled that mask over him again. 'Will have to follow us. Or endure. Or escape as the mageborn have. Or… if your brother is anything to go by, Officer Parry, find a way to profit. There are free mageborn out there, beyond our borders. Larks, I believe is the term. That's what they call them when they flee Rathlynn, isn't it? When you load them on ships and help them get away from collars and vassalage and days of homage?' Daniel flinched back and went silent. He eyed the Lord of Thorns more carefully. 'I am no threat, Daniel. You can see that. We want the same thing. Come now, if we are to make it to the Academy, we must leave.'

'Danny?' Grace asked. 'What's he talking about?'

'I… I can explain. Later. I promise. He's right. We have to leave.'

She nodded. She knew he was right. She didn't want him to be, but it didn't matter what she wanted. Not any more. He was the king, even if he would never wear the crown. And her duty was to him. Her heart… well, her heart didn't really get a say in this, but she already knew she would do anything to keep him safe.

*

The tunnels led down, into the lowest levels of the palace, places best forgotten about. They were only a small group, twenty mageborn, three officers and one king. And the bells followed them, mocking them all the way. One of the mageborn had a tattered cloak and they tried their best to disguise Bastien with it. It wouldn't hold up to more than a glance, Grace knew that, but it was the best they could do.

Bastien led them through the narrow, drain-like tunnels and then out into stables at the back of an abandoned inn. Grace had passed it a dozen times in the last five years and never looked at it twice. She'd thought she knew every inch of Rathlynn. Missing this seemed like an affront to her knowledge. She didn't like it. The blood royal of Larelwynn kept more secrets than the acolytes of the Little Goddess. They pushed open the doors lined with peeling paint and thick with ivy growth, and the mageborn – each of them taking Bastien's hand once, pressing it to their lips – took their leave and vanished into the city.

To Grace's surprise, Daniel had spoken to each of them in turn on the way down, his manner solemn and firm. The words had been the same.

'Go to the Larks' Rest in Eastferry. Ask for Kurt. Tell him *a bird must fly* and do what he says.'

Grace pulled him aside. 'What the hell does that mean?' she asked.

Daniel shrugged. 'It's a way out, Grace. What Bastien was saying. How do you think Kurt keeps in business?'

'Kurt? By cheating everyone and everything going.'

Daniel gave a brief, bitter laugh. 'You always thought the worst of him, didn't you? He gets mageborn out of Rathlynn. The Larks, Grace. It's so bloody obvious. I can't tell you the number of people I've sent to him over the years. Misha too. Misha gave me the idea. He started it.'

'Misha Harper? Your boyfriend?'

'He wasn't… I mean, he is now. I mean, I hope he is. I… I mean…'

This was getting her nowhere. 'Mageborn? Any of them? The ones we hunted, the ones who killed or controlled others… the ones who…'

'No! Not the dangerous ones, I promise. But the others. Like Katy Frewen and Styl Greysen, remember? The ones who were being exploited and used. The kids from the docks and… The ones who wouldn't be safe here… People like them.' He nodded after the now vanished group.

'I'm going to need to have words with Kurt,' she said. 'And this Misha character, leading you astray.'

'It isn't really astray if it's the right thing to do, Grace.'

She hated it when he was right.

The bells were still ringing, louder now, and clearer, the sound reverberating over the city. There was a mild air of panic to the place, a hum of danger and the threat of chaos. As if something might boil over at any moment.

It didn't take long until Ellyn spotted someone she knew. While Grace waited with Bastien and Daniel, the little Valenti Islander waved as if she hadn't a care in the world and chatted to the stallholder, buying a bag of sweet steamed buns while she did so.

Then she was back, handing out the pastries, her expression sombre.

'Eat them. They've just put the price up. All the prices are going to go up. The king is dead, the succession is up for grabs and the word is our boy here is the killer.'

Of course it was. Who better to blame than the monster from beneath the palace, the Lord of Thorns, the man who had run away from the bedside of the dying king.

'No one spoke for him?' Daniel asked, and Grace was sure he was genuinely surprised.

'A few did.' She glanced at Bastien, who was holding his bun like it was some kind of strange foreign object. Shock, Grace thought abstractly. Or trauma. Or grief… Perhaps all of them tangled together with guilt and magic.

Ellyn pointed up towards the hill and the palace walls which were just visible from where they were, the bells still ringing out, the statues lining the way, all graced with his face or something like it. And beyond the statues, above yellow stone walls curved inwards to the gate, above the bright blue tiles set with golden lions, the rising sun illuminated a small group of bodies impaled on spikes jutting from the barbican above the gates. The stomachs had been opened and guts spilled out like vines. The heads were missing because they'd dip them in pitch and mount them on spikes for later. It was the Tlachtlyan way. Made them last longer.

Bastien stared for the longest moment and slowly crushed the bun in his hand.

'Simona.' He whispered her name, as if he couldn't bear to say it any louder. 'And Lyssa. And…' he almost choked and then seemed to recover. The next words came out in a rush. 'They were my friends. All of them.'

The air trembled around him like a summer storm, the magic in him, even depleted, enraged and in agony over what he was seeing. They couldn't keep standing there staring, not with the whole market gathering around them. But he couldn't seem to move either. Everyone who cared about him. Everyone but her…

Ellyn spoke first. 'Sorry, your highness.'

'Bastien,' he replied absently and turned away. He wasn't forgetting the dead, Grace knew that, but he was filing it away, compartmentalising it to survive. 'The less we use titles the better from here on in.'

He was right, of course. There were probably hundreds of Bastiens in Rathlynn. Only one Lord of Thorns.

'Is there a warrant out for his arrest?' Grace asked.

'Worse, a reward. We've got to get out of this city and fast. I'm half-tempted to turn you in myself for the amount of gold they're offering.'

A reward meant anyone could try their luck if they recognised him. They needed to move fast. The Academy wasn't far, especially not using the back alleys and lanes Grace knew.

'Stay close,' she told him, even though she knew she didn't have to. 'Keep your head down and keep up.'

*

There was no one on guard duty at the door. That was the first thing that set her nerves on edge. There was always someone on guard duty, even if it was only a couple of recruits. That was Craine's way and it was unchanging.

Daniel came to a halt, uncertain. He noticed it too. The whole place was too quiet. It was past mid-morning, almost lunch. The Academy ought to have been a hive of activity.

But it was silent. Still.

Grace had to force herself to keep walking forwards. As she got nearer, she drew her sword and heard the others follow suit. She didn't think Bastien had a weapon other than magic but she hoped it would be enough. Something was wrong here. Terribly wrong.

'Report,' she called out, in as casual a voice as she could.

No one answered.

Shit.

She gave a brief hand signal to the others who fanned out on either side of her, flanking Bastien.

And then she smelled it.

'Divinities, no.' The rush of panic was more than she could control. The same stench, the same sickly sweet stench that had lingered after that Gore wherever he killed. She knew that smell.

It had cost her Kai. It wasn't going to cost her everyone else as well.

'Bastard,' she spat as she entered the marshalling square and knew it was too late. A Gore had been here, all right, more than one. And a Flint, a Shade, a Brawn... And others. Not ones born with their abilities perhaps, but just as powerful despite that. Powerful and wildly unstable. Without the limitations of a collar, or any real understanding of what they were doing.

The bodies were twisted, burned, broken. Some had the pallor of drowning victims, the blue lips, their skin and hair still wet, lying in puddles. Some were charred beyond recognition and still more had been unravelled from inside. Some looked to have choked to death, or died from fright. Some had simply been torn apart. People she had known all her life. People she had hardly known at all. Not one of them was mageborn.

The sound of retching made her turn, and Ellyn bent double, throwing up the mangled remains of the bun she'd managed to wolf down earlier. Daniel looked grim and terrible. Bastien's face was white with rage, his eyes so very dark, a study in contrasts.

'Any survivors?' Grace asked and her voice came out grating against her tight throat.

'It's a massacre,' Daniel replied. 'Whoever did this—'

'We know who did this,' she snapped. Mother Miranda, the queen, Lord Asher Kane… one of them anyway, all of them. 'Find Craine. She's got to be all right. She has to be here somewhere.'

They followed a trail of blood and scattered bodies, not Academy these ones. Royal Guards and others out of uniform. They'd tried to take on Craine. Maybe they'd thought a crippled commander wouldn't be a challenge. They'd learned differently.

Craine was in her office. And true to form, hard as nails, she wasn't dead. Not quite yet.

She'd propped herself up at her desk, somehow, and she was peppered with wounds. Some might have been recoverable from, if it hadn't been for the dozen that should have already killed her.

''Bout time you got here,' she rasped as Grace crashed through the open door.

'Craine?'

She tried to push herself up in the chair but didn't have the strength. 'They knew you were coming here. Simona…'

'She told them?'

Craine tried to smile. 'I doubt she had a lot of choice. Not when they cut off her head and pulled her thoughts out of her brain.'

'We saw the body. She's dead.'

'Tends to happen when you do that.'

'But her plan, her escape…'

'I'm not sure she had a plan for her own escape. Just yours… and his…' Her eyes focused past Grace's shoulder and the looming sense of Bastien filled Grace's senses. 'Hello, your majesty.'

'I'm not…' he started but his voice trailed off. For a moment he was silent and then he sighed. 'I can help. With the pain.'

Not to heal her. She was too far gone for that. Not that she would have let him.

'I'm sure you can. In a moment then. In a moment. I need to talk to Captain Marchant first.' She reached out.

Grace wrapped her own hand around her commander's. Blood covered it up to the wrist. It was slick and warm against her skin. The other hand she held pressed into her stomach, the wound there staining everything crimson and black.

'Tell me,' Grace said. 'Tell me whatever you can.'

'You can't leave by the gates. That was Simona's plan. They'll look for you overland. The quickest way to his stronghold… don't go that way now.'

'We won't. I'll find another—'

'Danny can sort that. Can't you, Danny? Larks' Path, wasn't it?'

Grace heard his voice from behind them, a small sob of despair. And then he found some strength to force out the words. 'I can. I will, I swear it.'

'And Ellyn... where is Ellyn?'

'Guarding the way in. She's... she's just...'

'I'll get her,' Daniel offered.

'No,' Craine replied before he could take off. 'No, leave it. She doesn't need to see this... Our mageborn... they took our mageborn. Those they could. We tried to hold ground. Took down some of them. But the other cadets... Don't... don't go down to the baths.' Her voice broke off and she swallowed hard, three or four times, choking. Daniel scrambled forward trying to reach her water jug which he lifted to her mouth. He cradled her head as he helped her drink. It helped, a little. But nothing was really going to help her now. 'Just leave. Be strong. And remember what you can do, Grace, what you can take. Remember your loyalties. And don't lose heart.'

'Where are the others?' Grace asked. 'Everyone can't have been here. Everyone can't be dead.'

Craine tried to shake her head but choked on blood as she did so. 'Not all. Some turned on us. Some were... were with them. They took the mageborn, the ones who couldn't fight back. Marched them off.'

Grace didn't ask where. She glanced at the pained and horrified expression on Bastien's face and she didn't have to.

'We can find them,' she whispered. 'We can—'

Craine's grip tightened abruptly, vice-like and terrible. The action brought Grace's attention back to her blood-smeared face, her ice-blue eyes, the glare that brooked no dissent.

'That would be just. And it would be honourable. But it isn't the time for those things. Not any more. Later perhaps… you'll know when. Lara will find you. I know she will. She'll be angry too. Tell her… tell her…' Craine choked, then swallowed hard, a gasp of pain cutting her off. 'Tell her I regret nothing. You get your king to safety. Otherwise… otherwise all is lost. Understand?'

What could she do but nod? What choice did she have?

Craine pulled her hand free of Grace's, briefly patted her cheek like a fond maiden aunt and fixed her arctic gaze on Bastien. 'If you would, your majesty?'

As far as Grace knew there was not a shred of magic in Craine. Never had been, never would be. But Bastien took her hand, and knelt beside her. The pulse of something passed through the air, through their touch, and the lines of pain on the older woman's face eased suddenly.

'Ah yes,' she said. 'I see it now. I chose well. That's good.'

And then she closed her eyes.

Carefully, almost reverently, Bastien put her hand on the desk. For all the world it might have looked like she'd had just closed her eyes to contemplate her work… if you ignored the blood, and the broken crutches. If you closed your eyes to the devastation around her.

Craine was at her desk in the Academy, doing her duty to the last. They couldn't let her death be in vain.

*

Ellyn found the bodies in the baths, the water turned red, the walls and ceiling dripping where it had surged up to take those not already dead. All the quotidian cadets, scattered across the now tranquil surface like flotsam and jetsam. Too many of them, too young, far too young. There hadn't been time to pass on Craine's warning and Ellyn had gone looking for survivors while they found the commander. She hadn't found a single living soul. She told them between sobs when they found her sitting in the corridor leading down there, her knees drawn up to her chest, her long white-blonde hair wet and bloodstained.

'I couldn't do anything to help. I was too late.'

Daniel gathered her up in his arms. 'We were all too late.'

'The commander?' Ellyn asked.

'She's dead.' The words came out with a bite of sharp reality and Grace instantly regretted it. 'We have to leave before the Royal Guard do another sweep looking for us here. If they know we were meant to come here, they know they missed us the first time—'

'They know,' Bastien interrupted.

Overhead, they heard horses' hooves, the courtyard filling with the shouts and cries of a mounted group. Orders being yelled, directions handed out.

'Fuck,' Grace said. 'Time's up. We have to get out of here. Weapons check.'

Ellyn was strapping a belt full of throwing knives and sigils around her waist. Tears still clung to her eyes. Daniel had found another sword from somewhere and slung it over his back. Grace nodded as he handed her more sigils, all designed to clip to her belt, and her baldric. They glowed when she touched them.

'But we don't have a plan,' Bastien said, looking at her helplessly.

'Simona told them.' She handed him a sword belt and waited until he finally moved to strap it across his back. It suited him.

'Then we do what we always do. We improvise. Danny, take point. You know the way best.'

'Wasn't that the only way in?' the Lord of Thorns asked, still bewildered by her cold efficiency. She wanted to explain that it was the only way to get through this, that if she stopped to feel any of this she'd be unable to continue. That seeing Craine like that had broken something inside her, something that might never recover. She couldn't feel anything now because there was just too much. There wasn't time.

'The Academy Gates?' Daniel gave a brief bitter laugh. 'For formal occasions, sure. You have the Rats' Path from the palace but we have the Cadet's Path to the bars. Ellyn?'

Ellyn shook herself back into a form of an Academy officer, even if no Academy of any worth existed any more. Divinities, Grace loved them. More than she could ever say out loud. They were her strength.

'Which way?' Bastien asked.

'Up,' said Ellyn. 'When in doubt, we go up.'

Chapter Twenty-One

The terracotta roof tiles slid and skittered underfoot. The wind whipped fiercely around them, blowing his black hair into his eyes, and Bastien, determined not to let the three Academy officers see how much heights bothered him, balled his fists up so tight that his nails dug painfully into his palms. He lived in a tower on top of a palace on top of a mountain, for the divinities' sakes. He walked along paths and ramparts a hundred times higher than this every day.

Of course the ramparts tended not to move beneath his feet or be so old and ill-cared for that they might give way under him at any second.

Up ahead, Grace moved, light-footed as a cat, following Daniel, and he was aware that Ellyn stayed cautiously behind him all the time. Ready to catch him if he fell, no doubt. Which he was certain he could do at any second.

His stomach lurched and the world around him seemed to spin. This wasn't any way to travel. How many of their cadets had tried this and broken limbs, if not their necks? How many had dropped through into whatever gaping chasm lurked below?

The city beneath them rippled with life, with magic. Bastien could sense something building, fear and panic. Or maybe that was just him. He couldn't place the creeping dread that swelled beneath him.

They danced across the rooftops and, when they reached the edge of one, either stepped up onto the next abutting it, or jumped through the air like squirrels, crossing narrow alleys and lanes of Rathlynn as if they were streams.

And suddenly the world ahead of him fell away. They'd reached the People's Plaza, the dull smudge of Eastferry on the other side. Grace waved them back and they ducked down, sheltered by the parapet on the edge of the roof, peering over the top. The square below was full of people, his people, all the citizens of Rathlynn, or so it seemed at a glance. There were soldiers everywhere, scarlet-clad Royal Guards rushing through the crowds, pushing people aside, shouting obscenities. And he could feel the energy pushing back, the same sense of panic and alarm he had sensed before, stronger now. It was as if the life force of the city balked at their treatment, shied back and then, like a wave, broke.

'Shit, that's not good,' he heard Ellyn say as she came up behind him.

'What is it? What are they doing?' Bastien asked, as the guards tore people apart, shoving some in one direction and some in others. It was like watching a cattle mart. The ones in the square looked frightened, huddled together, desperate.

Some of them... most of them... no, all of them wore collars.

'They're separating the mageborn.'

It was impossible to see who threw the first stone. Or if it even was a stone. It could have been horseshit for all he knew. That went flying too. One second the guards were standing firm, aggressive and threatening, and the next stones and shit and anything else to hand flew at them.

It drove them back, disorganised and shocked. The people of Rathlynn weren't meant to fight back. That was what everyone in the palace thought. The common people were supposed to take orders, do as commanded and pay their taxes no matter how high they went. They were meant to cheer for the king and queen, for the nobility. They were meant to offer up their mageborn children when told to do so to the service of the crown.

It was their honour to serve.

But this wasn't service. Those people weren't being taken willingly.

With a roar, Rathlynn rose up. His people, the people of Larel-wynn... Pride was an unaccustomed feeling to Bastien but this... it bubbled up in his chest, swelling and growing.

'We need to get out of here,' Grace said.

'We can help them,' Daniel said. 'We have to do something.'

Grace hissed between her teeth and looked right at Bastien. 'We already have the making of a riot down there. Imagine what'll happen if they see him.'

That seemed to sober Daniel up. His grim expression fixed on Bastien and he nodded.

The riot came anyway, surging forward, and the guards tried to hold it back. With a cry, the mageborn already corralled broke through the lines and scattered, down the narrow streets and laneways, into buildings and out the windows on the other side. While half the city fought, the rest hid or fled.

And to his eternal shame, Bastien knew he had to flee as well. Not because he wanted to. But because Grace was right. He knew the mageborn reaction to him, what they wanted of him, what so many others feared. He also knew the hatred Aurelie had managed to instil in many towards him, mageborn and quotidian alike, the fear with which she had wielded his name. She'd made the Lord of Thorns into another Hollow King in the popular imagination. He was a fool to think it wouldn't matter. That she'd someday bear Marius a son and be happy with that while he, as an uncle, would step aside to serve his new king. Or that somehow, someway, Marius would recover.

She had never wanted that.

Damn it, he had been such a fool. Perhaps he should have just done what she wanted, swallowed his pride and his loyalty, and provided her with an heir. But it would have meant betraying Marius. And he couldn't have done that. He could never have done that. The king, his cousin, had been the only one who hadn't wavered in his friendship. Marius had been the constant.

She had used him, they all had, even Marius. Bastien was the fear that governed, the hand raised in threat. Even if some people, the mageborn particularly, knew otherwise, knew how he cared for them, it didn't matter. The myth was all that mattered. That was what people believed. Not a barely glimpsed truth seen only from a distance.

He had never been good at playing these games. There had never been a need for him to do it. That had been Marius's skill.

A soft wind, like a whisper, carrying the scent of apple orchards, wafted over him and his feet stumbled to a stop. He stood there, transfixed.

Don't go. Don't leave me.

Celeste?

Brother, please. Don't leave me.

He looked back. He could make out the towers of the Great Temple, the rose windows blazing with the evening sun. She was in there, locked up and used, feeding the power of Mother Miranda and the divinities knew who else.

Celeste, I can't... I promise, I'll...

He almost heard her laugh, or felt it perhaps. Whatever spells she was weaving, or whatever madness was letting her contact him this way, he didn't know. It was beyond him. But not beyond her.

So many promises, little brother…

That didn't sound like Celeste. And yet it was her voice. His legs suddenly felt weak and his head swam again. When you reached into the pool of magic, he recalled being told once, long ago, other things can reach back. The more magic you pulled into yourself, or through yourself from its netherworld, the more you risked those other things finding a foothold as well.

Divinities, Celeste, what have you done?

He stood on a rooftop, over a city at war with itself, and wondered what had been unleashed here. And how.

A booming voice broke the silence around him.

'Guards of the blood royal, stand ready!'

Something in the air shuddered again. He felt it, like the threat of thunder in the distance. Something was happening. Something magical. Something that should never happen.

'Guards of the blood royal, prepare!'

He knew that voice. Knew it too well. It was artificially amplified, and that made it sound deeper, more resounding, more impressive. But he knew it.

Kane?

You were my friend once, remember? You and I were friends?

Kane didn't seem to remember one damned thing about him. And Kane's eyes, his deep blue eyes, were darker than ever before.

When you reach into the pool of magic…

You can't take the throne. Not you, nor your line…

Precious few people knew about his family line, or about Celeste. They knew about him, about the Lord of Thorns. And about his father who had been dead before he ever knew him. About his mother who had been called a glory and died while he lived.

But Asher Kane did. Or had. Once.

Asher's sister had died… he tried to focus on that. Asher's sister had died, there had been an accident and… But Bastien hadn't been responsible. He knew that. He was sure he knew that.

Asher's memories were as broken as Bastien's own. Which could mean only one thing. Aurelie hadn't been as hesitant about using the drug on others. Or about the use of magic.

How long had Miranda and Aurelie been feeding Kane stolen magic? How much damage had already been done?

'Guards of the blood royal…' The power in the air shimmered and shook, trembling like a wave about to crest.

'Grace! Get down!' Bastien yelled.

Up ahead, on the rooftop's edge, she hesitated, turning, confused by what he was saying, what she was feeling. Because she had to be feeling it too. He knew she was.

'Attack!' Kane yelled.

Fire and wind unleashed itself, water ripped through the mob. The earth itself reared up beneath them and flung them aside. The screams of people trapped in a moment of agony rose like the music of nightmares. The power of Flint, Gore, Loam and Tide eviscerated the people of Rathlynn trying to fight for their family members. The mageborn still trapped in the centre of the plaza screamed and fell, clutching their heads as their magic was ripped from them and used against their will.

And somewhere, because Bastien's instincts told him it was going to happen, someone with the stolen power of a Loam, who had no clear idea of what they were doing with it, wrenched up the wrong piece of earth, the wrong stones from the ground to hurl at an attacker, and the building they were perched upon gave a terrible groan and collapsed underneath them.

*

He struggled out of the devastation, coughing, his chest aching. There was no sign of Grace. No sign of anyone.

Bastien stumbled forward. 'Grace?' His voice came out harsh and breathless, no use at all. 'Grace?'

'Over here!' But it wasn't Grace's voice. It was Daniel Parry. 'Hurry up. Help!'

The officer was on his hands and knees, pulling at the rubble, his hands bleeding. Covered in dust and dirt, he didn't look up until Bastien joined him in the hollow he'd already managed to clear.

'She's down here. I heard her. She has to be…'

Bastien dropped to his knees beside him and started to haul stones and tiles off the area. 'Ellyn?'

'She's okay. Hurt her arm and shoulder but she's fine. We were at the edge, jumped clear. But Grace…'

'You're sure she's here?' If they were digging in the wrong place, if they were too late…

'I'm sure. See for yourself. You can do it, can't you? Lord of the Mageborn and all that.'

Normally Bastien would take slight at anyone talking to him like that. Normally. But nothing was normal any more.

He stretched out his senses and there it was, a glow, faint and fluttering, but he would have known it anywhere. That stubborn little flame at the heart of a Flint. His Flint.

Beneath them, something moved.

'Grace!' Daniel shouted, but Bastien just moved faster, tearing back rubble and debris. And there she was, curled up in the hollow they'd exposed, grey and dusty and so so small. Blood covered one side of her face. But that was nothing compared to the blood soaking the clothes around the shard of wood jutting from her side.

Daniel seemed to freeze as he saw it, the extent of Grace's injuries taking the strength out of him.

Bastien's stomach dropped as if he'd hurtled out of the tallest tower in the palace. This couldn't be happening. Not this. Not now. He hadn't even managed to tell her how he felt. He hadn't even managed to figure that out for himself, not really. It slammed into him with a force he could barely withstand now.

He needed her. Not to be his, or to be with him, or anything as facile as that. He simply needed her. To be. Alive. In this world.

'No,' he whispered and the dark pool of magic that always lurked below him shuddered to wakefulness.

But it was Daniel who reached for her first, scrambling to get to her. Bastien followed, hardly daring to breathe, lest he dislodge the remaining wall and rubble or lose the thin wedge of control still holding him together.

Daniel looked up at him, holding a slender hand in his. Grace's skin was far too pale and she didn't respond. She didn't even move. Not even a flicker of a breath.

If Daniel told him to leave, would he? If he told him she wasn't his concern, that she wouldn't want magic used upon her in any circumstances, would he actually be able to bring himself to back away? She'd told him. There could be no doubt of her wishes. He could save her but she'd been clear. No magic.

But Daniel's voice was fierce. It came out in a roar of pain and torment. It was unequivocal.

'Do something!'

Bastien didn't need to be told twice. Divinities forgive him, he didn't even argue. It was an instinct, a natural urge, something as easy as breathing. All his life magic had been something to control, something to be stamped down and yoked.

But now… now…

He sank to his knees beside her and felt it course through his veins like lightning.

'Hold her,' he told Daniel. His voice didn't even sound like his own voice. It reverberated, echoed, as if coming from far beyond him, from within the pool itself. There was so much power, more than he had ever imagined. He seized it all.

'*There's more magic in you than I've ever sensed,*' Grace had said. '*More than should be possible. More than should even be safe.*'

Was this what she had meant? What had she sensed in him that made her pull away from his magic so completely?

Daniel pulled Grace into his arms and she gave a soft cry. Still alive, still there… but the pain in it almost stopped his heart.

And something else, hungry and urgent, beat in its place.

It burned.

He worked on instinct, or perhaps memory. There was no telling which. As he pressed his hands to her wound, felt the kiss of her blood on his fingertips, that *other* took over.

Darkness rushed through him. It was strong, powerful, and it relished its sudden freedom. He struggled to contain it, to focus it and force it to do his will. He wrestled it into a tool instead of a weapon, even though he could suddenly see what a formidable weapon it could be.

Simona had said so many times that control was everything, that he should never do this. But Simona was dead. So was Marius. Everyone was dead.

He was not going to let Grace join them.

He forced the spear of wood from her body, commanded her skin and veins to reknit themselves, thrust the life back into her. He demanded that she breathe, that her heart keep beating, that her strength return. He made her whole again.

He poured his power into her and through her, emptying himself. And the dark pool of magic surged up inside him to take its place. Every time he thought there was no more of the Maegen to help him, something else appeared, more powerful than before, filling him.

Her eyes opened. So beautiful. A clear bright gold, like sunrise on a summer's day. She gasped, sitting up in Daniel's arms, shaking herself free of him. She grabbed Bastien's shoulders and pulled him to her.

'Bastien?'

Her voice sounded so far away. The edges of his vision clouded with shadows and he felt himself falling back, down into the pool. It swallowed him, down into its darkness, and he felt the currents of it tearing away all that made him himself

Grace's hands on his face burned against his skin. 'Don't go,' she whispered. 'Bastien, please… stay with me.'

But he couldn't. He knew that. It was too late. The darkness inside him reached every nerve ending, flooded every vein. It devoured him from within.

Instead of the light, the darkness swallowed him whole.

Chapter Twenty-Two

Grace sank in the light, the Maegen, the pool dragging her down. And for once she didn't need to fight it. This was where she was meant to be. Deep in the heart of the light, flowing with it, losing herself. It was peaceful, quiet. It murmured softly, sang snatches of old songs. It caressed her aching mind, soothed her broken body. It was her home. The place she had come from. The place she belonged.

And then the shadow appeared. It spread wide black wings, like a hawk overhead, searching for prey, silhouetted against the sun.

Then the wings folded and it dropped towards her like a stone, claws extended.

But they weren't claws. A hand. It was a hand.

Bastien pulled her back. Light surged inside her and the fire blazed into new life. Her power, her magic, responding to him.

*

Pain, everywhere, just pain. Darkness and pain. And his voice.

And then light.

She was sprawled in rubble, covered in blood, but the pain was gone. The physical pain.

But Bastien's eyes were filled with golden light and his face was white and bloodless. The contrast in him had never been starker, nor his features so sharp. He hardly looked like himself. It was the statue again, the way she had first seen him, cold as stone and barely human. It was the Lord of Thorns looking back at her, not Bastien.

'Grace?' Daniel's voice shook. 'Grace, let me explain…'

But there was no time for explanations. Something was wrong, terribly wrong.

'I told him to do it,' Daniel went on, even though she was hardly listening. 'I had to. I thought you were dying…'

She glanced at him, her hands trembling as she cradled Bastien's face. 'Don't go,' she whispered. 'Bastien, please… stay with me.'

So much magic flowed through him, but it wasn't the light that had killed Kai. This was something else, something other. Far more dangerous. And he was lost in it. Lost in the darkness beyond the magical pool of the Maegen.

'Find Ellyn,' she told Daniel in as gentle a voice as possible. She needed him to go. She needed to find a way to pull Bastien back to her but she couldn't do that with him here.

'But Grace—'

'Go, Danny! We need a moment. Go and find Ellyn. Just go!' If the tone in Grace's voice didn't warn him off, her frown did. But she couldn't look away from Bastien, not for more than a moment.

A monster, he'd called himself once, just after the Flint had. Lots of people did. She had done so herself. She could see it now. The monster lurking inside the man.

'Can you hear me? Understand me?' He nodded once, slowly. She stroked his face, pressed her fingers against his lips. 'Bastien, please. Talk to me. We have to go. I need you to—'

His voice rumbled to life, the darkness making it echo like distant thunder.

'*You... you need me.*'

Well, it was something. She wasn't entirely sure what.

'Yes.' Her lips replaced her fingertips and she felt him shudder.

'There is magic in all things,' he murmured, as if talking to someone else, sharing something intimate and clandestine. 'Bright and dark, a balance. It is a pool at the heart of the world, a deep and dark place, endless and filled with both wonders and terrors.'

It sounded like he was reciting a lesson. His fingers moved, threading with hers. She'd seen this pool. She'd been in it. With him.

'Some people spend their whole lives without seeing it, some catch brief glimpses, moments of synchronicity or good and ill fortune. Some are aware of it and find it hopelessly out of their reach. They long for it and no matter how greedily they stretch out their minds and hearts for it, they cannot touch it.'

'Like Aurelie and her court. They've found a way.'

'They have,' he agreed, and this time his hand touched her hair, but carefully, reverently, as if it was a jewel beyond price or a holy relic. 'And then there are mageborn... Like us. We sense that pool as part of ourselves, we dip our fingers into it as easily as breathing. For some that is all. That is all they want.'

'What have you done?' she whispered, leaning into him. She kissed his lips again.

'I can't let you die, Grace. I need you too.'

She smiled, a brief and wobbly smile, unsure and suddenly afraid. He didn't know what he was saying. He couldn't. 'Come back to me, Bastien.'

He blinked, confused for a moment, and she was reaching him, she knew that. She had to be reaching him. But the darkness didn't fade. The otherness was still there.

'For others the pool calls so strongly. It entices us. We slide into its cool embrace. We sink down into the endless depths, where the light is just a distant shimmer overhead. And the currents there are strongest. There is so much more darkness beneath than there is light.'

He shuddered again, closed his eyes as if forcing away a migraine. She had to keep him talking, make him aware of who he really was once more, draw him back. Another part of her screamed that there wasn't time for this. That they had to run.

'What happens if you go too deep, Bastien?' she asked.

'Those who go still deeper risk losing themselves in the darkness, sinking into the heart of magic, the primal urge of creation, and deeper still. Your memories, your personality can fade into it and be lost forever. I think... I think I was almost...' He blinked, and his eyes were his own again. But not the callous and cold gaze she had first seen, nor the blazing passion that they reflected on her last night, but these eyes, dark brown and beautiful, confused and afraid. Lost. His eyes.

'It's all right, Bastien. I'm here. You're here.'

'I... I... am.' He heaved in a breath. 'But I was almost swept away in the depths. I saw...' But his voice trailed off in confusion.

'What did you see?'

He pulled her closer, his arms encircling her, his body once stiff and cold, melting against her warmth.

'If I knew... if I could remember... I don't know if I'd say even then. To name something like that is to draw its attention. Grace... I'm sorry...'

'Don't be.'

'I used my magic on you. You... you said not to do that...'

She tried to draw him to his feet, to lead him out of the rubble and make their way out to where Ellyn and Daniel stood by the end of a laneway, furtively watching the square beyond.

Bastien spoke into the silence. 'You haven't answered.'

'You haven't asked a question.'

'Forgive me.'

'Sure,' she said lightly. But Bastien stilled against her and then released her. 'Bastien?'

'Kane,' he said. 'It's Asher.'

'I know. We saw him.'

He shook his head. 'No, he's coming. He's full of power, of stolen magic.' She studied his face, and saw him again, Bastien. But a Bastien who was afraid, and confused, who didn't know what to do. 'I have to…'

And his eyes filled with light again.

'What are you doing?' she snapped.

His face turned to her and the man was gone once more, fading into the monster, full of magic and lost to her. 'I can deal with him.'

'Prince Bastien!' The voice rang out. Kane's voice. Amplified somehow, dripping with Charm, the most trustworthy voice possible. The words had been chosen with deliberate cruelty. 'We know you're there. Please, be reasonable.'

Grace felt her skin shiver as it reached them and then the magic began its work. She saw Ellyn and Daniel relax their guard, their faces softening. She felt it too. This was wrong. What they were doing was wrong. Why were they even running? It had to be a mistake.

'You need to come out now, your highness. The Queen Regent will understand. She just wants you back safe and sound. She has the most wonderful news.'

Grace found herself smiling. Wonderful news? What was it? She needed to know. She looked at the others and saw the same delight on their faces.

'Captain Marchant, if you're there, please… we just want our prince back safely. That's all any of us want. The prince needs to be here for his little nephew or niece.'

The queen was pregnant? But that *was* wonderful news. A miracle. Grace turned to Bastien to say as much and the shock made her take a step back. His eyes had turned from black to golden and bright again, lacking iris or white. Like looking into the sun itself. Incandescent and terrible.

'It's a trick,' he said, his voice a low rumble. 'A lie. It has to be.'

She almost believed him but Kane sounded so convincing. And the moment she looked away she was sure of it, sure that Kane spoke the truth and Bastien lied.

If the queen was pregnant the child had to be his. It was like a punch to the guts. Of course he would lie.

'Come back, your highness. Your people need you. The mageborn need you. Who else will speak for them?'

'Grace…' Bastien's hand closed on her shoulder and the fire in her boiled up. 'Grace, hear the truth. She wants me under her control or dead.'

Around her neck, Zavi's sigil flared into life and Grace sucked in a breath. Bastien was right. Kane had to be lying. The queen didn't want Bastien back, not really. Not with his memories intact anyway.

'I… I'm okay,' she whispered, hardly able to make her voice louder. Bastien nodded and pressed his hand on Daniel's shoulder, then Ellyn, working the same magic, draining Kane's spell from them.

'We have to get away from here,' Ellyn said, shaking herself as if coming out of a bad dream. 'Away from him.'

'And we have to get the mageborn out of the city. Starting with him.' Daniel nodded at Bastien. 'Or they'll use him to command all the others. If they have him, the other mageborn won't stand a chance. Please, Grace…'

Grace knew it was true. Convincing Bastien to run before the others were free… that could be the trick. And still Asher Kane went on speaking, his voice melodious, his words… convincing… but not quite the lies they had been. A new tactic. A much more dangerous one.

'What about Celeste, Bastien? What should I tell her?'

For a moment Grace thought it would still be okay. But then Bastien tore himself free of them. He made it three or four steps before she caught up with him and hauled him back to relative safety.

'They won't hurt her. She's in the Temple. They need her.'

'Only because they don't have me.'

'And Danny's right. If they have you, the mageborn will end up like no more than cattle. Or dead. You can't let that happen.'

She watched the knowledge of it play out on his face. The abject misery that came on him when the truth of it settled in. Then something else. Resignation. Determination.

'But we could rescue her. We could get her out. They're using her. Feeding on her. And I think… I think, she's helping them with these tethers, these syphons. She must be. They've deceived her, or forced her to help. We have to rescue her.'

He made a good point. But there wasn't the time. A rescue operation like that would take planning, and far more people than the four of them. No, they needed to get him out of Rathlynn. Then, maybe, then she could work something out.

'Later. We'll talk. We'll make a plan. I'll go back for her if you want me to. But right now, Bastien, we have got to go.'

'Promise,' he whispered harshly. But she had learned long ago not to make any promises.

They were hard to keep.

'Later.' That was all she could say. 'Now shut up and move out.'

He didn't move. Perhaps he couldn't. Not with that much magic in him, that much power. He was fighting her, fighting Kane, fighting his own nature. Everything pulled him in different directions. And they were running out of time as Kane's people surrounded the area and started to move in. Basic tactics. Keep them talking. If that didn't work, use the time to get into position. He might have the power of a Charm now, but Asher Kane had the mind of a general.

Which left only one thing. If they were going to get out of this, Grace needed to take control, to make Bastien do as she said. She didn't want to. Every instinct told her it was wrong.

Grace grabbed Zavi's sigil, and pulled hard. The leather thong snapped and she lunged for Bastien. She couldn't think about what she was doing, what she was doing to him… It was wrong, but it was necessary. The sigil flared to brightness, stronger than any she had ever handled. Whatever Zavi had done to this thing, its power was beyond any other she'd ever used. The fire in her flared with it, the Flint powering the sigil. She pushed Bastien back against the wall, pinning him there with her body, and let it unfurl.

'No!' he managed, just that single word, as it seized him, bound him. His eyes widened, his own eyes once more as she snatched control away from him, but the deep soft brown was bewildered and angry. 'Grace, please… don't do this. You don't understand…'

Oh she did. That was the problem. She knew she was betraying him, yet another person taking his freedom and his choices from him, and she was going to do it anyway. Regardless of his feelings or hers. Because she had to. She wrapped her hand around the warrant and felt it warm beneath her touch. Bastien shuddered, staring at her, his eyes wide in horror, the pupils blown out to great dark holes.

'Do as I say,' she told him, the magic of the warrant commanding him, the magic of the sigil controlling him. 'And no more magic. We aren't facing Kane now. We run. We're heading into Eastferry and we'll hide. Then we'll find a way out of the city, without you using magic at all, understand? Celeste will have to wait. Danny, lead the way.'

For a moment she thought Daniel or Ellyn might argue, or tell her that what she was doing was wrong. Because it was. Everything about it was wrong. She loathed herself for it. But something could be awful, and still be necessary. The hard decisions required that understanding.

But his face... divinities, the betrayal on his face.

Ellyn and Daniel just nodded and fell into step. Bastien lurched into a forced march beside her, his mouth a thin hard line. And she hated herself for doing this to him.

*

The streets of the city were in chaos. People ran in panic, mageborn and quotidian alike. Those who could escape were fleeing, but the word was that the gates were already closed. The ports were still open, but not for long.

When they finally made it to Kurt's bar, the taproom was full of the City Watch.

Grace took one look, swore and pulled her sword.

Suddenly there were weapons everywhere, men and women on their feet, everyone shouting.

'Stand down!' Kurt yelled from the bar. He brandished the club he kept there like it was a blessed relic. 'This is my place and my rules. Anyone breaks my truce and you'll regret it. All of you.'

A brief moment of doubt passed over the crowd. 'We're here to parlay,' said the guard nearest the door. A lieutenant, Grace saw. Not much older than she was. But still about the oldest there.

'Where are your superiors?' she asked, praying Bastien was still behind her and out of sight.

'They're dead, Duchess,' Kurt said. 'Much like yours. The Royal Guard are all the law we have in Rathlynn now. And the army answers to them.'

The young lieutenant lowered his sword carefully, showed his hands and then sheathed the blade. A peace gesture. Slowly the others followed suit, as did Grace, after a moment or two.

'They came to the watch house. They… they were mageborn. But they weren't. I don't know. No collars so we didn't realise. But they just started killing everyone in their way. We only just got away.'

The law does not bend, and cannot break. She'd learned that in the Academy. The Watch held the same maxim. It was everything. And now… now the law wasn't just broken. It was shattered.

'No law in Eastferry though, Kurt?' she said, hoping it might lighten the mood.

'None but me,' he said. 'What have you been doing with my little brother? Misha sent you a message, Danny. It's behind the bar.' He shook his head as Daniel made a beeline for it. 'Look like you've all been in the wars.'

Who hadn't? Looking around the room, Grace could see nothing but wounds, haggard faces and tension.

Daniel unfolded a ragged bit of paper and turned away. He didn't look happy about it, whatever it was. Maybe his harper had already left town.

And that was the room Bastien walked into. There was a shocked silence and the guards stared. He wasn't meant to be here. Not him. They all recognised him instantly. The rush to bow or raise arms again left everyone in a tangle of confusion.

'Enough,' Grace snapped. 'Kurt, Danny, we need to get the hell out of Rathlynn and I need your help. Now.'

Kurt stared at Bastien. No bow from him. Not for anyone.

'All right. We can do something. Not right away. You'll have to hide out here until we're ready. You'll have to trust me, Duchess.' Easier said than done, but what choice did she have? She nodded, just once, and he grinned without humour before turning his attention back to the Lord of Thorns. 'Come in then, your highness. You wouldn't want to draw any undue attention, would you?'

If Bastien cared, he didn't show it. The sigil still glowed around his neck and every time she saw it, her stomach sank. She'd betrayed him. When he needed her most, when he'd saved her life, she'd collared him and commanded him with magic.

She needed to explain. She needed… no, it wasn't about what she needed right now. She had to think. She had to plan.

Prying eyes were their worst enemy. They might be safe in Eastferry, but with a pack of guards and a lot of people hungry and in need of money, not to mention the whole city in uproar… she wasn't so sure. Kurt's reputation might defend them a little. That was what she was counting on.

Getting away from Kane and his stolen magic had left them all drained. What they'd seen had left them reeling. Grace was half dead on her feet, the adrenaline wearing off.

'Bastien,' she said and he stopped beside her. She reached out to him to remove the sigil but he flinched back abruptly, just for a moment before he stopped himself. He lifted his chin, looking over her head, and she stared up at him. He looked every inch a king, or a martyr perhaps. 'I'm sorry,' she said. 'I had to.'

'You had to,' he repeated. She wasn't sure if he was agreeing with her or not. It didn't really sound like it.

The sigil came off easily and he sighed with relief, unable to keep it in. For a moment she thought he might shout or leave. He just looked down at the thing in her hand as if it was a scorpion. He'd never trust her again. Not so long as she had it. The feeling that she'd broken something between them was a barb deep in her heart. And there was nothing she could do about it now.

'Danny,' she said. 'Mind this for me, will you?'

'You sure?' He didn't look eager. His face was so pale, his mouth a grim line. 'That's... that's a strong one.'

'Zavi's best.' And possibly his last. She didn't want to say that. She didn't want to be reminded. No one knew what had happened to Zavi. There had been no trace of him at the Academy. Like so many others. 'Just... just take it.'

Daniel slid it into a pocket and turned to follow Kurt.

Kurt didn't lead them to one of the shabby rooms upstairs this time, but rather, once they reached the stairs and were out of sight, he led them to a panel in the wall which opened when he touched it in just the right place. From there, they went down into darkness.

In the cellars, there were more stairs, equally hidden.

'You have your own Rats' Path,' Bastien muttered and Kurt grinned back at him.

'The Larks' Path. Everyone needs a way out, don't they?'

Everyone. Especially criminals and royalty.

As they made their way down the two flights of creaking stairs, underneath the inn, a rabbit warren of tunnels spread out. The passage was narrow and dimly lit, a dirt floor underneath them swallowing sounds. It was bare and basic, all earth-colours and undecorated. Paint flaked from the mismatched doors and any repairs were haphazard. There were small rooms, and behind those doors sounds of life. But the doors were tightly closed and any still open were slammed shut before they got near.

'Friendly place,' Ellyn murmured.

'They're scared,' was all Daniel said in reply.

'Aren't we all?' Ahead of them Kurt stopped by an open door. 'What about the Watch upstairs?' she asked him.

'Don't think there is a Watch any more, gorgeous. Don't worry. I'll keep them up there and take care of them.'

'Take care or *take care*?' The emphasis was different and they all knew what Ellyn meant.

Kurt just grinned down at her. It wasn't an especially nice grin.

'Whatever do you take me for, Ellyn? They're desperate people in need of safe harbour. That's what Eastferry is, after all.'

'Parry's Watch now, is it?' Grace asked.

He just shrugged. 'They'll have to quit wearing uniforms and standing to attention but yeah, why not? Eastferry's mine. The people here, quots and mageborn, they live together peaceably enough. It's better for business this way.'

Bastien smiled. 'Are you declaring independence?' There was a strange edge to his voice.

Kurt's face went oddly still and the wheeler-dealer act fell away. Grace saw a man who had a community to care for and protect, by any means necessary. Much like Bastien.

'It won't be long before they come for us. I'm not a fool to think we're safe here. Eastferry's tough enough to get into but throw enough arms at it, especially if they have magic too... well...' He raked his hand through the scrappy dark hair. 'It's still my home, your high and mightiness. I don't like people interfering with my home.'

'Neither do I,' Bastien said.

It was as much of an agreement as they were likely to express outright. Kurt just nodded. 'There's rooms down here, not a lot of space but enough for a night or two. Beds, somewhere to wash. Hide out here and Danny and I can sort out passage for you out of Rathlynn. We'll need to go through Belport, but don't worry. It's in hand.'

Grace glanced at the closed doors they had passed. 'Why do I get the impression you do this a lot?'

Kurt laughed and slapped his brother on the shoulder. 'Many times, Duchess. Many times. Danny's idea. He's the mastermind.'

'And I presume you're the money man?' Grace said.

For a moment he actually looked offended. 'People pay what they can. If they can.'

Ellyn slung her arms around Daniel's neck as he turned scarlet and tried to splutter out an explanation. 'I always knew you were devious, Danny. Now, this one is mine. I could sleep for a week.' She flung herself into the nearest room, not much bigger than a cupboard, and with a pirouette kicked the door shut in their faces. 'Night!' she called.

Daniel left with Kurt, presumably to do something with the guards upstairs and make plans for their escape. Grace could hear their voices fading, something about Misha's note, something about who dropped it off.

Which left one room remaining, and one bed, narrow and unmade but with worn sheets folded up at the foot of it. Grace and Bastien both stared at it and she swallowed hard on a suddenly dry throat.

'Might as well…' She started unfolding the sheets, because it was something to do, something other than talking to him about everything that had happened, to them, between them. She didn't even know where to start.

His magic, and the darkness that came with it, Marius's death, the moment he saved her life, the massacre at the Academy and Craine's last words, being on the run with his oldest friend hunting them. Or the fact that the last time the two of them had been this close to an empty bed, they'd slept together. They'd made love.

It was only last night. Exhausted, dead on her feet, shell-shocked – Grace stared at the worn white material in her hands, trying to work out what to do next.

His hands, gentle and dexterous, took the other end of the sheet from her and spread it out over the lumpy mattress. They worked together, silently, making the bed – the sheets, the pillows and pillow cases, a grey blanket. He even straightened everything when she stepped back. The room was spinning just a little and she still didn't know what to say.

It ought to be easy. She should make a flippant comment, or flirt with him as if he didn't matter, as if what had happened was just a one-night thing. Which it had to be, really. She was nothing to him. He was… he *ought* to be king.

'Sit down,' he told her.

Alone together, she obeyed as if he held the warrant rather than her. As if she was the sigil-bound mageborn. She was too tired to argue, exhausted by even the idea of being in charge any longer.

'I should be dead.' The words came out suddenly. She didn't know where from, just that it was true and she couldn't hold it in any more.

'No,' he murmured gently and unbuckled her baldric. He placed it reverently on the stool in the corner. Her knives went next. And she just let him. She didn't know why. She just…

Divinities, she was still wearing his shirt, the rich sable material thick with sweat and blood, grey with dirt where once it had been the colour of the finest jet. The costliest material she'd ever had against her skin and she had to ruin it.

Just as she had ruined everything with him. She'd used the sigil against him. She'd promised she wouldn't and then, the first time he didn't agree with her, she'd forced him to obey her and leave his sister behind.

'Bastien… I'm sorry. I'm so sorry. I had to get you out of there. Kane's magic was just—'

'It isn't his magic. He's using mageborn, stealing their magic.'

'It's different from a syphon.'

He unbuckled her belt next and slid it off around her waist slowly. 'Tethering. It's slower than a syphon. But far more stable. We saw them in that room. Miranda's experiment. With my sister's help, no doubt, and Hale to supervise. They have more than one mageborn, if I'm any judge, all tethered to Asher.'

'It doesn't kill them.'

'It will eventually. It'll burn through them. They won't last.'

'How did you come up with such a thing?' she asked, leaning forward.

He glanced back at her over his shoulder and his expression had turned bleak. Then he looked away again, staring back at the sigils on her belt as if they could provide absolution. 'Celeste gave me the idea, I suppose. It was something she said, the way the Maegen runs through me, through us. I thought… I thought it would help people.

Make it easier and make life less restrictive for the mageborn. They could donate their services for a time. Imagine, skilled healers with the abilities of a Curer or even a Gore, that power put to good use instead of ill. A blacksmith with the powers of a Flint. Our navy with the power of a Zephyr on each ship, and not a conscripted one but an experienced sailor in his own right, or every field producing food for the city tended by a Loam.'

'If they agreed to be power sources?' Her stomach twisted as she spoke.

Bastien turned back to face her, lifting his hands as if begging her allow him to explain. 'Marius thought... he thought it was a terrible idea. I called him old-fashioned and repressive. Said he wanted to keep each mageborn indentured for all their lives. I was so caught up in how to make it work...'

'That you didn't ask what others would do with it when they found out. And of course, they found out.'

His shoulders slumped. Hale had betrayed him. He must have been working for them all along... Miranda and Asher, the Queen... She could see the horror of the realisation on his face. 'They have to be using Celeste to do it...'

'You can't go back for her, Bastien.'

He crossed the room suddenly and dropped to his knees suddenly. 'Please, Grace. You don't understand. She's all I have now. And if they are using her to do this then we can stop them. We just need...'

'You need to leave Rathlynn. That was Marius's last command, wasn't it?' Grace stroked his hair, thick and silky, so dark against her skin. He closed his eyes in resignation. Or maybe in exhaustion that mirrored her own.

'You should rest,' he told her, as if he felt her body aching for sleep.

'So should you. You must be exhausted.'

He shook his head beneath her touch. 'My magic sustains me.'

Too much of it, she wanted to say, recalling the brightness in his eyes, the way he had looked, lost and half mad, the darkness in him.

There he was, kneeling in front of her. He wrapped his hand around her calf and lifted her foot so he could start to tug off her boot. Then he set to work on the other one. The caress of his hands did funny things to her. Things she shouldn't be thinking about right now.

When he looked up again, when his gaze trapped hers, she suddenly couldn't think of another question. His hands came up to frame her face, cradling her, and a sad smile kissed the corners of his lips.

Her mouth parted by itself and she leaned towards him. No command this. No coercion. She wouldn't do that to him. The first kiss was tentative, an uncertain question. Last night could have been just an aberration, a moment of madness and stress spilling into sex. A mistake. He was a prince – no, a king, albeit one without a crown. She was no one. Nothing.

But his kiss said something else.

She pulled back, trying to focus, knowing that she had to speak, she had to explain. 'You don't have to do this, Bastien.'

'Yes I do.' His lips brushed against hers as he spoke, and his fingertips buried in her hair, caressing her neck, pushing back the neck of the shirt to reach her skin.

'I'm sorry,' she said again.

His mouth brushed her jaw, tilted her head back, nuzzled at her throat. 'Sorry for what?'

'For using the warrant and the sigil… I never meant to.' Tears started in her eyes, trailed from the corners, and he looked up, startled. Then he kissed them away.

'And I'm sorry too.'

The response almost startled her back to lucidity. 'For what?'

Bastien smiled, that brittle, heartbroken smile she had come to recognise as his. 'This.'

He dragged her mouth to his, kissing her more completely than she'd ever been kissed. It ought to have been bruising and desperate, a clash of teeth and lips, but it wasn't. He filled her, his tongue caressing her, teasing her. It was a kiss that seared promises onto her soul, a kiss that would winnow its way into her moth-eaten memories and every dream from this moment on. She gasped against him as his hands continued their teasing exploration. He eased her back onto the bed, taking control completely. The fire roared up inside her, demanding that he touch her more, that he make love to her, that he sink into her and be hers forever. The magic in her, so long denied, grew wild this close to him and he was making it worse with his tenderness.

But still, he kissed her, his tongue tormenting her until she gasped for breath, her body trembling, her hands clutching his shoulders, pulling him to her. She couldn't think. All she could do was feel.

Bastien made a sound deep in his throat, a groan or a moan smothered by desire, a sound of need as desperate as hers, but threaded with a taint of regret and loss. Like he knew something she didn't.

A warning thrummed at the back of her brain. She opened her frantic eyes and saw his, open just a slit, but beyond the lids they were endless and bright, filled with the radiance of a thousand stars, the eyes of a man consumed with magic from the deepest places in the pool, lost in its depths.

A wave of sleep swept over her, coupled with the shock of betrayal. He was doing this. It wasn't natural. He was making her go to sleep, stealing her consciousness.

She cried out, struggling to escape, to tear herself free, but it was already too late. The spell had her wrapped in its web and it was too powerful. Bastien caught her in the gentlest arms and slowly guided her back onto the pillow, settling her on the bed. Her mind struggled against what was happening.

He'd said he'd never use magic against her. A promise he had already broken. Using it to heal her was bad enough but this... this... he'd sworn...

But she was tired. So tired. Her body wouldn't obey her any more. Her voice wouldn't work.

He gazed down at her and she adored him, even as she hated him for doing this to her.

'I'm sorry, my love. But I have to go back. It's the only way.'

He placed a brief, tender kiss on her forehead and sealed his spell. Unable to fight any more, she slid into unconsciousness.

Chapter Twenty-Three

He hated himself. Nothing else came close to expressing it.

If he ever made it back to her, he'd be lucky if Grace didn't kill him. But what choice did he have?

He couldn't leave Celeste behind. He couldn't let her be used like that. She trusted Asher. She'd known him all her life. Of course she'd trust him.

She was like a child. He couldn't abandon her.

He should never have left her in the Temple. The moment he found out about Miranda… he should have believed her, the things Celeste said. He should have listened.

And he should never have used magic against Grace. Not once but twice. Saving her life might have been a reasonable excuse but this? She'd never forgive him for this.

In spite of that hellish sigil she had used… Where had she even found it? He'd never come across one as strong as that, strong enough to hold him. No matter how much grief it caused Grace, something in him was glad its creator was dead in the Academy.

He slipped back through the concealed door and found himself in the hallway of the inn. The taproom was quiet, the guards still there, drinking with a bleak determination while Kurt kept pouring cheap ale and hard spirits. What he planned to do with them, Bastien didn't have time to find out. There was no sign of Daniel, which was probably for the best. He wasn't sure how Grace's friend would take what he had just done to her.

No one was going to understand. If he made it back, if he could get Celeste and make it back to Eastferry... he'd spend every day trying to make it up to her. He'd do everything in his power to make amends. If she'd even deign to see him again. If he even made it back in time.

But for now... now...

He balled his hands into fists. He had to focus. He had to stop thinking about Grace, if he ever wanted to see her again. Celeste was what mattered now. If they didn't have Celeste, Aurelie and Miranda couldn't access her power, or use her brilliant mind to solve their problems stealing the magic of the mageborn.

All he had to do was get into the Temple, and get her out. With magic, he could do that. And now that magic was his.

A heavy black cloak hung by the end of the stairs. He grabbed it as he went by, opening the narrow door and stepping out into the night.

'Where do you think you're off to?'

Daniel stood a little way down the alleyway outside the inn, his expression dark with suspicion.

'I have to go.'

'For your sister? Where's Grace?'

The flinch of shame he felt inside him was a stab of pain. 'She's... she's sleeping.'

Daniel looked levelly at him, disbelief written all over his face. 'Sleeping...'

'I promise, that's all.'

'I've heard your promises, Lord of Thorns.'

'On my honour then. She's safe. She's sleeping.'

He didn't mention how she'd fallen asleep. Daniel didn't look like he believed him anyway.

'If you're caught…'

'I won't be. And even if I am, they can't make me tell them where you all are.'

'High opinion of yourself. I've seen the kind of things they can do. I felt Asher Kane reach into my head and make me believe him. What's to say he won't do the same to you?'

Bastien let his magic flood him again. It was easier each time, sinking into it, calling it to hand. Daniel took half a step back.

'He won't. I'm the Lord of Thorns, remember? The king of the mageborn.'

Stiffening his resolve, Daniel didn't look impressed. 'I thought the point of all of this was to avoid a mageborn king. Do you want to be another Hollow King? Doesn't sound like the best idea, does it?'

'Would you trust me if Grace kept the warrant?'

But Daniel didn't relent.

'And what's to stop something happening to Grace?'

The very thought. Bastien's anger surged and his magic with it. His voice came out thick and dark with menace. 'Me.'

Daniel lifted his chin. 'And what if you *are* the something?'

'What would you have me do, Daniel? Return to her? Stay here? Go now and never return?'

'You're going to get captured. She'll be so angry with us.'

That one word caught him. 'With us?'

'Well I'm not letting you go on your own.'

*

The streets were deserted. Everywhere they looked, doors were locked and windows shuttered. Royal Guards roved in packs but they didn't seem to be using the powers of the mageborn now. Just the threat of it was enough to subdue the city.

Cloaked and hooded, Bastien and Daniel walked in silence. There was nothing else to say. Daniel was protective of Grace, whatever scheme he and his brother had with the mageborn. Bastien knew he was a spanner in the works of that.

He'd used magic on Grace. Twice. She was never going to forgive him anyway. And neither was Daniel Parry.

The Temple square was empty too. The doors were firmly closed. High above them, the tower taunted him, the only lights in the upper rooms, where Celeste lived.

'Has she always lived there?' Daniel asked, staring up at it.

'As long as I can remember.' That was a joke, wasn't it? Bastien didn't know what he remembered and what he'd been told, didn't know the difference. 'She was… difficult as a child. So was I, I suppose. But she became dangerous.'

'Dangerous, how?'

'Someone died.' *Someone.* It was easy to just say someone. A woman. A lover. A sister. But he didn't want to talk about Hanna. Not now. ' I… find it difficult to remember.'

'Difficult to remember?' It wasn't a taunt exactly. There was an element of disbelief, an element of disgust. 'No one too important then. Doesn't it matter when someone dies?'

'Yes, Daniel. It matters.'

But his memory was hazy. Most of his memories were. The accident when he was eighteen or so, a blow to the head and much of his childhood was knocked out of it. That was how it had been explained. He'd tried to stop Celeste. He'd been too late. Hanna was already dead.

You tried, Bastien, Marius had said, his voice as gentle as a breeze through rose petals. *The powers know that you tried. You loved her so much. But it wasn't to be.*

He didn't owe anyone an explanation. Least of all a nosy Academy brat dragged out of the worst slums of Eastferry with an attitude problem.

Daniel snorted and dismissed it. Somehow that was worse. 'Doesn't look like it matters to you. How do you plan on getting in then?'

Bastien hadn't actually thought through that far. He'd never meant to just walk up to the main door and knock, but he didn't want say that out loud either because Daniel would decide that was exactly what he'd intended to do.

That *shouldn't* matter. He couldn't say why it did. He had a suspicion that it all circled around back to Grace. Daniel was her friend. And while he didn't give a damn if Daniel didn't like him, or even respected him, he cared what Grace thought, and Grace cared what Daniel thought and…

The Temple. Celeste. That was why they were here.

'I thought maybe a back door, a servants' entrance or…' his voice trailed off as Daniel raised his eyebrows in disbelief.

'O… kay? Any idea where?'

He didn't have a clue. Of course he didn't. But… Daniel Parry worked in this city, had grown up in its underworld and knew its secrets more intimately than anyone else. When you had information like that at hand, you used it.

'You tell me.'

'That's your plan? Lucky I came. This way.'

Bastien wanted to say he would have found another way, but what was the use in that? This was where they were now. He just followed Daniel down the side of the Temple, where a disreputable-looking alleyway led towards the market square. Daniel selected a door painted a bright blue and knocked, three swift knocks, like a signal.

'Whose house is this?'

'It's a… Look, never mind about that. Just shut up and let me talk.'

One look at the woman who opened the door told Bastien exactly what sort of house it was. She was draped in silks, her hair caught up in an elaborate style, and chains of gold hung around her neck. But she didn't look in any way alluring. She looked, if anything, terrified.

'Daniel darling,' she gasped. 'Thank the goddess you're here. This is a bad night to be out and about. Come inside. Both of you. Quickly.'

The door snapped shut behind them, the lock turning and bolts driven across.

'Madam Dean,' Daniel said in strangely formal tones. 'We need access to your vaults.'

Madam Dean peered at Bastien and, though the cloak hid him, he wasn't sure if that would be enough. If she recognised him, she was too well trained to react.

'Do you know what's happening, Danny?'

There was a group of young women and a few men huddled in the next room, peering at them from the doorway. They were all beautiful, all scared, and clearly all prostitutes. It wasn't as if Bastien had never seen one before. Just not so blatantly obvious. And not so filled with fear. The nearest, a Tlachtlyan boy with almond eyes and a luscious mouth, touched Daniel's shoulder, a soft caress that spoke of an intimacy.

Daniel pulled away. 'Nothing to worry about. Just… just stay indoors until morning. Don't let the guards in.'

'Misha isn't back. Have you seen him?'

Daniel's face went pale. He swallowed, his throat working hard.

He's hiding something, Bastien thought. Trying to protect them or... or perhaps me.

Who was Misha? And what was he to Daniel? More than just an acquaintance. The thought of him outside and possibly in danger clearly rattled the man.

'I got the message. That's why I'm here.' He glanced at Bastien, who didn't react. What message? What was he talking about? But before he could ask, Daniel went on. 'The vaults, Rina?'

Madam Dean just nodded carefully and once more they were descending stairs.

Rathlynn was old. It had been built upon its own bones, generation after generation of buildings. The further down it went the more it was interconnected. Bastien wanted to ask why a temple might have a passageway to a brothel but he knew the answer already. The brothers and sisters serving there might take vows of loyalty to the goddess alone, but they were human. And what the eyes of the goddess didn't see couldn't harm her.

The vaults were sparse compared to those beneath the inn, but wide. The passageway wound down to a door, old oak, with lines of iron curling across it like vines. Madam Dean produced a key from somewhere in her ample cleavage and fitted it to the lock.

'Are you sure?' she whispered to Daniel who just nodded.

'Just open it and go. It'll be okay.'

The key turned in the lock and the door burst open. Light flooded in around them, and so did a troop of Royal Guards. They surrounded Bastien, pressed close together, all armed, some carrying torches which spluttered with black choking smoke. He drew back, already letting the magic fill him, the shock of this turn of events barely slowing him. The pool filled him as naturally as breathing and the light within him roared to life.

Daniel's hand on his throat brought him stumbling forwards. A line like fire etched itself into Bastien's skin, encircling his neck and pressing down. He reached for the magic, desperate to defend himself, and found nothing.

A sigil. Daniel had caught him with a sigil.

And then he recognised it, because the bloody thing burned on his skin like nothing else ever had. Grace's sigil, the one she'd bound him with in order to escape to Eastferry. Daniel had taken it. And now it was being used again.

Rage replaced the magic but before he could use the strength it lent him, he was brought to his knees. Guards seized his arms and twisted them behind his back, manacles crushing his wrists together. They didn't draw back, pressed close in the darkness.

'Parry? What have you done?' Bastien gasped.

But Daniel had stepped away, unable to meet his gaze, his face pale, his eyes tormented. 'Careful with him. I don't know if it will hold for long.'

'I can take care of that, Officer Parry,' said a voice he knew far too well. It put all thoughts of Daniel Parry's betrayal right out of his mind. A matter of perspective. What Daniel had done was minor. This... Asher stepped from the doorway to the Temple. 'We have any number of sigils all ready and waiting for him. Hello Bastien. We missed you. Your sister is beside herself with worry.'

'What is this, Asher? What do you want?'

Asher grinned at him. 'You, of course, my Lord of Thorns. We have only ever wanted you.'

He grabbed a handful of Bastien's hair, the same hair that Grace had caressed, jerking it back by the fistful, making him bare his throat. He pulled Grace's sigil off and tossed it aside. For a moment a wild surge of hope seized Bastien and he drew on his magic again, but Asher was ready for him. A line of sigils appeared in his hands and in seconds they were around Bastien's neck like a collar, half a dozen of them interlinked, humming with power. The sigils flared even brighter than Grace's had, and the tiny ball of glass hanging around Asher's neck on a silver chain burned with an answering light.

In a rush, all the power was sucked from Bastien's body. Asher inhaled sharply, a gasp of delight. He closed his eyes, ecstasy written on his patrician features.

Bastien slumped forward but Asher grabbed another handful of his hair, dragging his head up again, making him look. 'Do you like them? Sigils to bind your power and an orb of my own to feed it all to me. Celeste perfected it herself, clever little thing that she is. Instead of a syphon, it's a direct connection. We found her someone to work with, someone she could encourage. They die so quickly though. Isn't she a marvel?' He almost purred the last words and released Bastien, who sagged in his captors' grip, bewildered.

A syphon and a tether working in tandem. That was what Miranda had done. They'd used his own ideas, and his own sister, against him. And now his own magic.

'Where's Misha?' Daniel interrupted.

Asher glanced at Daniel with a cruel glint in his eye. 'All in good time. Your boyfriend's been entertaining the ladies. Such a voice. Such a talent. I bet he even screams on key.'

Daniel's face went white and Bastien understood. Where Bastien had wanted to save his sister, Daniel had wanted to save his lover. And this was the price.

'We had a deal,' Daniel hissed. That wasn't the voice of a guard. Nor an officer. That was the voice of an Eastferry crime family member. If Asher didn't recognise the tone, Bastien did.

Kane curled his lip in disdain. 'And I keep my word. Where's the warrant?'

'The what?'

'The coin the girl was given. Where is it?'

Daniel drew a pair of daggers, his patience at an end. 'You didn't mention a coin. You just said bring him. So I did. Now give me—'

Asher just flicked his hands at Daniel. That was all. Just a flick of the wrist, dismissive and contemptuous.

Daniel dropped to his knees, gasping for breath. The daggers clattered from his hands, and he reached for his own throat, clawing at it. Asher watched for a minute, in horrid fascination. Daniel's eyes bulged, his face purpled, and then he fell like a rag doll.

Asher released him, and examined his nails while Daniel struggled to regain his breath. When his eyes met Bastien's, he grinned, as if they were co-conspirators. As if they were still friends.

'You really have no idea of the amount of power within you, Bastien. It's exhilarating.'

He wanted power? So be it.

Bastien narrowed his eyes.

Asher leaned forward to say more but suddenly the little globe hummed, vibrating far too strongly, the light intensifying. There was too much power, too much magic. Asher stepped back and tore it off before it exploded into dust.

He dropped the chain, disgusted.

Bastien smiled, heaving in breath after breath. 'Not so clever. When these sigils wear off—' The throb of pain eating into his flesh, he tried to draw his power into him again, the sigils still fighting him every step of the way. But it was there again, just out of reach.

'We'll apply more. And eventually we'll get it right. I'll have your magic, Bastien.'

'I will not cooperate with you.'

'Not even for Celeste? We can do this to her, you know. We have. She's harder to control, but it's worth it.'

Somewhere Bastien found the strength. The mention of Celeste, the thought of her bound and used like this, the *arrogance*…

One guard dropped to his knees, clawing at his own face and howling. The other held on grimly for a moment and then his neck twisted to one side. He didn't make a sound until he fell. Bastien rose to his feet, his hands still chained behind him, the sigils blazing like unholy fire around his neck, and advanced on Asher, blocking out the pain.

His friend, his oldest friend, didn't flinch or back away. He watched him, grinning that terrible grin, all teeth and superiority. Slowly he shook his head.

Lightning rushed along Bastien's veins, his blood boiling at its touch. He tried to breathe but it felt like inhaling glass shards. Inside his bones shattered and reformed and a broken cry forced its way out of him, more from shock than any ability to voice anything. He didn't know when he fell, only that the ground was cold and hard and the pain didn't ebb. But it wasn't Asher. He knew it didn't come from Asher.

No one else could inflict such power on him. No one else.

'You're taking far too long,' he heard Celeste's voice through his pain, different to how he'd heard her through the mirror, clearer now. 'We've been waiting. I don't like waiting.'

'Divinity,' Asher said, a mixture of awe and deliberate care threaded through his voice. 'I think he's ready for you now.'

She came on bare, silent feet, delicate as a dancer, the guards parting for her, and she crouched down, peering into his face.

'Hello, little brother. I've been waiting such a long time for this.' Then she frowned, screwing up her pretty face in consternation. 'Where's the warrant?'

'There's been a complication. It's in hand.'

For a moment, she just stared at him. 'Are you telling me you don't have it?' Then she laughed. So brightly, his heart ached. Because this was his sister, the sister he remembered. She was lucid and sweet. She was everything he remembered before it all went wrong. 'I was very specific. Bastien *and* the warrant. Aurelie was meant to get it from Marius but oh no. She couldn't even do that.'

'Celeste,' Bastien murmured, trying to reach her. 'Celeste, what's going on? What's happening?'

Her hands twitched against her sides, fingers worrying at the fabric of her gown, pulling at a thread. She shivered suddenly and she turned on Asher as if she would tear out his throat. Her voice became a roar. 'Where's the warrant? It won't work without it.'

For a moment the look on Asher's face was almost comical. All colour drained away and it was replaced with the knowledge that all the stolen power in the world wouldn't protect him from her.

'We'll get it. I swear. On my life.' He looked desperate. Terrified.

Celeste froze, and then she smiled again, her mood changing like quicksilver as she heard what she wanted. '*On. Your. Life.* I'll hold you to that. Where is it? Who has it?'

Bastien looked at Daniel who flinched back from them. He'd picked up Grace's sigil again, holding it as if it might defend him against them.

It wouldn't. Celeste followed his glance and instantly she was all pretty girl again, childish, the coquette. 'You?'

'No,' Bastien ground out the word before Daniel could find an answer. Not a denial. A warning.

Don't answer her. Don't be fooled. Don't do this.

'He was *meant* to bring both.' Asher's voice was cruel again, deflecting failure from himself to another as he always did. He was transparent to Bastien now. How had they ever been friends?

Celeste reached out a hand to Daniel, smiling as she did so. At least he had the good sense not to take it.

'You're the harper's lover, aren't you? He's so good. Aurelie is quite enamoured but she does love her music. I do hope I haven't broken him.'

Daniel's mouth opened in dismay but no words came out.

Bastien tried to struggle upright. 'Celeste, stop this. Please.'

'Oh shush,' she said. 'I'll get to you in a minute. I'm talking to… *Daniel*, isn't it?' She pressed her hand to his head and his face went blank, completely blank, eyes staring to nothing, jaw sagging. 'Go and get that warrant. By whatever means necessary. Understand? You know where it is and I want it. Kill anyone who tries to stop you. Now. Go.'

He moved like a puppet, controlled by strings of magic, staggering up onto uncertain feet, turning without a word and leaving.

'Now, my little brother,' said Celeste, more lucid and more terrifying than he had ever seen her. 'We really need to talk. A long talk. There is so much I have to tell you. There is so much for you to do.'

Chapter Twenty-Four

'Grace?'

Something shook her shoulder. But she didn't have to get up. She wasn't even on duty yet. There were no alarm bells. And it was still dark. Hours to go until reveille.

'Grace, please. Listen to me. You've got to wake up. Grace!'

'Five more minutes,' she mumbled, trying to pull the blankets over her head.

'Grace!' Ellyn grabbed her by the shirt and shook her until she thought her teeth would rattle. 'Wake up. Bastien and Daniel are missing. I don't know what he did to you, but you have to wake up now. Please.'

'Here.' That was Kurt's voice. Alarm bells were ringing now, not actual bells of course, but if Kurt was here as well… 'Allie's a Curer. Let her through.'

A mageborn? No.

That brought Grace up out of the dreams that dragged her back down. No mageborn was touching her again. Not after…

'Bastien,' she growled and rolled onto her side. The world spun around and came back into focus.

'Allie can help you, Duchess. Just—'

'No, just give me a minute.'

'Why won't you just listen, you stupid, stubborn woman?'

If anyone else had said it under any other circumstances... She glared at him and dragged herself up to sit on the edge of the bed. The carefully folded belt, baldric and the associated weapons swung into view and she remembered Bastien doing it. The fastidious way he'd undressed her, kissed her, used his magic on her...

'No mageborn is using magic on me again. No mageborn is ever going to *touch* me again.'

It would be more convincing if she wasn't remembering every kiss and every caress in detail. It would be more convincing if she wasn't mageborn herself.

She forced air into her lungs as deeply as she could and then exhaled.

'Did they go together?'

'We don't know.'

'I bet you don't know where they went either.'

'No,' Ellyn admitted. 'But Kurt has put the word out.'

'Well...' Grace groaned as she levered herself onto her feet. 'I have an idea. Bastien's gone back for Celeste.'

'Who's that?'

'His sister.'

Ellyn gasped. 'Isn't she a Temple acolyte?'

'More like a patient.' Grace shook her head. 'Doesn't matter now. We have to find them. Have you sorted passage?'

Kurt stepped back, folded his arms. 'The ship's sailing in a couple of hours. It can't wait for you, Duchess. Or him. I've too many people who need to get out of this shithole before Queen Nutjob rounds them all up and drains them, mageborn and their families. There are kids to think of. If they're found—'

Grace held up a hand to silence him. 'The boat sails when it's ready. Don't wait for us. Ellyn? You need to leave with—'

'Where am I going without you and Daniel? We're a team, remember?'

Speaking of whom… where was he? Why had he gone after Bastien? He didn't even like him.

'A couple of hours, Grace,' Kurt warned. 'That's all I can do.'

'I know,' she replied. 'I wouldn't expect anything else.'

And it was true. She knew that. That ship sailing on time was too important. Even more important than a missing king, a lost best friend or a vanished, treacherous lover.

*

The Vigil bells were sounding by the time they left Eastferry. Grace and Ellyn picked their way through the dark and silent city, keeping to the shadows. She'd never seen the area so subdued, not even at this hour. Eastferry was quiet, but the Temple quarter was dead.

So a figure standing alone in the square, sword drawn, really stood out.

It looked like Daniel. But something made her pause.

'Grace? What's he doing?'

'Waiting, I think.'

'Just like that. Out there. In the open?'

'Like he's waiting for us.' She tried to sound convinced but knew she'd failed. Every instinct warned her that this was wrong.

'He wouldn't wait out in the open like that.'

Daniel would never leave himself so exposed. So vulnerable. Everything about this rang wrong for her. A cold feeling clawed at her guts.

'No. No he wouldn't. I don't like this. Don't do anything. Just… keep an eye… Can you circle around? Get behind him?'

'Can a dog bark?' Ellyn slipped off into the shadows but not before Grace held up a warning hand. 'I know. Be careful.'

Grace gave it a count of ten and then walked out into the open, right towards him. Her footsteps rang out on the cobbles and she loosened the sword in its scabbard.

'Danny? We've been looking for you.'

The weird look on his face made her stomach clench. 'Grace.' That was all he said. No smile. No nothing. His face was like a mask.

'Are you just going to stand there?'

The sword came up and he studied it. Then he pointed it directly at her. 'I need that.'

Whatever *that* was, she didn't know and didn't have a second to ask. He came at her in a lunge, quicker than she ever remembered him being. Daniel was a good swordsman. Not as good as Ellyn perhaps, but easily Grace's equal. As Grace folded back out of his way, she drew her own weapon. His next attack drove her back across the square, the clash of blade on blade singing in the night's air.

'I don't want to kill you. But I have to. Give me the warrant. I'll make it quick.'

'The warrant?' She pressed an opening, a brief advantage. He took two steps back and grimaced. If they'd been fighting in a training session she'd have scored points. But they weren't.

The kick to her shin was a dirty move. He'd learned to fight in Eastferry where nothing was clean. But she'd fought with Daniel all her life. Knew his moves like her own. Daniel always pulled his punches. That was the one thing they all knew about him. Deep down he didn't like hurting anyone.

But in this fight he was different.

An elbow came up hard into her face, sending stars dancing all around her as she stumbled back from him. The fire inside her flared up. Utterly useless in this situation. She wasn't going to use it on Daniel. How could she?

But she'd been using it all her life. Not the actual powers of a Flint, but the instincts, the speed, the way she always had.

Grace rallied, fighting like with like. She had to. She pulled one knife free and went at him with two blades. He almost brought her down by the well but she spun around it, using it to block him. And seizing those brief moments to catch her breath.

'What the hell is going on, Danny? You can't take the warrant. It'll kill you. Talk to me. What are you doing?'

He faltered, as if struggling against something. He took two steps back and then shook his head. 'I have my orders. I need the warrant. That's all that matters, Grace.' His voice trembled. 'They'll kill Misha. They might have killed him already. I didn't want to do *any* of this but… she told me to… She said to take it and… and to kill anyone trying to stop me.'

The warrant itself hung like a cold weight against Grace's chest. She could feel it there, calling to him. Someone had told him, compelled him… she…Who was she?

Misha… that was the singer, wasn't it? The harpist. The one he'd been mooning over. More than mooning. Ellyn had said he was in love. Oh divinities, what had he done?

'Danny, listen to me. Where's Bastien?'

The concern melted away to disgust. The mask slid back into place. '*Him*… They took Misha so I'd bring Bastien to them, tortured him, told me that if I didn't they'd kill him. All for Bastien bloody Larelwynn. It's always about him, Grace. Has been since you met him. He's all that matters to you now.'

Another flurry of blows came out of nowhere and she blocked him, breathing hard. Damn this, where was Ellyn? She'd told her not to interfere, but that had been a mistake. Clearly. She needed help. What was wrong with him? This wasn't the Daniel she knew.

'He's... he's the king.'

'No king of mine. Or yours. Since when did you have time for kings? Oh, I know, when you screwed him. When you threw us all over and yourself into his bed.'

He scooped her foot out from under her and she came down hard. Before she knew where she was, her sword was on the ground and before she could bring the knife up, his blade was at her throat.

It pressed there, shaking. But it didn't bite. Not quite.

She drew in a shaky breath, gazing up into his face in dismay. Daniel was her weakness. She'd thought they were friends. They always had been. And now he was being used against her.

'If you're going to kill her, shouldn't you be getting on with it?' Ellyn called from the darkness, the singsong taunt making him scowl. About bloody time, Grace thought. What the hell was she waiting for? He jerked his head up, looking for her.

'This is none of your business, Ellyn,' Daniel snarled.

'Yes it is, mate. We're a team. You don't turn on your own team. Danny, what happened?' Grace said on a ragged breath, drawing his attention away from Ellyn and back to her.

'Give me the warrant, Grace.'

She lifted up her chin defiantly. 'Take it.'

The look of anguish that crossed his face made her heart twist inside her. He was her friend, her oldest friend. The sword pushed against her skin, pressing in, ready to slice her throat open. His hand shook more than ever.

Slowly, she reached out. He didn't even seem to notice. He fixed his gaze on her face and fought to kill her or release her. Grace narrowed her eyes. She could almost see it, lines of purple light twisting around him, binding him, compelling him.

'Is it a spell?'

'Such a spell. I... I can't fight her. I can't... please Grace...' Tears matted his eyelashes.

Her hand closed on his wrist and she let the fire flow through her fingers. Daniel screamed, trying to pull back from her, his sword falling free, and Grace felt the compulsion snap, threads of it incinerating around him. Daniel dropped to his knees beside her, his face stretched in pain.

A moment later, Ellyn was on him. She dragged him free of Grace even as his sword hit the cobbles, whirled him around and slammed him back against the side of the ornate well.

'You betrayed us for a bloody *singer*?' That one word didn't sound like any sort of compliment. 'Fuck's sakes, Danny.'

'Ellyn,' he sobbed. 'Ellyn, please listen...'

She slammed him back again, his head cracking off the stone. 'What? Like you were listening? He'd better be the love of your fucking life, Danny, because I'm going to—'

And her voice just stopped as she saw the look on his face. Grace felt the world drop out from under her. The love of his life. Oh divinities, glories, seraphs and powers, Grace thought. That was it, wasn't it?

'His name is Misha Estin... he calls himself Harper though...' Abject misery dripped off Daniel with blood and tears. Misha... Grace remembered him, golden-skinned, golden-haired, sunkissed, the golden boy who had played the harp in the Rowan, and Daniel hadn't been able to take his eyes off him.

'Aw shit, Danny,' Ellyn sighed. 'Why didn't you just tell us they'd taken him?'

'I wanted to. But…'

Grace glanced towards the Temple. 'Is he in there? With Bastien?'

He nodded.

If they hadn't killed his lover already. She couldn't say that to him. She just couldn't.

If they hadn't killed hers.

'Let him up, Ellyn,' she said, shocked at how steady her voice sounded.

He was still cradling his arm, staring at her warily. 'I always knew you were a Flint. Even when we were kids. I protected you and your secret. I never thought you'd turn it on me.'

'You don't get to talk about turning on people right now,' she warned him and he hung his head, avoiding her glare. 'Is the spell broken? Still feel the urge to kill me?'

'Yes.' His voice was a growl. 'But… the spell is broken. As far as I can tell.'

At least there was that. She couldn't see anything any more, couldn't sense the coils of it around him. He was himself again. Or at least, she hoped so.

Either Celeste was in on it, or Miranda was making her cooperate. Crazy or not, she was powerful. So was Miranda. So was Asher. Far more powerful than Grace. What could she do besides make things uncomfortably hot? What good was a Flint to anyone?

Bastien on the other hand…

If they could tether him… if they could syphon his magic… if they could make him share the things he'd discovered…

And they would. They didn't even have to drug him and wipe his memory this time. They had a way, a lever to make him do it.

Something he cared about. His sister.

'Do we have a plan, boss?' Ellyn asked, retrieving Daniel's sword. She didn't give it to him, Grace realised, but held onto it.

'Of course I don't have a plan. We'll do what we always do. We'll improvise.'

Chapter Twenty-Five

'Bastien, Bastien, Bastien,' Celeste sang. 'I tried to tell you but you would never listen. Why don't you remember? Why is it so hard?'

He couldn't keep explaining it. 'They're using you, Celeste.'

She laughed. His sister, the most important person in his life... she laughed. 'No, my sweet boy, I'm using them.'

She stroked his hair, her fingers digging too deep for comfort. She held him as he'd held her so many times. Sometimes she sang lullabies. They'd been together for an hour and once he would have thought it was all he wanted from life, to have her here, to have her lucid.

He had never imagined it would be a nightmare.

His sister wasn't just crazy. Not in the traditional sense. She was something else.

The room, her room, at the top of the tower was beautiful. Or had been once. Every so often she'd hurl things at the walls, tear the wallpaper or smash the windows. Things got repaired, patched up, but the scars still remained. One of the windows had been boarded up recently. The others had mismatched stained glass. Scratches like claw marks scoured the door.

'I'll try again,' she murmured. 'In the beginning there was just the two of us. We were free. We danced among the stars. We lived in the fire. Our tears were the oceans. Remember? Please remember?'

Another ripple of agony shuddered through him. He gasped and she purred at him. 'Remember.'

'We need more sigils to hold him,' Aurelie said, pacing the perimeter of the room, her gown swishing around her slippered feet, reflected in the polished floorboards. She sounded nervous. It made her irritable. There was a chair, one which had been brought in especially for her because it was undamaged. She ignored it. 'Where's Miranda?'

'The Atelier is exhausted. He says he can't make more. She's... encouraging him.' Asher didn't look down at Bastien. As if he couldn't bear to. He stood in front of the door, his arms crossed.

'Then find another Atelier,' she snapped. 'This isn't some game, Asher. Look at him. You can sense the power in him as well as I can. Without Marius, without that warrant... Look!'

But Asher didn't look.

Didn't look at Bastien, naked and bound with sigils glinting on his skin, muscles straining, drenched in sweat. Didn't look at the pathetic, broken mess he had made of his old friend. Perhaps he couldn't stand it. Bastien wished that was the case but he didn't believe it.

'Asher,' Bastien tried again. 'Please...'

'Why do you even bother?' the queen snapped at him as the door closed behind his friend with a soft click. 'He's the one who thought of this, you know? He's the one who suggested we use you and your sister in the first place. Divinities, Bastien, you're such a fool. We could have ruled this kingdom together. You and I. All you had to do was say *yes*.'

She slammed the door behind her so hard that the walls seemed to shake.

All he had to do was betray Marius, she meant. Something she had no problem with. He on the other hand...

'You never could,' Celeste crooned. She stroked the torc around his neck, wrapped her arm around his throat and squeezed. 'They always had you, those thieving Larelwynns. A way to control you. You were never one of them, neither of us were. They stole you. You loved them. All of them. And if they couldn't control you, they had me to compel you. They always made you forget but they couldn't make you forget me. Not entirely. You always remembered that I am your sister. I always will be. They locked me up, they trapped me here, but their drug doesn't work the same way on me. Oh, it makes me dream and makes me mad, but I don't forget. I never forget. But it's over, my darling love, they're gone. Every last one of them. There's only you and I left. We're going to be free again. We're going to purge it all with fire and flood. We're going to rain down vengeance. We're going to—'

'That's quite enough, Celeste,' Miranda said as she entered the chamber. 'We're going to do nothing of the sort. We're going to rule. As it should have been all along. As it was meant to be.'

Bastien looked up into the other woman's face. He knew her. But at the same time he didn't. Once he had thought her kind. She was Mother to the Temple faithful. She fed the poor, cared for the children.

And it had all been an act. Grace was right. She was a monster who fed on others. Not just a Leech of magic. Of life. Of freedom. Of everything.

'What do you mean?' he asked. She gave him a look like she pitied him.

'I'm not going to go on surviving on the scraps these morons feed us. Look at you,' she said, the words seething with disgust. 'You don't even know what you are any more.'

'Remember, Bastien,' Celeste murmured. 'Why won't you remember?'

'Because he can't. Not without his full power. And he can't have his full power without the warrant. If we had that, we could make the crown complete again, make it ours. But Marius gave it away.'

Celeste abruptly shoved Bastien aside with a snarl of impatience, a child whose favourite toy wouldn't work. He fell heavily to the ground, his hands barely able to hold him up.

The sigils digging into his skin were weakening. Any moment now, they'd go. He just had to wait. Wait for the right moment. Endure this.

'I'm getting the warrant,' Celeste snarled.

'You sent that Academy idiot. On his own. Like a halfwit.' Miranda sat down at the card table and shuffled her cards, before she spread them out face down. She flicked them over one at a time, studying the garish pictures. If they told her anything she didn't let on. 'We could have sent a whole battalion of Royal Guards. We should have—'

'He knows her. He'll get it.'

'We could have gone ourselves.'

'Outside?' Celeste shrank back from Miranda, backing towards Bastien again as she always did when something scared her. 'You want to go outside?'

'Oh for goodness sake, you're able to go outside, Celeste.'

Celeste shook her head, muttering to herself in a frenzy.

Bastien struggled to draw his body back under his own control. The sigils were definitely failing. The more he pushed the faster they went. He was burning through them but he wasn't strong enough yet. They still blocked him from the pool and the magic inside it. The pain was receding too, or perhaps he was just becoming accustomed to it. Whatever was happening, he had to keep his wits about him. Especially as Celeste had gone over the edge and had apparently taken Mother Miranda with her.

His breathing calmed and his racing heartbeat slowed. Focus, he told himself, focus. The pool of light was so close now. The Deep Dark beneath beckoned. It swirled up through the base of his spine, coiling around it like a snake, ready to rise, ready to strike.

'Oh look,' said Miranda, her voice bland. 'He's trying to draw on his power. How sweet. Here.'

And she reached across the table to pull a jar off the shelf. Not one of his. This was something else. She handed it to Celeste and then saw his look of confused alarm. She smiled.

'I improved on your design, Bastien.' Miranda grinned at him. 'You're not the only one in the family who can create such wonders.'

'You're not my family.'

And Celeste laughed, riotously, uproariously. She threw back her head and spun around, hugging the jar to her chest. 'Oh but she is. He doesn't remember you, sister. He doesn't remember at all.'

'No,' Bastien said, suddenly unsure. There were so many things he didn't remember. But he couldn't have forgotten another sister. Especially not Miranda. He knew he had to have forgotten something about her. She knew things she couldn't possibly know.

'Listen to yourself,' Miranda said. She looked at him with those disdainful, pale eyes that seemed to see inside him. 'You're such a fool, Bastien. Now try not to struggle. It'll hurt less... well, no. That's not quite true. It'll hurt like hell but you know that already. It always does. But you don't have to put any effort in with my syphons. I improved on your inventions. Took my time. I could only take a little to begin with, when they first wiped me from your memory and threw me out. But I'd worked on *our* project with you. It was as much *my* work as yours. I perfected it. Slowly. I could only take a little magic, scraps of power at first. It took an age to drain them.

I had to look after the little mageborn brats until it was done, until I was finished with them. For years, I hid in the pits of this city, hid from the Larelwynns and my bloody family, and I started there. And the more of them I kept, the more the word spread that I was saving them. Imagine. Saving runts and cast-offs, and suddenly I'm a saint.' She laughed. She actually laughed. 'My reputation made me Mother of the Temple, goodness personified. They're so gullible, the people of Rathlynn. They believe you're a monster when you keep them safe. They believe I'm a saint when all I wanted to do was drain every last drop of magic from their children.'

'It can't be done,' he said. 'Not… not safely.'

'No… not safely. But when they died, all those years ago, who missed them? No one was looking. Your Captain Marchant was the first one to survive and it wiped away everything she knew. I thought she'd die when I dumped her at the Academy. She should have died, but she was always stubborn.' She leaned in, gazing into his eyes, and suddenly she seemed younger, like a girl staring at her lover. 'I perfected it, Bastien. Everything we worked on. You'll see. It takes everything and there's nothing you can do to stop it. Don't worry. You're strong, like Celeste.'

The burns on their hands, the failed syphon, all those dead kids dumped in the alleys of Rathlynn and the divinities knew where else. And before that… Grace…

She stole my magic, Grace had said. *I know her.*

All he'd had to do was listen. And believe her. No, he'd just told her it was impossible.

Celeste cradled the jar like a baby as she approached. 'Take it. It… it isn't the worst thing, Bastien. It hurts but—"

He shuffled back. 'No.'

'You don't get to avoid this,' Miranda laughed. 'Don't you remember, really? You said you loved me. So many times. And I, like a fool, believed you.'

'I... I never...'

'You *don't remember*, the Larelwynns made sure of that, with that cursed potion of theirs. Aurelie would have done it again if I hadn't offered her another way. You were *mine*, Bastien. You loved me. We had a plan. You taught me and I learned well. And then the Larelwynns stole your memories and tossed me out on the street. I survived on scraps, on whatever magic I could scrape from the underbelly of this wretched city.'

'Why won't you remember?' Celeste chimed in again. 'Please, Bastien, remember.'

'Because if he remembers that, he'll have to forget her. *Marchant.*' Miranda spat out the name like a curse. 'If he draws on his powers as deeply as we need him to, the man he is now will be gone. And do you know what, Bastien, I don't care. This man you've become is pathetic. Just get it over with, Celeste. Now.'

Light encircled him, wires in his skin, barbs digging into his bones. Bastien fought her but she was too strong.

Miranda rose gracefully and approached him slowly. The pain increased with every footstep. 'You'll feed us for millennia, Bastien. Tethering won't work on you yet. You're too powerful, you burn right through them in no time at all if left alone. I'll perfect it eventually, you'll see. I can tether a weaker mageborn for days, sometimes weeks. They don't even remember it. I combined the two. Drain them down and then tie them to another, use them both ways. But not for you. Not yet. Until then syphoning will have to do. Even with the pittance we give those stupid quots. And they are so hungry for you. To drink of the magic of a god, from the Maegen itself… Now do as you're told and play nice.'

'No.' He had to bite out the word, but it did no good. His body bent to her whim and he was on his knees, his hands outstretched.

Celeste kissed his feverish forehead and then pressed the jar between his palms. It was cold as a block of ice, painfully hard.

The rush of the void within it seized hold of him, dragged the magic from him, raking along the insides of his veins like acid, scourging the power from within him.

The scream that came with it tore its way out of his throat, light pouring from his eyes and mouth, every iota of it burning as it ravaged through him.

'Don't,' he gasped in the moments between. 'Please. Don't.' He knew it wouldn't do any good. He just couldn't help himself.

If anything the pain lurched up a notch, into blinding agony. Miranda watched him, smiling. She was enjoying this. Enjoying all of it.

'You always were so superior, weren't you?'

'It's not his fault, Miranda,' Celeste said, stroking his hair, trying and failing to soothe the pain. Her touch made it worse. 'We were gods once, divinities, all powerful. We danced in the pool's depths, we sang up the stars. Before Larelwynn.'

Light and flames burned his flesh and boiled his blood. Celeste murmured on and on as if he would listen and finally understand her, as if she could hypnotise him with her voice. The last dregs of magic guttered out inside him and the jar, glowing like a new sun, slipped from his numb grip, his hands burned and raw. It didn't fall. He prayed it would, that it would shatter and the magic would be gone and they'd be cheated. But they were ready for that.

Miranda took it in greedy hands, lifted it to her mouth and began to drink. Glowing magic poured down her throat, illuminating her from within.

'Me!' Celeste cried out. 'My turn. Give it to me!'

Either they forgot about him or they didn't need him any more. Whatever held him vanished and he collapsed slowly, weak sobs racking his body, sounds he couldn't even give voice to. Darkness pooled around him. He faded into it but it didn't fill him. Not this time. He was lost, empty and broken inside.

Chapter Twenty-Six

In retrospect, a plan would have been better. Grace knew that the moment she laid eyes on the queen. They'd made it as far as the Temple gates, the great filigree-like arches opening onto Temple square, aglow and empty in the moonlight. The gates stood open, waiting, and guards fell in around them, silent and grim. In moments they were surrounded and led inside, up the stairs to the tower and into a simple corridor, panelled in gleaming wood, lit by candles. The light reflected like stars in the polished surface and the dark glass of the windows. Aurelie was there, like she'd been waiting for them. But clearly, she wasn't. She knotted her hands together in front of her and, when she saw them, her mouth twisted in disgust.

'What is *she* doing here?'

'She has the warrant.' Daniel shoved Grace down on her knees. He didn't 'your majesty' Aurelie, or bow. He was too angry. So long as he didn't mess this up, Grace didn't care about the bruises he caused her. She'd had worse treatment. Looking at Aurelie, worse was coming.

Aurelie's fingers twitched at the sumptuous folds of her dress. 'Give it to me.'

Grace smiled up at her. She'd love to see that pretty face burn. Call it spiteful. 'No.'

'Asher,' she snapped but he didn't move either.

'Go on, take it. I dare you.'

Clearly they both had heard what happened the last time someone tried that.

'Let Miranda deal with her,' Asher said.

'Where's Misha?' Daniel cut in before they could leave.

Aurelie rolled her eyes. 'We kept our word. Take him. Much good he'll do you now.' She swept off but Kane stood there a moment longer. He dragged his gaze over Grace and then fixed Daniel with his darkest glare.

'He'll be brought to you. You'll have to put him together again, but if you don't get out of the city before they get control of Bastien's powers it'll be too late. No one will be getting out. Understand?'

'Where are the mageborn?' Grace asked, forgetting that she was meant to be a prisoner. 'What have they done with them?'

Asher shook his head, his mouth lifting on one side in a sneer. 'Your precious Academy friends? She's got them lined up like chickens in a coop, and they're not coming out again. The dead don't. Down there they won't see the light of day again, but they won't miss it. Parry, tell your *brother*, all debts are off now. Understand? Once that ship has sailed there will be no others. This isn't his city. Now get out.'

'Giving up?' Grace needled him. 'Running away?'

He laughed, a deep, bitter sound. For a moment she thought he might ignore her. But he couldn't. Not Asher Kane. Not when she called him a coward. No, he couldn't stand that.

'Not at all. Grace Marchant... you should know Bastien at this stage. How powerful he is... They think they can control him. But they can't. Celeste is crazy and Miranda... well... *Miranda* is a dangerous narcissist who wants to be a goddess in her own right.' Oh, he was one to talk. 'But there are other ways to control them, all of them. Ways for a queen of Larelwynn to rule.'

'With you at her side.'

He hit her in the face, just once with all his strength, sending her down on the ground with the force of a battering ram. And then he spat on the floorboards beside her. 'It takes a man to wield a sword.'

Then he was gone too.

Grace felt like throwing up. Daniel didn't look much better. He tried to help her up, tried to wipe the blood from her face. 'Doesn't matter,' she said. 'More convincing anyway.'

He swallowed hard, clearly distraught, and Grace wondered once more how he had ever survived growing up in Eastferry with Kurt.

'They have them in the catacombs underneath us,' Daniel said. 'It has to be. There are ways in there. And ways out. Kurt even uses some of them.'

'Kurt betrayed us. Weren't you listening?'

Daniel shook his head. '*I* betrayed you. Kurt… Kurt tried to make sure it was just Bastien. He hates Kane, but he likes his debts. Kane owes my brother. That's the only reason they're letting Misha and I go. And the ship with the mageborn who are in Eastferry.'

Grace grabbed his hand, pulling him close. He pressed something into her hands, something cold and hard, humming with magic. She looked down to see Zavi's sigil glowing softly in her hands. She almost smiled except it would hurt too much, and she forced herself to breathe.

'You messed up, Parry. Don't do it again. Now, get Misha and then get out while you can. You and Ellyn can get the others out through the catacombs. You make that ship. All of you.'

'But Grace—'

'That's an order, Daniel.'

'But I—'

'You have to do what I say. Don't try to go off script again, under-stand? We are not leaving the mageborn behind. Especially not our own. An order, Daniel. Remember them?'

He almost snapped to attention, but there was unspoken pain in his voice. She hated herself for putting it there. 'Yes, Captain.'

All she could do now was stall for time. The door opened and he shoved her inside. She tried to fall convincingly, but ended up just thudding to the floor on her face, right beside Bastien.

The broken wreck of the man who had been Bastien.

He tried to say her name. This was bad. Unbearably bad. What had they done to him? Sigils peppered his sweat-drenched, gleaming skin, humming with fading power. But he didn't shake them off. He couldn't. He was too weak. His magic was a faint glimmer now.

'Bastien? What happened?'

Daniel was gone. Ellyn was under orders not to come back for her. Grace had hoped Bastien would be in a fit state to help her, to work with her.

A plan would have been a really good idea.

She didn't think. She just pulled him into her arms, held him. When she looked up again, both Miranda and Celeste were back in the room, staring at her like magpies ready to play.

'What have you done to him?' she hissed at them.

He lay in her arms, helpless, shattered.

Mother Miranda gave her a withering look. 'Nothing he won't recover from, eventually.' She turned to her companion, dismissing Grace. 'We just want the warrant. Not the girl. Celeste, make yourself useful and kill her.'

'No!'

Out of nowhere, Bastien surged back into life, holding onto her fiercely, his grip painfully tight. He seemed more animal than human, pain making muscles stand out on his body, his skin on fire to the touch. Celeste, on the other hand, didn't move an inch. Like Miranda, she had no intention of getting her hands dirty. She ignored the command, like she hadn't heard it at all.

'He loves her,' Celeste said, every inch the bratty sister. 'I don't know why.'

'Because I *do*, Celeste,' Bastien replied. 'There's no reason to it.'

This couldn't be true. He didn't know what he was doing. He'd just handed them the leverage they needed. Besides which, it… it couldn't be true.

Miranda's eyes glowed with that unholy golden light Grace had seen fill Bastien. His magic, she realised. They had stolen his magic. That was why he was so weak, why those almost burnt-out sigils were still holding him.

'He loves her.' Miranda made it sound like something craven and disgusting. 'And I suppose you love him too. He said as much to me once, when I was Hanna, when I was just a girl.'

Hanna? Asher's sister? Grace had imagined her younger than him, not older, but now… now she started to understand. Had they been working together all along? Or had Miranda, disgraced and cast out, made her own way in the world until she got herself into a position of power? And then she had reeled her little brother back into her sphere of influence.

'You're Kane's sister?'

'Yes. Or rather he's *my* brother. Our parents had such plans. They were idiots, of course, but ambitious idiots. The Larelwynns stole him from me, wiped his memory with their potions and cast me out. Even my parents rejected me. And Asher, poor little Asher, had to go along with it. Until one day, when I'd established myself as Mother of the Temple, we invited them to dinner and we slaughtered them all, our parents, grandparents, siblings… Delicious vengeance. It almost made it worthwhile, losing Bastien. But that was long ago. Bastien forgets so easily. A certain drink, a long sleep and he's born anew. They've done it for centuries, the royal family and the marshals. Even Simona did it, when I was young, poison from a trusted hand. He never saw it coming. If he did… well, they could force him to drink and he'd forget. They'd just tell him there was an accident. Blame Celeste…'

'I didn't do anything,' Celeste crooned. 'They lied and lied and lied. I didn't hurt anyone. I'm a glory.'

'Of course you are, my darling girl,' Miranda replied, smiling at Celeste. 'My glory. And now we have the captain, Bastien will do exactly what we want. With or without the warrant. Isn't that right, oh Lord of Thorns? We have you as long as we have her. You've just secured her survival. Well, maybe. If she can stand to live when I'm finished with her. Do you know why the Larelwynns call him the Lord of Thorns?'

Grace had to be brash, harsh. She had to make Miranda believe that even if Bastien cared for her she didn't care for him. She had to make Bastien believe it. It might be the only way to protect him now.

She scowled. 'Because he's a massive prick?'

Miranda's eyes narrowed. She didn't bite, or get the joke. Why would she? It wasn't a joke to her. Nothing had ever been as serious. She was so close to her goal, she could taste it. 'No, foolish child. Because everyone who touches him gets hurt.'

Something unseen wrapped itself around Grace, cold as ice and twice as strong. It wound itself around her like a python, squeezing her, lifting her, wrenching her away from him. She hung in the air, a specimen to be examined, her body crushed by an unseen force. Bones ground together, her breath shortened and constricted, muscles straining but unable to move.

A scuffle behind her told her Bastien was trying to fight but Celeste was on him already, murmuring away, her magic almost his match at the best of times, now easily overwhelming him.

'You see, I know you.' Miranda peered closer at her face, as if she was examining a holy book, or, more probably, a small and helpless child. 'From years ago. I was on the street, starving, desperate after the Larelwynns had cast me out. I had to find a way to use what I'd learned from him. I made those mageborn street rats sustain me. I remember you. You were a Flint, weren't you? Let me in. Let me see.'

'No.' It was a trial to even force out that one word. The need to obey, to submit, to do whatever was demanded ground down on her, Miranda's magic, the compulsion and the weight of her magic combined. 'You can't make me.'

'Oh, child,' Miranda said, almost amused. And Grace realised the woman wasn't even trying yet.

It was just pressure at first, pressure at her temples, behind her eyes, like a headache from trying to focus too hard. And then it pushed harder. Explosions of pain burst at the back of her brain and her whole body tensed. A knot of agony unfurled along her spine, lancing up to the base of her skull, like a white-hot wire snapping taut. Her scream was strangled and cracked.

From somewhere far away, Bastien howled her name. But he couldn't help her now.

Miranda was in her mind, in her memories, rifling through them, looking for her most intimate secrets, her forgotten memories, dragging her past back into agonising clarity.

Sunlight filtering through long grass and a woman with red hair like her own, laughing, spinning her around. A pair of hands in hers, so strong, so gentle. And that song. That voice.

Tears stung her eyes, burned like acid down her cheeks. It wasn't fair. This wasn't fair. She didn't want to know. Didn't need to know. Not like this. Not like this.

'Show me,' Miranda snarled. She gripped Grace's jaw with iron fingers and forced her way even further into Grace's mind.

*

The sound of the smithy rang through her, the clang of the hammer on the anvil, horseshoes and bits, farm equipment, gleaming in the sunlight, the smell of wood smoke, the fire warm against her skin.

'Gracie, come away from there,' the voice, that voice. 'It's dangerous.' Her mother. It was her mother. Her voice, sweet and gentle.

'Don't worry, love. I have my eye on her. She's happy here.' Her father. Strength, surety, a man who never failed her, never let her down. And she was happy. There was nothing to fear. Nothing to worry about at all.

Flames came easily...

She moved her hands slowly, and made fire dance out of the dust. It swirled in a spiral, growing stronger, but perfectly under her control.

The water came out of nowhere. It splashed everywhere, soaking the front of her pretty dress, and she wailed in shock and betrayal. Her fire was gone.

Her mother swept her up into her arms. 'Are you all right?' Her voice tender but concerned.

'Not a mark on her,' Father said, setting down the bucket.

'Never do that again, Gracie,' her mother whispered, urgent in fear, crushing her against her. 'Never ever. Promise me now. Never again.'

And she promised. Oh how she promised. But she hadn't kept the promise. She couldn't. That was her fault. It was all her fault.

There was a fire. The house burned. The house burned down.

But she didn't do it.

They came with torches, in the night. The village was in the middle of nowhere and there were others who could work the forge. People without a mageborn daughter.

She had woken coughing, hardly able to breathe, unable to see more than a foot or so in front of her. She crawled through the house, trying to cry out but unable to find her voice. She dragged herself into the night, gasping for breath.

All Grace remembered were the flames that didn't touch her, the smoke that didn't kill her. But it killed her family.

Hands seized her as she made it outside the burning house, not gentle this time, not kind. Hard and heartless, hands that hated, that bruised, that hurt.

'What do we do with it?' someone snarled. It sounded like one of the farmers. Her father had helped him when the crops failed. Her mother had baked with his wife. Grace had played with their children that very morning.

'Fire didn't kill it. Maybe water?'

They dragged her off to the river, and she kicked and screamed and sobbed every step of the way.

They threw her in, they held her down, but every time, every single time, she came up gasping for breath and fighting. She remembered kicking, scratching, biting, and the same hands kept pushing her under the surface until…

Someone else found her, a merchant travelling through. He fished her out of the water and called her a pathetic catch. The road to Rathlynn wasn't kind to her and neither was he. But he took her there. She was starving and wretched, begging for scraps and trying to duck the myriad blows raining down on her, trying to cling to her memories of another life, tormenting herself with thoughts of her lost family.

Rathlynn was a yellow-red smudge on the edge of the gleaming sea. The palace loomed overhead like something from a fairy tale. He dragged her along to the docks and made her help unload the goods he'd brought. She struggled with crates far too big for her to manage. When she dropped one, he whipped her.

And then he sold her.

The woman on the quays had held her chin in a grip like iron, wrenched her face this way and that as she studied her. Her hair was a riot of chestnut curls, tangled and wild.

'She's weak.'

'She'll grow,' said the merchant. 'And she's tough. You'll see.'

'She'll do, I suppose. Waste not want not.' The woman threw a few copper coins at him and pulled her off to the miserable hovel which was her home, and Grace's prison for the next three years.

'They call me Auntie,' the woman said. She held a glass ball, like a soothsayer, and offered it to Grace. 'And you'll do exactly what I say, understand? I own you now. Body and soul. I can feel the magic in you and it is mine. Now… take this.'

Grace didn't know what else to do. The glass was cool and hard in her small hands. For a moment she thought it was a game, a present. Something special. And she started to smile.

Until everything became fire and pain, a void sucking out all the magic inside her.

*

Somewhere Grace found her voice. Somewhere. Because she wanted to scream and sob and swear. But she didn't. 'They called you Auntie. But you… you…'

She burned me and she burned me, over and over again until there was no fire left to burn.

'I fed you.'

You want to eat, you earn your keep. Each phrase punctuated by a slap. *Just another mouth to feed.* A punch. *There's been a war, everyone's hungry.*

A kick. A slap. A hard floor to sleep on, exhausted and hurting. Miranda's hands cruel and unkind, forcing a glass ball into her grip. And it burned. It burned and burned and burned. Until there was no magic left in her. She was a Flint without fire, her magic swallowed down by a woman who didn't care if she lived or died in the process. Burning glass orbs in her hands, searing the skin of her palms, scarring them. A monster. All her life, all she encountered were monsters. Until Bastien, the one who was meant to be a monster, but wasn't. He wasn't.

You're no use to me.

It wasn't her parents. They hadn't handed her over. They were already dead. They had already burned, but it wasn't her fault, and Grace had crawled out of the fire. It wasn't her fire. She hadn't caused it. And her parents… just normal, everyday people. No one special. Just… normal. And special beyond imagining to her.

All these years… all this time… she'd thought it was her fault. She didn't know how or why but she had believed it, because of this woman.

It was Miranda who cast her out.

She had sold her to the Academy and forgotten about her.

Miranda gave a derisive snort. 'You're nothing. No one.'

The force holding her collapsed. Grace crashed onto the floor again, her heart broken, her lost life exposed.

Bastien had said they weren't missing any princesses. She had been no one all along.

And yet… and yet she had been someone, to some people. She'd had a family who loved her. She'd lost them. She'd lost her magic.

But she'd found the Academy, somehow. Found a family there instead. A purpose. A life.

Truth and justice. And protection of the mageborn.

But she had the truth of it now. The truth of who she was. Of what had happened.

'Grace…' Bastien strained against whatever Celeste was using to hold him, bands of air like iron cutting into his skin as the sigils faded. He was still fighting, burning through them. 'Grace, talk to me. Are you okay? Please… please…'

Everything hurt. Blood and snot dripped from her nose, covering her face, filling her mouth, mingling with the dried blood from earlier. She was a mess.

'Still here.' Her voice sounded like it had been run through a grater. It hurt to speak.

'For now.' Miranda's foot pressed onto her outstretched hand, grinding down with her full weight. 'The warrant. Give it to me.'

'Take it.'

The bones in her hand cracked under the heel and Grace couldn't hold in the cry any longer.

'I'm not a fool,' Miranda said. 'It was made to bind a divinity. It immolates anyone who tries to take it by force.'

Bastien was on his knees, his voice desperate. 'Grace, just give it to her. It's okay. It doesn't matter. Please. Just…'

'No.'

The kick lifted her off the ground. She felt her rib break, felt it stab into her lung as she landed. Not good. Not good at all.

Waste their time. Easier said than done. She was running out of time to waste.

'The Lord of Thorns said he loved me once, too. He made me believe it. Years ago, during the last war. Before that bastard king made him forget me. But I waited, bided my time, built my power. I'm going to be a goddess, with or without Bastien. Celeste promised.'

At the mention of her name Celeste started laughing again. And Grace's lips twitched into a smile too, in spite of the pain. Divinities were fickle. Divinities were like magic. They wanted what they wanted. And they used people.

And Grace understood.

'Celeste played you, *Auntie*. Just like you played Asher and Aurelie. There's no way to make yourself a goddess.'

The same power seized her again, shaking her like a rag doll, closing on her throat, crushing and bruising. Grace wheezed, trying to catch a breath as spots danced before her eyes. With a jerk, Miranda released her and she hit the wall, sliding down to a crumpled heap.

Arm's broken, she thought, in spite of the fact there was no one source of the agony coursing through her. Unless you counted Miranda. Grace tried to move and it blinded her. Definitely broken. Shoulder… dislocated…

'Bastien can't remember. He needs to remember. I can make him.' His sister spoke through her mirth, laughter breaking through the words. Oh, she was loving this.

'That poison took his memories,' Grace said. 'Only getting his powers back can help him. You just drained him.'

Miranda's face fell in loathing. Maybe it hadn't occurred to her, but Grace didn't doubt that it had occurred to her companion. Celeste had played her indeed.

'Celeste, kill her and take the warrant.' Miranda almost purred as she said it. 'You can do it, can't you? There's nothing you can't do, my sister. Make her give it to me. Make her obey.'

A strange look came over Celeste's face at the word 'sister', distant with half-forgotten dreams.

And suddenly Grace felt something else, far stronger than Miranda. Stronger than anything she had ever encountered. It wove its way through the elements inside her, it stoked the fire, and turned it white hot. She was burning now, burning from inside. The fire was her own, her powers as a Flint, so long ago taken away, came back all at once, years of fire.

She didn't just scream this time. The sound of agony she produced transcended that.

'No!' Bastien yelled in wild desperation. 'No please, I'll do anything. Anything. Just don't... please Celeste. Don't.'

His sister turned to look at him, her eyes brighter than ever, and she nodded.

This time when Grace fell, he was there to catch her.

And she was ready. She grabbed the warrant in her hand and pressed it to the torc around his neck, slotting it into the space. A perfect fit. Of course it was.

He jerked back, horrified. 'Grace, what are you doing?'

What was she doing? She was using her fire. She might be the weakest mageborn left in Rathlynn, but with him so close, her magic was stronger. And Celeste had just ignited it. The fire burned hotter than ever now. Grace looked up into his horrified eyes and kissed him, drinking him down and making her own meagre flame burn even brighter. It blazed from her hands, melting the gold, sealing the circle around his neck.

And the circle changed. It came alive within her hands, glowing and expanding. It rose, dragging itself out of her grip. It slid up his face, moulding around the line of his jaw, crawling over his sensuous mouth, his high cheekbones, closing over his eyes, a mask of liquid living gold, glowing like the light inside him, like the light of the Maegen. It ran fingers of light through his black hair, just as she had. Finally, it reformed itself as a simple band on his head.

A crown. A golden crown.

Grace slid to the ground, exhausted, the pain strangely distant now, ebbing. Not a good sign.

Bastien Larelwynn threw back his newly crowned head and howled.

Light flooded him, sucked from everywhere, from the other women, from the lamps, from the orbs, from the world itself. Even the sky outside darkened. The pool of light within him surged up to meet it.

Such power. More magic than she had ever sensed before. Anywhere.

Miranda shrieked, clawing at the table in an effort to anchor herself. Celeste's screams joined hers in a fierce and terrible harmony. Bastien stretched his arms out wide, raking in more and more power from them, everything they had stolen, absorbing it into himself. He radiated light, so beautiful that Grace could hardly look upon him.

And then, just as suddenly, everything stopped.

He stood there, breathing slowly, his eyes wide.

'I… remember…'

Celeste dragged herself up first, her face aglow, her smile iridescent. 'My brother, my king.' She spread her arms wide.

An unseen force flung her back, lines of gold appearing all over her skin, binding her, sealing her magic inside her again.

'What are you doing?' Miranda yelled. 'Stop it. Stop at once.'

'*You are not what you claim to be.*' Each word was the sound of a deep bell tolling, each breath the rush of the waves against the shore. '*You never were. I loved you. You betrayed me. Used my work against me. You are nothing but a lie made flesh.*'

'I know what I am. I made you anew, Hollow King. You owe me. You owe me everything.'

He stepped forward, glowing and glorious. Grace watched him… *it*… a divinity, the highest form of magic. Larelwynn had trapped the Hollow King, but no one had ever known what he did with him.

Now she did.

Miranda did too. 'They made you forget what you were, made you part of their family… and each time you supposedly died, they fed you that poison, made you forget, reinvented you… Please try to understand, my king.' He hesitated and she smiled, pressing her case. 'King of all kings, master of the mageborn… they used you. They made you control the mageborn.'

They had. All but Marius, who loved him like a brother. Like more than a brother. Who wanted it all to end with him. The last Larelwynn.

'*And you released me…*'

Music in his voice. Grace could drown in it. She wanted to lose herself in him as she had that night. She wanted… and she would never have it.

Another wave of cold swept up over her. She was fading. Dying. She could recognise it now.

'Yes. I released you,' Miranda said, desperate for him to agree.

No, Grace thought. *She's lying. I released him. I set loose the Hollow King. He'll lose all that makes him human. He'll forget me and Marius, forget anyone who cared for him. I've set him free to bring his revenge onto the city, on the kingdom, on all my people.*

But he'd been forced to live a lie. And now there needed to be truth. In all things. She had always believed in truth.

I had to do it, Bastien. I had to. Truth and justice.

He gazed down at Miranda's trembling form, reached out a hand to touch her forehead. She went still, smiling in triumph, convinced that she had him now, that she had won.

'*Liar*,' he said.

The movement shivered through the air, light and dark and filled with shadows. For a moment an expression of pure horror stained Miranda's features, and then she unravelled. Her mouth opened wide as her body unknit itself. She tried to scream, but it never made it from her lungs before she was all whispers and smoke and nothingness.

Bastien shook his hand, as if ridding it of dust.

'Bastien! Bastien what have you done?' Celeste sobbed. 'She was one of us, part of us. She was my friend.'

'*No*,' he told her, turning to face her. She shied back from him, horrified by what she saw there. '*She was not one of us, sister. She made herself what you wanted her to be. As she was for me, a short time ago. But she was not one of us.*'

'She loved you.'

'*And hated me. Like you.*'

'I didn't… I didn't mean to hurt you, Bastien…'

He drifted towards her, his face a mask of sorrow. '*You did. I know you did. No one loves their captor. But not any more. Never again, Celeste.*'

'You… you remember?'

'*Everything.*'

'And you won't forget again? Please, Bastien. We can rule. We can be free. We can do whatever we want. The first Larelwynn king said we'd protect the mageborn, control the Maegen and keep it at bay, but he lied. They all lied. They used us. This place is ours. Everything is ours. They'll do what we want. We can make them.'

He frowned, looking away, down at Grace, where she lay in her own blood, her breath fading, her eyes dimming. Strange she could still see him, still read every emotion on his face. Celeste was a pale shadow, but Bastien… Bastien was the sun in her sky.

She could hear her heart thudding out of rhythm, slowing, fading as her vision was fading. But she wanted to look at him for as long as she could. To drink in that light.

'What about her?' Celeste asked. 'You can have her if you want. Make her love you. Make her adore you, obey your every word. Just do it. We are gods, Bastien.'

'Oh Celeste, you will never understand,' he whispered. And it was his own voice. Just his own human voice. Not a god, just a man.

He reached out and Celeste shied back, terror of Miranda's fate making her pull away, but there was nowhere to run. He pressed his hand to her cheek, so tender a gesture that tears spilled out of her eyes, real tears. Bastien smiled and from somewhere he took a sigil. Grace recognised it at once – Zavi's sigil. He'd taken it from her pocket when he held her. She hadn't even noticed. It blazed like the sun in his hand, his magic powering it beyond any strength a sigil had held before.

'No,' Celeste said. 'Please don't. Bastien, please…'

'I'm sorry, Celeste. I have to. You're too dangerous, love. The Maegen still has to be controlled, the mageborn protected. I can't let you hurt them any more.'

The sigil wrapped around her neck and the power inside her, which had desperately struggled to match his, shut off. Zavi's sigil glowed, brighter than ever before, burning itself into her skin, fixing itself there forever. Celeste gave a simple gasp of dismay, her eyes open in shock, and then she slumped down the wall.

Outside someone was hammering on the door. Grace could hear Asher's calm voice trying to reason, and Aurelie screaming orders. Darkness clung to the edges of her vision. They were coming. They'd gone back for whatever secret weapon they thought could destroy Bastien.

The one that had bound him before, Grace realised. The sword. Larelwynn's sword, that hung above the thrones in the palace of Rathlynn. The weapon that had destroyed the Hollow King.

Aurelie's voice came through strident and shrill. 'Kill whatever you find in there. Tear them apart. I want them dead. All of them.'

The spell holding Grace had fallen away. Whatever compulsion Miranda had used was gone. Many spells would be falling apart right now, many eyes opening. How would Aurelie and Asher deal with that, she wondered. How many of their actions would they blame on the Mother of the Temple? How many excuses would she provide? No one needed to know she was Asher's lost sister. No one needed to know the truth of that at all. There would be no justice.

Grace's eyes were drifting shut. When she forced herself to open them again, she saw Bastien's face. He slipped one hand under her head, the other under her body, lifting her. He was so gentle, even with such power flowing through him.

'Don't go,' he whispered. 'Not yet.'

'I… I don't have… much of a choice.'

'Then I'll go with you.'

'Bastien… you can't… You may still make the ship. Go.'

Go, so easy to say. She didn't want him to go. She didn't want to go. His face blurred and when it reformed she saw tears burning in his eyes.

'I won't,' he said, his voice shaking. 'I won't let you.'

'I'm tired, Bastien. It's… it's cold… it's dark…' But the pain was ebbing away now, drifting off as her mind drifted in the other direction. His grip was so strong, but she hardly felt it any more.

'Grace. Please…'

But she was drifting and she couldn't fight it. There were tears on her face. His tears. They glowed.

*

Light faded. Darkness beckoned. Worse than before, when the building had collapsed and she had fallen. Bastien was gone. She knew that. Lost to her. His power was loose and what hope would she have had anyway without him?

'There's more magic in you than I've ever sensed,' she had once said, kneeling before him. She hadn't even known what he was, but somehow she had sensed it. 'More than should be possible. More than should even be safe.'

So much more than could ever be safe.

Unless he wasn't human at all but a god.

She had been such a fool. Falling in love with him. What had she been thinking? Except she hadn't been thinking, had she?

The Deep Dark was calling. She had cheated it once, or rather Bastien had cheated it to save her. And now… now… it wound greedy arms around her and pulled her into its embrace.

'Grace,' his voice was a whisper. 'Grace, don't go.'

Easier said than done. She had already gone. The darkness was calling. She couldn't deny it any longer. On the brink of death, she released her hold on life, and fell.

The explosion of radiance shook the world, the Maegen pulsating with it. Encircled in shadows, Grace watched it billow towards her, and he was there with her, in the depths, in the darkness.

A divinity, he bled light into a world which should have no light. Beyond the shadows, she could see other things, other beings, creatures of teeth and eyes, claws and barbs, poison dripping from a stinger, glistening in a glow of life that should never have been shed on it. As Bastien drew closer, so did they.

The Hollow King… this was the place he came from, the Deep Dark, the endless night. It wasn't Bastien. Not really. It was the thing that Bastien could become if he lingered here too long. If those creatures got loose and made him their host…

The light made them hungry.

And she was the bait, the lure.

'You have to go,' she said.

'Not without you.' *And this was the core of him. Loyal, stubborn, honourable.*

All she wanted to do was sink down to oblivion. Everything in the light was pain. Agony. Suffering. And him…

His eyes were the eyes of a god, his power leaving her helpless. He was everything. Bastien could be gone. She knew that. So much magic, so much power, delving so deep into the Maegen and its shadowy underbelly, it would all change him.

'You have to let me go.'

'Never.' *The darkness pressed closer and he raised a hand, his light driving it back. She could feel the ripples of its rage. Its grip on her tightened still further. She couldn't fight it any more.*

'Bastien…'

'I can't force you to do anything, Grace. I know that. But I won't go without you. I refuse to.'

'You'll lose everything. Your identity… your memories…'

'If I lose you it won't matter.'

And still Bastien didn't go. Like ink in the water, the Deep Dark crept behind him, curling around to envelop him as well, to claim him.

'You can still escape and live a life.'

'There is no life without you.'

The words hung there, startling and honest. And true. He meant it with all his heart. She could see that now. She reached out one hand, tearing through the black spider webs of nothingness clinging to her, and his hand met hers, light driving them back as his fingers threaded with her own.

Grace's consciousness entwined with his, knowing what he knew… That long ago he had been part of the Maegen, part of the Deep Dark beneath. That the light had brought him power and glory, joy. That the Larelwynns had stolen that from him. That the Hollow King was made of raw magic and they had tricked him into forgetting, time and time again, what he really was. That they had promised him a way to protect the mageborn, those born of the Maegen, and then used him to enslave them instead. That the light in her, that broken flame of Flint magic, reminded him of everything he had once been.

And that now he was beyond any of them. He was the last Larelwynn because they were all his line. Not the other way around. Everyone that had deceived, coerced, drugged or seduced him… even those he thought he loved.

Celeste had, in her own way, been right. She had tried to free him. But that wasn't freedom to Bastien any more.

The endless deep coiled around him. He wouldn't fight it while he waited for her. He wouldn't struggle or resist. If she was gone it could take him too. He wouldn't know anything any more. He wouldn't feel the pain of loss. He wouldn't know of all the betrayal threaded through his life. He wouldn't know what might have been. He welcomed oblivion too.

'Go,' she told him. *'Please. Before it's too late.'*

Too late. It was already too late. The man she knew – the man she loved, though she could never tell him that – was already fading in his golden eyes. The light was too bright, the darkness too dark. He was a shape made of pure magic, the heart of the Maegen.

Without her, he didn't care. He had come back for her and he wasn't going to leave without her.

No choice left. No other path. She had to stop this. All she wanted to do was rest but her duty was greater than that desire. Duty and honour over everything, truth and justice etched at her core.

Whatever else, I charge you, protect him, *Marius had said.* He must live.

It was the last wish of her dying king. A king who wanted a curse to be lifted, who wanted to set right an ancient wrong. A man who loved far too much. The only man who had ever shown Bastien love and what it really meant.

Grace wrapped her arms around Bastien's blazing form, and the fire in her rose to meet it. It was a faint, flickering thing, but it was hers. It was all she had. Like him. The Deep Dark recoiled, and all those eyes and teeth, the tentacles and barbs, couldn't touch them. They burned too brightly.

*

The door burst open. Bastien turned, still holding Grace in his arms to face this new threat.

'Where's Miranda?' Aurelie yelled. 'What have you done with her?'

Grace shivered, trying to get her strength back. She needed to stand on her own feet, needed to help him. Now more than ever. For a moment he didn't seem to understand what was happening, half in this world and still half in the Maegen. He tilted his head slowly to one side, studying this new arrival with eyes glowing gold beneath the fall of his black hair.

Slowly, carefully, Grace regained her feet. She still hurt everywhere. Whatever he had done, she wasn't healed but it was enough. For now. Enough to keep going. She coughed and it almost made her drop to her knees in agony but she couldn't let them know that. Behind them Celeste slumped, limp and unconscious, the sigil still blazing at her throat, part of her, binding her. Bastien glowed with power, filled with a light like the sun. The air hummed with energy and Grace's own fingers were ringed with tiny flames. His magic bled into everything.

'We're leaving,' Grace said.

'You? You're not going anywhere.' The queen's tone seethed with malice. 'Asher.'

Asher Kane held a sword. Not just any sword. Grace knew it instantly, although she had only seen it once. Even at this distance waves of cold came off the metal, ice emanating from it. It looked at home in his hands, part of him... or perhaps he was part of it. It seemed so much greater than the man holding it. It was called Godslayer for a reason.

'Larelwynn's sword,' Grace said.

Aurelie sneered at her. 'Yes. I will control him. Or I'll kill him.' Her voice turned mock simpering. '*A tragic turn of events. A spurned lover. A trained swordswoman. We just couldn't stop her in time.*'

Grace forced herself to keep breathing, through the pain. Something stabbed into her lungs, almost dropping her. She held on, barely. '*Her?*'

One side of Aurelie's lips twisted up. She eyed Grace like a piece of dirt. 'You.'

Half a dozen crossbows trained on her from the guards accompanying the queen.

So this was how it ended. He'd brought her back from the brink of death to face this.

'Give me the warrant,' Aurelie said, pronouncing each word like she was biting them off her tongue.

Grace reached back and felt Bastien's hand slip into hers. The hum of his power echoed through her body. She didn't exactly know why, but she smiled. She didn't have the warrant any more. It wasn't hers to give.

'No.'

It was a word people like Aurelie were not used to hearing. Which made it even sweeter to say.

The queen nodded. The crossbows snapped.

Halfway towards her, fire consumed the bolts, turning them to ashes in seconds. The bows themselves ignited next, the guards dropping them, scattering backwards in alarm.

Grace forced her breath to stay calm, even though her heart thundered inside her chest. Every beat was agony.

'*We are leaving*,' Bastien said, his voice as cold as winter's wind.

Aurelie didn't even spare him a glance. Her fury was fixed on Grace alone. 'So he obeys you now? Don't you know what he is?'

What he is? She might as well just call him it.

'You control the most powerful weapon in the world,' Asher said, before Grace could answer. 'The most terrible weapon ever conceived. Marchant, you serve the crown. Your duty demands—'

'I serve the crown, yes,' she smiled sweetly, hating him with every fibre of her being. 'I serve the king, the *true* king. And it *is* my honour to serve.'

Asher lunged at her, the sword a blunt instrument in his hand. Grace twisted aside, pulling Bastien with her. The blade had to weigh a tonne, because Asher carried on past them, momentum sending the blade crashing through the table.

He hauled it back, breathing hard, looking for them again.

Grace's professional mind kicked in. The sword was far too big for him. You'd need to be as big as Kai to wield it and Asher was slim and elegant. He needed his rapier, not a broadsword. A general he might have been, but not a soldier. Not really. That was the sword of someone who took battle to others, not one who directed it from behind the lines.

'*Asher, enough.*' Bastien's voice reverberated with magic again and this time when Asher swung the huge sword, Bastien didn't move aside. He reached up and caught it. With the Maegen's glow wreathing his hand, he squeezed, and the ancient metal gave beneath his grip. It buckled, his hand imprinted in the blade.

'What... what *are* you...?' Asher Kane stammered.

'*I was your friend.*'

'You're a monster. You killed my sister. You were *never* my friend.'

A look of such sorrow ghosted over Bastien's luminous face. '*But I was. And this thing...*' He wrenched the sword from Asher's hands and flung it aside. '*It was never Larelwynn's weapon. I was.*'

Asher dropped to his knees, defiant. 'Hanna knew what you were. She warned us all, knew you needed to be controlled. Rightly. Look at you.'

Look at him. It was hard to tear your eyes off him. The magic coursed through him and the more he used it...

'*Hanna?*' Bastien said, as if he couldn't remember. And he couldn't, Grace realised. More of his memories were gone. The Maegen was already eating away at his mind, his past, devouring who he was.

'Bastien,' she called urgently.

He bent down and seized Asher by the throat. He looked at Grace, a question. She shook her head, hoping... no, praying he would understand.

Asher Kane wasn't worth it. Neither was the queen. Miranda, or Hanna, or whoever she had ended up being, was gone. Bastien's sister was insane but he had bound her magic and if he gave up now, if he let rage and power destroy what made him Bastien rather than the Hollow King, Celeste would still win.

How could Grace make him understand? How could she make him see? She couldn't lose him, not now. Not like this. Tears spilled from her eyes, tears she couldn't hold back any longer.

She reached out her hand to him and Bastien dropped Asher Kane like a sack of rocks. Aurelie and the guards were in retreat, shielding their eyes from the glow, but Grace couldn't move.

He was full of light, full of the sun, fire and rage, pure unadulterated power. His form barely contained it any more. It would eat through him eventually and Bastien would be gone.

'Bastien,' she whispered. 'I may not know what you are, but I know *who* you are, my love. Please, I want you back. Just you. Please…'

And the light turned incandescent, like an exploding sun in the night's sky. It was everything, all around her. His light which drove away all the darkness, more powerful, more dreadful than ever before. He was that light.

Light filled her. She opened her arms to him and let in the fire.

Chapter Twenty-Seven

Grace woke to a gentle rocking. For a moment she thought Bastien was still holding her, still saying her name, still glowing. But she found herself alone, in a simple wood-panelled cabin, tucked into a bunk. Her body ached everywhere but there were no obvious wounds. Certainly none as severe as she could recall Miranda inflicting on her. And this was not the Temple.

Grace got up on unsteady feet and pushed open the narrow cabin door. Beyond it she found a passageway with similar slender doors. At the far end, steep steps led up on deck, and a hole with a ladder led down into the hold.

Part of her wanted to call out, to find someone and ask where she was and what had happened. The rest of her didn't dare.

Instead she broke down what she knew, what she could see, what she could remember.

She was clearly on a ship, but she had no idea how she'd got there or which ship it might be. It didn't stink. It looked in good order. That had to be considered promising.

She reached the steps and forced herself upwards. Overhead she could hear the wind in the sails, the shouts of sailors at work and the sea humming all around her while the hull creaked gently. They were under full sail in open water.

As she got to the top of the steps, she heard something else; singing.

On the deck, tucked out of the way beside a lower access hatch, a man sat, bent over a harp. He played with exquisite delicacy, and some care. Bandages swathed his hands, but they didn't stop him playing. He sang gently, softly, a love song. Before him, watching and listening with rapt attention, Daniel Parry sat with his back to her.

'It's good luck to have a harper aboard,' said a voice beside her. Grace turned, hand already reaching for a knife that wasn't there. It was the Leanese captain whose daughter had been killed, Captain Vayden. He tilted his head. 'We know the truth now. For that I thank you. And for the justice you brought.'

'You came back?'

'The Parrys sent word. Kurt was most insistent but then, that *is* his little brother. A host of blessed waited for us, he said, and there they were. Your mageborn. Refugees on the quay. *You* were more of a surprise. We were already clear of the harbour when you appeared.'

Grace caught sight of Ellyn climbing up the rigging like some kind of imp. As she watched, her friend did something, twisted herself around and dangled there laughing at the amazement of the sailors with her. Then she spotted Grace below and her smile turned even brighter.

'Valenti,' said the captain. 'I sometimes think they're half spirit.'

'So do I,' Grace agreed. But she had to get back to the matter in hand. 'You said appeared…'

'You'd better ask him about it. He brought you with him. Just appeared on deck in a halo of light. He drank deep of the pool, that one. What he remembers and what he had to offer in sacrifice… well, that's another question. It's a wonder he came back at all.'

A wonder. That was one word for it.

Bastien.

'Where is he?'

'At the stern, looking back. I offered him my cabin, but he wouldn't hear of it. He let our healer examine you, just to double-check his own work, I think. The rest of the time, when he isn't watching over you, he's back there, looking aft.'

At Rathlynn, she realised, at the kingdom of Larelwynn. At his home. His kingdom. Even if they couldn't see it any more. Even though all around them was sea.

'How long ago did we…'

Leave? Arrive? Her brain wasn't managing this.

'A day and a half.'

So long. Had she slept all that time? But she knew the answer to that. Many others remained.

'Be gentle with him, Captain Marchant,' the old man said. 'He lost much. And his memories are scattered. He is greatly blessed now. The divine is on him.'

That didn't sound good.

'Grace!' Ellyn had climbed down and ran towards her across the deck. The warm embrace was just what Grace needed, though she would never have admitted it.

'How much has he forgotten?' she asked, her throat closing even as she said the words. She couldn't bear the thought that he might not remember her. That he might have no idea what had happened between them.

'He doesn't… he hasn't really talked about it. What happened, Grace? He said you were hurt but…'

But she wasn't now. There were bruises but that was all. And Ellyn had no idea how badly she was hurt. But Grace did. Not so much hurt as dead…

The divine is on him, the captain had said. That was a euphemism for insane, wasn't it? Was Bastien like Celeste now? Had he lost himself in the pool completely?

She drew in the deepest breath she could and let it out in a long shaky exhalation. There was only one way to find out.

Bastien was leaning on the carved rail of the aft deck, his shoulders stooped, his dark gaze fixed on the receding horizon as if he couldn't bear to look away. He wore a pale blue shirt, the colour of the sky overhead, simple homespun fabric such as the sailors wore. Grace had never seen him wear anything but black before. Blue suited him.

'Bastien?'

She watched his shoulders tighten and he turned sharply, ready for an attack. She took a step back but then stopped, staring at him.

He looked the same. The light was gone. He was the man she'd made love to, whose body she had explored, who had brought her such joy.

And such pain.

'Grace,' he said. So simple a sound, her name on his lips, and inside her something fluttered desperately. He'd been a god. An actual god. Soaked in magic, more powerful than anything she had ever encountered. He'd worn a crown. The torc had been...

It was just a torc again, heavy gold, ancient and rose-toned, resting against his collarbones.

He held out his hand to her. In his palm, she could see the gold coin, the warrant, hanging on the thong which had held Zavi's sigil.

'What did you do?' she murmured.

Bastien looked down at it again and frowned. 'I thought...'

'Bastien! You had your powers back. You had your freedom. You had everything.'

He closed his fingers around the coin and turned away, looking back out to sea.

'I didn't.' His voice was no more than a whisper. 'Not... not everything.'

Forcing herself to move towards him, she stretched out her arm, fingers trembling. He *had* been a god. There was no other word for it. The Hollow King. She'd seen the crown, felt the power in him, the otherness. She had wanted nothing more than to fall at his feet and worship him. What else would a mageborn do to the god of magic?

Her hand touched his shoulder. He felt real. He felt warm. Slowly she flattened her fingers and palm, rubbed between his shoulder blades. He stiffened and then relaxed slowly, unwinding, as a soft groan escaped his lips.

'How much did you forget?'

'Some things. Not... not anything important... at least... I mean, if it was important, would I even know now?' He looked like he was hoping she would laugh, but there was no laughter in her. 'I remember Celeste, and Miranda... I mean Hanna... I remember Asher. That he was my friend until... until he wasn't. Maybe he never was. I remember what Celeste did... tried to do. What Hanna... Miranda did... I remember the Deep Dark...'

He turned and suddenly she was within the sphere of his arms, looking up into his perfect face, gazing into his endless eyes. There was no magic in them now. They didn't glow and burn. But there were tears.

'I remember you,' he whispered. 'You and me.'

'You were a divinity, Bastien. You were...'

'I was lost. You brought me back. It's as simple as that. I could have transcended, it's true. But then what? Apotheosis isn't worth it if you lose what matters.'

Apotheosis. Trust him to find a big word she didn't understand.

'Your sister…'

'Is insane. And easily led. And vulnerable. And terribly dangerous. She can't leave the Temple. The Larelwynns saw to that. The whole thing is a spell to hold her. It should stay that way. I made sure of it.'

'Zavi's sigil…'

'Is that who made it?' He gave a brief, joyless laugh. 'He was a master Atelier.'

'You remember him?'

'I don't know. There are some things I remember. Important things.'

He leaned forward and Grace couldn't move. It wasn't magic. Not *his* magic anyway. Nothing held her. Except herself.

His lips brushed against hers. Soft, enquiring, hopeful.

'Aurelie will rule,' she said, breaking away, trying to distract him.

'With Asher as her iron fist, I suspect. They're welcome to each other.'

'And Rathlynn, the kingdom…'

He closed his eyes, shame making the blood drain from his face. 'Grace, I… I will find a way, I swear it.' He fought to find the words, to explain. 'To… to go back… to… I won't abandon them. I won't.'

Divinities bless him, she believed him. He'd never abandon them, his people, both quotidian and mageborn.

'I know. I'll be there with you.' She had to. She could do no less. He kissed her again, lingering this time, and the urge to stop this happening ebbed. But she had to know. 'Do you think she is pregnant?'

He frowned, pain flickering through those endless eyes. 'If she isn't, she will be soon. She'll make sure of it. Aurelie is nothing if not thorough. She'll be a tyrant. But she isn't Miranda.'

'And the mageborn left behind?'

'She won't be able to control them. Not as Marius could. Not that he ever did. He wasn't ever… like that… Grace, we'll find a way to free them. I swear it. Kurt Parry will help. There will be others. There have to be. I can't just give up and abandon them. Not just the mageborn. All of them.' He pressed his forehead against hers, his hands ghosting up her spine. The wind lifted her hair, entwining it with his, red and black. She held his shoulders, her thumbs resting on the torc. 'But I need you to do this for me. Take the warrant. It's a protection, a promise. And it is yours. Always.'

'I don't want it. You don't have to do that.'

'Yes. I do. Grace…'

She kissed him. Whatever the future brought, wherever they ended up, she just needed him. His kiss, his touch, just him. Not the warrant. Not control. Him.

'Come back to the cabin, Bastien.'

He let her lead him below decks, her fingers threaded with his, her hand tugging him onward. She closed the door behind them.

'You don't have to do this,' he told her. 'I'm giving you the warrant because…'

'And I'm not taking it. Not yet. Bastien, listen to me…'

But he didn't. He went on, trying to explain instead of hearing her. 'It's too great a temptation for me, Grace. That sort of power, the ability to lose myself in it, to be… that thing…'

'You're not a *thing*, Bastien. And I… You think I won't feel tempted? The warrant *commands* you. If I have it, if I hold it, how do I know… I mean… I could make you… like Aurelie wanted, I could…'

His eyes went round and his mouth parted. It hadn't occurred to him, she realised, and her heart gave a jerk. He didn't believe she was capable of doing that to him.

'It's not the same, Grace.'

A flicker of hope joined the flame inside her.

Bastien closed the space between them in the blink of an eye. His arms encircled her again. His lips found hers, the need and desperation making her groan into his mouth, a soft noise of surrender and need. Her hands buried themselves in his hair, and this time it was his turn to make a noise like that. She pushed at his clothes, felt hers fall away, and suddenly they were skin to skin, unable to stop touching, kissing, caressing. He cupped her breasts, brushing the pads of his thumbs over the tightening nipples and then bent to take each one in his mouth in turn, making her gasp. She wound her legs around him as he lifted her, murmuring her name like a prayer as he carried her to the bunk. He laid her down and worshipped her, this god made flesh.

He dipped his head between her thighs and she arched her back, stuttering out a cry.

'Stop,' she told him. 'Not yet. Not…'

He pulled back, gazing down at her, his eyes so dark with desire and confusion.

Swift and strong, she pushed him onto his back and straddled him.

'Tell me you want me,' she said. 'That you want this. Please…'

'Is that a command?' She froze for a moment and then saw the teasing lift of the corner of his lips. The Lord of Thorns was teasing her. He smiled that broad and beautiful smile and glanced down between them. 'Of course I want you. Can you doubt it?'

Grace's answering grin was a surprise even to her. 'Not for a moment. But I mean it, Bastien. I want you. Freely, completely. I need you. But I won't... I won't make you...'

His hands closed in a firm but gentle grip on her hips, guiding her gently down onto him, filling her, making them both whole at last.

'You can make me do anything, my little Flint. You don't even have to ask.'

Epilogue

The light of the Maegen swirled and glimmered, reflecting back up onto the glass-smooth roof of the cave. From the depths, the darkness stirred, pushing itself upwards, straining for the surface. He had been there, so deep, so close, and in tearing the girl out of its embrace he had opened a way for the Deep Dark. It reached out, towards the life. The life which had been snatched away from it so long ago. So much life. And it was hungry. So hungry. It had hungered for hundreds of years and now it would feed again. It reached out, searching, ravenous. Insane with need.

*

In her tower above the Temple, Celeste stirred. She opened her eyes, as dark and endless as her brother's, and she saw something far beyond the walls that imprisoned her. Light swirled up inside her, and she reached out blindly, her mind aching for what had been lost so many years ago. Slowly, she began to laugh, a soft chuckle at first, which built like a wave, a laugh, a scream, a howl.

*

In the palace Aurelie slept in her royal bed, wrapped in silken sheets and cushioned on swan feathers, and whimpered in her sleep, curling in around her belly. Tears stained the pillows where she lay. She reached out across the vast, empty bed but Asher wasn't there. No one was there.

*

In another palace many miles away, perched on another shore of another sea, another queen studied a report from her spies. Her network spread out spider-like across a dozen kingdoms and brought her news of all that happened. She frowned at what she read there and finally crushed the parchment in her aged hands.

*

And beside the pool, in a barren valley thick with thorns, another pair of eyes opened, eyes that didn't know life, eyes that were made of stone, eyes that suddenly spilled gold from their depths.

'He's coming,' said a voice which had not spoken in three hundred years. 'Coming back. At long last.'

A Letter from Jessica

I want to say a huge thank you for choosing to read *Mageborn*. If you did enjoy it, and want to keep up to date with all my latest releases, just sign up at the following link. Your email address will never be shared and you can unsubscribe at any time.

www.bookouture.com/jessica-thorne

When Bookouture asked me if I would be interested in writing a fantasy romance series – and a sexy romance no less! – for them, I was so excited. And slightly terrified. I have loved fantasy romance for as long as I can remember. Even if a fantasy book or movie didn't have a romance element in it, I would find one for myself. Adventure, magic and love just seem to belong together. To get to write this book is a dream come true.

I hope you loved *Mageborn* and if you did I would be very grateful if you could write a review. I'd love to hear what you think, and it makes such a difference helping new readers to discover one of my books for the first time.

I love hearing from my readers – you can get in touch on my Facebook page, through Twitter, Goodreads or my website.

Thanks,
Jessica Thorne

JessThorneBooks

@JessThorneBooks

www.rflong.com/jessicathorne

Acknowledgements

Many thanks for all the wonderful support from my writing friends, especially the Lady Writers' Social Club – C.E. Murphy, Sarah Rees Brennan and Susan Connolly – for constant support and endless entertainment. Thanks to the Naughty Kitchen – Rhoda Baxter, Kate Johnson, Janet Gover, Alison May Imogen Howson & Daisy Tate – who saw the beginnings of this world on a writers' retreat in snowy Shropshire, and to Kate Pearce for years of writerly friendship. Thanks also to Helen Corcoran, a new star in the making, for her keen eye and her helpful comments.

Thanks to everyone at Bookouture for their trust and faith in me, especially Kathryn and Ellen, and to my agent Sallyanne.

And of course all my love and gratitude to my fabulous family who put up with so much.